The Muse

V. KAY MARTIN

For Maleah ~ my forever muse.

February

One

NOCTURNE IN BLACK AND GOLD

CHARLIE

"Where am I?"

For some time, all I can hear is beeping. My eyes peel open to a grid of white speckled ceiling tiles. I take a deep breath, and the beeping lurches in tempo. My throat is scratchy and burns as I attempt to clear it.

A woman in blue scrubs jolts, turning to face me. The rasp of my voice must have startled her. She catches her breath, one hand splayed over her heart, the other hovering over a bag of clear liquid she'd been securing to an IV pole.

"You—you're at Argale General, Mr. Bensley," she stammers.

My eyes flit around the room, catching a glimpse of the night sky behind the sheer curtains drawn across the windows.

What am I doing here? What day is it?

The digital clock on the wall reads *3:46AM — 02.26 SUN — 34 degrees.*

Sunday... I furrow my brow, trying to remember what happened—what landed me here. The monitors tracking my heart rate crescendo as I recall the sound of gunfire. The heat of the bullet that scorched my flesh. The projectile that ripped through me...

Rachel.

It was a bad dream. It had to be. My recollection and my reality cannot possibly be the same. The pain that I'm feeling—it must be work related. Getting injured on the job makes more sense. It's a far more welcomed conclusion than the twisted images and distorted echoes looping in my head.

Rachel is just downstairs in the cafeteria, hunting down more caffeine. She's tired, sure. She's been at my bedside all night, anxious to see me recover. That's all. She didn't do this. None of what I eerily recall happened. She isn't gone.

She can't be.

I heave myself onto an elbow, groaning as pain shoots up my abdomen and into my shoulder. My movement is restricted with my arm caught in a sling.

"Please be careful," the nurse insists, adjusting the pillow behind my back. "How's that?"

I hear her voice, I feel her kindness—but it's background noise. There's only one thought on my mind. One question.

"Where's my wife?" I ask, staring past her. My fist clenches the blanket, desperate for a version of events that makes more sense than the one I remember.

Her silence is infuriating. My enraged eyes cut to hers, only to find them glistening with empathy.

"I'm so sorry for your loss, Mr. Bensley."

My jaw clenches and ticks as I bite down to subdue the rise of emotions that whip through me like a hurricane, wreaking havoc beneath my still and silent demeanor. This storm might shred everything inside me, doing far more damage than the tip of a hollow-point round ever could.

"Do you think that I'd let you leave me?"

Her words echo like gunfire. Our final encounter flashes before my eyes, so vividly—like I'm watching it all play out on a movie screen. The tears in her eyes. The rage in her voice. The shattered glass, and the *click* as she loads a bullet into the chamber of my gun...

I fixate on the ceiling's recessed lights until my sight blurs. A hard blink releasing a pool of tears, now streaming freely into the wells of my ears.

"Mr. Bensley," the nurse says, her voice garbled beneath the pounding of my heart and the racing of the monitor. "Mr. Bensley," she repeats, quieter than before, voice trembling.

I put myself in her shoes, if only to be rid of my own existence for a merciful moment. Maybe she can see the pain that I'm in, recognizing it as an injury beyond the physical discomfort of my wounds. Something deeper—*anger, grief, disbelief*—emotions I'm sure she can't begin to reconcile. I can only imagine she's treading lightly for fear of stepping on a landmine. To her, I'm probably a ticking time bomb, ready to blow at the wrong sentiment.

"Is there anything I can do for you?" she finally asks.

Like what?

Could she erase the last 24 hours? Could she bring my wife back so that my sons don't have to mourn the loss of their mother? *My sons.* They'll hate me for this. Despite my earnest attempt to keep my family together, I've destroyed us.

"Where are my sons?"

GLORIA

I didn't know what time it was
Then I met you...

Sweet, melodic jazz bops through my condo. The corners of my mouth curl up into a smile—a smile that I have had the damnedest time chasing away. It's become almost involuntary. Half the time, I don't even notice it until my cheeks begin to ache or I happen upon my reflection and see a gushing Gloria gazing back at me. Apparently, others have noticed it too. Ms. Judy happily pointed it out to me as I arrived at the office Friday morning.

"You look like a flower in bloom," she'd said sweetly.

The blush only deepened. I'd resigned myself to blaming my ethereal glow on the fact that it was simply Friday, objectively the best day of the work week.

She'd only smiled politely, suspicion glinting over the rim of her glasses.

Is it really that obvious?

I cover my mouth to stifle yet another swiftly approaching grin. I'm home alone, and still I conceal my coyness in an attempt to avoid any further judgment from these walls.

God knows they've seen enough.

A certain budding artist has evidently painted a permanent smile on my face and colored me happier than I can honestly say I've ever been. Hunched over the cocktail table, I push the handles of the rolling pin across the puzzle, ensuring that every piece is locked into place.

"The flatter, the better," my mother would say.

It's been more than fifteen years since she and I framed a puzzle together like this. Fortunately, I've committed most of her lessons to memory. Those priceless memories I'll treasure forever—her lingering legacy. And for the tidbits I struggle to recall, I can feel her guiding me.

Thank you, Mama.

My hands move in the way I remember her hands moved, applying her technique. Rolling the pin upward and then bringing it back down to the base of the puzzle to start again, all while she hummed one of her favorite Nancy Wilson tunes.

"Looks good," I murmur aloud. I gently swipe my hand over the puzzle to feel for any protruding pieces. My fingers pause over the last piece he placed the night that he... that we... became something more.

Charlie and I are something more.

More than just secret lovers and stolen moments. More than the mystery behind our smiles. More than what was best left unsaid but has since been declared. I light up at the thought of how beautiful the finished product might be, my heart tumbling like a tiny acrobat inside my chest.

One coat should do, I decide, dragging a doused sponge brush over the puzzle to seal it.

I glance over at the frame that sits across the room, leaning against my favorite chair. The store clerk was right. A frame trimmed in gold perfectly compliments the metallic gold specks shimmering from the Eiffel Tower, making yesterday's trip to the custom frame shop exceedingly worthwhile.

All done.

With at least twenty minutes before the glue dries, I follow my bare feet to the stove to start the kettle then drift toward my window nook. What better way to kill time than to sink into the coziness of my chair and get lost in the haze of a lazy Sunday? I rest my chin on one hand, curling my feet beneath me. Today's view could inspire even the most well-traveled landscape painter. The sky is a shade of ocean blue, littered with pearly white clouds poised like beckoning islands. The rows of bare trees that line the lakefront patiently wait to blossom. *Patiently waiting...*

"...to be yours, alone."

The divine voice from the speaker croons aloud my heart's whisper. *So this is love...* I muse. This view has comforted me in so many different ways—soothing me after a long day at the office, inspiring me to immerse myself into the city's offerings, consoling me when my heart was breaking, and is ever the gracious provider of a perfect backdrop for moonlit lovemaking.

Oh, the love we make. My eyes fall shut, feeling the warmth of his hands caressing my face. His beautiful eyes gaze at me, and I drink in their deep, earthy browns. With a hint of a smile, he lowers his plush lips to mine, whispering as they brush, *"I love you."*

My eyes spring open as the kettle whistles, breaking the spell. A laugh escapes me as I realize yet again how easily carried away I've become. I pour myself a warm mug of tea and return to the puzzle, scooping up the frame on my way.

I check the surface—*almost dry*. The puzzle gleams up at me expectantly. Again, my eyes fall on the piece I left for Charlie to place at the very tip of the Eiffel Tower.

"I'm fully invested in finishing this puzzle," he'd said, wearing that roguish grin.

They say you can't help who you fall in love with. I don't know if I agree with that, but I do know that I built a wall as high as the Eiffel Tower, a fortress to protect me from deceivers and heartbreakers—the kind of men who will hurt you more than they will heal you.

But then there was you.

My fortress and its broken drawbridge never stood a chance. And now, I'm defenseless and vulnerable. I've allowed love to leave me completely exposed, and yet somehow, I have never felt more safe. There was nothing left to do but surrender.

Where do we go from here?

The question nagging my mind, I slide the puzzle onto the foam board. I suppose it's just my nature to consider all scenarios. I could easily produce a list of issues that come with this kind of relationship. *It's complicated*, as they say—an expression I've never subscribed to. Our love, on the other hand, is simple. So today, I choose to bask in the beauty of it.

An enticing plume of steam rises from my mug of tea. Bringing it to my nose, I breathe in the sweet smell of chamomile before indulging in a sip.

Just then, my phone chimes on the table, screen glowing.

"Domestic Dispute Escalates to Fatal Shooting," the notification reads.

My brows knit instinctively. I hate headlines like this. I could easily ignore it, preserving my good mood and rose-colored view of love and domesticity—but something compels me to read. Maybe it's knowing he's out there, helping people, solving these cases. Oddly, it makes me feel *closer* to him. With a sigh, I tap the screen and scroll.

"The community is reeling after a shocking attempted murder-suicide in Argale on Saturday night. One person is dead, and another has been rushed to Argale General after suffering from multiple gunshot wounds, according to police."

How awful. I can't help but wonder if Charlie is lead on the case. I read on.

"Just after 6:15 PM, officers with the Argale Police Department responded to a residence on the 1200th block of Moonpath Lane. A male and female were found inside suffering from gunshot wounds. Both have now been identified and authorities are continuing to investigate.

"Upon arrival, officers found Police Detective Charles Bensley clinging to life after sustaining two gunshot wounds to the abdomen and shoulder."

I freeze. My eyes close on impact—my brain needing a hard restart.

Opening them again, I re-read the words: *"...officers found Police Detective Charles Bensley clinging to life..."*

I haven't taken a breath since seeing Charlie's name, so the frantic gulp of air dizzies me. The words blur on the screen as my hands tremble.

"His spouse Rachel Bensley lay unresponsive with a fatal gunshot wound."

No. My heart thuds painfully in my chest. *This can't be happening.*

"Charles Bensley was taken to the hospital for emergency medical treatment. Sources at the scene say that Rachel Bensley's death appears to be a suicide."

My phone slips from my hand onto the table with a distant clatter.

Charlie.

What have I done?

A golden glow illuminates the room as fire rains down from the sky like a thousand shooting stars. Fierce winds howl and thunder roars just outside my window while the Earth tremors and shifts beneath us. With only a pane of glass separating us from destruction, Charlie and I lay quietly on the sofa. His arms wrap tightly around my waist, our heartbeats thrumming in sync. I link my fingers with his until they're laced together, as if I could physically hold onto whatever time we have left. But devastation consumes the world around us, and I have nothing to leverage for our survival. Charlie nuzzles against my neck.

"Perhaps in another life," he whispers.

A single tear drips down my cheek. *This is the end.*

My eyes ease open, and I wipe the mist from them. I'm lying in the very spot that I'd just dreamt I was in, but now there's no fire, no storm, and no Charlie. Only a tear-stained pillow. I never knew that the tears shed in a dream could actually fall in reality.

With a soft groan, I pull myself up to sit on the sofa's edge. My feet are sore. I must've paced for hours before collapsing onto the cushions. I don't remember falling asleep.

The view outside my window is now an overcast, midnight blue, offering no solace for the heavy hearted. Earlier, the sky was tranquil, but now it appears troubled and overwrought. Evidently, as I slept, the heavens wept too.

Clinging to the pillow, I reach for my phone on the table. I haven't touched it since it fell from my hand earlier this afternoon. It glows on contact—the only light in the room apart from the dim lights of Argale.

Two missed calls and a text. Both Luci and my father have tried to reach me.

Nothing from Charlie.

I'm a fool. Why would he be among the missed calls? And I'm insane to consider calling him. Even so, I pull up his contact on my phone. *I'm desperate.* I need the only balm that could soothe my panic—*his voice.* God, just to hear it when he answers. I don't even know what he sounds like when he answers the phone. Phone calls always felt reckless and unnecessary during our tryst. It wasn't worth the indiscretion.

How would he answer my call? A simple and sweet *"Hello?"* or perhaps something more flirtatious? Both preceding that signature Charlie smile that I'd certainly hear in his voice. This, among many other things, might now only be left to my imagination.

Did he survive the night?

My fingers feel heavy as I draft a text.

Tell me you're okay.

I stare at the unsent message. I want to press send, to make contact. To comfort him. But I can't. His wife is—gone. Who am I to want to console him when I'm the reason he's grieving? I have no right. I was wrong to have pursued him, a married man, and this is my punishment. This despair is only retribution for falling in love with him—for falling in love with *her* husband.

Rachel Bensley.

Her name punches through me, learning it like this. I was so selfish. What kind of woman causes this kind of devastation? I'm complicit. I deserve no consolation for the anguish I've caused.

The agony I feel.

I shudder, hearing my mother's voice from another lifetime. Recalling all the hateful things that she said about my father's then-mistress, now-longtime girlfriend.

"What kind of woman fucks married men!" she'd screamed at him. "Trash! A homewrecker! A selfish bitch! A whore!"

Today, those words carve through me. *Is that what I've become? Trash, Homewrecker, Selfish Bitch, Whore*—and perhaps worst of all—*the object of my mother's fury?*

Desperate for an outlet, I hone in on the yet-to-be hung puzzle that still sits on the cocktail table. My despair turns to rage as I shove my feet into a pair of sneakers and throw on my long puffer coat. I snatch the petrified puzzle from the table and head for the door, keys jangling in my pocket. The door's slam echoes down the hallway, following me to the elevator.

Outside, the air is bitter cold, gnawing against my face and neck as I march across the lot to the dumpster. Lifting the lid, I command my arm to chuck it in, to rid myself of this ridiculous symbol of glittering hope for a future with him. *Our future.*

My defiant extremity betrays me. I can't do it.

I groan in aggravation, letting the lid fall shut and blow the putrid scent of rotten garbage on me. I hear my mother's voice again—*Trash!*

Before I know what I'm doing, I've tossed the puzzle into the trunk of my car and cranked the ignition. I don't have my purse or my phone—just the need to drive. *Anywhere but here.*

I have no destination in mind, simply seeking the welcome distraction of the city's bustle and the therapeutic hypnosis of passing streetlights. The streets are disappointingly empty tonight, like a ghost town with no pedestrians or motorists. It's just quiet. *Too quiet.* Just when I need the busyness of Argale to relieve me of the misery of the unknown, it sleeps. I glance at the dashboard. It's 1AM.

I rev the engine, letting the fog of my misery carry me from point A to wherever point B will take me. My knuckles bulge as I grip the steering wheel, navigating purely on autopilot. The car lurches to a stop as I pull into a bare parking lot.

How did I get here? I drove blindly. Irrationally. Aimlessly.

Through the windshield, a grid of lights peek out from the windows of the brutalistic building. The bold and boxy letters of the overhanging sign beam a bright, oppressive white—*Argale General Hospital.*

I sink into my seat, wondering if any one of these windows could be his. Is there any chance he might peer out of one of them?

I shouldn't be here.

Still, I open the car door and follow my feet toward the entrance. Crossing the silent parking lot feels like stepping through a lucid dream—more so a nightmare. The only proof that I'm really here and any of this is real is the intermittent puff of my breath against the cold winter's air.

I pause before the revolving doors. *What is my next move?* Visiting hours are long over, and I don't even know what floor he's on. I linger on the sidewalk, but the sensor above decides for me, activating the door like an open invitation. I stand there for a moment, letting it revolve three times before I relent and step inside.

A pleasant voice calls out to me from the hospitality desk. "Gloria?"

Behind the desk sits a familiar face, her hair pulled up into a sharp bun. It's Ava—one of my classmates from Friday morning yoga. An employee lanyard hangs around her neck.

"Ava," I say, a bit nervous. It feels as though I've been spotted somewhere I don't belong. "I didn't know that you worked here."

She smiles, miraculously chipper for such a late hour. "Yeah, been here for about five years now. As you can see, it's quiet, perfect for studying." She tips a textbook on healthcare management in my direction.

She'd once shared with me her desire to pursue her Master's degree. "Good for you," I offer. Ava doesn't see the mess I am. And I suppose that's good for me.

Checking her watch. "Are you visiting someone?"

"Uh, yes." I lie without lying. "I was in the area. I just wanted to check on a friend. I didn't even realize how late it was. I'll come back another time." My sneakers squeak as I begin my retreat.

"Wait," Ava whispers, waving me back to her desk. "What's the patient's name? I'll look up the room number for you. You're a family member, right?" Her wink tells me to say *yes*.

I force a half-smile and a nod. "Right. His name is, um, Charles Bensley?

My heart races, worried that Ava might recognize his name from the news. Fortunately, her smile remains unbothered. She pecks away at the keys.

"Bensley, got it," she says. "He's on the fifth floor, Room 5324."

"Thank you," I say with complete sincerity. "You know, I really don't need to go up there. It's so late. I don't want to disturb him or get you in any kind of trouble. Does it say how he's doing? I just wanted to check his status."

"It doesn't," she says, tilting her head sympathetically. "Once you're upstairs, you can stop at the nurse's station to inquire. They should be able to help you."

With parting thanks, I walk across the hospital's expansive lobby to the elevators. Pushing the button feels ominous as the numbers on the digital display begin their countdown.

Escape now, while you still can, they seem to say. *3... 2... 1...*

Just then, Ava swings around the corner, waving a small white tag.

"Glad I caught you," she pants. "Here, take this, just in case anyone asks." It's a visitor's pass with *G. Gatlin* scribbled on it in permanent marker. "Technically, it's after hours," she explains, "so I couldn't key you in the system in an official capacity, but this'll do in case anyone has questions."

My heart constricts in my chest. "Thanks, Ava."

"No problem. See you Friday?"

"Yeah, see you then."

The elevator delivers me to the fifth floor, where I slowly make my way down the corridor, scanning the room numbers. *5322... 5323...* There—*5324.*

I hover at the door. The nurse's station is further down the hallway. I could just walk down there and ask them how he's doing. Or I could see him for myself, just through this door...

"You can go in," says a soft voice from behind me. A young nurse pushing a medical cart passes by, nodding toward the door. "He's asleep though. He won't be coming out of his sedation for another few hours."

"Thank you," I whisper before she disappears into the room next door.

After a moment's hesitation, the door opens with very little effort. The sounds of softly beeping monitors reach my ears, careening me back in time. *The last time I was in a position like this was with my mother.* The realization grips me by the throat, but still I press on, moving the curtain aside.

He's asleep, fresh bandages peeking out from beneath a light blue blanket. The muted TV flickers, casting the room in a dim light. The overhead lamp above his bed is turned off, giving him a peaceful look. Holding my breath, I tip toe closer to him—but not too close.

At his bedside are bouquets of colorful flowers and stacks of unopened cards. Even more litter various surfaces on the other side of the room, proof that he is loved.

I'm not needed here.

I find the solace I need in watching his chest rise and fall. This beautiful man, whose face I could sketch with my eyes closed, is alive. I dread the moment he opens his eyes to a life completely changed—a world totally altered by tragedy.

"Hopefully, you can just forget about me," I'd said that fateful night.

Instead, he made love to me. Tears prick at the corners of my eyes. He probably regrets that now. He probably regrets it all. *How could he not?*

"I'm so sorry, Charlie," I breathe, quieter than a whisper.

Damn it. I should've just asked the nurse how he was doing. That was all I needed.

I swipe at the tears that drench my cheeks. I can feel *goodbye* on the tip of my tongue, but my lips stand guard, refusing to allow the word to pass.

Perhaps in another life.

CHARLIE

The machine whirs as I operate the hospital bed remote, tilting myself upright.

"Ugh," I wince aloud, releasing the button as a sharp pain shoots through my abdomen. Breathing through the shock, I push a bit further to bring myself up to seated, straining the arm confined to a sling. I heave for air until I feel stable again. I haven't felt pain like this ever before—sharp, digging pain that radiates through my whole body. I'm desperate enough for a distraction that I un-mute the TV.

Surfing the channels, I come across a commercial for an indoor waterpark that the boys have been asking to go to. Now, my heart aches with a different kind of pain.

"Grandma Mona is here!" my youngest shrieked over the phone yesterday. *"We're making brownies!"*

"Lucky you," I chuckled, remembering my mother's homemade brownies fondly.

It took some convincing, but the doctors agreed to lower my pain meds so that I could talk to my sons without feeling completely out of it. Once I felt like I could string full sentences together, I called to let them know that they'd need to spend a few more days with Uncle Jack.

Jack has always been one of my emergency contacts. The nurses told me he was here for the surgery, only leaving once he knew I'd make it through the night. Since I woke up, he's wanted to visit me, called to say as much, but I asked him to keep my boys preoccupied until I could explain it all to them myself. Since then, Jack has done everything in his power to keep them from the news—even mentioned keeping them home from school for a few days while I muster up my strength.

During yesterday evening's call, the boys wrestled for the phone.

"Alright, guys" I scolded, *"you two are too old for this. Share the phone."*

"Hi, Dad," came CJ's voice with Cam's grumbling in the background.

"Hey, CJ."

"Where's Mom?"

Like a switch flipped in my chest, my heart just—stopped. *"She can't talk right now, son."*

"Okay," he sighed. *"Tell her goodnight for me."*

"I will," I whispered around the lump in my throat.

The TV drones overhead as my mind wanders, fresh tears stinging my eyes. *How do I tell them?* They need to know. They deserve to know what happened to their mother. *But how do I say that they'll never speak to her again?*

"Good morning," sing-songs the cheery food-service aide. She barges through the door, pushing a cart with a platter on top—breakfast, presumably. *I'm not hungry though.*

"Good morning," I mumble.

"I have something yummy for you!" Her Russian accent softens the room. "How are you this morning?"

I mute the TV again. *How do I answer that?*

It's the simplest, most complex question anyone has ever asked me. A question I've asked many grieving people after years of consoling and advocating on behalf of victims and their families. Intellectually, I know how one feels after losing a loved one so tragically—sad, hurt, numb, betrayed, afraid. But now that I'm the one having come so close to death, I can't land on a response. My feelings are all over the place. *I* am all over the place.

This sweet lady isn't asking for a full diagnosis. I scroll through my mental Rolodex of responses—*I'm hanging in there. As good as can be expected. Taking it day by day.* They're all pretty safe choices, even though I'd prefer no comment at all.

Instead, I settle on, "I'm okay. Thanks for asking."

With a nod, she parks the cart and carries the tray to the overbed table. She swings it across my lap, and with a flourish, she lifts the cover to reveal a less than appetizing platter of dry scrambled eggs, pale sausage links, and a pair of microwavable waffles.

"Voila!" she declares.

I force a half-smile.

"No good?"

My smile is more genuine now, and I shake my head.

"How about some fruit?" She offers. "Maybe an apple, a banana, or an orange?" I don't have time to respond before she makes the decision herself. Reclaiming the platter, she pushes the cart back to the door, pausing to stare at the floor. "Tsk, tsk, tsk, we must keep this room clean for you, eh?" She squats to pick up a scrap of paper, reading aloud, "G. Gatlin?"

My head spins so fast in her direction I nearly give myself whiplash.

"I put in trash," she mutters to herself.

I extend a shaking hand. "Uh no, may I have that, please?"

"Yes. It is old visitor's pass. I throw away for you, yes?"

"No," I say firmly, softening my tone with a smile. "I've got it. Thank you."

"Okay," she shrugs, not realizing the value in what she's discovered.

My eyes scan each letter of her name. *G. Gatlin* scribbled in marker, done in a rush. It's not her handwriting, but it's her pass.

Gloria.

She doesn't know it, but she was there with me during those last few moments of consciousness. Feeling the warmth of her presence was enough to make me feel safe again. That was just an illusion, but here? *Was she really here?* I stare down at the tangible piece of evidence between my fingers. *Did she really come to visit me?*

If she knew I was here, then the incident has certainly reached the media, just as I feared.

Ignoring the pain that shoots through my shoulder, I reach for my phone and Google my own name for the first time. A recent news report populates on the screen.

"Domestic Dispute Escalates to Fatal Shooting," the headline reads. My eyes shutter closed in disbelief. *Damn.* And all of Argale knows too.

I read the article against my better judgment. It's a bizarre thing to see one's own name in the description of a crime, rather than simply being quoted as a reliable source on the scene.

Gloria's name stares up at me from the pass, now resting innocently in my lap. I drag my fingers over each letter, my soul burning with shame. My heart aches for what I've lost—*Rachel.* Yet, I long for the comfort of Gloria's embrace.

After this, I know I'll never feel her love again. Ultimately, I've lost it all.

My weary eyes open to the sound of the door. I don't remember falling asleep, but the clock seems to have fast-forwarded into the late afternoon. Footsteps prompt me to look up and see a familiar face. He's the spitting image of my father with a fitted baseball cap on his head and a long, expertly groomed beard hanging from his jaw.

"Jack," I croak. If I needed anyone right now, it's him. *My big brother.*

He sits on the edge of my bed, staring straight ahead until his eyes fall to his fidgeting hands. The breath he exhales seems to quiver in the air between us.

"You scared me baby bro," he says. "I thought I'd lost you."

His face twists with emotion, thumb and index finger catching his tears before they can even fall. Mine don't bother asking permission. They slide freely down my cheeks. Jack leans in to hug me gently—careful of my injuries. He kisses the top of my head, cradling the back of my neck, like I'm just a kid again.

Jack has never been one to conceal his love for me. He's always been in my corner, rooting for me, guiding me. No matter the issue, he has always been there to listen. Always there to learn from.

"How you feeling?" he asks. "Because you look like shit."

I chuckle lightly, wiping tears away. "I've been better. How are the boys?"

"They're fine," he assures me. Jack rises from the bed and wanders over to the collection of greeting cards. I've only opened a few at the nurses' behest, finding a mixture of *Get Well Soon* and sympathy cards—mostly sympathy. "I can tell that CJ suspects something might be wrong. But Cam, he's just happy to be out of school for a few days."

"That boy," I sigh, a fond smile on my face.

"Sounds like someone I know."

We scoff at the truth of it. Jack, like CJ, always had a heightened sense of awareness as the more mature child. Cam, on the other hand, is more like I used to be—content with just being a kid.

Jack goes on to tell me what they've been doing to keep themselves occupied. The boys have been gaming with their cousin Royce, helping their grandma make a big Sunday dinner...

"She went all out," he says. "A roast and mashed potatoes with onions and carrots swimming in gravy—just like back in the day."

"Sounds amazing," I say, staring at the orange the aide must have dropped off while I was out. *What I wouldn't give to have some of my mom's cooking right about now.*

"Tonight is game night," Jack continues. "Aries is at the house preparing as we speak." His whole face lifts when he says her name. They have the kind of marriage I always wanted—intimate, loving, and solid.

"I will not let you disgrace me this way," my wife vowed. *"A failed marriage—the shame. The embarrassment."*

Rachel's voice rips through my memory like wind through broken glass. My chest constricts as I force the echoes from my mind and focus on the present. Knowing that my boys are surrounded by their family brings me some sense of bittersweet solace, considering how much their lives are about to change.

"Thanks, Jack," is all I can manage.

"We got you." He sets the card he was reading back on the table, meeting my eyes. His forehead creases with concern. "Bro, what the hell happened?"

I sigh, unready to answer the inevitable question. "We were arguing, and it escalated," I explain, straight-faced and guarded. The words sound clinical. Flat. Like I'm debriefing the team on a domestic call. I'm not even sure why. Jack is the last person that I'd ever have to worry about providing a socially acceptable answer to. He would never judge me or make me feel like shit, even if I deserved to.

Jack leans back against the wall, unconvinced. "Arguing about what?" he probes, folding his arms across his chest.

I avert my eyes. "I've been seeing someone else."

It's the first time I've admitted it aloud to anyone but Rachel. Unsure if he even heard me, my eyes return to his, only to find them sitting wide on his face inches beneath his raised brows—utterly dumbfounded.

"Wait, what?" Jack chuckles in disbelief. Realizing I'm not joking, he moves swiftly back to the bed, this time pulling up a chair, ready to dive into the details of my life turned soap opera. "Are you serious?"

I nod.

Jack scoots forward to the edge of his seat, his expression both intrigued and confused like his brain is working overtime to process it all. Finally, he fires off his first question: "For how long?"

"About eight months."

"Eight months! Why didn't you tell me?"

As if telling him could've changed the outcome. I begin to wonder if it might have. If I had confided in my brother, what advice would he have given me? *Would Rachel still be alive?*

But I have no words to answer him. I simply shrug, shaking my head.

"Shit," Jack mutters to himself. He sinks back into the chair, raking his fingers through his beard. "Was it serious?"

"Yeah."

He shakes his head. "Damn it, Charlie. You supposed to die with the lie, bro..."

I shoot him a sarcastically scathing look.

Jack's eyes soften. "What do you want me to tell Mom?"

"I don't know. Nothing. I'll talk to her when I'm... when I'm settled."

"Okay." He frowns, contemplating. "What are you going to tell Rachel's family?"

The answer that slips from my mouth surprises us both. "The truth."

March

Two

MELANCHOLY

CHARLIE

The bandage tears open easily between my teeth. Watching my reflection in the full size mirror, I quickly redress my wounds, pressing fresh gauze over my still-discolored flesh. It's unsettling, getting ready in the master bedroom that I no longer share. For a moment, I just stand there, looking in the mirror, trying to recognize the brutalized man in my place. All I see is sleep deprivation, swollen eyes, and a desensitized spirit. At this point, all of my injuries seem self-inflicted. *I did this to myself.*

The day I was discharged, I told my mother.

"I'm sorry," I concluded, my voice hoarse with the burden of my choices.

She was silent for a good, long while. I could see the weight of my confession crushing her pride—the pride she took in having a son that she could dote on for being a good man, husband, and father.

I certainly tried to be.

The look of disappointment quickly crystalized into derision. No doubt was she processing the fact that her son had taken the same disgraceful path as her former husband. Her disgusted stare cut deep as she saw in me the very man that I despised for abandoning his family. The man that carelessly hurt her. The man that I devoted my life to being nothing like.

Perhaps the apple doesn't fall far from the tree after all.

"Bensley men," she said, venom in her voice.

Telling the in-laws was even worse.

"What happened?" Vivian pleaded through the phone, her despair evident.

Seconds of silence turned into horrible minutes. Vivian sliced through the quiet, demanding a prompt explanation. I found it hard to be sincere, despite my plans of being upfront with them out of respect for their daughter and their unthinkable loss. But honesty was already leaving a trail of destruction behind it. *Hurting the ones I love.*

Maybe Jack was right. In the hospital, he'd urged me not to tell the whole truth. To Jack, the truth isn't always a kindness. Since we were kids, he's tried to teach me that sometimes, the truth can cut deeper than a simple, white lie. The least that I could do was spare them any further pain.

So I began cautiously, leaving out the more unsavory pieces. *"We were discussing divorce,"* I explained—which was true.

My tattered version of events proved insufficient to my in-laws. It didn't explain the devastation they were left to sort through. They interrogated me, refusing to accept my superficial recap as the entire story—a story with two sides. Yet, there I was, left with the task of telling it alone.

"Who wanted a divorce?" Vivian demanded. *"You?"*

"No," I said impulsively, *"I mean—"*

"There's something you're not telling us," Wesley added. The heartbreak in his accusation shattered any sense of self-preservation I had left.

So the truth came out. Having to confess my adultery was mortifyingly painful. Shame clung to my every word, and each horrified gasp and wailing scream was completely deserved. I'd broken the promise that I made to them, after all—the promise to love and cherish their daughter, forever.

The funeral director had called earlier this week about arrangements. It seemed that Vivian had submitted her own specifications, which needed my approval: A dove release. A white suit that she'd already ordered and overnighted to the funeral home. And for the floral arrangements, white lilies—*Rachel's favorite.*

I chuckled dryly to myself.

Tulips. Her favorite flowers were tulips.

Even still, I was happy to incorporate all her requests. It was the least that I could do.

Today, we bury my wife. My bedroom door creaks open, and Cam peers at me through the reflection in the mirror. Quickly, I button up my shirt, concealing my injuries.

"Hey bud," I say, adjusting my sling.

His necktie is knotted poorly around his neck. "Dad, do I have to wear this?"

My lips lift into a half-hearted smile. "C'mere." I gesture him over to the bed, where I take a seat. Cam sulks the few steps over to stand between my knees. "Let's do it together—over, under, around and down," I say, hiding a wince as I overexert my bad arm. "Around again, under and down again. Good."

"Is Mom in Heaven?" Cameron asks, trading his sullen expression for curiosity.

"Yep. And she's smiling down on you Cam, you know that, right?"

Cameron nods, his eyes pooling with tears. Swallowing hard, I smooth the knot of his black tie before squeezing his shoulder.

"Okay," I say. "Go get your jacket. I'll be ready in a minute."

The March air whips through the cracked windows of our car. We could have gone with the rest of the family, but I opted to drive the boys myself. Outside, the flowers are budding and the sky is blue—arguably too beautiful for a funeral.

At the funeral home, we join the early-comers walking up toward the front doors. Cam holds my free hand tight while CJ hovers close at my other side. As we approach the steps, I catch Vivian looking my way. It's the first I've seen of her since Christmas, and even behind her sunglasses, I can tell that her face is contorted with unimaginable grief.

Before I can say a word, her hand connects with my face. It's a blow she's probably been waiting to deliver since the ugly call we shared—*my public execution.*

I tense, dropping my eyes to the pavement. Cam squeezes my hand. Jack, seeing the altercation, steps down from the entryway. I turn to my kids with a neutral expression.

"CJ, take your brother, and go to Uncle Jack."

CJ does what he's told, ushering Cam away from the tense scene. Wesley hurries to Vivian's side, gently taking her arm. I can feel Vivian's glare boring into me from behind her dark lenses. A single tear falls from beneath the frames, justification hanging from the quivering down-turn of her pursed lips.

"Vivian," Wesley whispers, but she stands resolute. "Let's go inside. Rachel is inside."

It's then that Vivian breaks down, her chest heaving with sobs. Wesley guides his bereaved wife away, leaving me with a look of disappointment that shatters my resolve. My only remaining father figure doesn't have to say a word for me to know that his adulterous son-in-law has been well and truly disowned.

After the service, I follow a narrow path that winds around the back of the funeral home. It's a peaceful memorial garden, brimming with freshly budding flowers and trimmed shrubs. It's here, seated on a cold, concrete bench, that I finally allow myself to cry.

My wife is gone. The woman I once loved with all of my heart, who bore my children—came to see me as the enemy. *How did we unravel so completely?*

I hunch over, elbows perched on my knees, eyes locked on the cobblestones beneath my feet. Tears rush down my cheeks in uninterrupted streams, soaking the hands I keep tightly clasped over my mouth. I won't make a sound, or else run the risk of someone finding me here.

As if on cue, the sound of approaching footsteps has me wiping my face dry. I look up to see Jack's eyes as watery as mine.

"The boys are with Aries," he assures me before I can even ask, taking a seat next to me. It's exactly what I need—quiet solidarity. The kind that doesn't ask me to speak. The kind that knows the words wouldn't be enough anyway.

It's far too beautiful of a day for a funeral.

The house is quiet, and we three Bensley men are exhausted. My necktie hangs loosely around my neck as I sink into the sofa. The boys curl against me like bookends, my arms holding us all together like the weathered binding of a worn family photo album. Their heads rest on my chest, and I ignore the ache of my injuries. I wonder if they can hear the way my heart breaks.

"Dad," CJ whispers.

"Yeah?"

"Why did Grandma Vivian hit you?"

And here it is—the question that I've been dreading all day. The moment that the boys come to realize that all of this is my fault. *Completely.*

"Because Mom and I were fighting," I whisper back, my voice cracking, heavy with emotion.

"But Dad, you said—"

"I know, CJ. I know what I said."

I said that everything would be alright. A promise to him that I failed to keep.

CJ's shoulders shake as he begins to cry, and then Cameron does too.

Guilt pours out of me in torrents. "I'm so sorry," I murmur, dropping a kiss onto each of their heads as I pull them even closer. My wounds are screaming with the exertion, but I don't care. I need to hold my sons tonight.

One day, they'll want more answers. They'll need a deeper explanation. One day, when they're older, they'll hold me accountable. And I'll be preparing for it every day until the time comes. Until then, I'll carry this. And hope, one day... they'll forgive me.

CHARLIE

My alarm drags me from my dreams. No longer am I in the perfumed embrace of the only woman who's ever loved me for me. Instead, I lay alone in my bed, struggling to remember what she even smelled like. *I don't even dare let myself think her name.*

It's a school day, and the first day that Cam and CJ will be returning to class. CJ has been a bit closed off since the funeral. Seeing his grandmother slap his dad was undoubtedly a shock, as well as the realization that his dad is a hugely flawed person who's been struggling to keep promises lately.

How can I ever make CJ understand that I thought I was doing the right thing, keeping my family together? How is it possible to make a right from an egregious wrong—to justify it? *Won't that only make the wounds deeper?*

I just wanted them to have what I didn't—*a complete family.* I didn't want a divorce, at least not right away. Not until the boys were older. I was ready to play the good husband as long as it allowed me to be the best father I could be.

Birdsong lilts through the window, a gentle breeze coaxing me from my bed. I consider keeping the boys home from school for just one more day, but they've missed all of last week, and I don't want them to fall further behind. Their teachers were kind enough to email their assignments to me. A week's worth of make-up assignments proved to be the perfect excuse for CJ to lock himself away in his room all of yesterday. *Avoiding me.*

It's only five in the morning. *Go back to sleep*, I tell myself.

God, I wish I could.

Sleep hasn't come easily to me since the incident. My thoughts are louder than they've ever been, my brain constantly running like an engine that just won't quit. No amount of white noise or melatonin can drown out my regrets, let alone lull me to sleep.

I got a solid two hours, and a dream out of it too. I'll just be grateful for that. It's the most I've had all week. I pull myself up with a little effort, sitting on the bed's edge for a moment as I wait for the ache of my slowly healing wounds to subside.

Showering with open wounds isn't easy. Lately, a sponge bath has been a half-decent solution. Since I have the time, I wrap my torso in plastic so I can stand under the hot stream and let it work out the tension in my neck and shoulders. *Drown out my thoughts.* When I'm done, the house is still quiet, the boys still asleep.

In the kitchen, I linger next to the island, memories of broken glass, screaming wails, and gunfire ringing in my ears.

I steady myself against the counter, feeling suddenly nauseous. I don't want the boys to know just how volatile that night was. I want them to know that they are safe—that their mother loved them more than anything, even if she...

With unsteady steps, I reach the table, finding one of Cam's school notebooks, math problems scribbled across the pages. He won't mind if I take a few sheets for myself. The sun is just cresting over the trees when I begin to write.

To my sons,

Forgive me.

I'm sorry for the hurt that I've caused. Mom is no longer here for you, and I take responsibility for that. I betrayed her trust, I hurt her, and that was wrong. From this experience, I find it essential to reiterate the significance of integrity, good character, and taking accountability for one's actions. I hope that your hearts aren't too jaded to receive a bit of hard-won insight from me, and I pray that you know that I only have your best interests at heart.

When you were born, like every parent, I promised you the life that I didn't have. I wanted nothing but the best for you and was determined to make the world a better place for you to live in. Perhaps my promise was a bit lofty, and I was unprepared for some of the challenges I would face trying to stay true to the commitment I made to you.

If I could go back and add an addendum, it'd be to forewarn you that I would fall short. A promise more plausible than the first. Time and time again, my humanity will mock me, bitterly reminding me I'm flawed, limited and incapable of being a perfect man. And despite my earnest desire to be everything that you need, I will disappoint you, make mistakes, and perhaps even let you down.

However, I will never lose the zeal for growth, if only for your sake.

Your life looks different than what you or I undoubtedly planned. Nevertheless, I pray you will live and take risks. Be a meaningful contribution to the world and approach each day with wonder and excitement. Be exceedingly optimistic. Seek counsel and wisdom. Have good character and hold tight to those that matter the most. Learn from your failures and seek to extract every ounce of wisdom that you can from their lessons. Help others. If you fall, get back up. If you make a mistake, correct it. If you hurt someone, make amends. Try not to lose yourself in the sorrow of making mistakes, don't cling to the hurts of the past, and proactively forgive others and yourself.

There aren't words that can express what you mean to me.

You add texture to the fabric of my life. You are my greatest adventure. Your potential is limitless, and I am eager to witness all that you will achieve. I know that you will make a difference—you already have. It is an honor to be your father, my life is truly better for it.

I love you.

Dad

I find an envelope in my office to seal the letter away, tucking it into the top drawer of my desk, for safekeeping. Until they're older, until they can understand.

Coffee percolates in the machine, filling the kitchen with the enticing scent of fresh caffeine. It's domestic but I close my eyes, pretending I'm just waiting for the Keurig at work to finish brewing my morning coffee. When I open them again, I survey the room like I'm looking at crime scene photos. As a detective, I'm naturally inclined to investigate, to determine how an event can escalate to a crime. Taking a sip of coffee, I resolve to understand what happened—to uncover the facts, retrace the steps, and piece together the fragments to form the whole story.

To make it make sense.

Was it merely a crime of passion? Or had she already devised a plan—a contingency to an unaccepted ultimatum? Had she already determined that the marriage would end only on her terms?

"Divorce is not an option," she'd said.

The idea that her actions might have been premeditated spark a flame of fury from the ashes of my grief. I shake away the thought of it. I'm angry but not enough to believe that she would hurt us this way. Or at least I hope not. That night, I questioned if she ever loved me, if she was only willing to stay in this marriage for appearances.

Is that so much worse than staying in it for the kids?

I had hope for us. Until I didn't. *Until...*

A shuffle of feet precedes CJ's appearance at the bottom of the stairs, interrupting my thoughts.

"Good morning," I say.

"Good morning," he grumbles, only shooting a quick glance in my direction.

He doesn't want to look at me.

CJ saunters up to the cabinet, pulling two bowls from overhead to place on the island.

"Did you sleep okay?" I ask.

He nods, retrieving a pair of spoons for him and his brother.

"CJ, look at me."

He does, but not without apprehension. It's like he thinks I'll be able to see exactly what he's thinking, just by looking into his eyes.

I can't read his mind though. *What is he thinking?*

"I know that I promised you that everything would be okay. I'm sorry," I plead, internally kicking myself for bringing this up so early in the morning. *Find a better time.*

Cam stumbles down the stairs before CJ can form any sort of response. We both look in his direction, which stops him in his tracks.

"What?" he yawns.

CJ takes the opportunity to ignore my apology, grabbing a box of cereal.

"Nothing bud," I say, beckoning him inside with a wave.

Cam makes himself comfortable on a stool at the breakfast bar, jolting when his brother slams the cereal box on the counter.

"Cameron!" CJ gripes. "You ate all the cereal!"

"No, I didn't!" Cam whines.

"Yes, you did!"

My shock at the sudden outburst quickly devolves into something darker, my ears echoing with their mother's enraged screams around this very island.

"Stop!" I yell. The boys freeze, staring at me with wide eyes. "We'll pick something up on the way. Get your bags, and go get in the car. Now!"

CJ storms away, knocking over the mostly empty box of cereal in his wake. Cameron follows timidly behind his older brother, startled out of his sleepiness.

I've never been one to yell at my sons. *Damn it.*

Later when we're pulling out of the drive-through, I find the words for an apology.

"I didn't mean to yell at you two like that," I say, locking eyes with Cam in the rearview while CJ stares out the window. "I'm sorry for raising my voice. I'll grab some cereal on the way home. You don't need to fight like that over something so small."

"Okay, Dad," Cam says, chewing on his ham and cheese croissant sandwich. CJ's breakfast sits uneaten in his lap.

"Eat up, CJ. They won't let you eat that at school," I say, making an effort to keep my tone soft. Reluctantly, he opens the parchment paper and takes a bite. The rest of the ride is silent. When I pull into the drop-off lane, I turn around and say, "Alright, listen. At any point, if you're not feeling great and want to come home, just go to the office and have them call me. I'll come get you, okay?"

"Okay, Dad," Cam repeats.

"CJ?"

My oldest finally meets my eyes, but his expression is heartbreakingly sullen. "Okay."

Together, they exit the vehicle, the door slamming behind CJ before I can wish them well. I sit and stare at the school's front doors long after they disappear through them. A car idling behind me honks softly, and I wave an apology out the window as I pull out of the way.

Seems like I have a lot of apologizing to do these days.

CHARLIE

Friday night means movie night, or at least it did before our whole world upended. It's the least I can do to try to keep our traditions alive—to restore some sense of normalcy.

Normalcy is a long road ahead.

As T'Challa dons the Black Panther suit on screen, I recall my own masking, albeit much less heroic. Now, even simple cereal runs feel awkward. At the grocery store, I pulled the hood of my hoodie over my head after spotting a woman whispering to her friend as I walked by. Did she recognize me? My photo had been included in the article about the incident. Probably not, I told myself. But what if she did? Is this my new norm—the constant ping-ponging of paranoia? Either way, it's uncomfortable as hell.

All the more reason to have groceries delivered to the house from now on.

When the credits roll, I yawn, rolling my shoulders back. "Alright, bedtime."

No one fusses when I turn off the TV, rising to their feet and heading for the stairs.

"And Cameron," I call, "you need to brush for at least two minutes."

"I know," he calls back, a hint of annoyance in his tone.

"Just a reminder," I say gently. "I'll be up in a bit to say goodnight."

I take my time cleaning up the living room, raking popcorn crumbs into my hands and dumping them into the trash. When all the blankets have been neatly folded and placed back in the ottoman, I climb up the stairs after them.

CJ is still awake, sitting up in bed with his Nintendo Switch illuminating his face.

"Time to power down," I say.

He does as he's told, placing the device in his nightstand. *He's so quiet lately.*

With a sigh, I sit on the edge of his bed, choosing my next words carefully. "How has school been, son? Has anyone been unkind to you? You can tell me if they have. Because, if anyone has been mean to you or your brother, I'll—"

"Dad," he interrupts. "No one's been mean."

"Okay." I raise my hands in surrender. *So the problem is me.* "I love you, CJ."

Dead air hangs between us.

"Love you too," he finally says, pulling his blanket over his head. *End of conversation.*

Turning off the light on my way out the door, I head to Cam's room next.

"Hey, Cam," I whisper through the cracked door, but my youngest is already asleep, sprawled across his bed with one arm hanging loose over the edge. I smile to myself, stepping inside to adjust his position into something more comfortable.

"Good night," I murmur, kissing the top of his head.

When it's time to tuck myself in, I can't seem to fall asleep. Night after night, I lie awake in the loneliest place in this whole house—our bed. The empty space beside me is a constant reminder of all the reasons I don't deserve a good night's rest.

I still listen for her footsteps. It's a habit I can't shake. My mind returns to a pamphlet that I read at the funeral home on the stages of grief. I struggle to determine which phase I'm in. Denial? Anger? Depression?

Does it matter?

If I've learned anything from this harrowing experience, it's that what goes around comes around. I tried to carve some happiness for myself out of this life and only ended up back in the same prison I was trying to escape. *Loneliness.* For hours, I toss and turn on the mattress until my wounds begin to ache again. I twist the switch on my bedside lamp, casting the room in a warm glow that does nothing to chase away the cold I feel inside.

Downstairs, my pain meds go down nice and easy with a glass of cold water. My eyes catch on the bar cart, a bottle of bourbon gleaming enticingly in the low lamp light.

I need sleep, one way or another.

The bourbon is warm in my throat. I toss the tumbler back—savoring just a shot's worth, so as not to interact with my pain meds too dramatically.

Outside the sliding glass doors, I can see that the patio lights have been left on. The wind rattles the hanging bulb, casting our outdoor enclosure in strange and unfamiliar shadows. I step outside, and the night air wraps cold hands around my bare chest.

"*Make some time for us, Rach,*" I begged of her.

"*Charlie, please don't start.*"

I turn off the lights and lock the patio door behind me. No amount of water or bourbon or well-placed guilt could wash down the lump in my throat. Upstairs, light peeks out from under the doorway to my bedroom, like it might have on a normal night.

She could be on the other side of this door, sitting at her vanity.

But Rachel's stool is empty, the mirror in her vanity only reflecting our empty bed. Her makeup and jewelry sit untouched, exactly as she left them, like she was planning to come back to them the next morning. Whatever she decided, whatever she felt, it was in the moment. It wasn't premeditated. The detective in me knows that such little evidence can't excuse the possibility, but the husband in me knows that Rachel didn't mean for it to go as far as it did.

This relief is bittersweet.

I stare at the traces of her until they lose their meaning, like words I've forgotten how to read. They're nothing if they're not in her hands anymore. I even lift her perfume to my nose—her signature scent—but still I feel empty. In the closet, I find a hat box that will serve as an adequate resting place. Lifting the lid, I empty the vanity to the brim.

When I'm done, my dual medication swirls in my gut. I let my head drop to my hands as I sit on her stool, facing away from the mirror. The room stills when I fixate on the bed, the symbol of our failed marriage. Except for the turned down duvet on my side, it sits like a photo from a magazine or a display in a furniture store. *Not real. Not warm. Not love-worn.*

A lovers' bed should be a refuge from the world, a sanctuary where reality can slow down and the bad days can fade away into distant memories. A lover's bed is for tangled sheets, pillow talk, and loving whispers.

Instead, our bed was one of absence, distance, and rejection. It was a slow death.

I can't help feeling sad, but it's a familiar sadness, the same I felt throughout our marriage. I lost Rachel long before the day she left us behind. Is that why my grief is so disjointed and strange? Have I been grieving for years already? Do I now just grieve for my sons, who lost their mother?

I spin my wedding ring on my finger. The pain in my heart is dull as ever, like a chronic ache I've learned to live with. It'll always be there, but it doesn't have to rule me. Everyone else's grief is a fresh wound. Mine is already scarring. *I'm done picking at scabs.*

For the first time in years, I slide my ring off my finger. Slowly, I rise to my feet, flexing my newly bare hand. The box of Rachel's things stares up at me, an accumulation of all of the tools my wife used to create an appearance of perfection. The ring drops into the box without a sound, resting easily in the midst of Rachel's tokens of image.

Like it belongs there.

It's only when I put the lid back on top of my melancholy that I'm finally able to sleep.

April

Three

THE PERSISTENCE OF MEMORY

GLORIA

It's been a day.

My trench coat swishes against the grocery basket in my hand. Now that the winter has begun to thaw, I've traded my puffer coat for something more breezy.

"How's your friend?" Ava had asked in the yoga studio's parking garage earlier this morning. *"Is he still in the hospital?"*

Luci stared at me with her brows raised, waiting for my response with her suspicious sister senses simmering. I wonder which word triggered this impulse. *Friend? Or He?*

"I'm not sure. How's school going?" I asked, changing the subject. At the push of a button, my car started a few rows down. I was ready to make a break for it if I had to.

Just as Ava opened her mouth to answer, Luci interrupted, circling back. *"Who's in the hospital?"* she probed.

"No one you know," I said curtly. After a purely performative glance at my watch, I made up some excuse about having to go to work early. Luci was still asking questions when I kissed her on the cheek and waved goodbye to a perfectly clueless Ava. I couldn't very well fault the girl for her sincerity. It was equal parts lucky and unlucky that she was my ticket to seeing Charlie that day.

I spent the rest of the day preparing a solid case for trial. It's rare that complaints against the city go beyond pre-trial motions. Generally, it's in the best interest of both parties to reach a settlement out of court, avoiding court costs and time.

However, with both sides standing firm on their positions, this case will be heard and decided by a judge and jury. These trials can take weeks with jury selection, presentation of evidence and cross-examinations. Needless to say, I've got my work cut out for me. Buried in briefs, I barely noticed when the sun went down. To be honest, I don't mind the workload these past few weeks.

I've needed the distraction.

In the grocery store, I add another bottle of red wine to my basket. I'll be pulling an all-nighter to ensure that I'll have everything needed for discovery tomorrow.

Shockingly, I haven't heard from Luci yet. My sister is a natural born litigator despite her decision to go into education. I've never asked, but I think she chose otherwise to spite our father. After our parents split,

Luci wasn't as forgiving as I was, and it's an issue that still lingers between them to this day.

Unlike my father, I managed to escape with my secret still intact.

What would I even say? I can't imagine that my married sister would understand how I fell for a man that was beyond off-limits. I found that Big Love she's been wanting for me, that she foretold, but it came with an expiration date. How could I expect her to be happy about it? How could I tell her that I'm in love with him without offending her principles? And how on Earth could I bring her up to speed without her losing her mind and going all kinds of apeshit on me.

I just wish I'd clocked his ring before I was so changed by his smile. Maybe then I could have chalked up the attraction to a taste for the forbidden. I could have written him off like any other married man on the prowl with a wife and kids at home.

Truth be told, Charlie is special. I knew it the moment that I placed my hand in his that night at Swank. Our first handshake was magnetic, and it scared me more than I can say. There was something between us that not even a ring could chase away.

Pure lust inspired me to boldly invite him into the Bassment for a secretive rendezvous, finding a bit of security in knowing he had very little to say in how the relationship could progress. But it was something else that coaxed me into inviting him to all my favorite places—my sacred spaces. The Hot House, Hurley Park, my own bedroom... He was the only man that ever proved capable of unraveling me. Ghosting him was the right move. But despite my best efforts to discount our connection, he was impossible to ignore. The magnetism never faded, and seeing him across any room always sent a delicious shiver down my spine. No matter where I turned, he was there, as if an invisible string hung taut between us, tying him to me. Now, I haven't spoken to my fated in weeks, and the string tugs tighter than ever, yanking my heart back toward—

My phone rings in my pocket. I blink, realizing I've been standing here for God knows how long, staring blindly at the ingredients on the side of a box of cereal. *Get it together, Gloria.*

"Hey Daddy," I say, smiling into the phone I've wedged against my shoulder.

"Well, good evening, Counselor. Whatcha up to?"

"Just a quick after-work grocery run," I say, placing the cereal back on the shelf and continuing down the aisle.

"Speaking of work, have you found a better job yet?"

I roll my eyes. "Dad, please don't start..."

He sighs, relenting. "Okay. How's work then?"

Turning into the produce section, I simply say, "It keeps me busy."

"Is that why you graduated law school at the top of your class? To be kept busy?"

"Yep!" I tease, but he's unamused.

"Gloria," he asserts. "It's just not exactly the future that I hoped for you, sweetheart. You're a brilliant lawyer, and you should be working for a prestigious firm or running your own practice. Not working for the state—making peanuts, I would imagine."

"No complaints here, Daddy. And I appreciate that. Really, I do. I'm happy here. That's what matters, right?"

"I suppose," he grumbles.

"So, to what do I owe the pleasure of this call?" I ask, feeling a mango for bruises.

"Ev and I are planning an anniversary party. So put it on your calendar."

"An anniversary party," I repeat slowly.

"Yep, it's been 25 years." He sounds proud, but I know they've been together for longer. It makes sense why they'd opt not to celebrate the years before the divorce.

"Wow, Daddy, that's really something. Hold on."

I stop for a moment to plug the details into my calendar. I suppose I was never really able to appreciate their love for one another until now. I recall the look on Charlie's face when I told him about my dad and Evelyn. When he learned how long they'd been together, hope seemed to spill from his eyes. Sleeping in his arms that night, I couldn't help but long for the same, praying that we'd end up together too—*eventually.*

But Charlie and I—our situation—is different. I want to believe he'll find his way back to me but the circumstances feel so extreme.

What happened that night?

"Okay," I say, lifting the phone back to my ear. "I'll be there."

"Thank you, baby. I can't wait to see you. And sometime between now and then, perhaps you'll give some serious consideration to staying in D.C. You know, to retire me." The line goes quiet as I take his joke to heart. "Gloria, you there?"

"Yeah, I'm here. Sorry, I was just thinking. Maybe you're right... Maybe I should come back."

"What's wrong?" I can hear his frown through the phone.

"What do you mean?"

"I've been battling with you for years about coming back to D.C., and then suddenly without a fight, it's a consideration?"

"Nothing's wrong," I laugh, trying to sound convincing. "And since when do you argue with someone telling you that you may be right?"

He chuckles. "I must've missed that."

"Hey listen, let me wrap this up here. I've got you locked in. Say hey to Evelyn for me. I'll see you in November. Okay?"

"Alright, sweetheart. Take care of yourself. Love you, darling."

"Love you too, Dad."

Even though I drop my phone back into my tote, our conversation doesn't leave my mind. As amazing as it's been, living here in Argale, I mull over the possibility of returning to my home base. I load my groceries into my trunk, considering the pros and cons. Being close to Luci has been the top-most perk of living here. Immersing myself into a community that I've come to love has been a joy in itself. Maybe Argale isn't the forever home that it began to feel like it could be, especially now that even a restaurant sign reminds me of my heartache. The glowing, green Milligan's sign hovers over my car as I drive past, remembering the first time I invited him over for takeout—the first time I let anything besides our physical chemistry spark between us.

It wouldn't be so bad, heading back to D.C. I could just pick up where I left off. Maybe I'll add that to tomorrow's to-do list. I begin a mental checklist. *Update my resume. Search for apartments. Explore new career opportunities.*

Crossing Moonpath Lane, I remember the article stating that he lived on the 1200th block. I chide my memory for retaining such a useless detail. It's not like I could go visit him. I'm left out in the cold, as any woman in my position would be.

Under the circumstances, the fact that we fell in love is... insignificant. It's time to move on. *He's trying to move on, Gloria. Let him be.*

Still—

Charlie, am I waiting for you? I wonder, my heart whispering the answer.

Because I would.

CHARLIE

It's been a long time since the swing of a ponytail stopped my heart. The woman who just walked into the coffee shop isn't Gloria Gatlin, but damn does she remind me of her. She's strikingly elegant with her pumps and designer bag. Beautiful, but none compare to my girl.

My girl.

The woman has her phone tucked sweetly against her smile. She blushes, like the person on the other end just made her day.

What if that was us? What if Gloria answered my call and smiled just like that?

"Just checking in," I'd say. *"How's your day going?"*

"Good," she'd giggle. *"Will I see you tonight?"* she'd ask, already knowing the answer.

As the woman joins the line, I focus back on the work in front of me. Frequenting the coffee shop has become something of a routine in my new life as a single dad. The boys and I have found a flow that's led us somewhere next to normal. I, for one, have started jogging again. It helps me clear my mind and tricks me into thinking that normalcy is within reach. I haven't been cleared to return to work yet, and that giant sarcophagus of a house is the last place I want to be. So, while the boys are at school, I camp out at a local cafe to get back into the swing of things. It feels good to be busy again, but even so, I still war with the anxiety that comes with sitting in public. I do my best to ignore the occasional whisper and wide-eyed stare from other cafe-goers.

Life must go on.

In the spirit of returning to work, I've been responding to security inquiries all morning. Jeremiah, one of my leads, took up the mantle while I was out of commission, and I owe him thanks and a bonus for good measure for all the work he's done. *Good looking out, J.*

The door chimes, and I look up to see a detective that I know all too well.

"Bens," Graham says, a wide grin across his face.

I stand, pulling my friend into a hug. "It's good to see you."

Lifting the strap of his leather messenger bag over his head, Graham takes the seat opposite of me. "How you been, CB? No more sling I see. The office hasn't been the same without you."

"Yeah, I miss you guys."

The team is short-staffed with me waiting for clearance and Anderson gone on maternity leave. Graham texted earlier this morning to ask me to put eyes on an ongoing case—the Minter case, in which the senator's daughter was found dead in the river. It's a high-profile case, and I jumped at the opportunity to meet him for some good, old-fashioned think-tanking.

"You coming back any time soon?" he asks.

"Hopefully," I sigh, leaning back in my chair. "I have a few more weeks of physical therapy, and I'll need to get cleared at the range after that."

"Happy to hear it, brother. I'm looking forward to having you back on the job. And grateful for no new cases since you've been gone." Graham knocks on the wooden table, his eyes fall on the mystery novel I purchased at the local book store. "Brushing up?"

"Something like that," I chuckle, my mind wandering back to Gloria. She's the one who got me hooked on mystery novels, and reading this one makes me feel closer to her. *Wonder if she's read it yet?*

"Well," Graham says, "here's what we've got..."

Before he can pull his laptop onto the table, I say, "Yo G, before we dive in, I just wanted to say thank you for your friendship. You've always had my back, and I appreciate that."

"You know you're my boy, CB," Graham says with his goonish smile.

"I feel like I owe you an explanation."

"Listen, you can tell me anything. You can also not tell me a damn thing if you don't want to."

Graham has always met me where I'm at. It feels like an invitation to come clean.

"I should've said something sooner, but I..." I sigh, searching for the right words. I'm closer to accepting that the *right words* might not exist. I lower my voice, clasping my hand on the table. "That night. With Rachel... I'd been having an affair. And when she confronted me about it, I was honest. I'd hoped that she and I could have had a reasonable conversation about how to move forward, but I guess I was kinda naïve about that. I know that you thought my marriage was perfect but... not even close."

Graham doesn't look shocked—just solemn. He nods. "No one's perfect, Bens."

"Yeah, I know."

"I'm sorry for your loss, man. I'm glad your boys didn't lose you too."

I crack a half-smile. "Me too, Graham. Me too."

"So..." he begins, something mischievous in his eyes. "Who is she? Anyone I know?"

I peer up at him from over the rim of my mug—contemplating. A large part of me is still hesitant to say. I want to protect Gloria, but I know Graham wouldn't betray my trust. All this time, I've just been hiding behind the preservation of her reputation rather than seeking camaraderie with my trusted friend. This will probably be the first and last time I'll ever get to tell another soul what she means to me.

How much I love her.

"Gloria Gatlin," I say.

His eyes just about bug out of his head. "Get the fuck outta here!" Catching the looks of fellow cafe-goers, he drops his voice to a whisper. "ASA Gloria Gatlin?"

"Yep."

He's speechless for a moment, opting to simply nod with approval. "I mean, it's fucked up what happened, but, yeah, she *bad*, man."

"Yeah," I agree, snickering before sobering. "But it wasn't just sex, you know. Our connection is—*was* amazing. Honestly, I didn't even know that she was a prosecutor when we met. I saw her, and it was like the world stopped spinning. I've never felt that way before. And then to be with her... to get to know her. I could spend the rest of my life with her. I'm in love with her, G."

The words spill out of me like a dam burst free, weight lifting off my shoulders as the rapids of my truth wash my burden away. It's damn near baptismal.

"I know that's a lot, so thanks for listening," I add. "It's been a secret for so long, and I needed to tell someone. Thanks for being someone I can trust."

There's pride in the quirk of his smile. "Your secret is safe with me. So, where do the two of you stand now?"

I shrug. "I don't know. I haven't spoken to her since the incident."

"What? Why not?"

"I don't know what to say. I'm ashamed. She didn't sign up for this shit. And I'm not quite ready to add heartache to my list of troubles right now."

Graham shakes his head vehemently. "You need to talk to her. Call her, Bens. You just told me that you love her, that you could spend the rest of your life with her. The timing isn't great, and what happened between you and Rachel is fucked up but you deserve to pursue your happiness now more than ever. Go get your woman, man."

A half-smile finds its way to my lips, even though reluctance still sits heavy on my heart. Graham's support and words of encouragement, it's everything I needed to hear and more. I'm happy that I confided in him. And as much as I want to pull out my phone and call her, to hear her voice, her smile on the other end—as tempting as it would be to run down to her office and knock on her door, flowers in my hand, my heart on my sleeve...

I can't. I have to let her go. She deserves better than what I've become—*broken.*

How could she ever trust me?

He's right about one thing though, we need to talk. I owe her that. *A respectable goodbye.*

But first, business.

"Thanks, G." I point to the laptop in his hands. "Show me what you got."

GLORIA

An email from a recruiter in D.C. sits open on my laptop, waiting for my response. The list of opportunities should feel exciting, but my fingers hesitate at the keyboard.

The doorbell rings. I look down at my watch—9:06 PM. My neighbor must've locked herself out again. I peek through the peephole before reaching for the knob, and what I see sets my heart racing.

Charlie.

Butterflies swarm wildly in the pit of my stomach. I didn't know he was coming, or else I would've worn.... something else. My cropped Howard sweatshirt and cozy joggers are hardly the usual ensemble I would greet him in.

Relax, Gloria. He couldn't possibly be here to just pick up where we left off.

With a deep breath for good measure, I open the door.

He lifts his eyes to mine, then says, "Hey."

"Hey," I return, heart in my throat.

"I should have called." His five o'clock shadow has filled out into a well-groomed beard, elevating his sophistication.

"That's okay," I insist, stepping aside. "Come in."

I wasn't expecting a guest, let alone the man that makes my heart smile. Files lie haphazardly across the counter, and my glass of wine sits waiting.

"Were you working?" he asks.

"Yeah, just doing a little research for a case. Have a seat."

I gesture to the stool next to mine. He joins me, propping his feet on the lower rungs and clasping his hands between his legs. I close my laptop as if to say, *you have my full attention.*

"I'm sorry that it took me so long to reach out," he begins, staring at the floor. "I've had a lot going on."

"I know. I'm... I'm so sorry for your loss, Charlie," I whisper. My fingers twitch around my wine glass, wanting nothing but to entangle with his. *Better not.*

"Thanks," he murmurs. "I don't usually make it a habit to show up anywhere unannounced. I've just had so much that I've wanted to say to you, and every time I begin to draft a text, I'd talk myself out of sending it. So I just followed my feet today." His smile is only half-full but still softens his features. "I figured I couldn't back out once I was here."

A smile blossoms on my own face. *I'm so glad you're here.*

As if reading my mind, Charlie holds his hands out between us, silently asking for mine. I place my hands in his, helpless to his magnetism. We slide closer, our knees interlacing.

"Gloria," he sighs, voice thin. "I..." His mouth opens then closes, like he's struggling to find the words. He strokes my knuckles with the soft pad of his thumb. Finally, he asks, "Do you know what a red nova is?"

I shake my head.

"It's a stellar explosion. It occurs when two stars collide."

"Okay...?" I cock my head to the side, trying to understand.

"Fun fact..." He smiles, eyes sparkling. "Stars rarely collide. I learned that while I was helping my son with his science project last year." As he reminisces, I chew on a smile, imagining him erecting a model of the solar system with one of his boys. "I remember thinking of you, of us. A red nova, stars destined to collide—a grand design. His smile fades, the light in his eyes dimming. The air hangs empty and heavy between us, like gravity just pulled us back down to Earth, slowly drifting us back to reality.

Finally, he draws a shaky breath to speak. "It was a mistake..."

I knew it.

It's one thing to anticipate it, chew on it, try your best to break it down to nothing so that it's easier to digest. But his confirmation of my worst fear goes down whole, and I can barely breathe around it. We were a mistake, one that he would clearly take back if he could. History he'd rewrite, if given the chance. My heart aches like an old wound reopening in my chest.

"A mistake…" I breathe uneasily.

"Yeah." He nods, staring off into space. "I should have ended it with Rachel years ago. I should have sorted this out with her long before resentment had a chance to fester between us. It was a mistake, thinking that staying was the right thing to do. That night at Swank, I should have already closed one chapter—free to begin another. *Available.* No ring on my finger."

I realize that his wedding ring is gone now, his ring finger bare. My memories flood with our first clandestine meeting at Swank—one of my favorite places. The dark, sharply cut vest he wore, the ring on his finger he never once tried to hide…

The warmth of his eyes.

I blink the mist from mine, hoping he can't see the hope in them. I should be ashamed of how relieved I feel, but I can't help it any more than I can help clinging to his hand right now.

Exhale, Gloria.

Charlie graciously breaks the silence again. "That mistake has left me with very little to offer you. I'm hardly the man that destiny designed for you. The man that you need—that you deserve."

"Charlie…" I lift my hand to his cheek, slowly, carefully. His beard is as soft as it looks, and I relish in the new but gentle abrasion against my fingertips. He covers my hand with his own, drawing the sensitive flutter of my wrist's pulse to his lips. I feel that kiss everywhere I shouldn't, but I remain perfectly still.

Charlie lowers our hands between us again. "Let's cash in while we're up. There's no telling what our next hand will look like, and I'm afraid it's a hand that we can't win with, baby."

He's right. My head tells my lips to agree with him, but my heart aches to object—to give us the chance that we deserve. I've been here before, after all. Not so long ago, I too was afraid of the overwhelming energy that binds us together. If we really are just two entities spinning through the vast canopy of space, there's a high probability that we could be ejected from our personal utopia. *Maybe we already were.* It feels easier to just let go on our own terms rather than risk losing each other to the unknown.

My lips ache with everything I'm holding back. *I know, Charlie.*

I want to assure him. *I've tried.* I want to tell him that I've done everything in my power to let go. I made many earnest attempts to push him away, but random run-ins turned into secret rendezvous, and the forbidden taste of each other's lips turned into the sweet wine of a love confession. *One that I tried to dismiss.*

I want to remind him that something cosmic worked awfully hard to bring us together. Even now, it's trying to keep us together—to keep him here with me after a brush with death. *Something written in the stars?*

We collided—lit up the sky red, the color of love. And our luminous glow has only just begun. We're still in orbit.

"My poker knowledge is limited," I finally say, "so from what I do know, you can still win, even when dealt a bad hand... right?"

Charlie's eyes brim with tears. They leave glossy stains in their wake, and I want nothing more than to wipe them away. Instead, I wait patiently for his answer.

"Yes, baby—you can," he says to the floor beneath our feet. My heart soars as his ebony eyes rise to meet mine.

"So, deal me in."

May

Four

VENUS AND MARS

CHARLIE

Jazz echoes through the kitchen, mingling with the smell of basil, tomatoes, and cheese. I open the oven to check on the lasagna, mouth watering at the sight of bubbling mozzarella. The timer on the stove says ten more minutes until done. It looks ready to me, but I check the recipe to be sure.

Cook for 50 minutes at 375 degrees, it reads in Aries' handwriting. *Who am I to argue with her?*

My sister-in-law was kind enough to prep and pack the meal with easy instructions. As the consolation casseroles depleted, *"What's for dinner?"* quickly became the most dreaded question of the day. I have a few go-to meals in my repertoire, but my once fan faves now get pushed around on the plate like unwanted vegetables.

Aries soon got wind of our exclusively take-out dinners and graciously took matters into her own hands. A professional dietician, she has been a Godsend, preparing meals once a week for us in addition to setting up a meal kit delivery that arrives every Monday night. Hats off to parents who meal prep on a daily basis. It's a skill that I have a newfound appreciation for.

Thank God for sisters-in-law.

I suppose Aries is my only sister-in-law now. At the funeral, I was met with stares, whispers, and frowns from the Evans family—as to be expected. But not from Leah. Rachel's little sister still held empathy for me in her eyes, subtle as it was. They were close, and she was the only relative that was willing to call my wife on her shit for neglecting our marriage.

I wince slightly at the heat of my thoughts, hot enough to scald. With a deep breath, I urge the negative thoughts away, focusing back on Leah's kindness. She's been an ally to me, all these years. I'll need her help to ensure that the boys stay in touch with the Evans side. I don't foresee any forgiveness from my in-laws in my future, but my boys shouldn't suffer for my choices. They should have a relationship with their grandparents.

My jaw tingles where Vivian struck me, weeks ago.

My phone buzzes on the counter nearby. A winky face from Gloria is a very welcome distraction. I thumb her contact open and give her a call.

"Hi," she answers. I can hear her smile through the phone, just as I imagined it that day in the café.

"Hey, whatcha up to?" I wedge the phone between my shoulder and ear, shaking a bag of croutons into a premade salad, courtesy of Aries.

"Picking up some dinner."

"What are you having?"

"A dragon roll and a bowl of miso soup."

Sushi. "Sounds good."

"Is that Coltrane I hear?"

"Yep," I chuckle, turning up the speaker ever so slightly.

She giggles. "'I'm Old Fashioned,' huh? Suits you."

"I could use an old fashioned right about now, actually."

We should grab a drink sometime. That's the subtext that never actually leaves my lips. It feels absurd to suggest something as pedestrian as a drink with this woman—this relentless spirit, who has deigned to stay in touch with me in the aftermath. She could have ended it that night—shut the door and left me standing in the past. *But she didn't.*

"Well, hey," I say, clearing my throat. "I'm about to call the boys down for dinner. Can I call you later?"

"Of course."

"Okay."

I'm about to bid her goodbye for now when she says, "Hey."

"Yeah?"

"Your boys—what are their names?"

A slow smile stretches across my face. "Hang on." I lower my phone to scroll through a photo album. There's a picture of the three of us that I like, and I shoot it her way. "On the left is my oldest, Charles Michael Jr. We call him CJ. And on the right is my youngest, Cameron."

Gloria sighs softly. "They're beautiful, Charlie."

"Thank you."

After a brief, blush-filled silence, she says, "Okay, go enjoy your dinner."

"Gloria?"

"Yeah?"

We're both slow to release the call. I let my instincts take over, for better or for worse. *I just want her to know...* "I love you."

"I love you too," she whispers back.

The call ends, and I sigh from the bottom of my lungs. Turning the music down again, I realize that I hadn't only wanted to let Gloria enjoy it with me. I didn't want the boys to overhear. They're all the way upstairs, and sound doesn't travel like that in this house. But some discretion is wise, considering how our relationship began—rather, *when* it began.

My eagerness swirls in tandem with my reservations in a constant battle. We're getting to know each other again, taking it slow. We have the privilege of learning about each other beyond the boundaries we once held. It's freedom, but it's not—not really. *Not yet.*

Will we ever be free to love one another in the open?

The morning after I dropped in on her unannounced, I woke to a text from Gloria.

When I can't find the words... ♡

The same, sweet sentiment came every morning thereafter, in addition to midday check ins and end of day recaps after the boys are in bed. We're in no rush, factoring in our reality and allowing ourselves only baby steps. So far, I'm enjoying every inch. I'm falling in love with her all over again, living for the hope of it all.

I glance at the timer—two more minutes. I've always been a patient man, but I'm unaccustomed to this kind of anticipation. The inability to think of anything else. That night, I left her place with hope in my heart, and I could swear that I could feel hope in hers too when I tied her arms around my neck and held her close.

She wants this. Us. *Me.*

I never expected my feelings to be reciprocated like this. I hoped, certainly, but I was resigned to keep up the charade—to walk away and end it like a good man should. The revelation of her shared sentiments emboldens me to never let her go again.

Is it destiny?

I blink, breathing in deep through my nose—basil, tomatoes, and cheese. *Ground yourself, Charlie. You're taking it slow, remember?* But I can't lie—*I miss her.*

Carrying the salad to the table, I remember the first dinner we shared. The weight of her in my arms as we made love. The warmth of her kiss, the silk of her bare skin on mine...

The oven chimes. As I retrieve the lasagna, I shake my head at how worked up I can get when Gloria is on my mind. Washing my hands in ice cold water, I take my damp fingers to the back of my neck before drying them on a towel, slung over my shoulder.

"Bensleys," I yell up the stairs. "Let's eat!"

GLORIA

The cool spring breeze rustles the leaves above me, sending their shadows into a languid sort of dance on the sidewalk. Planting one foot on the bench, I lunge into a gentle stretch, preparing my body for a run around the park. My disposition is just as sunny as this weather, and I smile as my playlist shuffles to a song I've had on repeat lately—*a love song.*

I quickly school my expression back to neutral as a group of teens walk by. I must look silly, standing here all love-dazed like a girl half my age. I pull out my phone to check the time, instead finding a new message.

♡

It's from Charlie, in response to the one I sent earlier today. Exchanging hearts has become something of a daily greeting for us. I scroll up, admiring the photo of him and his boys. It's taken some unlearning to get to this point. I'd formed a habit of not asking questions about his family so as not to blur the lines. *Overstep.* It wasn't until the other day that it even occurred to me that I never learned their names.

CJ and Cameron.

The oldest has eyes that gleam just like his, and the youngest brags his exact smile—my favorite feature of Charlie's. I've never dated a man with children before, and I hadn't even considered what it would be like to develop a relationship with Charlie, let alone his sons. I only ever pictured myself in the shadows of his life. *Is that horrible?*

It feels hauntingly possible that I could meet Charlie's sons someday. *What would they think of me?*

I remember what I thought of Evelyn. We met on a spring day much like this one when I was ten. Evelyn was tall, thin, and exceedingly beautiful—flawless brown skin and long straight hair swept over one shoulder. A ballet dancer, Dad had said, who once toured the world with one of the top leading classical dance companies before settling down to open her own studio in D.C. That day, Evelyn was undeniably gorgeous, but she may as well have had three heads, the tongue of a serpent, and glowing yellow eyes.

Dad introduced her to us with a proud smile. "This is Evelyn."

"Hi," Luci said sharply, rolling her eyes.

I had no words for her.

"GG?" A nickname my father rarely used. With raised brows, he urged me, "Say hello."

"Hello."

"It's so nice to meet you both," she'd said with a smile I came to understand as genuine—though at the time, her pleasantness sounded more like a hiss to my jaded little ears.

Still, I couldn't help but notice how Dad was with her—lighter, happier even. It was as if her mere presence had a way of melting away his worries, making the world a brighter place. His laughter came more easily, his contented sighs more often. With her, he'd seemed to have found a joy once unfamiliar to him.

A joy he never shared with our mother.

Perhaps, with time, CJ and Cameron will see that I'm not the monster I seem to be. Maybe—someday—they'll forgive me for my part in the tragedy that upturned their lives.

I'd have to forgive myself first.

My stomach churns a bit as I stare at their smiling faces. This must have been taken prior to that awful night. *Maybe it's their mother behind the camera.*

I tuck my phone into my leggings pocket, setting a gentle pace as I begin to jog. Running helps me clear my head, giving me the space to process my thoughts and find solutions to overwhelming problems. With each hit of rubber against pavement, the noise of daily life fades away, leaving behind a sense of clarity.

For the first time, I've found myself in a situation that just feels right. Charlie makes me desire the once undesirable—*partnership*. No other man has ever had this effect on me. My innate ability to keep the butterflies at bay, to compartmentalize, to separate fact from feeling has all but evaporated. The lines I used to draw in the sand don't seem to hold anymore. I love the way we do what we do. The way we get carried away, like dandelion fluff on a springtime breeze.

The wind is cool against my cheeks, soothing like the sweep of his thumb. The early morning air pricks at my nose with the scent of dew-kissed grass. I shiver through the chill, focusing on the music in my ears and the feeling of my feet against the sidewalk as I pick up my pace into a sprint.

Loving him feels natural, like breathing.

How can I live without breathing?

We're no longer on borrowed time—rather the contrary. And the idea of a lifetime of making dinner plans for two, no, four, sparks a joy that I never imagined it could. *How terrifying.*

I'm not sure what I'm more afraid of—what I've come to feel for him, how much further I might fall, or the thought of being without him. I'm tempted to go back to him and say, *"Maybe you were right. Maybe we should examine our hand more closely and fold. With so much stacked against us, are we too risky?"*

Is there too much to lose?

Once upon a time, I made no room for a relationship. I went from being a focused college student to an ambitious young professional, securing a leading spot in my field. Love never seemed to glint as brightly as chasing down my dreams did. Even so, watching Luci and Peter's romance blossom into an engagement was awe-inspiring. They're a classic, melanin-Hallmark couple with a love that makes even a love-skeptic like myself hopeful. A love that can only be described as exceptional.

However, with the pros and cons weighed—love, relationships, and especially marriage were never found to be worth the buy-in that they required.

I suppose I'd hoped to find someone to love one day, down the line. Maybe somewhere between making partner at the firm and adopting a cat? I giggle to myself, recalling the checklist that I shared with Charlie that night at my condo.

"I had a pretty solid plan, back in D.C... Senior Associate. General Counsel. Partner. Buy a luxury condo. Maybe get a cat."

But what does a real relationship look like for me? Is it explosive like my parents'? Or enduring like Dad and Evelyn's? What about Luci and Peter's? *Their love seems so effortless.*

My sprint slows to a jog, then a halt. My mind is moving faster than my feet, and slowing down hasn't done much to calm my thoughts. I hunch over, bracing my hands against my knees as I try to catch my breath. The sun still peeks through the trees, shining down onto the path ahead, bringing with it a fresh perspective.

This is no ordinary love. It was well worth the wait—an *exceptional* love.

The path that we're on blazes far beyond what I can see, but I've made up my mind to travel it, my hand in his, curious to see what waits for us ahead.

GLORIA

The floor numbers tick by as the elevator rises. I'm returning from city hall after researching at the law library for an upcoming trial. With the date quickly approaching, I had to dedicate time to finding relevant laws, case summaries, and other information to support the State's position.

After some copious note-taking, I'm confident that I can build a strong argument to secure a favorable verdict.

The doors open to Judy's smile. "Welcome back!" she sings.

I've come to rely on her smile like a fresh brew—contagious and energizing. I can only recall once when that smile of hers faltered, on a day not so long ago. I walked in the office as usual that fateful day, surprised to see her smile at half-mast, not quite reaching her eyes.

"Good morning, Ms. Gloria," she said, her usual warmth lukewarm at best.

"Judy, are you okay?"

Tears formed faster than she could blink them away.

"I'm sorry," she sighed, dabbing at her eyes. *"I shouldn't cry like this at work."*

"No worries. What's going on?"

Judy took a shuddering breath. *"I just heard about what happened to Detective Bensley. You remember him, right?"*

I had to pretend to vaguely recall the man I'd spent the last several months falling in love with. Pretend I didn't know he'd been lying helpless in a hospital bed—on the heels of a tragedy I likely caused. I had to pretend I wasn't seconds from falling apart myself.

Keep it together, Gloria, I told myself.

I tucked my feelings away. *"Yes, I do."*

It was agony, listening to her recount the article about the incident, speculating on what could have happened. She never once judged him. She was only concerned.

"I just can't imagine what this was about or what he must be going through," she hiccuped, clutching at her heart like it hurt to breathe.

Little did she know what role I played in Detective Bensley's tragedy.

In the present, I smile at Judy, sunnier now than she was that somber day.

"Having a good day?" I ask, crossing the lobby with my briefcase rolling behind me. A stunning bouquet sits on her desk. "Beautiful flowers, by the way."

"They're yours," she sings after me.

I stop in my tracks, slowly turning to face the colorful arrangement with fresh eyes.

Charlie.

Fighting my blush, I return to the desk, anticipating Judy's piqued interest.

"Gorgeous, aren't they?" she asks, waggling her eyebrows.

"They really are."

Charlie outdid himself. I know the names of these flowers from my brief stint as a florist, DIY-ing Luci's bouquet for her tenth wedding anniversary last year. Purple hydrangea, pink roses, yellow spray roses, orange asiatic lilies, purple alstroemeria-peruvian lilies, blue delphinium, pink snapdragons, Israeli ruscus, sword fern, silver dollar eucalyptus, and lemon leaf... I reach for the little card nestled between two roses.

Thinking of you, it reads, with a little heart in the lower right corner.

"Someone special?" Judy asks.

I smile at the understatement of the year. "Yeah."

Judy beams. "I'm so happy for you, Ms. Gloria."

I wish that I could tell her that it was Charlie. That he's the one that's responsible for my happiness lately. That despite his unthinkable loss and the unforgivable actions that lead up to it... our love is a real one.

But at a glance, the portrait of us is distorted. Our love story doesn't shape up nearly as nicely as this bouquet. *How can we expect anyone to be happy for us?*

Judy's opinion of me may soon change. If the truth ever comes to light, what will she think of Charlie? The beloved detective she thinks so highly of... and me, the *other woman* masquerading as a cupid's latest victim.

I pick the pinkest rose and hand it to Judy before retreating back to my office. There, I'm free to bask in the bouquet's beauty, to sit and breathe in the intoxicating aroma without worrying about letting my love show.

I retrieve my notebook from my briefcase, fully intending to get back to work. Instead, I lose time sketching the flowers before me.

Like an epiphany, I suddenly realize—love is a lot like art. Its focal point, something your eye is meant to be drawn to, something that takes a trained eye to truly see—*to appreciate*. For so long, I was looking at it all wrong. I had trained my eye to see the pain rather than the beauty, missing the focal point entirely.

When I'm finished, I've been adrift for over thirty minutes, just living between the lines of this still life.

I've missed this—being in the flow, suspended in time by the sheer beauty of a thing. I hold the card between two fingers, letting loose a long sigh.

I've missed him too. *My man.*

With a smile on my lips, I snap a picture of the bouquet and draft a text.

Thank you. ♡

CHARLIE

The buzzing drags me from my sleep. I fumble for the phone on the nightstand, its glow cutting through the dark. 2:01 AM. Her name lights the screen.

Gloria.

I answer the call. "Babe, you alright?"

"No." Her voice is soft, needy. The shadows in her room are looser than mine, moonlight spilling through her tall windows. The phone is propped. Her hair is wild across her pillow, a halo of curls. Her lips pout when she whispers, "I miss you. Do you miss me?"

"Like crazy."

"I wish you were here." She whines as she shifts, her mesh nightgown slipping lower. Her breasts spill into view, taut nipples straining against the fabric. She bites her bottom lip—slow, deliberate.

And damn, does that shit undo me every time.

"Gloria..." It comes out a groan.

"Yes?"

"Close your eyes."

She obeys, her lashes casting dark shadows on her cheeks. *Beautiful.*

"Relax for me, okay?" I murmur, easing back onto my pillow.

She nods, breathing in through her nose and out through slightly parted lips.

"I'm right next to you. Can you feel me?"

"Yes."

"Good. Picture it. We had a nice night in, just the two of us. Dinner and dessert, maybe a glass of wine. I lit candles around the room, giving everything that syrupy glow—like a sunset. I want to touch you, babe. Can I touch you?"

She nods, shivering, lips trembling—eager for my phantom touch.

I drag her deeper into the fantasy. "Can you feel my breath on your skin, just where your jaw curves into your neck? I leave kisses there, dragging my tongue down to your collarbone, across your chest. More babe, will you show me more?"

She whimpers in desperation, dragging her fingers across her nightgown. She tugs the mesh fabric down, freeing her breasts. I ache to suck them into my mouth, recalling the way her nipples pebbled between my lips, how she gasped when I sucked harder. I describe it for her now—how they feel against my tongue, how they taste.

"Mmm, sweet, like candy," I say, watching Gloria trace her peaks, imagining with me. "I want to taste more."

She bites her lip, as one hand slips down her belly, dipping into her panties. I follow her lead, letting my own hand wander down to the tension in my shorts. I palm myself, groaning at the sight of her face lit by moonlight, the skyline behind her glowing like a sensual backdrop to her lovemaking.

"You wet for me?"

"Yes..." Her voice is breathless, broken.

"Good girl. Now, stroke yourself—slow. Feel me tasting you, spreading you open, taking you higher."

She moans, her hips shifting against her hand, fingers deepening their exploration. "Mmmm..."

"Sounds like you're ready for me," I murmur, her moans betraying her. "Can I have you baby... the way I want you?"

"Yes," she gasps, desperate.

"Then take me, babe—*deep*." I groan, reminiscing on the indescribable feeling of easing into her essence. "Can you feel me, Gloria? Can you feel me inside you?"

She hums, biting her lip again. *Shattering.* Watching my woman pleasure herself—only to the sensations my voice can conjure—is sexier than I could have ever imagined. With each stroke, I feel my own fire inch toward eruption, awakening the sleeping volcano within me. *God, she's probably so warm inside...*

Her head tips back, mouth open, voice ragged. "Charlie—"

Damn that sounds good—*so* good. My name on her lips, the name that she screams at the peak of her pleasure. *She's almost there too.*

"Let it go, Gloria..."

"Shit..." Her breasts heave with each quickened breath, rising and falling in time with my strokes.

"That's it, babe. Let me love you." For a moment, even through a screen, it feels like we're in the same bed—lost in each other. God, I want her. *Right now.* "Come for me."

And when she does, her body quakes as she clutches the sheet. Moonlight illuminates the rapture on her face as she comes to the sound of my voice—*and my voice alone.*

CHARLIE

Her heart comes through at its usual time. I lie quietly on my back, watching my phone light up on the nightstand—savoring the moment. Truthfully, I wake up minutes before my alarm every day, preparing my heart for hers. A smile graces my face every time, as if I weren't expecting it.

♡

Reaching for my phone, I reply, *Take the day off*—followed by a heart of my own. I wonder if it's even possible for her to do such a thing. It doesn't seem too outlandish of a suggestion, considering it's Friday.

Not even a minute later, a thumbs up emoji sets my heart racing.

Hopping up, I spring right into my new home workout routine. Being a single dad no longer affords me the luxury of hitting the gym first thing in the morning. It's a good set up, with a variety of weights and an elliptical to get the blood moving.

Not that my blood wasn't already moving... elsewhere.

Knowing that I get to see Gloria today is a rush of its own. I stifle the smile on my face when the boys shuffle down the steps for breakfast. They're finally settling back into school, and I worry less and less about them as I drop them off in the mornings. Instead of turning back toward home today, I take the car in another familiar direction.

Before long, I'm in the elevator of Gloria's building, anticipation rising with every floor.

Standing at her door makes me appreciate every moment we've shared, each etched into my mind like a work of art, adding to the tapestry of our time together. I try to envision what awaits behind this door moments before it's revealed—like guessing a gift before it's unwrapped. This drought ends today. *I'm about to tear her ass up...*

The door opens to an exquisite sight. Lingerie peeks up at me in a blush pink. The satin ties at the hips of her lacy panties beg to be undone.

"Good morning," she breathes.

Her place looks so different in the daytime, natural light streaming in through those tall, magnificent windows, illuminating the space with vitality. As much as I like it and want to say as much, I have more pressing matters to attend to.

I cross the threshold in one stride, my hand slipping behind her neck. She's eager to be pulled into me, meeting my lips with a hungry kiss. I slip my free arm around her waist, kicking the door shut behind us. Liplocked, we waltz into the bedroom—of the same mind.

"You have missed me..." she murmurs against my lips.

"How can you tell?" I nibble at her shoulder, inspiring a shiver down her spine.

We linger at the foot of the bed, content to just kiss for now. Her lips taste like everything I've missed—*excitement, acceptance, love...*

Her arms cling to my neck as I travel one hand down to her ass, squeezing once, then twice for good measure. Trailing gentle caresses up the center of her back, I tease the curve of her spine, fingers catching on the clasp of her corset.

Gloria loosens her hold, leaning back as if to give herself to me. I ease the lingerie down her shoulders, baring her skin to my hungry eyes. I tug my shirt off in one motion, surprised to see her eyes widen with emotion, her breath stutters.

My scars.

Her hands hover, trembling. I hook my finger beneath her chin and lift her eyes back to mine. Our lips meet again, slow and reverent, until she dares to touch me—palms pressing to my chest, sliding down with bold fingers that toy with the drawstring of my shorts.

Gloria sinks down onto the foot of the bed like temptation itself, lashes low, lips parted. The picture of a good girl begging to be ruined. Her dainty fingers pull my shorts down, and my erection twitches beneath my briefs, waiting to be freed. *She doesn't make me wait.* The elastic-banded garment follows soon after, and Gloria wastes no time licking me into her mouth.

My head falls back, hips twitching as she devours me. My fists clench uselessly at my sides, resisting the urge to bury my fingers in her hair. *If I touch her, I'll lose it.* She hollows her cheeks and takes me deeper, every muscle straining, every nerve screaming as I savor the hot, wet pull.

"Gloria, please..." *I know I won't last long like this.*

She releases me, then eases back onto the bed. Her body, an offering. *An invitation I couldn't refuse.*

I kneel between her legs, tugging at the knots that decorate her waist. "I like this," I murmur, kissing the trail of skin it reveals.

Her only response is a smile, followed by the slow, delicious parting of her thighs.

Gloria's taste floods my tongue—sweet, intoxicating. I groan against her, lapping at her until she's trembling, moaning, clutching the sheets. Her legs quiver around my head, muffling her cries as she shatters.

Before her climax can fully fade, I climb her body, trailing kisses until my lips claim hers again. She's still trembling as she spreads her legs wide for my hips. Her hands slide down to grip my ass, urging me forward. With a soul-deep sigh, I enter her warmth, filling her with everything I've held back.

"You love me?" I grit, barely a whisper.

"Yes," she moans, clutching me tighter.

"Tell me you love me."

"I love you, Charlie," she gasps, and I lose the last thread of control.

I can't form words any longer, releasing only a throaty groan. I drive into her, deep, relentless. She whimpers beneath me, meeting my hips thrust for quickening thrust.

"I love you," she gasps again as she tightens around me, pulling me deeper into our already fathomless connection. Our bodies hum together in a sensual duet, harmonizing like a classic love song. When she falls apart again, her walls fluttering, I break too, spilling into her with a guttural groan, collapsing into the warmth of her body.

When she opens her eyes, a tear falls.

"What's wrong?"

"Nothing." Her eyes are bright but bleary when they find mine. She lets out a small chuckle, almost embarrassed by her own emotion. "I'm happy." She smiles, but yet another tear chases the first one. "It's just... I thought we'd never make love again."

"So did I," I admit softly, swiping her tears away with my thumb. "You don't ever have to worry about that again." My voice dips, steady, to assure her. "I'm yours—okay? *Only yours.*"

A promise I seal with a kiss.

Afterwards, I drape over her, cheek to cheek, our arms entwined around our heads, our legs tangled. I close my eyes, the room around us fading to black. There's nothing here but this bed and Gloria's arms.

I could stay here forever.

"Am I too heavy?" I whisper into her ear.

"No." She giggles. "I missed you."

"I missed you too," I murmur, playing with a strand of her hair.

"Charlie?"

"Hmm?"

She pauses, her voice only a breath. "What happened..."

My eyes slowly creep open, taking in the sights of Argale through the window. I recall the light-speckled pavement on my way home that night. It had rained earlier in the day, and the street lights cast a hazy glow on the road, reflecting a warped vision of my beloved city.

I knew this question would come. *She deserves an explanation.*

Where do I even start? Do I tell her about the open marriage proposal? The desperate lengths I was willing to go to keep her in my life? What would have happened between us, had that night never happened? What would Gloria come to expect from me? Did she see a future for us? Would she have waited for me?

"For weeks," I begin, taking it slow, "she refused to discuss it. Or much else, for that matter. Then one day—that day—she did. Finally, she wanted to talk."

"I didn't have some master plan devised, you know?" She nods. "I only wanted to have a conversation. To talk it out. To figure out how to move forward. We needed some kind of resolution—*something* that didn't amount to me losing you."

Listening intently, her arms tighten around me, and I draw strength from it.

"I told her the truth—that I wanted to keep seeing you. I refused to hide it anymore. I was in love with you, Gloria. *I only wanted you.* But I couldn't keep lying to her. She deserved better than that. What I wanted was simple—to do whatever was best for the boys. Even if that meant staying in the marriage." The words scrape on the way out, but they're true. "You mean the world to me, Gloria. But my sons—I'd do anything for them."

She nods, eyes soft with understanding. "I know."

My throat tightens as I approach the part of the story I have yet to tell anyone in full, beyond the facts that went into the police report.

"That night, I dropped the boys off at my brother's house. They were sleeping over so we could have the time and space to hash out our issues. When I got home, she wasn't interested in talking. She had one demand..." I trail off, scrubbing a hand over my face, dragging the memory with it.

Gloria's question is a gentle prompt. "Which was?"

"We could never get a divorce," I say, pausing before I speak again. "I couldn't agree to those terms. So..."

Silence hangs heavily around us, cloaking our peaceful haven with words unsaid.

"I'm sorry, Charlie."

My half-smile is pained. "Yeah, me too. Waking up in the hospital, it felt like I was in a fog..." A memory floats to the forefront of my mind—a slip of paper. "Gloria?"

"Yeah?"

"Did you come to the hospital?"

She nods, sheepish. "How'd you know?"

"You dropped your pass."

She scoffs a bit, saying, "I shouldn't have. It wasn't my place to..."

"Gloria," I interrupt, lifting my head to gaze into her eyes. "Thank you... for loving me."

She reaches for my face, stroking a gentle line from my temple to my jaw. The kiss that follows is softer than my heart can handle.

"You make it really hard not to."

Five

UNTITLED

GLORIA

Sunlight pours through my windows in generous streams. The gold specks of the Eiffel Tower puzzle glimmer, catching rays from where it sits on the coffee table.

"God, yes..." I murmur, letting my head fall back.

It's a slow morning—ripe for lovemaking. With Charlie's breath in my ear and his fingers between my legs, I could live in this slow morning forever. Coffee brews in the background, intermingling with the lilt of music. Just minutes ago, we settled into my chair together, him seated on the plush cushion, and me, splayed wide and submissive on his lap. Now, my legs cling to each arm rest as I bear down on his impossibly hard length, taking him inside of me inch by glorious inch.

As he shudders beneath me, I drag my lips over the shell of his ear, whispering, "That feels so good..."

Leaning back, I can see in his eyes that he feels the same. We gaze at each other like star-crossed lovers, finally occupying the same galaxy. I cling to the back of the chair as Charlie gently rocks his hips, deepening our connection. It's a ride that rewrites my appreciation for this chair, this private sanctuary turned love nest.

With a gentle grip, Charlie pulls my hair, and I arch my neck in response. He drags his tongue up the stretch of my neck before wrapping his lips around my jaw. With a groan, he releases my hair so I can bring my lips back down to his. He pulls me in even closer than I thought possible. Wrapped in my man's arms, I feel—whole again.

When we're both satisfied and spent, we enjoy a shower together, sudsing each other's bodies and rinsing under the hot stream. Opting to work from home a few days this week means he's been coming over most mornings after dropping his boys off at school, enjoying what's left of his time off with me. Today, Charlie takes it upon himself to hang the puzzle on the wall, and I can't help but admire his shirtless form. In that pair of low hanging joggers, he looks like a model. As he measures the wall and hammers in the nail, the muscles of his bare back ripple deliciously. He lifts the puzzle into place, and my eyes linger on the dimples in the small of his back, right above his waistline.

Genetically blessed, he is...

Charlie joins me at the counter, where I pour each of us a cup of steaming coffee.

"It looks good," I say. "Thank you." I lean forward to kiss him across the island.

With a roguish smile, he sits on one of the stools, pulling out his laptop from his backpack along with a pair of readers. He pushes the glasses onto the bridge of his nose, and I resist the urge to kiss him again, just for being so cute. Instead, I glide his mug closer to him, giddy with the domesticity of this whole scenario.

"Thanks, babe," he says, bringing the coffee to his lips. He hums in delight at the taste, eyes catching on the glass cake pedestal I've filled with muffins from the local bakery. "May I?"

"Of course, help yourself."

He lifts the lid and retrieves a chocolate chip muffin, thanking me again after his first bite. I chuckle to myself, pulling my laptop from my briefcase and setting up my own little work station across from him. I never could have imagined us together like this, having downtime and finding joy in the simplest moments. These little domestic moments feel so effortlessly perfect, providing me with a sense of belonging I never knew I needed and discovering a depth of connection I never dreamed I could have.

Look at us being something more.

A few minutes into our little work-from-home date, Charlie slips off his readers and sets them on the counter. His hand lingers at his temple, fingers pressing lightly as his posture softens, a quiet shift that doesn't go unnoticed.

"Everything okay?" I ask.

The corner of his mouth lifts into a half-hearted smile that doesn't quite reach his eyes, an attempt to mask his clear concern. "Yeah…"

I tilt my head. "What is it?"

He sighs deeply, glancing at his laptop. "A rejection email."

My stomach tightens. "May I?" asking to see it.

He turns his screen around for me to see. "I was really looking forward to this."

The email came only minutes ago.

Dear Mr. Bensley,

Thank you for expressing your interest in our recent project opportunity. After careful consideration, we have made the difficult decision to reject your application.

Please note that our decision was based on a thorough assessment of various factors, including your experience and suitability for the project. Although we appreciate your efforts in submitting your application and the time invested during the selection process, unfortunately, we have decided to move forward with another firm who aligns more closely with our requirements and objectives.

In the future, we may have other projects or opportunities that align better with your expertise. Therefore, we will keep your information on file, and we may reach out to you should any suitable opportunities arise.

Thank you once again for your interest in partnering with us. We believe in maintaining strong relationships with potential contractors, and we hope to have the opportunity to collaborate in the future.

Best regards,

Miles Lofton

I look up from the screen to see Charlie staring contemplatively into his cup of coffee.

"Lofton approached me at the Forester on New Years Eve," he explains. "He wanted to set up a meeting to discuss a contract for the city's summer festivals. I was floored. That's a huge contract, you know? We met a couple weeks later and discussed the logistics. He said he'd be in touch. Just needed to draw up the paperwork and get the official sign off. I followed up with his office last week..."

My resolve caves as I put the pieces together. Charlie's recent tragedy had been covered in the news. Was the publicity enough to dissuade Loften from investing in his security firm? *Is this all my fault?*

Charlie looks up at me, concern lining his eyes. "What are you thinking about?"

"This is because..."

"Nope," he cuts in, reading between the lines. "You saw what it said. They went with a better firm, and they'll keep my info on file for future projects." His tone is convincing, but his eyes give him away. *He's wondering the same.* Still, he smiles. "Can I have a kiss?"

This time, I step around the island to close the distance between us. Standing between his legs, I take comfort in his big, warm hands coming to rest on my hips.

"How can I help?" I ask, clasping my hands behind his neck.

"Just like this."

"It's their loss, Charlie."

"Thank you, baby."

I kiss him then, fulfilling his request. Before I can lean back, Charlie pulls me into a tender hug. My arms snake around his neck, tugging his heart to mine. Maybe if we stand like this forever, so tightly wound, the world outside will forget about us altogether and leave us to our love.

CHARLIE

A tennis ball flies through the air, a streak of black following it across the green grass. The labrador catches it in its grinning mouth, carrying it back to its owner. The park is well attended today as Argaleans soak up the warmer weather. Young children frolic around the playground while couples enjoy leisurely walks around the perimeter. Meanwhile, my boys and I sit shoulder to shoulder at a picnic table, waiting for the first applicant to arrive.

"It should be a girl," CJ announces, consulting his notebook.

"Oh yeah? Any other requirements?" I'd asked each of them to bring their own lists, since they'll be spending the most time with their sitter.

"Um, responsible?"

"Agreed."

I have a list of my own. I was recently cleared by both physical therapy and the gun range to return to work. As ready as I am to get back to my regular life, there are important steps left before I feel comfortable leaving my boys alone with just anyone. To start, I decided to do our sitter interviews in a public place. Lately, *home* doesn't necessarily equate to *safety*. Maybe it's a cop thing, maybe it's just my recent experiences, but I want to be sure about the person I'm letting into my house around my boys.

I turn to my youngest. "What about you, Cam?"

"Not old!" he says matter-of-factly.

"Got it. A young, responsible female."

Back in my day, a sitter was your older cousin or a teenage neighbor looking to make an extra buck. Rachel and I rarely needed a sitter for the boys, as one of us was usually home if the other was away. When we did need an extra pair of hands, we could usually count on family to watch the kids. These days, I can count on my nephew, Royce—Jack's son. He's mature, responsible, has his own car, and the boys adore him. But Royce will be off to college in just a few short months, so a longer-term solution is needed.

CJ revises his list with a thoughtful frown while Cam doodles in his notebook. These boys are incredible. They've bounced back from an unimaginable loss with a resilience that humbles me. It's only been a few months of this new normal, but we've found something of a flow that works for us.

Still, single-parent multitasking is relentless—a juggling act of school drop offs and pickups, healthy-ish meals and takeout, mundane chores and unexpected demands. Being at home these past few months has certainly given me a better understanding of our overall needs.

Stability is the number one priority.

I shudder to recall those first few weeks after the incident. Each day was a grief-stricken haze of blunders and ball-drops—parental missteps that had me feeling uncertain of my ability to be the man they needed me to be. It certainly hasn't been seamless since, but with a little time, focus, and resilience, I've managed to keep most of the balls in the air.

Returning to work feels like taking the new juggling act onto a tightrope, suspended a hundred feet in the air. I need a safety net.

I need help.

A responsible-looking young woman waves at us from the sidewalk.

"Alright, here we go, guys," I say, waving back.

While CJ holds his notebook close to his chest, Cam mimics my friendliness, waving with me as he sing-songs, "Here we gooo..."

When all the interviews are complete, I treat the boys to dinner at our favorite spot, a retro diner named after the owner, Pop's, and co-run with his better half, Claudette. She greets us straightaway, smiling from behind a pair of cat-eye glasses.

"Welcome to Pop's! Well, if it isn't my favorite trio, C3!"

"It is!" Cam insists with glee.

She waves us over to the counter where we take our seats. As we wait to place our orders, I take a moment to simply admire the atmosphere. There's nothing quite like a diner that celebrates the unique African

American cultural experience. Pop's has colorful, vintage decor, its counter lined with vinyl-padded bar stools and its walls with comfortable booths. Vintage album covers adorn the walls, featuring famous music acts like The Temptations, The Jackson 5, The Supremes, and Gladys Knight and the Pips. The jukebox in the far corner only plays the best old-school jams, reminding me of songs my mom used to listen to while cleaning the house every Saturday morning. The nostalgia is as much a part of the experience as the delicious comfort food.

"So, what'll it be, gentlemen? The usual?" Claudette asks, hand on her hip.

CJ and Cameron nod enthusiastically.

"Alright, then. Two hot dogs with the works, a hamburger—hold the onions—with fries, and three strawberry milkshakes."

An incredulous laugh escapes me. "You are amazing."

"And fabulous, Suga!" She twirls to show off her colorfully coordinated outfit.

"And fabulous," I agree. "Say thank you, boys."

"Thank you, Ms. Claudette," they recite in unison.

"You are very welcome." She swipes the menus from the counter and leaves us with a wink.

When she's gone, I tap the notepad in front of CJ. "Thoughts on the candidates?"

We run through pros and cons until CJ's face brightens. "I really like Sienna," he gushes.

"Yeah, I noticed."

CJ blushes, eyes wide. Although my son is fixated on the young graduate student for pre-teen boy related reasons, I'm more impressed with her qualifications: a babysitting certification, CPR training, five years of childcare experience, references—and a flexible schedule, priceless for a detective on call.

"She's studying to be a pediatric nurse," I add.

"*Qualified*," CJ says, like a miniature HR manager.

Moments later, old Pops appears with our food, wearing a handsome apron around his potbelly to match Claudette's colorful ensemble.

"Order up!" he bellows, passing us our plates with the ease of a lifetime server.

We dig in like we haven't eaten in weeks. Halfway through my burger, I wipe my mouth with my napkin. "So, who's it gonna be?"

The boys lean forward to look at each other. "Sienna!" they proclaim in unison.

We raise our half-empty milkshakes to toast, clinking the fountain glasses together.

"To Sienna," I declare.

"To Sienna," they repeat, delighted in the decision.

"What do you guys want to do for the summer?" I ask, popping a fry into my mouth.

The boys and I toss around a few ideas—camp, maybe an academic summer program, and even a weekend road trip. Recently Leah had proposed a trip to Tennessee for Cam and CJ to visit their grandparents. It's something to consider, though I haven't suggested it to the boys yet.

My phone pings in my pocket with a text from my realtor. A listing populates the small screen—*a townhouse rental.*

I reached out a few weeks back to toss around the idea of selling the house. Ever since, my guy has been sending me rentals around town. The goal is to stay in the area, to keep the boys in the same school for their own sake. Staying close to work is also a perk.

The townhouse is a decent price for an impressive amount of space. I scroll through the photos, my excitement growing. *I suppose it's time to bring the boys into the conversation.*

"So, I was thinking. Our home has some amazing memories, but it also has some really sad ones too. What do you guys think about a new place? A new adventure?"

The boys look at each other before they dare meet my eyes. I recognize their expression as one I've worn myself—*uncertainty.* We've lived in our house for their whole lives. It's all they've ever known.

"I know that these past few months have been kinda rough. I really think that a fresh start could do us some good," I explain. "But ultimately, we won't do anything that the three of us don't agree to as a unit. Okay?"

That seems to ease CJ and Cam, and for the rest of the meal, they toss around ideas for what their new home could have.

"A pool," CJ suggests through a mouthful of hotdog.

"A basketball hoop in the backyard," Cam adds. "Actually, a whole basketball *court.*"

I laugh, humoring their imaginations with a hand on each of their backs.

Thank you for trusting me.

We box our leftovers, settle the bill, and say our goodbyes to Pops and Claudette with a promise to return soon. Before I pull the car out of the lot, I type a quick message to the realtor.

Can we set up a showing?

GLORIA

"So, what's new?" Luci asks, setting the table.

Most weekends, I have dinner with Luci and her family. This weekend is no exception, even if everything these days feels like it has a shiny, new exterior. It's tempting to tell Luci about Charlie. But she will have a million questions—none of them the easy kind. I'm not prepared to be interrogated just yet.

Instead I say, "Same ol'."

Luci is never convinced. "If you say so."

I ignore the comment, placing a serving dish of sesame-glazed salmon topped with fresh parsley in the center of the table. It's a recipe I've been perfecting over the years, but I anticipate that my other offering might outshine it. One of Ms. Judy's famous sweet potato pies waits for us on the counter. Earlier this week, I ordered one special to share with my family.

Could I ever share Charlie with my family too?

Luci gestures toward the antique hutch that she inherited from our mother. "Would you grab the wine glasses?"

Plucking them one by one from the cabinet, I can't help but wonder what it would be like to integrate Charlie into my family. Our relationship is still so new and undefined. I mean, we know what we have, but we're still in the process of shaping it, understanding how to nurture it, and uncovering what it truly means for both of us. A small part of me likes our secret relationship, enjoying the intimacy and the thrill that comes with keeping our connection just between us. Together, we catch fire—a blaze that I'm content to let burn for a while. Sharing it too soon might risk dousing the flame.

The doorbell rings, pulling me from my thoughts.

"That must be Courtney," Luci says. "I invited my new colleague to dinner."

As Luci scurries away to answer the door, Peter and the kids shuffle down the stairs, like the doorbell was their cue to come to dinner. The kids each greet me with a hug before settling into their spots at the table. Pete steps up to the counter, where I'm pouring glasses of wine.

"I'll take care of that," he says. "You and Luci have already done so much."

Luci bustles through the door, a tall man in tow.

"And this is my sister that I was telling you about," she proclaims, practically pushing Courtney in my direction. I exchange a look with Peter before smiling Courtney's way.

He smiles back, flashing a mouth full of braces. *Oh my.*

"Luci sings your praises," he says. "It's really nice to finally meet you, Gloria."

"Courtney is an art professor at the university," my sister adds proudly. "He's from New York."

Courtney is handsome. His hazel eyes seem sensitive, and his six-foot frame adds a layer of attractiveness. He's a lean man with a tapered hairline and dreads pulled up into a neat ponytail.

But then there's the braces.

When we all sit down to dinner, Courtney is placed right next to me. Luci isn't even trying to be subtle anymore with these matchmaking efforts.

"Wow, Luci, this salmon is amazing," Courtney says.

"I'm glad you like it," she smirks. "GG made it."

"Impressive," he compliments, tipping his wine glass toward mine. When I reciprocate the cheers with a quiet *thank you*, he leans in, lowering his voice. "Your sister seems to think we might have a real *love connection.*" He says it jokingly, which puts me at ease. "Something about our shared love for art."

"Does she?"

He nods. "Well, what do you think?"

I smile politely. "I think that my sister is a bit more eager to see me settled down than I am. Growing more and more impatient by the day."

Courtney is unperturbed. "Hey, I get it. I have three sisters, and they're always trying to set me up." He looks across the table, laughing softly. "Don't look now, but I think your sister is onto us."

I raise my eyes to meet hers, which are wide and insistent as if to say, *Isn't he great?* When I don't acknowledge the silent message, Luci pours the last of the Riesling into her own glass.

"Babe," she says, "can you grab another bottle of wine?"

"Sure thing," her husband replies, standing.

Now's my chance. "I'll get dessert."

In the kitchen, Pete is already laughing under his breath. "Not your type, huh?"

I shake my head, nose scrunched as I retrieve cake plates and fresh utensils. He nods knowingly, retrieving a bottle of white from the fridge.

"It's the braces, right?"

I can't help but laugh. "Lu is *relentless.*"

"Yeah," he agrees, "but only because she loves you, GG."

"I know." I roll my eyes, more exasperated than I am flattered. *Why is she so over the top about it?*

"Just say the word if you need a diversion," Pete offers, inspiring a shared laugh. "I can fake a heart attack, make bird calls, or even start vacuuming."

"Vacuuming?"

"Yeah, it's a universal language. Everyone knows it means 'Party's over. *Go home.*'"

"Got it, will do," I snicker. I really am grateful to have Pete on my team. "Thank you."

He fist bumps me across the island. "I got you."

As Pete rifles around for a wine opener, I slice the pie into even eighths. I love the way that Luci and Peter love each other, with a tenderness and mutual respect that is both inspiring and heartwarming. His easy going personality perfectly complements her spunk. Simply put, they seem to bring out the best in one another.

As good friends do.

I sigh, thinking of our parents. They *weren't* friends. The rift between them created a callus around my heart that Charlie is gently chiseling away, revealing a deeper, more vulnerable part of me. Their failed marriage obviously didn't have the same effect on Luci. She and Pete have always been so open with one another, since day one. I've always admired their relationship, but for the first time in my life, I find myself wanting what they have—*true love.*

"Pete?"

He spins a newly discovered wine opener in his free hand. "Yeah?"

"What's the secret—to what you and Luci have?"

One of his thick eyebrows rises. "Who's asking?"

I hide my shyness by focusing back on plating the pie. "I am... for a friend."

He hums to himself thoughtfully. "Okay. I don't know if it's a secret, but I'd like to believe it's because we choose each other every day. We make a conscious effort to nurture our relationship and grow together, even when things get hard."

I smile. *He loves my sister so well.* "Please don't tell Luci I asked."

Pete zips his lips, tosses the invisible key over his shoulder, and smiles.

The rest of the evening is pleasant. There is no weird vibe from Courtney or undue pressure from Luci—and therefore, no vacuum. I said goodbye to the professor, sending him off with my salmon recipe and some art-inspired spots around town.

My heart does a little leap when my phone buzzes. The heart emoji seems to smile up at me—*Miss me?*

I reply with the same heart. *Like crazy.*

Six

LOVING KINDNESS

GLORIA

My laptop clicks pleasantly beneath my fingertips. I'm working from home today, curled up in my chair with my diffuser on high. Lavender vanilla has been my scent of choice lately, creating a cozy and sweet environment.

Speaking of cozy and sweet...

I glance to the couch, where Charlie lounges with a book propped on his chest. The glance turns into a full blown gaze as I rest my chin on my fist and take in the sight of this man. He looks casually cool in his cotton white tee and gray sweatpants. His feet are up on the arm rest with his ankles crossed, and—as if just for me—his bicep is on full display as he angles his head on the pillow with one hand. He wets his thumb with his tongue to turn the page, totally engrossed.

While I work today, Charlie is playing catch-up on our shared reading list. He fell behind this week because of house tours and various extracurriculars for the boys. On the coffee table next to him sits a plate practically licked clean where a slice of Ms. Judy's pie once was. I earned a peculiar look from Luci as I carefully packed up the final two pieces to bring back home.

"That for someone special?" she'd asked.

"Thanks for a lovely evening," I'd deflected, kissing her on the cheek before I made my escape. *"No more surprise guests."*

As much as Charlie continues to surprise me, he's more than a guest in my home. In fact, I've never been this comfortable with anyone in my space before. He looks like he belongs here, like his presence completes the environment. Even with another person present, it's still as quiet as any other day when I'm here by myself. I'm the first to admit that I like my alone time, but this feels just as nice, maybe even nicer. Like something I could get used to.

Pete's words echo in my memory. *We choose each other every day.*

I like that. I can understand why that sort of intentionality could be so important, what with the hustle and bustle of day to day life. It could be so easy to lose sight of what's supposed to matter the most. *I wonder...*

Turning my attention back to work, I refocus on preparing for trial. With the date just weeks away, I have to ensure that every detail is covered and every argument well-crafted. This is a big case for the city, so I reached out to my dad for advice.

"What about D.C.?" he asked, clearly confused by my change of heart.

I'd chalked my emotional overflow over the phone earlier in the year to a heavy week at work. No need to mention the mess I'd made of my life—or the fact that I'm just now starting to piece it back together. He wasn't thrilled to hear about my decision to stay in Argale, but as ever, he remains supportive when it matters most. He'll always be my mentor. I may have to sit through a lecture, but his knowledge is worth its weight in gold.

The sun is high in the sky by the time I look up from my laptop again. It's a beautiful view, and if I squint, I can make out people wandering the streets, enjoying their afternoon. I imagine—just for a moment—that Charlie and I are among them, hand in hand. It would be nice to share our love beyond these walls. But despite how perfect we are together in our little bubble, the shadow of everything that's happened still looms over us. I wonder... Do we stand a chance out there?

Where it's real.

I rub my eyes, adjusting to the room's shifting light. On the couch, Charlie has fallen asleep, the book lying open on his chest. At first glance, he seems so peaceful, except for a crease between his brows. Suddenly, he jolts, and the book falls to the floor with a thud. He stirs in his sleep, clearly distressed.

He's having a nightmare.

His eyes snap open—wild, afraid. He's nearly hyperventilating, struggling to orient himself.

"Charlie?" I call to him softly.

As the seconds tick by, his labored breathing slows by degrees. Finally, his eyes meet mine, less afraid now than they were. There's still something guarded in them though—an emotion I haven't seen from him before.

"Are you okay?"

"Yeah," he says, sitting upright. The corded muscles of his neck are tight, like he's barely holding on. "Just a bad dream."

Setting my laptop aside, I rise from my chair, joining him on the couch. My hand finds his knee, and his hand finds mine, our fingers threading in his lap.

"Have you talked to anyone?" I ask tentatively. He seems to know what I mean—not just anyone. *A therapist.*

He shakes his head.

"Are you opposed to therapy?"

"I'm not," he says simply. "It's just... I think I'm okay."

"Okay," I relent, tracing his thumb with my own. "Or perhaps... you're simply coping. You've been through a lot, Charlie, and I get that you want to navigate things in your own way, but please just remember that it's okay to seek—"

"—Babe. I'm okay."

"Okay." That's my cue to let up. I retrieve the book from the floor, handing it to him. "Here."

"Thanks."

I'm about to step away from the couch, but Charlie squeezes my hand, pulling me back.

"Hey, listen, you're probably right." He sets the book aside to cup my face, brushing his thumb along my chin. "I'll give it some thought, okay?"

"Yeah," I nod, hopeful. "Want some tea?"

"Sure. Thanks, Gloria."

A few minutes later, I'm standing over the stove, waiting for the kettle to heat up. He's apprehensive about therapy, and I get it. The idea of opening up to a stranger to face even surface level issues can be daunting, let alone deep-seated ones. But I've slept next to this man many nights, and never has he had such an episode. The fear in his eyes was real. If he has demons, he shouldn't have to fight them alone. *Not anymore.*

The kettle whistles, pulling me back. Until he's ready to talk, a cup of peppermint tea will just have to do.

CHARLIE

The office is quiet this morning. Folks usually don't arrive for another thirty minutes, and I decided to avoid the spotlight by arriving before anyone else. Passing by the empty desks, I adjust my tie in the reflective glass of the chief's office door.

Months ago, I was the subject of an investigation—interrogated in my hospital bed the same way I might grill a murder suspect. Crimes committed by police officers are typically investigated by their own police department's internal affairs division. They ensure that officers uphold the law and departmental regulations, regardless of whether the alleged misconduct occurred during official duties or personal time. In my case, Internal Affairs took the reins to ensure impartiality and transparency in the investigation.

My cubicle waits for me, untouched since that fateful day. I drop my bag on the floor by my desk, plopping into my chair with a sigh. *I missed this.*

It takes a while, but I finally work through all the daunting security measures on my computer and reset my passwords. Once I'm in, I'm met with a truly obscene amount of unread emails.

Damn it.

I recline in my chair, fingers pressed to my temples. Before I can fully humor the idea of quitting this career altogether, I hear familiar voices.

"I never even see any workers out there!" Anderson is saying. "If they don't finish construction before the summer starts, I'll repave the damn road myself..."

Rising to my feet, I wave from my cubicle. "Good morning."

Their faces are priceless, but Graham's smile is what really gets me.

"CB!" he sings. "Welcome back, my man!"

I chuckle, meeting him with open arms. As I hug Graham, I catch Anderson staring. I don't know what she thinks of me these days. I can't say for sure, but I wouldn't be surprised if the women in my life had branded me with the Scarlet Letter. I cringe a bit, remembering Anderson's words around a domestic violence case we worked on last year.

"Well, if I ever found out that my husband was messing around on me, I'm cutting it off."

Surprisingly, she embraces me, giving me an extra squeeze before she lets go.

"Congratulations on the baby," I say. "I'm sorry I wasn't here for the shower."

Anderson just shrugs, pulling out her phone. "Want to see some pictures?"

Nyla Anderson is a tiny, pink potato of a baby with big, brown eyes and thick lashes.

"She's beautiful," I say, scrolling through the photos. "I love her name. *Nyla.*"

"What time did you get here?" Graham interjects, tossing his bag into his cubicle.

"About seven o'clock," I sigh. "Been trying to get back into the system the entire time. Just managed to get back into my email account, so there's that."

"I had the exact same headache when I got back from maternity leave," Anderson relates. She heads back to her desk down the aisle, tossing a knowing smile over her shoulder. "Good to have you back, Bens."

"Thanks."

"You go be great, Anderson!" Graham yells behind her.

She waves him off without another look back. Graham follows me back to my cubicle, collapsing into my chair with a grunt. He looks around, wheeling the rolling chair around to make sure we're alone.

"Did you talk to...?"

I lean against the frame of the cubicle, staying straight-faced. "I did."

"And?"

"We're taking it slow, but... we're good."

Graham grins for the both of us. "Good for you, man."

"Thanks."

"How are the boys?"

"They're doing alright. We signed a lease for a new spot—a townhouse on Wood Street with three beds and two baths. Still in the school district, so it's perfect for us. We move in next week. You'll have to come see it."

"Word?"

"Yeah, we just needed a fresh start, you know?"

Graham nods. "Need any help with the move?"

"Nah, I hired movers. I can't afford an injury, what with just getting back and all."

"Smart."

Graham updates me on the Minter case—the senator's daughter. He pulls the file from his neighboring desk and walks me through the latest. There's a suspect we want to question but no one's been able to locate him yet.

"I was just about to type up a BOLO—"

"I got it," I offer. "Email me the details."

"Thanks, man."

The sooner I get acclimated, the sooner I'll be back to my old self. The sooner I'm back to my old self, the sooner I can convince Gloria that I'm doing better than coping.

I'm doing just fine.

CHARLIE

The packing tape squeaks out of the depleting roll as I tear a new piece. Boxes lay in piles around me, marked with sharpie. Our entire lives, packed up into boxes labeled *Kitchen, Office, Garage, CJ's Room, Cameron's Room, Dad's Room...*

I wasn't surprised when the realtor came back with a few enticing offers, only two weeks after our house was listed. It made sense. It's in a great neighborhood, filled with schools, parks, and small businesses. The house itself has a Colonial charm with modern updates throughout. It's what drew Rachel and me to it in the first place, making it our home. We'd planned our entire lives here. And now, after only two weeks listed, I accepted the best offer.

Last week, Leah drove up from Atlanta to retrieve some of Rachel's things. Save for a stack of photos I intend to give to the boys someday, I'd boxed all of her belongings up long before even considering moving to a new house. It didn't make much sense to bring the boxes with us, only to stay sealed away in some dark corner. That wasn't right, so I called her parents, to offer them the chance to look through everything and decide what they'd like to hold onto.

I only ever reached their voicemail. Eventually, Leah was the one to get back to me.

"They don't want to talk to you right now."

I assumed as much. It's hard not to wonder what kind of relationship—if any—the Evans family will have with my boys going forward. Before their mother died, CJ and Cam only saw their grandparents twice a year. Coming from a close-knit family myself, I'd always hoped to change that dynamic. But I knew from the moment I married into her family that they weren't an affectionate bunch, nor were they big on quality time.

Still, they're the only tie that my boys have to their mother—apart from Leah. Wesley is the only grandfather they've ever known. And while Vivian and Wesley Evans may not win "Grandparents of the Year," I'm hopeful that, in time, we can all find common ground.

For now, I'm grateful for Leah—a facilitator, a lifeline for the boys, and the only semi-healthy relationship left with the Evans family.

Rachel's sister didn't say much when she was here. I gave her space, let her take the time she needed to sort through the boxes and decide what to take with her. When she was done, eyes red and swollen from crying, I helped load Rachel's treasures into her car—so many tokens for the family to remember her by.

"Alright, Charlie," she'd said. "Take care of yourself."

She drew me into her arms then, giving me a hug that shook my resolve. I'd done so much to damage this family. I didn't deserve this kindness, but I needed it. I hugged her back, thinking all the while, *I'll miss you.*

I tear a new piece of tape, sealing a box labeled *Bar Cart* with all my liquor inside. I'd long since gotten rid of the bottle Rachel drank from that awful night, dumping it down the drain and disposing of the glass bottle.

"That's the last of it," I say aloud to no one in particular.

My life lay in tidy piles around me, dismantled but contained—packed up but brimming with memories. I remember carrying Rachel over the threshold that very first day, keys in her hand as she smiled up at me. The boys took their first steps here. We hosted backyard birthday parties. There were good times here amidst the rejection, loneliness, and loss.

"*Answer me!*" she screamed, gun aimed and rattling in her shaking hand.

Months later, I can still hear myself pleading. "*Rachel, put it down. Rachel!*"

My head spins as the memories threaten to drown me in their dark waters. Instead, I make for the sliding door, cracking it open to invite the breeze on my damp skin.

I'm okay. I'm fine.

The earthy scent of the outdoors anchors me. I can only do my best for my boys and myself, one day at a time. The future seems so unclear right now, and leasing a new house feels like an escape hatch out of the past. For now, I'm looking forward to a new beginning, despite the unknown.

With a flick of the switch, our home and the memories within darken to nothing but an empty house—*for someone else's family to call home.*

June

Seven

PROTUBERANCE

CHARLIE

Tonight is the first night that I've had to call Sienna to watch the boys last minute. She'd arrived within ten minutes of the call, a backpack slung over her shoulder and an understanding smile on her face. Because of the hour, the boys were already in bed. My day was only just beginning.

The call came in from a quiet, suburban street in North Argale. The flashing lights of emergency vehicles paint the entire block alternating blues and reds. I pull my unmarked SUV into an open spot on the street. Following the lights, I walk up to the scene, catching the eye of the responding officer.

"What d'we got?" I ask, pulling out my notepad.

The young officer runs down the scene for me. It's dark, so I have to wedge my flashlight between my cheek and my shoulder to see what I'm writing.

"Domestic dispute," he says. "One victim. Male. Late thirties. It's a stabbing. He was DOA upon arrival. His spouse is the 911 caller and the offender. She claims self-defense. She's currently being assessed for injuries and will be transported to headquarters for questioning."

I glance in the direction of the ambulance, parked in the driveway. A woman sits on a stretcher inside, a paramedic briefly shining a light in her eyes, asking questions. She tugs the blanket around her shoulders a little tighter.

The officer lifts the police tape, nodding. Ducking beneath, I step up onto the front porch, crossing the threshold into the house. The first detail I notice is a framed photo on the wall—likely of the couple. Past the foyer is the kitchen where two uniformed officers stand guard, securing the perimeter. I flash my badge, and they both nod, stepping aside to let me enter.

Damn, that's a lot of blood.

A medical examiner and two crime scene investigators process the grisly scene. The one with a camera snaps a photo of a bloodstained knife before the other bags it. Curled up in front of the oven is the corpse of a man not much older than myself. Blood pools around him, inching further and further from the body—so recently alive.

The medical examiner looks up, saying something to me. It's only then that I realize that I can't hear him over the pounding of my own heart.

I pocket my notepad, afraid that the trembling of my hands might send it flying. When I open my mouth to speak, nothing comes out—a tightness in my chest holding my voice hostage.

"What a mess," someone says in my ear. I jolt, recognizing the voice a second too late. Graham looks over the scene with the familiar air of detachment necessary for this line of work.

Is this how they looked over my scene? My blood on the tile...

"Yeah," I manage. "I'll be right back."

Outside, I drink the night air in hungry gulps. Eventually, my heart beat slows, and my hands start to feel like my own again. A migraine begins to throb in my temple as footsteps approach, a hand landing gently on my shoulder.

"You good, CB?" Graham asks.

"Yeah," I sigh. "I just needed some air. Let's get back to it."

At the department, I stand outside of the interrogation room, watching the monitor's feed of the woman from the scene—Keri—who clutches the blanket the paramedics gave her, dabbing streaks of mascara from her tear-stained cheeks.

I'm still a bit shaken up. So many times I've processed similar scenes—what's another victim? But still, every time I close my eyes, I see that man, lying helplessly on the floor in a pool of his own blood.

What could he possibly have done to deserve to die like that?

"Ready?" Graham asks.

I nod and twist the knob, entering the interrogation room with him close behind. I take a seat at the table across from her, while Graham pulls over a chair, still keeping some distance.

"Keri, I'm Detective Bensley and this is my partner, Detective Graham. Can you walk me through what happened tonight?" I keep my tone calm. Neutral. Betraying none of my inner turmoil from earlier in the evening. *I'm fine.*

Keri sniffles, and her voice is hoarse when she speaks. "Today is our tenth anniversary. We had a reservation for dinner at eight o'clock. He wasn't home until after ten. He was drunk. I demanded an explanation. He cursed me out, saying I was ungrateful." She rolls her bloodshot eyes. "I slapped him. That's when he grabbed me by the hair and threw me to the ground. While I was laying there, he stormed off. Said he was gonna teach me a lesson." She lowers her voice now, barely a whisper. "I knew what that meant."

"Okay, what did that mean?"

Keri glares up at me. "That he was going to hurt me. Probably kill me this time. I couldn't take it anymore. I grabbed the knife to defend myself."

I lean in. "So, you're saying your husband was violent."

"Yes. Abusive. Has been for years."

"Okay." I jot down as much in my notepad. "He stormed off. When he returned, did he have a weapon?"

"No, but he..." Her voice seems to collapse in her throat as a sob escapes.

"So, he came at you, and you stabbed him. He went down, right?"

"Yes... but—"

"—but you didn't call the police," I say, my calm deteriorating. I can feel Graham's eyes on me. "When he was bleeding out, why didn't you call for help?"

"I—" she sobs, unable to get a word out. Her despair inspires no pity in me—only rage.

"Because you wanted him to die," I insist, rising to my feet, glowering. "You were angry. He stood you up on your anniversary, right? You say he was abusive. This was your opportunity to put an end to it, to get rid of his ass. So you stood there and watched him die."

"He was going to kill me," she chokes out, lips trembling. "If not today, then soon..."

There's a knock at the door just before it swings open.

"Bensley," Sarge barks. He jerks his head, calling me out of the room. "My office. Graham, take over."

"Yes, sir," Graham says. I can feel his concern boring a hole in the back of my head as I follow Sarge out the door.

"Have a seat," the boss man instructs, settling into his own chair. At first, he just looks at me, his brow furrowed, mouth drawn in a frown. "You okay on this case? I can reassign it."

"I got it."

"You got what exactly? Because what I just saw was a version of you that I've never seen before. That isn't you. You're one of my sharpest detectives. You can read a suspect like a book. That wasn't so much book reading as it was throwing the book at a suspect prematurely. It's out of character, Bensley."

"Trust me, Sarge. This is manslaughter. She *wanted* him dead."

"Maybe," he concedes. "But there is a documented history of domestic violence. We can't dismiss self-defense when we have reports of abuse in the past. You know that."

My self-righteous defenses topple with every reprimanding word. *I feel like shit.* Under my shirt, my scars itch. The tape rolls back, my own words coming back to haunt me.

"This was your opportunity to put an end to it, to get rid of his ass. So you stood there and watched him die."

What was I doing? I just attacked a domestic violence survivor. *Good job, Charlie.*

Sarge leans his elbows on the desk, templing his fingers. "Bensley, you're one of my best investigators. That's why I threw your name in the hat for promotion. You're a leader. And you're ready for an upgrade. A tragedy like you've experienced is enough to really shake up your world and test your resilience. You think you might need more time off? That would be understandable."

I shake my head. I need my life to go back to normal. *I need to be fine.*

"Well, then, this is not a suggestion," he says, holding his hands out in surrender. "Therapy. It's the only way that you're staying on. You hear me?"

The ultimatum hangs heavy between us, waiting for my acknowledgment. *First Gloria, now Sarge.* Two people who know me well have recommended I seek therapy as a way to process the tragedy I thought I'd already processed. *Maybe I'm not as in control as I thought.*

"Okay."

"Good. I'll have HR hook you up with a therapist that suits your needs. The office will call you to set up that first intake appointment. Don't ignore the call."

"Yes, sir," I say, nodding solemnly. Sarge isn't giving up on me. He just needs me to get on the other side of this thing. *I need that too.*

He leans back in his chair, rapping his knuckles on the desk. "You have a great career ahead of you, Bensley. Don't mess it up. Get the help you need."

GLORIA

Meet me here, his text read, followed by a link to coordinates about thirty minutes outside Argale's city limits. I drive with the windows down, letting the air whip through my hair and caress the back of my neck. It's starting to smell like summer these days, days holding on for hours longer. This time a few months ago, the road would have been lit only by street lights and other passing cars.

Tonight, an amber glow from the setting sun casts everything in a romantic hue.

My GPS chirps my impending arrival, and I slow the car to pull off onto a dirt path, nearing my destination. The trees lining the road open up to reveal a cliffside view overlooking the valley-set city of Argale. *Stunning.*

Charlie stands near the cliff's edge, sun reflecting off of his bare shoulders. His tank hangs loosely on his muscular frame. With his hands in his pockets, his shorts are pulled taut against his perfect backside. Hearing the crunch of my tires against the gravel, he turns around, offering me a wide smile.

"You made it," he calls.

I hop out of the car. "I did." And in a few short strides, I'm in his arms. "Hey, there."

He leans down to kiss me. "Hey, yourself."

Without another word, Charlie leads me by the hand closer to the view. The sunset is exquisite here, painting the world in cotton candy pinks and blues. Together, we gaze out over the city of Argale, so small and precious from such a height.

"This is gorgeous," I breathe. "How'd you find this place?"

Charlie hugs me from behind, his palms settling on the waist of my loose-fitting romper. He nestles his chin against my neck, planting butterfly soft kisses there. "I used to chase teenagers off this cliff when I was on patrol. The kids call it The Peak."

"Oh, that's elusive," I say with a sarcastic chuckle.

"Right?"

"Is that what we're here for?" I tease, grinding my ass against his hips. "To hook up like a couple of teenagers?"

Charlie chuckles, burying his face in the crook of my neck. He squeezes me a little tighter but doesn't make any other moves.

I loosen his grip on me to turn and face him. "You okay?"

Something in his eyes says, *Not exactly*. Without a verbal answer, he leads me back to his Jeep, where we climb into the back seat. The top of the car is off, giving us a front seat view of nature's wonders. Even so, I turn to face him, folding one leg up on the cognac colored seat. He gazes up at the sky, neck tilted back against the headrest, hand on my knee.

"What's going on?" I ask, gently prodding him.

"I had a hard day."

"Tell me about it," I sigh, rolling my eyes. *My day wasn't exactly cotton candy colored.*

He smiles. "After you."

"Well, I overslept. Had to rush to work. Spilled coffee all over my favorite silk blouse. Got chewed out by a judge for showing up to court unprepared, and then I got a flat on my way home."

"Why didn't you call me?" Concern creasing his forehead.

I shrug. "I didn't realize that was an option—yet," I explain sheepishly. "It worked out. I called AAA."

"It *is* an option," he assures. "If you ever need help. If you need *anything*—call me."

I nod, smiling at his sweetness. "Okay. Your turn."

He fidgets with his car keys, running his thumb nail over the ridges. Finally, he says, "We got a call last night. A domestic. The victim—he was on the kitchen floor. Lying in a pool of blood. His wife had stabbed him to death. During the interrogation, she claimed it was self-defense.

She said that he was abusive, that she was in fear for her life. I didn't believe her. No, the problem was that I didn't *want* to believe her. I was being completely subjective. I've always been able to trust my instinct. But now... How can I trust myself? My judgment? My ability to do my job." He swallows hard, like more fears would spill out if he let them.

"Give yourself a little grace," I say softly.

He flashes a not-so-confident smile in my direction. "Well, Sarge saw me verbally attacking a domestic abuse survivor and mandated therapy." My hand finds his on top of my knee, giving it a comforting squeeze. "Seems to be a running theme, huh? I should have taken your advice. And now I don't have a choice. It's not that I don't think that therapy is helpful. I've seen it help other people before. I just didn't think it was for me. I mean, what do I even say?"

"Whatever's on your mind," I offer. "Therapy isn't so bad, you know. It can help you through some real challenges."

He turns his head, blinking at me. "Have you ever seen a therapist?"

"Yeah."

"What for? I mean, if you don't mind me asking. You always seem like you've got it all together."

I laugh, mostly at myself, and his eyebrows raise. Looking up at the sky, I say, "When my mom died, my dad found a grief counselor for Luci and me. It helped. Back in D.C., my career could be demanding and stressful at times. Every once in a while, I needed a safe space to explore and express my thoughts and feelings. And then, more recently, I found myself falling in love with a man who belonged to someone else... It wasn't the easiest thing to navigate. Therapy helps. Wine does too," I say, giggling, attempting to lighten the mood.

His eyes overflow with empathy, fingers lacing into mine. "Babe, I'm sorry, I—"

"—Don't apologize. There are so many things that I wish happened differently, but falling in love with you is not one of them."

He leans in for a kiss, one hand coming to cup my cheek. "Thank you for loving me," he murmurs against my lips.

I sigh into his open mouth, savoring how he takes the lead, angling my jaw to kiss me properly. "You make it really hard not to."

Soon, we're making out like the teenagers he used to chase away, our kisses slow and searching, seamlessly blending with the slow groove playing softly from the dash. Each time I open my eyes, the light around us dims, welcoming the night. Stars hang above us like shimmering jewels scattered across a velvet sky, each one winking their celestial approval.

Charlie's lips are on my neck now, his hand tugging greedily at my hip, urging me into his lap. I am eager to comply, splaying my legs across his as I capture his lips with mine. He peels the straps of my romper from my shoulders, lips mapping every inch of skin he uncovers. The cool night air licks the heat from my chest, goosebumps rising beneath his mouth. When he discovers I'm braless, a growl builds low in his throat. The discovery is like a drug to him. He surges forward, capturing one taut breast between his lips while his fingers tease the other. He kisses and teases and sucks, alternating between the two, making me dizzy with desire.

My head falls back as I grind on his lap, aching to feel every inch of him inside me. His bulge is deliciously hard beneath me. With eager hands, I lift his shirt over his head so we can be flesh to flesh, if only from the waist up. Taking the cue, he lifts his hips to pull his shorts down, releasing himself to rub against the cotton of my romper. I'm too worked up to wait for either of us to undress any further, so I reach down between us to pull my romper and panties aside, welcoming him into my warmth.

He eases inside me with a low moan that echoes my own. I brace my hand on the window.

Anyone could see us.

I ride him with renewed enthusiasm, a rhythm born of longing and trust. His hands grip my waist helplessly, anchoring us together. Fingers slipping beneath the loose fabric of my romper to squeeze my ass. Each thrust is deeper, more desperate. I kiss him fiercely, caressing his beard, clinging to his lips, to this moment, to this man who's all mine. It's a rush—being so uninhibited.

Only with him. Only for him. He is the only man for me.

I bounce on his lap with a feverish pace, gripping the bars of the Jeep's frame above me until I'm crying out, undone by the pleasure, undone by his love. Charlie follows with a guttural moan, clutching my hips like I'm his only lifeline. *Ruined. Replenished.*

Above us, the heavens twinkle in quiet celebration. *Written in the stars.*

CHARLIE

I don't want to be here.

This single thought reverberates in my mind like thunder echoing through a canyon. I sit in the waiting room, staring at the white letters on the frosted glass door—*Dr. Kevin Solomon.* My knee bounces restlessly. To calm my nerves, I scan the room, cataloging details. The more I know about this man, the easier this interaction will be.

The decor is sophisticated and modern with dark grays and earth tones. The small coffee station is well stocked with espresso pods and bottled water. A neat stack of magazines sits on the end table next to the row of seats. There's at least two potted plants within sight—real, from the looks of it. The wall opposite Dr. Solomon's office features inlaid bookshelves filled floor to ceiling with a mix of classic novels and psychology texts.

None of this says much about the man behind the door, other than the fact that he cares a lot about the comfort of his guests. *Patients,* I correct myself. The space is open and inviting, like a hip cafe in downtown Argale. Like somewhere you could brew some tea, pull a book off the shelf, and lose yourself for hours.

I don't buy it.

A shadow forms behind the frosted glass just before the door creeps open. A tall, bald man with a dark complexion and graying goatee enters the waiting room, locking eyes with me.

"Charles?"

I stand and approach him, hand outstretched. "Call me Charlie."

He accepts my hand with a firm grip. "I'm Kevin. Come on in, have a seat."

Dr. Solomon's office continues the theme—sleek, personal. More books, more curated art. Framed black-and-white photos line the wall behind his brown leather armchair—landscapes from across the country. I wonder if he took them himself.

I catch sight of an oversized analog clock, situated behind a charcoal colored sofa. *So Doc can kick out his patients when time's up, I guess.* I take my seat on the sofa, hands clasped and elbows propped on my knees.

"First therapy session?" he asks, sinking into the armchair across from me.

"Yeah."

"Okay, well let me start by saying this is a safe space, everything that we discuss is confidential unless I believe you're a danger to yourself or someone else. Ok?"

I nod, resisting the urge to rush things.

"So, tell me a little bit about yourself, Charlie. What do you do?"

"I'm in law enforcement."

Doc nods. "Thank you for keeping our community safe."

I offer a half-smile. *Why can't I seem to act normal?*

"So, what brings you in today, Charlie?"

He's cutting to the chase, and I'm grateful for it. I hesitate, revisiting the script I'd prepared for myself earlier today. "My girlfriend thinks therapy might help me sort through some recent trauma." It occurs to me that this is the first time I've referred to Gloria as my girlfriend out loud to anyone. Doc only nods. "My sergeant does too. In fact, he mandated it."

"And what do you think?"

"Maybe."

He writes something down on a notepad nestled in a leather portfolio. "Well, let's start with any questions you may have."

"How many sessions do I need?"

"That depends on what you want to get out of therapy. What do you hope to achieve?"

"I don't know. To be okay again, I guess."

Doc nods, taking another note. "Therapy is collaborative," he finally says. "It requires transparency—vulnerability, even—which can feel uncomfortable. But without that, therapy's just a waste of time. The more open and honest you are, the easier it is to start working toward your goal."

I nod. I can be vulnerable.

"I know this wasn't entirely your idea," Doc continues, "but together, we'll dive deep into what truly inspired you to seek therapy. That might mean working through trauma and learning better tools for coping. Make sense?"

I nod again, appreciative of how he's laying it all out for me. The more I understand how this all works, the faster I can go through the motions and get it done.

"Just remember," he says, "I'm here to be a sounding board and to provide resources and tools when needed. But my ultimate goal is to help you learn how to better help yourself."

"Alright," I sigh. "Can we just jump right in, or do you have to ask me about my parents or whatever?"

"We can talk about anything you want to talk about. At some point, we will want to talk about the incident that brought you here."

I feel myself bristling and force a deep breath. "What about it?"

"Well, let's start with what happened."

I wring my hands together. "My wife shot me. Then took her own life."

Most people's faces change when they hear that kind of story, but Doc's expression remains neutral. No shock. No pity. Just calm focus.

"I'm sorry to hear that. Why do you think things escalated?"

"We were arguing."

"Okay. What were you arguing about?"

"Some issues in our marriage."

"And how would you describe the issues?" The conversation is feeling a little less like an intake session and more like an interrogation. *Is this how my suspects feel on the other side of the table?*

"I had been having an affair. Divorce came up. It went left from there."

"Okay. Who brought up divorce?"

"She did."

"Was she asking for one?"

"No. She said it wasn't an option, that it would never be."

"Okay, did you ask her for a divorce?"

"No."

"But divorce was a wildcard for you," Doc states, though his eyebrows raise in question.

My jaw clenches. *Wow.*

Jack's voice rings in my ears. *"The truth isn't always a kindness, bro."*

Doc taps his pen lightly on his notepad. "I sense something has shifted. Have I offended you? Are you feeling upset right now?"

"Am I..." I trail off into a mirthless laugh. *Do all therapists talk like aliens on their Earth internship?*

"As we spoke about your wife, I noticed a difference in how you held yourself. We can change subjects if you don't want to talk about what's upsetting you."

"What's upsetting me is that my wife shot me. Then herself. If I hadn't survived, our children would be orphans." My voice hardens. "I take full responsibility for what I did. I was wrong for cheating, but we were supposed to be able to talk through it, figure it out *civilly.* My father—he left my mother. Left us. I could never do that to my boys. I stayed in a marriage with a woman that didn't even love me—"

Rachel's humorless laugh fills my ears. *"I will not let you disgrace me this way. A failed marriage—the* shame. *The embarrassment."*

"—She was going to leave our kids with no parents. Are you married, Doc?"

"No."

"Kids?"

"No. Would you prefer a therapist with a wife and kids?" he asks, unperturbed. His sincerity makes me want to throw something.

I'd prefer not to be here.

Without another word, I stand, turning for the door. "I don't think this is for me. Thanks for your time."

My head buzzes the whole walk back to the parking garage. I slam the door of my Jeep behind me, the buzzing following me into the claustrophobic space. Just recently, this vehicle was home to one of the many amazing moments I've created with Gloria. Today, it feels like my personal prison. My whole body shivers with an unnamed emotion, and I worry that I might burst through my skin. I can't still my bouncing knee, and I won't even try to slow my pounding heart. Instead, I pull my fist from my gritted teeth and hit the steering wheel full force. The horn blares, echoing through the garage, shrill and furious.

Shit. Sarge is gonna kick my ass.

CHARLIE

The week following my first and probably last session with Dr. Solomon is a chaotic blur of unpacking boxes, arranging utilities, and getting the boys settled into their new home. I hadn't realized how scraggly we were all getting until Jack called to inquire about missing our standing weekly appointment at the shop.

My older brother has always had a penchant for the barbering arts. He would cut hair between classes and on weekends for extra cash. His skill set made him quite the commodity among the other Black, male students at the predominantly white college he attended for Finance. He also got popular with the ladies, meeting Aries as a sophomore.

The summer before his junior year, Jack learned he had a son on the way. It made more sense for him to sharpen his natural talents rather than waste any more time on a degree he had no real interest in. It took some serious persuasion—and no shortage of begging—but he managed to convince our mother to loan him the tuition for a barber college. Needless to say, he completed his program and got to work, repaying every penny, plus interest.

The rest is history. By the age of twenty-five, Jack opened his own shop right here in Argale. *The Cut* is a sleek spot, just off Main Street. The black leather barber chairs speak to Jack's sense of style. Large round mirrors line the walls, strip lights behind them, casting the whole room in a soothing yet masculine glow. The best part might be the sixty-five-inch TV mounted above the blacktop billiards table.

"What do you think, little man?" Jack asks, spinning Cameron in the vinyl chair to see himself in the mirror. "Looks fresh to me."

"Looks fresh to me too," Cam agrees, admiring his low fade.

"Dope," I say, clapping a hand on his shoulder. "Right, CJ?"

CJ only gives him a distracted thumbs up, never once looking up from his game. Jack and I exchange a knowing glance in the mirror. I'll let it slide. CJ was first in the chair today—a low taper with a part. He's growing it out a bit, coming into his own sense of style. Cameron scoots off the chair and discards the smock, running over to his brother to get his approval. Seeing them together, I'm amazed at how much they've grown—right before my eyes. Becoming little men.

We've come so far.

I'm grateful for summer sports and programs that keep the boys busy. Cameron's on the little league baseball team, and CJ is doing an early learners' computer sciences program offered through the local community center. Oftentimes, it feels busier than I have enough energy for but somehow, together, we manage. *We're managing.*

"You're next, bro," Jack instructs, flinging a fresh cape over my shoulders. He knows what I want before I do, so I don't even bother to give him a vision. *Just trust.* Jack takes the trimmers to the back of my neck to start. "Y'all settling into the new crib alright?"

"It's coming along. Most of the boxes are unpacked. The boys love their new rooms."

For weeks after Rachel died, Cameron would climb into bed with me, missing his mom. I think that sometimes he just misses the spot that he used to claim between us, those nights that a nightmare or a scary shadow on the wall would bring him into our bed.

That doesn't happen much anymore. My highest priority after the move was to make their bedrooms as comfortable as possible. I knew they'd miss the only place that they'd ever known as home, but I wanted to make our new place as safe, warm, and homey as possible. I wanted them to know that home is anywhere that we are—*together*.

"CJ showed me some pictures of his gaming setup. You went all out," Jack says with a whistle. "And Cam says you're gonna loft his bed. Need an extra pair of hands?"

"I just might," I chuckle. "It's been so busy lately. I've barely moved into my own room yet, to be honest. Just so focused on the boys."

"And..." He lowers his voice to ask, "How are things going with your lady? Gloria, right?"

I smile. "Yeah. All good."

Jack trades the trimmer for a pair of shears. "Tell me about her."

"She's smart and beautiful. She's funny and just good to be around. Strong but delicate, you know what I mean? I can talk to her about anything. She makes me feel equally vulnerable and invincible. And man, when she smiles…" I trail off, at a loss for words. "I just… I just want to be with her."

Jack catches my eyes in the mirror. "When do you get to be with her?"

"Whenever we can. We try to make time for each other, but with me back to work and my schedule at home, it's a bit harder. We're making it work though."

"Well, check this out. Just bring the boys over every other weekend. Drop 'em off on Friday, pick 'em up on Sunday. That ought to give you two a little quality time for a while," he says with a mischievous grin. "Will that help?"

I can't believe his generous offer. "Yeah, man. That would help. Thank you."

"Don't worry about it. It takes a village…" It's hard to hide the small smile tugging at the corner of my mouth, moved by his sentiment and support.

"Bro, I know how much you loved Rachel, but it's obvious you've got it bad. I'm happy for you—all in love and shit," he chuckles.

I laugh, shushing him as I glance around to make sure the boys didn't overhear. Jack lowers his voice again. "Besides, it'll keep Aries busy after Royce leaves."

"Damn, I can't believe that boy's about to head off to college."

"That's right! We're almost empty nesters! Now, sit still for a minute so I can line up this beard you've got going on." After a few minutes shaping up my facial hair, Jack passes me a hand mirror to see the finished product. "What do you think?"

I study my reflection, impressed as always by how Jack can elevate any man's look.

"Thanks, Jack." I draw him into my arms, holding tight. "Love you."

Jack squeezes back. "Love you too, little bro. Next time, wait 'til the cape's off—I probably got your fuzz all over me now..."

"Aww, shit—sorry."

He *tsks* to himself but doesn't let go. "You deserve to be happy, Charlie. Not just your boys—you too. After what you've been through, you deserve happiness of your own."

Later, when I'm ushering the boys back to the car with the promise to drop them off for a weekend visit, I return to his words.

"You deserve happiness of your own."

With all that's happened, with all the hurt I've caused... *Do I?*

July

Eight

LOVE IN VIVID BRUSHSTROKES

GLORIA

I peek at Charlie from around my easel, admiring how he looks in an apron. A little smudge of deep, crimson paint blooms along his cheekbone like a kiss as he focuses on his own canvas. *I wonder what his painting looks like.* Today, we're making up for some lost time with a little arts and crafts—painting still lifes of a glass of wine, a cork and a half-empty bottle set in the center of our makeshift studio in the living room. *Merlot.* This summer proved to be busier than either of us expected. Last time we were together, he hadn't seen his new therapist yet. The curiosity gets the better of me.

"So..." I begin, adding paint to my brush, "how was your first session?"

"I walked out," he says simply.

I raise my eyebrows, "That bad, huh?"

He pokes his head out from behind his canvas, meeting my eyes. "It wasn't, I was just... I suppose the truth was just a little too much for me to handle. Anyway, I scheduled another appointment for next week. Not so much because of the job, but because of my reaction. I've never been quick-tempered like that before. *Angry.* I wanted to rip his head off, and the man barely said anything worth that kind of reaction."

I nod solemnly. "I don't know how you've survived all this time without therapy. I mean, seeing the things I can only imagine you've seen..."

Something sad hangs off the edge of his smile. "I'm not sure I have survived." It's quiet for some time before he speaks up again. "Babe, I don't know that I'm inspired by this setup."

"Okay," I chuckle. "What would you like to paint, then?"

His silence makes me peek around my canvas. Our eyes meet over the arrangement, and his lips curl into a smile both wicked and reverent as he looks me up and down.

My chuckle turns into a full laugh. "Need a muse?"

"Mmhmm."

"Okay. How do you see me?" With slow fingers, I unbutton my blouse, watching his expression darken from playful to hungry. I rise to my feet, letting my shirt fall to the floor as I approach his easel. "Where do you want me?"

His eyes speak for him—the couch.

Piece by piece, I undress, leaving a trail behind me as I move to the couch. Charlie follows, waiting until I'm completely nude to pose me how he wants me—comfortably on my knees with my hands in my lap. With the gentlest of touches, he brushes my hair out from behind my ear and lets it cascade over my shoulder. Lifting my chin, he drops a kiss on my lips before retreating to his workspace.

Charlie paints with the focus of a master. His brush glides over the canvas, looking between my body and the piece before him—like a true artist, trying to capture the essence of his muse. Occasionally, our eyes meet in a loving glimpse, sharing a smile.

I'm afraid to love him the way that he loves me—fearlessly.

He's so patient with me. As the days go by, I can feel the anxiety around our future subside. His warmth thawing my iciest defenses—his whispers soothe my anxious heart. Charlie's eyes linger on my lips, and my heart swells, overwhelmed by it all.

"You okay," he asks after I release a long sigh.

"Mmhmm." *I need to break the silence.* "So, tell me. Why homicide?"

Charlie blinks, surprised by the question but doesn't back down from it. "For the trench coat and fedora."

I laugh, my loose hair tickling the bare skin of my exposed chest. "Seriously."

He's thoughtful for a moment before he decides to speak again. "After three years on patrol, I wanted to—level up. Being a homicide detective was one of the most prestigious positions in the police department. The elite team. So, I expressed an interest. I remember thinking to myself, I can do homicide. I mean, on patrol you see a little bit of everything."

"Okay," I say. "I hear a *but* coming."

"Yeah, a big *but*." He chuckles to himself before getting serious again. "It's pretty standard for all the qualified applicants to be given an opportunity to get a feel for it, assist on a case, like a trial run."

"Mmhmm."

"It's typically a natural causes case or something like that. To get you used to dealing with death—understand stages of decomp, the smells, the sights, the way a scene feels when you walk into it. It prepares you for what's to come." Charlie shakes his head, his eyes going distant. "That first scene... G baby, it was like something from a horror movie. The smell. A body badly decomposed. Maggots." I grimace with him, bracing myself for more grotesque detail. "I hate maggots. It completely freaked me out. I threw up all over the place."

We laugh in melodic unison.

"Are you serious?"

"I'm pretty sure I sharted too," he confesses. *He's so ridiculous.* When we're done laughing, he sighs deeply. "I was pretty confident that I blew my chance at the promotion. My training officer couldn't stop laughing. When he finally regained his composure, he ordered me to process and help the ME bag the body. I told myself, if they didn't tell me to kick rocks, I was done. I wasn't going back."

"But you did," I say with a knowing smile.

"Yeah, I did," he says, a little stunned by his own memory. "Eventually, I adapted, learned the ropes, earned my keep, found my flow, and learned how to solve a murder. This job, it's not just about catching the bad guy. It's about standing in the middle of someone's worst day and trying to make sense of it all." His quiet is loud, and his reflection appears far heavier than his words let on. I can only imagine what it was like—*his worst day.*

I can laugh now, but that day I was like, let me see what they got going on in narcotics—maybe the gang unit or robbery."

We laugh again, finding the humor in even the macabre.

He shakes off a residual chill. "That experience shook me to my core, but it made me a better detective." Suddenly, Charlie lowers his brush, looking at his work with a discerning eye.

"All done?"

He meets my eyes like he has a secret to tell. "Yep."

"Can I see?" I rise from the couch, stretching my joints after being in the same pose for some time. Tugging a throw blanket from the couch to wrap around my shoulders, I venture toward Charlie and his easel, settling myself on his lap.

"What do you think?" he asks.

He's painted my side profile, a faceless silhouette with beautiful brown skin and shiny black hair. I don't expect it to be as lovely as it is, but I should have expected as much from such an attentive and creative man.

I tap my chin, feigning deep consideration. "Well, the last person to paint a portrait of me was my niece, Penelope..."

He shakes his head ruefully. "How can I compete?"

"This is amazing, babe," I whisper, my enthusiasm growing. "You know, faceless portraits are good for highlighting other aspects of the subject, like their body language or their relationship with others. Most artists use this style to capture more intimate moments without facial expressions distracting from the tone. Is that what you were going for?"

"Uh, yup. For sure."

I laugh. "She's beautiful."

"Yes, you are."

"And this is how you see me?"

"Gloria," he murmurs, angling my face toward his so we're looking eye to eye, "I don't have the skillset to capture how I see you."

Staring into his eyes, I can almost see myself reflected in them. His point of view seems to overlook all the ugly parts of me. *My fear. My guilt. My shame.*

I pull back ever so slightly. "Maybe I can put it on display at my art exhibition."

"You're putting on an exhibition?"

"No, but I've been daydreaming about it a lot lately."

"You should do it."

"Yeah, we'll see. Only if you'll be my featured artist."

"I'd love to," he whispers, already leaning in.

The kiss starts slow, soft, exploratory, like so many of our kisses do. We're in no rush these days, exploring each other and finding new ways to love one another. Rising up from his lap, I turn to face him, letting the blanket draped around my shoulders fall like silk to the floor. He lifts his shirt over his head as I help him out of his shorts. We're only flesh and heat and breath now—artists and muses, sculptors of each other's desire. Our love, like clay, to mold and shape with our hands.

Charlie lifts me, and my legs wrap around him instinctively. He carries me to the sofa, kissing me the whole way, then kneels on the cushions as he places me on top of the backrest. My back rests comfortably against the wall between two paintings hanging side by side, like I am part of the gallery too.

When Charlie pushes inside of me, I gasp, splaying my legs wide, toes pointed and pressed delicately into the plush cushions of the sofa, welcoming him deeper—*closer*. His long, deep strokes remind me of his brush strokes in their confidence. *Paint me with your love, baby*. My nails drag down his back as one of his hands grips my ass, the other braced against the wall. We come together, with his face buried in my neck, and my eyes on the loveliest portrait anyone has ever made of me, drying in the setting sun.

Waking up in his arms feels surreal. No watch alarm, reminding him of where he's supposed to be, pulling him from my arms—from the space in my bed that had become his, the spot I was happy to keep warm for him. I'd only ever dreamed this.

Somebody pinch me.

I peek toward the window, noting the gray tint to the sky—still early. I'm more than happy to forgo my morning meditation just to stay tangled up in his embrace. I used to think my reading chair was my favorite place on Earth, but that was before now.

No, there's no need to manifest anything today. *I'm already in my happy place.*

Charlie stirs beside me, sighing softly. I can feel his readiness pressed intimately against my thigh before he even opens his eyes. He pulls me closer, waking slowly.

I could get used to this.

"Good morning," he grumbles softly into my ear. I smile against his cheek. "Finally... I get to wake up with you in my arms."

Read my mind. "It's nice."

"What time is it?"

I have to wrestle out of his arms a bit to see the clock on the nightstand. "7:17AM. Breakfast?"

"Mmhmm," he murmurs, tugging me back in place to brush his lips against my neck. My body comes alive at his touch, and I hum with pleasure. "But first..."

I turn to face him, and he catches my giggles with his lips, kissing me languidly, trailing his fingers under the hem of my sleep shorts.

Yes, I could get used to this.

"Let me get the door for you."

Ever the gentleman, Charlie reaches around me to open the passenger side door. It's the first time we've gone out in public together, and it feels like a first date. Through the windshield, I watch him move in slow motion, eyes catching on the way his short sleeved shirt hugs his perfect biceps. That Beyoncé song plays in my head...

Driver, roll up the partition pleaseI don't need you seeing GG on her knees...

I bite my lip as I smile up at him, blushing when he grins back at me with all the swagger of the sun. He settles into the driver's seat, taking the wheel.

"What?" he asks, and only then do I realize I'm still staring at him all googly-eyed.

"Nothing," I say, floundering in my flush. "Where are we headed?"

"I know the perfect spot. I think you'll love it." He leans in, cupping my jaw, planting the sweetest of kisses on my lips. Then, he throws on his sunglasses and revs the engine.

Off we go.

We don't get far before Charlie turns on the stereo. "I Will Die For You" by Prince pulses through the speakers, and of course, Charlie Bensley knows every word. With one arm extended to grip the wheel, he tangles his free hand in mine, bopping his head to the music and singing along.

He's so cute.

"You," he croons, "I Would. Die For. You."

I grin so hard my cheeks hurt, chiming in, "Darling, if you want me to..."

Our own version of carpool karaoke—Prince Edition. I'm obsessed.

A phone call abruptly cuts through the song, and Charlie squeezes my hand briefly before letting it go to accept the call.

"Good morning," he declares.

"Hey, Dad!" a tiny, jovial voice rings through the car's speakers. *My heart.*

Charlie's smile is contagious. "Hey Cam! What's up, bud?"

"Whatcha doin?" Cameron sings.

"'Bout to grab a bite to eat. How about you? Have you had breakfast?"

"Yep! Auntie Aries made French toast with strawberries, blueberries, *and* bananas."

"Aww man, anything left?"

"Nope," he reports. "Whatcha doin today, Dad?"

"Hopefully, after I eat, I'm heading back to bed." He looks over at me with a devilish smile, and I feel my blush trickle down my cheeks to the rest of my body too. *Troublemaker.*

As they speak, Charlie pulls into the restaurant's parking lot. It's a cute little spot called Toast that I've never tried before. The black awning promises French toast and mimosas.

"Alright, Cam, talk to you later. Tell everyone I said hey. Love you, son."

"Love you too, Dad."

Dad. Cam sounds so adorable. Their bond has my heart screaming, and I feel so honored to have witnessed it. Oblivious to my swoon, Charlie simply hangs up, gets out of the car, opens my door for me.

"Ready?"

I nod. "Starving."

The hostess seats us on the covered patio. Colorful flowers hang from the rafters of a bright orange pergola. *Wisteria, pink bougainvillea, climbing roses...* A brick wall frames the space with an urban charm, complete with a mural of a saxophonist and a woman mid-dance.

"You like it?" Charlie whispers in my ear.

"I *love* it."

Once we've placed our orders, conversation comes easily.

"What's your favorite color?" I ask.

"Blue. Yours?"

"Fuchsia."

Charlie clicks his tongue, grinning. "Should've known yours would be specific. I'm in love with an artist."

"Yes, you are," I confirm, loving the sound of it. *An artist.*

"Fuchsia—that's like pink, right?"

I twirl my glass of water, watching the ice cubes clink together. "It gives pink energy, but it's bold like purple."

"I like that. Then mine's navy."

"Those colors go really well together."

"So, we're perfect for each other?"

"I didn't say all that."

"Oh, okay," he laughs. "So what are you saying?"

"That navy and fuchsia complement each other, yet contrast in just the right way. Like we do," I spell out, batting my eyelashes.

Our food arrives with time to spare, and soon we're talking about our favorite meals when something over my shoulder catches Charlie's eye.

"Camille?"

An older woman, barely sixty, approaches, wide-eyed and carrying a to-go bag.   "Charles?"

Charlie stands to embrace her. She's graceful, with fine lines around her smile that speak of laughter and experience. As they speak, her name tugs at my memory. Camille...

"Camille, this is my girlfriend, Gloria."

My heart skips a beat—*girlfriend*. I ignore my impulse to grab Charlie and kiss him. Instead, I behave myself and smile up at Camille. "Lovely to meet you."

"It's my pleasure, Gloria," Camille says sweetly. We clasp hands.

"It was Gloria who encouraged me to reach out to you," Charlie adds.

Her smile deepens, and suddenly it clicks. *This* is Camille—wife of the officer that inspired Charlie to become an officer of the law himself.

"I'm so glad that you did," she says to me. "It meant so much to me to hear about the impact my husband had on his life."

Charlie and Camille chat for a minute or so longer before she wraps him up in another hug. When she turns to say goodbye to me, she bypasses my hand and opens up for a hug. I pull her in without hesitation, so grateful for the gesture.

"Thank you," she whispers in my ear. "Thank you."

Charlie and I sit and watch Camille scurry away with her to-go bag. When we turn back to one another, both our eyes are glossy with emotion. We burst into laughter.

"To Camille," Charlie says, lifting his mimosa glass to mine.

"To Camille."

"Was that okay?" he asks. "Introducing you as my girlfriend?"

I nod, hiding my smile in my mimosa glass. "Yeah..."

He reaches across the table, his fingers curling around mine. The wind blows gently around us, showering our table with flower petals. Together, we look up to watch the wisteria sway, its delicate vines dancing in the breeze. Smiles tug at our lips as the world around us slows, as if time itself is holding its breath.

I couldn't paint a more perfect scene.

CHARLIE

The sound of the pen against the fresh page is comforting. Last week, I returned to Dr. Solomon's office with an apology and a promise to try more earnestly.

"I appreciate your apology," Doc had said with a kind smile, *"but I assure you it's unnecessary. Vulnerability doesn't come easy, especially in new spaces. I recommend you start writing in a journal, just to practice using honest language around your feelings. Consider it self-care."*

"Self-care?" I asked, skeptical. *"I'm fine. It's my boys I'm worried about."*

"It's natural to be concerned about your children, to want to support them through this. However, you can't guide them unless you're grounded yourself. That's why self-care is so important. For you and for them."

For me, journaling is new territory. I start a new page each day—my daily page, as I've come to call the routine. So far, it feels a little forced, like a grocery list of feelings. The more I do it, however, the more naturally the words come to me.

By the time I've filled my page, the doorbell rings. Gloria waits for me behind the door. It's her first time spending the night at my place, and I feel my heart pounding in my chest with anticipation. I wonder if she heeded my instruction over text earlier this morning—*No panties.*

I open the door wide, met with her smile.

"Well, hi," she says, sweet as sugar.

"Hi," I say back, reaching for her overnight bag. She steps inside at my beckon, the sway of her backless halter dress hypnotic. "Want a tour?"

I lead her through the townhouse, room by room, pointing out my favorite features—sunlight in the stairwell and the quiet corners I've claimed for myself. At some point, I lose her. I double back to find her in the living room, standing quietly before a framed photo. It's all of us—Rachel and myself bookends to the boys.

"That's Rachel," I provide needlessly. It doesn't feel as strange as it should.

"She's beautiful."

"Yeah," I sigh. "I keep it out for the boys."

Gloria nods in understanding, accepting my hand when I offer it. No judgment. Just grace.

Out back, I show her what I've been dying to share. An oversized tent covers most of the yard, lanterns planted around the perimeter and a large blanket and plush pillows arranged within. On it, a game of giant checkers awaits us. We're on game number two when I realize that Gloria has a competitive streak. We sprawl across the blanket, stealing each other's pieces with strategy and luck.

"King me," I proclaim after a double jump.

Gloria grimaces as she stacks a checker onto mine.

"You don't like to lose, do you?"

"No..." she chuckles. "I wouldn't be a very good lawyer if I did."

"Touché."

"I want to be your husband."

We're both surprised by the words that just fell out of my mouth. Gloria pauses mid-bite around a chip topped with ceviche, staring up at me in disbelief.

"I'm not proposing. Breathe," I laugh. "Just letting you know the end game."

She blinks, chewing the rest of her chip. Her silence is a little unsettling.

"We've never discussed marriage before. How do you feel about it? Ever been engaged?"

"No," she says quietly. "I think that marriage corrupts good relationships."

I remember her telling me about her parents' divorce. Flipping a checker between my fingers, I divert the subject. "Tell me about your last relationship."

She shrugs. "It was back in D.C. I was working on a tough case, and he was the opposing counsel. After we settled, he asked me out."

"Okay, well, what happened?"

"We dated for almost a year. He wanted to get married. He wanted a family. And I didn't. So I ended it."

"Heartbreaker."

She laughs, lifting her margarita to her lips. "It was for the best. He would have made a great husband if all I needed was a trophy."

"A trophy?"

She looks up at me slyly. "Yeah, men can be trophies too. You know—someone that makes you look good, makes your life look complete. Like you've accomplished something. An accolade. Know what I mean?"

"Yep," I sigh. *I know that life all too well.* "Any regrets?"

"None," she says with a smile, shaking her head. "I actually ran into him a few years later. He was married. Had a baby on the way. I was really happy for him. Like I said, he was a good guy. Just not for me."

"Damn right."

She laughs again—my favorite sound on this planet. I take the opportunity to make my case, or at least start to. Something tells me this will be a conversation we'll have again.

"I can't blame him for wanting to marry you. I'm probably not a good spokesperson for marriage, but I believe in love, marriage, and family. Marriage can be very rewarding, especially when you have the right partner. When your goals and your souls align."

"You sound like my sister," Gloria teases.

"Then I agree with her. But you're not wrong. Marriage is hard. Has its challenges. My parents were the first people that I've ever known to get a divorce. Now, it seems like a common practice." I trail off, sipping on my glass of whiskey. "I'll get off my soapbox now."

She has the chance to change the subject now, but Gloria just smiles. "Luci and her husband Peter are the only married couple that make me believe it's possible to have a good marriage."

"How long have they been married?"

She calculates in her head. "About eleven years."

"Any kids?"

"Yep," she sighs happily. "My niece Penelope and my nephew Preston."

"Ah, the famous artist Penelope," I chuckle, inspiring a giggle from Gloria. "What about your dad and Evelyn?"

"They never married. I think that it was a mutual agreement. Perhaps they have the formula figured out. Marriage complicates things."

"Perhaps."

"How long were you married?"

"Thirteen years, last June."

Gloria's gaze drifts, but she doesn't say anything.

"What are you thinking?" I ask.

"Nothing." But her eyes suggest otherwise.

For a moment, silence lingers between us. Discussing marriage—*my* marriage—has to be uncomfortable for her. I wonder if that's what she's holding back, or if it's something else—something she isn't ready to name.

Later, we dance under the string lights, swaying slow until the blanket beneath her feet bunches. Gloria topples toward me with a laugh, catching herself in my arms. I brace her, steady and ready—always ready. I'm content to just stand here, holding her, so I'm surprised when she steps back. With a sly smile, she moves to the rhythm, fingertips trailing up her curves landing on the knot around her neck. Her dress melts to the floor, revealing a feast for my eyes. She's completely nude underneath, just as I instructed.

Good girl.

Bare. She undresses me with her eyes, head tilted as if to say, *your turn.* I obey, shedding my clothes in a pile at our feet. With the crook of a finger, I beckon her to me. And she comes. Willingly. Wantingly. Our bodies glow in the lantern light, golden and bare, like stars in the night sky—*cosmic.* I hold her face and kiss her slow, then spin her gently, fingers weaving into her hair as I massage her scalp. She moans, hands gripping my thighs for balance.

"I love you," I whisper into her ear.

"I love you," she whimpers back.

We make a home together on the blanket. Gloria lies back, legs draped over mine, her skin flushed and radiant. I slide my thumb down her slick center, caressing her with reverence, watching the pleasure play across her heated expression. She gasps. Arches. Writhes—every motion a prayer for more. The lights above us dance over her skin—her cheekbones, her throat, the perfect curve of her breasts. I commit every inch of her to memory. Her hands clutch the pillow beneath her, hips rising to meet the rhythm of my touch. I'm hard and aching for her, but I don't rush. I savor. *I worship.*

We have all the time in the world now.

When she shudders with her first orgasm, she grips my wrist, trying to catch her breath. *First orgasm of many, if I have anything to say about it.* I realize that I could do this forever. Love her forever. Bring her to pieces with just the touch of one finger—*forever.* I bring my thumb to my lips, tasting her. Her sweetness blooms on my tongue. Gloria reaches for me, her eyes soft and full and pleading. I fall into her—into everything we are.

Into everything we're becoming.

Charlie

"Detective Bensley," Jonas begins, adjusting his tie as he scans the page before him, "when you arrived on the scene, what did you observe?"

It's a mock cross-examination, routine procedure for Jonas and me with a trial upcoming. Together, we sharpen the police's testimony, leaving little to no room for jury speculation. Once upon a time, I used to fidget in the hot seat, but Jonas has done amazing work preparing me for a day in court.

"There were clear signs of forced entry," I respond. "The front door appeared to have been pried open. I identified pry marks and a damaged lock on the jamb. Upon entering the residence, there was evidence of a struggle—glass everywhere, broken and overturned furniture. The entire entryway was in disarray. There was also a blood trail from the entryway leading to the living room."

Jonas nods, pacing slowly around the room. "And what did you find in the living room?"

"Mr. Hall. He had been dragged there, where he was found bound and beaten to death.

A satisfied smile flashes across Jonas's face. "Thank you, Detective. As you know, defense will cross. Keep it cool. Stick to the facts."

"I got you. We're the dream team."

He meets my fist with a bump. "That we are, my friend. Which brings me to the other reason I asked you here." Jonas takes a seat behind his desk, tugging at his tie for more breathing room. It's hot in the office today—something about the HVAC system being down—so Jonas smooths his light brown hair off of his forehead. "I'm running for circuit court judge. I'll officially begin campaigning next month."

"Wow, Jonas, that's incredible," I say, folding my arms and shaking my head. Jonas has always been an ambitious man, and I respect his hustle. "Congratulations."

"Well, let's not celebrate too soon. I've got an uphill race to run."

"You got this, J. Anything that I can do to help, you let me know."

Jonas stands again, circling the desk to shake my hand. "You're a good man, CB."

I ignore the usual social decorum of these situations and pull the man into a hug. Dr. Solomon has been urging me to act more honestly on my feelings, and I've known Jonas too long to celebrate with a handshake. He returns the embrace with a hearty slap on my back.

"I'll keep you posted," he says, releasing me. "You headed back to HQ?"

"I am," I say, heading for the door. "I'll see you later, your honor."

Jonas barks a laugh, waving me off as he returns to his desktop computer.

Instead of heading straight for the elevator, I duck toward a certain special lady's office.

G. Gatlin, the frosted window beside her door reads. I shake my head fondly, remembering our second chance meeting. I close my eyes, unsurprised to realize that I can picture exactly what she was wearing—an ivory suit jacket with a black blouse underneath, her hair down in loose waves. *What is she wearing today?*

I knock gently.

"Come in," comes her voice. *Deja vu.*

Gloria looks up from her desk with an adoring smile, completely surprised to see me.

"Hi," she chirps like a songbird, flushed from the heat.

"Hey," I say back, closing the door behind me.

Gloria's hair is half up today, a bouquet of soft curls. She wears a solid white top, tucked into a black skirt. I smile to myself, appreciating the similarities. So many parallels, but much has changed. *We're together now.*

"Meeting with Jonas?" she asks.

I step further into the room. "Yep."

She meets me halfway. "How'd it go?"

"Pretty good. Prepping for court next week. You look nice today," I say, cutting to the chase. She giggles as I sit on the edge of her desk, yanking her gently into my arms for a kiss. She fits so perfectly between my knees—puzzle pieces clicking into place.

"Thank you," she murmurs against my mouth, tying her arms around my neck.

I slide my hands down the curve of her skirt. "How's your day been?"

"Sweaty. HVAC system is down."

"I heard."

Her watch chimes, and she lifts her dainty wrist to check the notification. "My next meeting is in fifteen minutes," she sighs.

"Okay, I just wanted to stop by and say hi."

"I'm glad you did."

"Walk me to the door?"

Her smile all twinkle and tease. "Sure."

"After you."

I can't help but watch the sway of her hips as she leads me back toward the door. I'm not quite ready to leave yet. *Fifteen minutes is a lot of time.*

At the door, I spin her around, cornering her against the mahogany wood. Holding her in place with one hand on the back of her neck, the other the curve of her hip, I kiss her deeper now—more deliberate. She responds enthusiastically, caressing the back of my head, fingernails scraping gently. Tongues tangling, breath thickening—I trail my hand under the hem of her skirt, feeling the heat of her. She quivers as I inch upwards, hooking my thumb on the edge of her panties to pull them down.

You won't need these.

She's trembling as she steps out of them, her legs looking so sexy as they taper down into black stiletto heels. *What will those look like, hanging off my back?* I toss my tie over my shoulder—then her leg. She gasps as I push her skirt high on her waist and lower my face to her heat. My tongue moves slowly, intentionally, licking along her seam. She bucks against my mouth, her moans stifled behind pressed lips. I hold her steady, coaxing her to the edge and over it.

Gloria clutches the back of my head, breathless. "I hope no one heard me."

"They didn't." I swipe her taste from my lips, press a sweet kiss to her mouth, as I pocket her panties. She raises a brow at me but doesn't object. "Don't want you to be late."

With an extra skip in my step, I head for the elevator.

"Stay cool, Coach B," Ms. Judy comments, fanning herself with a packet of papers. "It's a hot one!"

I just smile and wish her well before I depart.

Not as hot as what just happened behind G. Gatlin's door.

August

Nine

HONEYMOONERS

CHARLIE

"I think we got Royce enough stuff," I scoff, eyeing the haul of gifts piled in the back of the Jeep for my nephew's trunk party. "We ready?"

"Yep!" Cameron chirps, hopping in after CJ.

For the first time in a while, Life is not life-ing. In fact, it's been dealing me a better hand. The boys seem themselves again, enjoying a summer break with the perfect balance of structure and spontaneity. Our boxes are all unpacked now—even my own—and our new place is finally starting to feel like a home.

Peering into the rearview mirror, I glance at them and wonder if maybe Lady Life has seen how hard we've had it, and she's decided to be a little kinder to us.

"Is Grandma going to be there?" CJ suddenly asks.

"She is," I confirm.

I think back to the call earlier this week when she confirmed she'd be coming. Excited about the party. Excited to see us all.

After Rachel's funeral, we'd kept up our weekly calls as if nothing had changed. She was distant those first few weeks, the warmth in her voice replaced with something guarded. She'd answer my questions about her garden or her plans for the week, but there was a tightness there, a subtle shift that told me she wasn't ready to touch the deeper stuff.

Slowly but surely, we found our way back to something resembling normal. Distance gave way to shared laughs and light-hearted questions about the boys again. Just when it felt like we were in a good place—

"You have any plans with the boys this weekend?" she'd asked.

"Nah, they'll be with Jack and Aries."

"Oh, good. You should catch up on some rest."

I'd chuckled softly. *"I should."*

"But knowing you, you won't." She'd sighed, knowing me too well. *"So, what are you planning to do with yourself then?"*

I'd hesitated, knowing the next words could crack the fragile foundation we'd just rebuilt. *"Um, a movie night—with Gloria."*

Silence.

It stretched out, long enough that I'd checked my phone to make sure the call hadn't dropped. *It hadn't.*

"Hmm," she'd finally uttered. One syllable. Flat. Emotionless. Then, without missing a beat, she'd changed the subject. *"You won't believe how beautifully my tomatoes are coming in. I may have to start my own farmer's market..."*

That was weeks ago, and we've talked plenty since. All signs point to us still being in a good place, but I can't help wondering if we truly are.

The sun is beating down on us as we pull into the drive. Presents in tow, we walk up the path to the back gate. Smoke billows up from the barbeque grill, floating over the top of the house. Music pumps from beyond the wooden gate, promising a good time. I grin at the boys before pulling the handle and letting them scurry ahead of me into the backyard.

The event is decked out in maroon and white—the official colors of Royce's future alma mater, Morehouse College. He's set to major in mechanical engineering, and his parents have clearly already familiarized themselves with the college's paraphernalia. Balloons, pennants, a tower of red velvet cupcakes—excuse me, *maroon velvet*—adorn the lawn.

A sea of smiling faces greet us, arms open and inviting. About ten or so hugs later, I finally clock the reason we're gathering today—Royce, posing in the DIY photo booth with his parents. All of them are decked out in Morehouse swag, smiles bright. My heart swells, seeing the pride of Jack and Aries' faces. They sacrificed so much to make sure that this opportunity would be possible for their only child.

"Royce!" I call, drawing their attention. He strides over—taller, prouder, like he grew overnight. I pull my nephew into an embrace. "I'm so proud of you, man."

"Thanks, Uncle Charlie," he gleams.

"My nephew, a Maroon Tiger!"

Jack throws his arm around my shoulder. "Thanks for coming, bro."

"Wouldn't miss it for the world."

He nods toward the cupcakes. "Now you know damn well she would've made us scrape all that frosting off before we could eat it." I follow his gaze to our mother—who is, at this very moment, handing cupcakes with frosting piled high on them to Cam and CJ.

I shake my head, laughing. "I was literally just thinking the same thing."

It's the first I've seen of her since the funeral, and it's a nice sight. She looks happy, beaming at her grandchildren. It's as if the hour-long drive from our hometown where she still lives was worth every mile just to be here—with them, with her family. And the smile she gave me, the embrace that lingered just a little bit longer than usual, the deep sigh—each gesture let me know that she was happy to see me too.

The boys catch me watching, and Cameron scampers up to me, frosting residue clinging to the corner of his mouth.

"Can we take some pictures?" he begs, already reaching for the props. "Grandma!"

She joins us, giving me a quick hug before we all squeeze together into the photo booth, dressing up with oversized glasses, makeshift hats, and a big "Congratulations" sign. In the final picture, I scoop my mother up into a hug, kissing her on the cheek.

Later, I find Jack manning the grill, flipping burgers.

"Aye, just a reminder, the boys are going to Tennessee next weekend," I say, clapping him on the shoulder. Jack has followed through on his promise to take the boys every other weekend so I can spend time with Gloria.

"Oh yeah, to visit Rachel's parents, right?

"Yeah."

Jack leans in, lowering his voice. "You still on ice with her family?"

"Sure am. But Wesley called to iron out logistics."

"That's something," Jack muses. "They flying?"

I nod. "Can't believe I'm putting them on a plane by themselves. I don't like it."

"They'll be fine," my brother reassures. "Royce was about CJ's age when he went on his first plane alone. He loved the independence. Came back half-grown." Jack chuckles to himself, laying slices of American cheese across the glistening beef. "A whole week, huh. What you gon' do with yourself?"

"Well, assuming that work doesn't keep me chained to my desk, I'm sure I'll find something to do."

He smirks. "Oh, I know you will. Something or some*one*..."

As anxious as I am about sending the boys off to Tennessee, I am looking forward to more time with Gloria. We've never spent more than a day or two together, so this is completely new territory that I'm eager to explore. She'll be staying over the entire week, sleeping in my bed, watching movies on my TV, making dinner with me in my kitchen...

We've spent so much of our relationship in her realm—an honor to inhabit, for sure. But I'm even more excited to bring her into my orbit. Show her my way of life.

"What are you two over here talking about?" Aries asks, wrapping her arm around Jack's waist. He returns the gesture, hanging an arm off of his wife's shoulders.

"Charlie's new boo," he says.

"I figured that," she says slyly. "I could see him blushing from across the yard."

"He's only blushing because he's been *getting some ass* on a regular basis now."

"Jack!" I scold. "There's a lady present, man."

Sorry babe. He apologizes as he tightens his hold around her neck, pulling her into a kiss. My brother looks down at his wife, who's still tucked under his arm. "You weren't a lady last night, now were you?"

She blushes a shade darker, slapping his chest. "Jackson Bensley..." He whispers something in her ear that makes her laugh. Her eyes are bright and loving as she says, "You're a real savage, you know that?"

He nuzzles against her. "Yeah, but you like it..."

More than 15 years in and still so in love.

Aries turns my way again, as if remembering I'm still there. "I'm happy for you, Charlie. Can't wait to meet her. Bring her around next time, okay?"

"Thanks, sis. I will."

What would that look like?

Gloria, meeting my family—meeting my mom? Would she give Gloria a chance?

I have no doubt that my mom would love her—that they'd hit it off instantly. But I'm confident that Gloria represents something... *unresolved.* Something Mom buried long ago that my indiscretion unearthed. My father left her with the ache of inadequacy—a wound she forged into armor. Mona Bensley, the most resilient person I know, took that pain and turned it into strength. She put herself through school, became a nurse, worked hard as hell, and raised her kids—*alone.* Talk about making lemonade from the sourest lemons. I can't think of a better way to say "fuck you" than to raise two good men without their father.

She took such good care of us. I wonder if she cared for herself half as well.

I wonder if she ever sought therapy.

GLORIA

The door is unlocked when I arrive, and the aroma of dinner wafts down the front hall.

"It smells amazing in here," I call down the hall, slipping off my sneakers, leaving my overnight bag by the door, and following my nose. Music hums from the smart speaker in the living room, gliding seamlessly into the open-concept kitchen where Charlie stands at the counter, mixing ingredients in a bowl—cabbage, red onions, cilantro, apple cider vinegar. A slaw, maybe?

He looks up and smiles, that signature smile I've come to crave. "Hey."

"Hello, handsome." I set my offering of a bottle of wine on the counter.

"You hungry?" he asks, reaching for my hand. I take it, and he tugs me around the island into the comfort of his strong arms.

"Mmhmm," I murmur into his chest. "What do we have here?"

"Baja fish tacos."

I hum in delight. "Sounds incredible."

"Well, it's almost ready." He plants a kiss on top of my head.

While Charlie finishes prepping our plates, I set the table with silverware and cloth napkins. He has a table for four, and I find myself wondering where his boys usually sit in this arrangement. I pour each of us a tall glass of wine—Sauvignon Blanc, a serendipitous pairing. Once we're both seated with our steaming plates, Charlie leans across the table to light the candle in the middle, adding notes of lavender to the dining experience.

"How's work?" he asks.

"Now that the trial is over, I can finally catch my breath. This one was brutal. Two continuances—" I huff, rolling my eyes at the memory of my frustration. "—plus, jury trials come with their own brand of anxiety, you know?" He nods in understanding just before taking a sip from his glass. "They can go either way and I just couldn't get a read on the box. In the eleventh hour, all I could do was shoot my shot. I'd saved my most compelling argument for the very end, but I needed a Hail Mary. The defense came ready to play."

"And how long did it take the jury to deliberate?"

"Six grueling hours," I drag out with a sardonic smile.

"Bet you were on pins and needles."

"Let's just say, I stress-ate a giant chocolate chip cookie."

Charlie chuckles. "But you brought home a win, right?"

I nod, smiling around a bite of the most delicious fish taco. My eyelids flutter closed at the taste. "Mmm... Charlie, this is amazing."

His grin stretches across the table. "So what's up with the art show?"

"What art show?"

"Your art show."

"Nothing, I was just dreaming aloud. That's all."

"Okay, so maybe it's time to turn your dream into a reality."

I scoff a little, swirling my wine. "Yeah, we'll see. How about you? Things going well with the company?"

"Yes, still in the black. And for that, I'm grateful," he says, lighting up. "I mean, I lost a few accounts, but I've had some pretty substantial deals come my way too. I'm beyond grateful, that's for sure. I just want to keep growing, you know?" We flow from topic to topic, easy as breath.

Eventually, he gestures toward my empty plate. "Was the food okay?"

"I inhaled it."

"Seconds?"

Man after my own heart. "Yes, please!

After dinner, I trail him into the kitchen as he rinses our plates and places them in the dishwasher. He has a dish towel slung over his shoulder, and it's undeniably doing something for me. He dries his hands on it, saying, "You're really into yoga, right?" he asks, like he doesn't already know.

I narrow my eyes. "Yes..."

"So, I got YouTube University certified to instruct a yoga class."

The laugh bubbles out of me like it's starved for air. "Okay?"

"And I was thinking you could be my first student. Did you bring some work out gear?"

Soon, Charlie is chasing me up the stairs with my luggage in hand, ushering me toward the master bath. I change quickly, excited to see what foolishness this man is up to. This is a new set—a mustard yellow leggings and sports bra combo that brings out the golden tones in my skin. *I can't wait for him to see it.*

Downstairs, I'm met with a shirtless Charlie, wearing only a pair of athletic shorts. I can't say I've ever had an instructor that looked quite as yummy as he does. His chest is a whole *situation*, every line and groove a carved temptation. I can't help imagining running my tongue over the divots between his abs... Warmth pools between my legs at the thought.

Focus, Gloria.

While I was upstairs, Charlie did more than lose his shirt. He moved the coffee table aside, laid out two yoga mats, a couple of water bottles, and dimmed the lights.

"Are you familiar with tantric yoga?" he asks with a sly grin.

"I am."

One brow raises. "How familiar?"

"Not *that* familiar, but I know what it is."

"Then I guess you'll have to follow my lead."

First, Charlie coaches me on the ideology behind tantric yoga. "The aim is to establish a spiritual bond with your partner through a sensual experience. It's not inherently sexual, but that doesn't mean it can't be." He winks. "Ready?"

We begin with light stretches, his fingers brushing mine, his arms ghosting around my frame. His touch sends little flares up my spine. I try to focus on breath, posture, intention—but with him behind me, correcting my stance, murmuring instructions against my ear, I'm unraveling by the second.

"Clear your mind," he instructs. *Yeah... not happening.* "We'll start in Warrior 2."

He aligns his arms with mine, grazing my wrist with his fingertips. We breathe together, moving backward and forward in gentle rhythm.

We move to the floor, seated back-to-back, twisting in tandem.

"Focus on your breathing," he says, "and move with me."

When my hand touches his knee, and his grazes mine, it feels like choreography born of instinct. Eventually, he eases me to the ground, letting my head rest in his lap. He massages my temples, fingers scratching softly at my scalp until I feel like I could melt into the floor.

It's his turn now. I take my time, fingers dancing along his jaw, slipping behind his neck. His eyes close under my touch. I lean in to kiss him, and when our lips meet, he smiles into it.

The final pose has me in his lap—yab yum, as it's called. *An intimate, lover's embrace.* We stare into each other's eyes, giggling at the vulnerability, but soon, the silence stretches. I realize our hearts are in sync. *Ba-dum... Ba-dum... Ba-dum...*

I close my eyes, nestling my forehead against his. I don't need to see him to feel his energy. His hands are warm on my back, his breath soft on my face.

I can feel him all around me.
Sacred.

GLORIA

"Hey, sister," Luci answers after just two rings. "What's up?"

"Mind if I pop by real quick? I'm in the area and need to grab those shoes. I've got a wedding to attend soon." I turn the car toward her side of town before she even says yes.

"I'm just grading papers," she sighs. "Reading this shit is giving me a migraine. Come save me."

Ten minutes later, I'm knocking on Luci's door.

"Come on in," she groans. "It's unlocked."

The kitchen is warm and fragrant—the savory scent of something baking in the oven. Luci sits at the counter, laptop open and glasses sliding down her nose. She groans, rubbing the back of her neck like she's been at it for hours.

"Rough batch?" I ask.

"This paper is completely AI written," she scowls. "I remember when we had to sit in the library for hours, take notes, write essays—*in our own words!*"

I lean my elbows against the counter. "It's a new day, I suppose."

"Bullshit, is what it is. I should fail this lazy child." She yanks off her glasses and massages the headache brewing in her temples. Then, pointing to a shoebox on the far end of the counter, she asks, "Who's getting married?"

"Oh, a colleague."

"Boring."

The truth is that Charlie's colleague is getting married. Last night, while we were tangled up on the couch, he invited me to be his plus one. I said yes before I could overthink the overlap in our circles. *One thing at a time.*

Instead of lingering in wedding talk, I pivot. "You know, I've been thinking about putting together a little art showcase. Maybe in the fall."

Luci's eyes widen, instantly misty. "Oh, GG. Mom would be proud."

"You think so?"

"Yes! I'm so glad that you've picked up a paintbrush again. It's been a long time. What inspired this?"

I shrug my shoulders, looking toward the stairs as the sound of a scuffle echoes down.

"Those kids," Luci mutters. "Hey! Be careful up there!"

"Okay, Mom!" two voices call down.

Just then, the back door swings open.

"I'm home," Peter sings, tossing his briefcase on the ground. "Hey! My favorite sister in love is here."

"Your *only* sister in love," I correct.

"That's true, but if you guys had more siblings, you'd still be my favorite."

"Kiss-ass," Luci mumbles.

"You still keeping everybody civil, sis?" he asks, all the while rounding the counter to kiss his miserable wife on the cheek. She leans into his touch, like a simple kiss is enough to heal her migraine.

"One day at a time," I report.

"Sensational!" He sniffs the air. "Dinner smells good, babe."

"Meatloaf," she says with a smile.

"My favorite."

"Go get settled and tell your kids to wash up for dinner," she instructs. "It'll be ready in a few minutes." Pete salutes and departs, and Luci turns back to me. "You staying for dinner?"

"Not tonight, thanks though. In fact, I need to get going," I say, glancing at my watch. "I'm gonna run to the bathroom first. Be right back."

I wander down the hall, admiring the gallery of my sister's family photos on the walls. Charlie and I have been playing house these past few days—coming home to each other like real partners. Kisses in the kitchen. Inside jokes on the couch. A rhythm that feels easy. Natural.

Could this be us someday?

As we were entangled in the tent all those nights ago, Charlie said something as he was nodding off. Something that lives in my heart still.

"I could do this forever," he murmured. *"Love you forever. And I don't care what forever looks like as long as we're together."*

Forever. What would that look like for us?

I can't imagine his boys will take to me well. I remember how I was when my mother passed and we moved in with my dad. I was an absolute terror to Evelyn, never giving her a chance until well into adulthood. *Would they hate me?* My father used to demand that we treat Evelyn with more respect.

"She's not trying to be your mother," he would say. *"She just wants to be in your life."*

I wonder how much Charlie would intervene on my behalf. Would it be too difficult to—

"Gloria Michelle!"

My name rings down the hall like a gavel. "Uh, yes?"

No response. *Uh oh*. We don't middle-name each other lightly. I shake my hands dry in the sink and emerge from the bathroom, dreading what I'm about to walk into. Back in the kitchen, Luci stands at the kitchen counter, my phone in her hand. She's grinning from ear to ear like a cat who just caught a mouse.

"Who's Charlie?"

Oh God. What did she see?

I freeze, debating my next move. Do I raise my hands and surrender? Try to make a run for it, leave my phone behind, go on the lam? Or do I argue my way out of interrogation like any good lawyer would?

I resolve to stand my ground, hand extended, requesting the return of my phone with only a pointed look. I need to see the evidence before mounting a defense.

Luci giggles, passing my phone back to me with a look so smug it could be framed. On the lock screen:

Hey babe, chicken or fish?

I roll my eyes, landing on Luci with a glare. Thank God for lock screen privacy. Our actual thread? *Indecent.*

"Put your damn eyebrows down," I demand.

She does as instructed, but they creep back up with each prying question she asks. And she has a million and one locked and loaded, like she's been waiting for this day her whole life.

"The police officer from the picnic? The one that you were working with?"

"Yeah."

"He was fine! Is it serious?"

"It's complicated."

"Why, because of your professional relationship?"

"Sure."

"Well…" she trails off, likely gearing up for a big sister monologue when I cut her off. *No thanks.*

"Hey, Lu, I gotta get going." As I'm bolting for the door, she calls after me.

"Gloria?" she sings, her voice rising in a melodious question.

"*What?*"

Snickering to herself, she points to the shoebox I'd completely forgotten on the counter. With a scowl, I stomp back, snatch it off the counter, and tuck it tightly under my arm.

"Oh, sis, one more thing," she calls sweetly as I reach the door. *Dear God.* "What, Lu?"

"Chicken or fish?"

I shoot her a look that could kill and turn on my heel.

"Enjoy your dinner," she yells before the door swings shut behind me.

The cat's officially out of the bag. God help me.

CHARLIE

My work bag lands with a thud in the back seat of my car. *Finally, the day is done.*

Settling behind the wheel, my mind naturally drifts to my boys. Now would be the time I'd be picking up CJ from his computer sciences program—though that wrapped the week before he and Cameron left for Tennessee.

I miss them.

I sent an iPad with them to share, and they communicate with me daily. The pictures have been the best part. The Evans have a pool, and it seems the majority of their time there has been in it. I would send them reminders to wear sunscreen, but I trust that Vivian wouldn't let them outside without slathering it on herself.

With a heavy sigh, I start the engine.

I shoot off a text to my girl—*Heading home.*

Gloria's response is immediate—*On my way.*

After hours of staring at surveillance footage, all I want to do right now is peel off these clothes and unwind with her.

Not an hour later, she's in my arms, rocking with me gently in the hammock I've installed between two sturdy trees in the backyard. This is it. Heaven. The feeling of being tangled up in her with nowhere else to be.

"I could get away and chill like this for a few days," I muse, playing with a strand of her hair. "How about you?"

Her voice thrums against my chest. "Any place in particular?"

"I heard about this place. It's about an hour and a half away. Cozy cabin, real sexy vibe. Jack and Aries went a few years back. Said it sits on a lake, real picturesque and quiet. We should go."

"Let's do it." She drags her finger across my thin shirt, tracing delicious little lines between my abs. "Wanna come with me to dinner at Luci and Peter's? Maybe in a few weeks, sometime after the wedding? We can go on a weekend when the boys are with Jack and Aries."

"Definitely," I sigh contentedly. "I'd love to meet your family. I can't wait to introduce you to mine. Jack and Aries are always asking about you. Asking when they'll meet you."

"Really?"

"Yeah."

We don't speak for a few minutes, content to just marinate in the quiet of nature, listening to the distant bird calls and the chirp of cicadas.

"Charlie?"

"Yeah?"

"Your mom... Were she and Rachel close?"

"I wouldn't say close, but they were cool." The words leave me easily, but my mind drifts back to the awkward pause on the call when I mentioned Gloria's name. Leaning in, I whisper the next part into her hair. "I think she's really gonna love you though." And I mean it—*if she truly gives you a chance.*

She doesn't respond, just nestles closer to me. *Is she anxious to meet my family?* I wouldn't blame her. I've put her in a difficult position. Still, only Jack knows that she was once the *other woman*, if she could be called such a thing. I press a gentle kiss to the top of her head, imparting whatever comfort I can muster.

Later that night, I write about it. *Doc was onto something with this journaling thing.* I don't have a regular schedule with it. Sometimes, it's the way I start my day. Today, it's the way I'm ending it. With my readers on, I sit back against the headboard, pen in hand.

The door creaks open, and I lift my eyes to see Gloria in the doorway, looking like something out of a movie. She glides across the room like a vision. Her hair tied down with a satin scarf, her face freshly washed and dewy. She massages moisturizer onto her hands as she makes her way from the en suite to the other side of the bed—*her side.* And I can't look away from the way her navy blue cami nightdress swishes around her thighs.

My favorite color.

"Are you journaling?" She climbs under the sheets next to me, and I have to remind myself to breathe.

"Yep, I've been writing for a few weeks now. Doctor's orders."

"How do you like it?"

"I can't believe I'm saying this, but a lot. Expressing myself this way has been... liberating. It's for my eyes and no one else's, so it feels very safe. Doc even gave me some prompts to get me started, but he encouraged me to just write whatever I'm feeling and the context around it. Some days, I only write two lines. Other days, a four page letter."

"Do you write everyday?"

"No, but definitely a few times a week."

"What do you write about?"

"Whatever's in my heart or on my mind. Gratitude. Goals. Things I want to unlearn. Situations that I encounter and how I react to them. My goal is to be able to measure my growth, to look back through these pages and see how far I've come—the changes I've undergone."

"That's amazing," she says so earnestly. "I'm really happy that it's working for you. The prompts—can I hear some of them?"

I reach into the back of the journal and pull out a folded sheet of paper, reading aloud.

"*Write about one thing you want to forgive yourself for. What is something that you are still harboring from your parents? List the things you had to learn the hard way. What from your past still needs healing? Where do you feel most loved and safe? Name five memories that fill you with joy. During hard times, who do you rely on the most?*"

"Which one are you working on tonight?" she asks softly.

"Just some thoughts from today. But yesterday? '*Where do you feel most loved and safe.*'"

She chews her lip. "Can I ask you a question?"

"Of course."

"It's not a loaded question."

I swallow my laugh, nodding. "Okay. Ask."

"Do I make you feel loved? Safe?"

I lean in to kiss her. "You have no idea."

It starts sweet. Just a brush of lips. "I didn't mean to interrupt," she whispers against my mouth.

"I like it when you interrupt."

"Well, in that case..." With gentle fingers, she removes my glasses, bringing my lips back to hers in a less than chaste kiss.

Safe is the word I'm thinking when I have Gloria naked, cheek pressed to the mattress. She clings to the sheets with her ass hiked high in the air while I make love to her from behind. I hold her steady and take her slow, drinking in each moan she releases.

The arch of her back, the sweat along her spine, the way she gasps when I grind deeper, the pleasure on her face...

I'm committing it to memory as I bury myself in her, pushing into her sex and filling her, again and again and again. Her essence wraps around me with each thrust, clenching tight, stretching around my length. I have an unobstructed view of her—*all of her*, glistening on my manhood.

"Charlie," she whimpers. "Baby... punish me."

I groan. *How could I deny such a desperate plea?*

"You think you can handle it?" I know she can, but I want her to be sure.

She says nothing, instead putting her arms behind her back, offering herself completely.

Submission—loud and clear.

I pin her wrists with one hand, the other gripping the back of her neck. I lean in, whispering in her ear, "We need a safe word, baby."

"Paris," she breathes.

Paris it is.

With a hard jerk of my hips, I give her body every bit of what it's begging for. She gasps, meeting my hips thrust for thrust. We fall into a relentless rhythm—our lovemaking is feral and unrestrained, brutal even.

"Tell me it's mine," I growl.

"It's yours!"

"Tell me you'll always be mine."

"Always, babe," she whines.

"Louder!"

"*Always!*"

I lose myself, half-crazed as I pound into her pleasure faster and faster. It feels unreal, this intensity, and I don't ever want it to end. I break with her, completely undone. My release is coming fast, but I manage to hold on until Gloria cries out, shattering beneath me. Her climax sets mine off like a fuse—my license to drive into her until I have nothing left to give.

Handled—like a champ.

We collapse, spent, sprawled across the bed. Her night gown and hair scarf are scattered on opposite sides of the room, and my briefs are nowhere to be seen. Suffice it to say, my new California king is suitably broken in.

We curl into one another, foreheads touching, heartbeats slowing in sync.

"I've never felt this way before," she murmurs.

I can relate, but I want to hear her say it. "How do you feel?"

"Loved. Safe." Her eyes sparkle with emotion, voice wavering. "I've given you my heart, Charlie. Please don't break it."

If only she knew how sacred these moments are to me, how coveted her heart is—one of my most prized possessions. I wish I had the words to convey the depth of my devotion, how fiercely I'd protect her and her heart.

I swipe my thumb across her cheek, choosing my next words carefully. "Your heart is *safe* with me."

Ten

RECLINING NUDE

GLORIA

The late afternoon air feels stifling as I exit the office and make for my car. Nothing like this morning, when Charlie and I woke up around dawn to go for a run. We've had some pretty late nights and early mornings, barely dragging ourselves out of bed—from exhaustion or simply the desire to stay cuddled up together for just a little bit longer.

A little bit of both, I suppose.

But this morning, we managed to get up, get dressed, and get moving. Our run was accompanied by a stunning backdrop—a soft watercolor of peach and coral hues as the sun slowly rose over the horizon. What started as a simple attempt at exercising together ended in playful chasing and tackling in the dewy grass. Back at home, we made love in the shower.

"Fuck, Gloria," he gasped in my ear as he came, pressing me against the cool tile.

Now, in the car, I fan myself, feeling a little worked up at the memory. Our stamina is undefeated, but our week of bliss is coming to a close. *Just one more day.* I reminisce on the time we've shared on the drive home from work.

Home. That's what it feels like, being in Charlie's realm.

We had so much fun this morning that we were both tempted to take the day off completely and make the most of our final days together. But we both have a heavy workload that would only get heavier if we slacked on our duties.

Leave it to me to fall for a man who cares as much about his work as I do mine.

It occurs to me that I screened a call from Luci earlier—mid-deposition. I use the car's Bluetooth to give her a call.

"Hey, Lu. Sorry for missing you earlier. It's been a pretty busy day. What's up?"

Luci only has some work gossip to share, and I'm happy to distract myself by listening to the latest on who's sleeping with who in the English department. At Charlie's house, I press the remote clipped to my visor to activate the garage door. Inside, I can hear music bumping from within the house.

"Where are you? Where's that music coming from?" Luci asks.

"I just got home," I say simply. *There I go again with that word.* Inside, the lights are dimmed, and the sultry music draws me like a siren call. I follow the beat to find Charlie, lounging across the leather sofa with nothing on, only a hand towel across his lap. His arm is propped up, showcasing his biteable bicep. He's the picture of relaxed, ankles crossed, a drink sweating on the table beside him. And that smirk on his lips? *Devilish.*

Looks like he got a head start—no fair. I drop my tote on the counter, licking my lips.

"Hey Lu, I'll call you tomorrow," I say, disconnecting the call before my sister can get a word in edgewise. Stepping out of my heels, I free my hair from its tie and let it cascade over my shoulders. I run my fingers through it slowly, enjoying how Charlie's fingers twitch on the couch. *Patience, love.*

Slowly, I drag my fingers down the zipper of my pencil skirt, easing it down my hips. My draped-neck bodysuit follows, stepping out of my clothes entirely. All that's left are my lacy black bra and panties, and I want to draw that reveal out a little while longer.

Sauntering around him on the sofa, I drag my fingers along his arm, biting my lip when goosebumps erupt at my touch. Once I'm behind him, I reach around to run my hands up and down his chest, pausing only to circle the pebbled skin of his nipples.

He groans, cocking his head back for a kiss. I indulge him—briefly—savoring the whiskey on his lips.

Delicious.

Parading to the beat of the music, I circle around to the front of the couch to give him the full show, running my hands over my body as if they were his—*his sensual touch.* Just the thought turns me on. My hips sway seductively to the music as I trace my curves, grazing between my breasts, up into my hair. One bra strap slips down my shoulder as I bite the tip of my finger.

He blushes, the towel on his lap rising with his growing erection. Turning around, I sink slowly into a squat, swirling my hips in a circle, charming the snake with my dance. I let my head fall back, tossing it from side to side, my hair dancing down my back like a wild, rebellious current of midnight waves. I unclasp my bra with one hand and let it fall to the floor.

When I face him again, Charlie's lips are parted with desire, his eyes devouring every inch of my body.

Who knew that dancing for a man could turn me on? I just wanna be the kind of girl he likes, and if I know anything about the look on this man's face, it's that he likes what he sees. *God, I'm so into him.* I feel utterly high on him and his sexy bedroom eyes.

I pinch my nipple with one hand, letting the other wander between my legs to give me the pressure I so desperately need. He licks his lower lip, as if he could taste me from where he sits. I moan for him, slow and sultry, rutting against my own hand, wanting to show him how good he makes me feel. He sips his drink, enjoying the show.

I love the way that he looks at me, like I'm all that he needs.

The song changes, the beat easing into a slower, more deliberate tempo. *A little sexier.*

I cross the space between us, only in my panties. Running my fingers gently over his lids to close them, relishing his gasp as I sit in his lap and grind. His hands come to grasp at my hips, desperate and firm. *Just how I like him.* Leaning back against him, I let his hands explore—one slipping into my soaked panties, while the other grips my tit like it's his personal obsession, pinching my nipple, tugging just right.

"Babe," he whispers, fingers curling inside me.

"Yes, baby?"

"Fuck me."

A grin overtakes my face. I'm drunk on power, on pleasure. I turn around to straddle him, tossing aside the towel and slipping my panties to the side. His head falls back with a guttural moan, undone as I sink onto him in one, slow glide, gripping the cotton of my panties like a pair of reins.

Giddy up.

I ride him with filthy intent, slick and ravenous. I ride him like he belongs to me. *Because he does.* He grips my ass, keeping me right where he wants me—impaled, writhing. His hips piston up into me with brutal precision, and I meet him stroke for stroke, chasing the burn.

He buries his face in my neck, groaning curses that melt into my skin. "Goddamn it, Gloria... the fuck are you trying to do to me?"

Our bodies slap together with obscene rhythm—soaked skin, and carnal need.

I'm so far gone.

Then—the slap lands hard.

"Mmm..." I gasp, breath hitching as heat blooms beneath his palm—it stings. *It sings.*

I take it. Beg for it. My core flutters around him, need-drunk and greedy. "Again," I breathe.

And he delivers.

Another strike. Fiercer. Then another, just as sharp. The sound—lewd and primal—rings out, reverberating through the room each time his palm meets my ass.

"You like it rough, don't you?" he growls. "You like when I take what's mine."

"You know I do," I moan for him, filthy and unashamed. "And you love drowning in how wet I get for you."

His eyes darken, grip tightening like my words unspooled him, before his mouth claims mine.

His kiss is slow but searing, full of heat and hunger—until I break it off with a gasp, taking him deeper.

I ride him shamelessly. Lips dripping with words no good girl should ever say—nasty little truths I grind into him, one roll of my hips at a time. Filthy confessions poured straight into his mouth, until he's choking on the taste of how good I feel.

My thighs tremble, and yet—I ride him with no mercy, teasing the edge, my core tightening like a fist. Then it hits—my orgasm—like a thunderclap. Loud. Sudden. Impossible to ignore. My walls clamp down on him, orgasm detonating like a supernova. I scream his name—not whispering, not moaning—*screaming*. I want the neighbors to know who's breaking me open.

Charlie!

"Shit," he pants, clawing at my ass. His grip bruises. His hips punish. I can feel his breaking point—how close he is. I smile down at him, feeling the way he pulses inside me. Needy. Wild... *Ready*.

I lean in, lips at his ear. "You don't come until I say so."

His brows knit. Jaw clenched. A hiss escapes through his gritted teeth—equal parts arousal and restraint. His eyes lock on mine. Desperate. Helpless. Turned on. Owned.

And that's when I take everything.

I take him slow—tormenting him with every grind. Making him ache for it. Making him earn it.

Showing him who's really in control.

"Say my name," I command, breath ragged, eyes locked on his.

He bares his teeth, eyes blazing as he chokes on a moan.

"Glo—" *a thrust* "—ri—" *another* "—a."

His voice is gravel. His length like steel. His control—unraveling.

"You're close," I whisper, taking him in completely as I bare down on him. "Aren't you?"

"So fucking close," he chokes. "Babe..." he pleads. "I'm gonna—..." His restraint is a live wire, fraying.

I clench down around him, savoring his gasp. "You're gonna what?" I purr, cruel and sweet.

"Fuck, Gloria—I can't—" His voice breaks. "I'm gonna—"

I cut him off, whispering, "Come for me, baby."

My voice is the match that lights the fuse.

His eyes shift—from pleading to dark, dangerous, defiant as he bites his bottom lip, teeth bared. Like I just whispered the keyword that unlocks the beast I've kept caged. *Savage.*

"Come for me."

He shudders, seizing inside me, gasping curses that collapse against my throat. *Fuck.* Teeth scraping my collarbone as he slams up into me once, twice—then breaks in his release with a strangled cry, gripping my hips, pulling me flush against him, burying himself with one final thrust.

"Gloria," he grits between his teeth, sweat clinging to his skin. "Fuck—baby—I'm coming."

And he does—with a roar that rips through the room. His whole body trembles beneath me as I ride him through it, wild and unrepentant. His release is so raw, so overwhelming, I fall with him.

I cry out, arms wrapping around his neck, anchoring myself as our center of gravity tips and the world tilts with it.

Damn—that was good.

CHARLIE

I wake to the feeling of velvety lips against my own.

"Good morning," a siren whispers.

Blinking my sleepy eyes open, I take in the sight of her—*the love of my life.*

"Morning, babe," I murmur with a lazy smile.

"How'd you sleep?" she asks beneath gentle kisses on my chest.

"Like a man in love."

"With me?" She looks up at me, batting her eyelashes.

"With you."

She beams triumphantly before returning to her conquest—kisses trailing down like a benediction.

"How about you?" I ask, scrambling for control.

She answers with a playful tongue over my nipple. Senses heightened by such a pleasant awakening, my ever-ready arousal twitches on its way up. Her lips drag down my body until she disappears completely beneath the sheets. My lips curl up into a smile as my eyes fall shut. I shake my head at the thought—*What did I do to deserve this woman?*

Her mouth is hot and wet around the length of me. I moan as pleasure pulses through my veins, trickling up from my toes to my fingers. Her hand glides slowly up my torso, peeking out from under the sheet. It lands over my thundering heart before I cover it with my own.

She's taking me there—dragging me closer with every stroke of her tongue, every erotic bob of her head beneath the sheets. Between the sensation of her perfect lips wrapped around me and her silky tongue massaging me, I'm losing my shit.

"Ah, baby," I groan.

She releases me, slowly slithering up my body to bring her lips back up to mine. I capture them in a hungry kiss, reaching for her as she rocks herself onto me. She takes me so well, this beautiful creature. The sheet falls away, and I watch, spellbound, as every damn inch of me disappears in between her legs. With her hands on my chest for leverage, her breasts crowd deliciously together. I cup them, thumbing her nipples as she rides me like a wave, her hips moving with the grace of a reef on the sea.

"Babe," she moans sweetly as she collapses on my chest, drawing dangerously close to her peak. With one hand at the nape of her neck, I pull her into a kiss while the other hand presses into the small of her back, deepening our connection. *I can't get enough.*

Just as I feel her tighten around me, siphoning my climax, I roll us over. Pressing her legs tightly to my chest, I nuzzle my nose against her inner ankle as I drive deeper and deeper into her ocean. She moans, and I feel her body ready itself to wash over me. The look of pure adoration on her face is enough to do me in with her.

Finally, our waves smash into one another, pulling us under until we are drowning in its ecstasy.

It feels silly to have more than one pillow on this bed, since we only ever share mine. Face to face, I admire the sunlight illuminating her face. She is something to behold. I look into her beautiful brown eyes and it hits me that this is our last day together. We should make the most of it, spend it doing something memorable. I smile sadly, grateful for a tiny glimpse into what awaits us.

"Is this what forever with you looks like?" I murmur, tracing the length of her spine. "Making love to you every morning?"

"I sure hope so," she says, her smile both sweet and seductive, her voice low and full of promise.

"You hungry?"

"Mmhmm, but I could stay like this a little longer."

Eventually, we make breakfast together, Gloria at the stove preparing blueberry pancakes and turkey sausage while I cut up a melon to share.

We managed to put some clothes on—just a pair of pajama pants for me and one of my police shirts for her. She's drowning in it but it hikes up just enough to give me a peek of her ass every time she reaches for a slice of honeydew.

We eat in comfortable silence, me seated at the island and her standing between my legs. The pancakes are delicious even without maple syrup, but Gloria drowns hers in it nevertheless. We're almost done when she swipes a stripe of syrup from her plate with her finger. I catch her wrist before she can taste it, leaning in and sucking her finger clean. She gasps, laughing—but it fades when I pull her into a kiss, stealing her breath and every giggle with it.

Standing, I lift her onto the counter, dragging sticky kisses to her neck. Her legs tie securely around my waist, and I sweep her from the counter, liplocked—one destination in mind.

Maybe we won't make it out of the bedroom today after all.

That's fine by me.

CHARLIE

The airport is a maze of travelers today—folks coming home from weekend trips or squeezing in last minute vacations in these final vestiges of summer. I keep my eyes peeled, sign in hand reading BENSLEY MEN.

As much as I've cherished every minute spent alone with Gloria, life isn't complete without my boys in it.

When the monitor overhead flashes their flight's arrival, a weight lifts from my chest. *Thank God.* Only He knows how shattered my life would be if I were to lose them too.

Soon enough, the crowd spills out of the gate, each face a fleeting blur. My heart leaps when I finally spot them.

They're home!

The boys' faces light up when they see me. "Dad!"

They practically sprint, their rolling bags flying behind them, almost knocking me over.

"Hey," I laugh, barely managing to stay on my feet. *Man, I missed them.* Their laughter charges my battery. "Welcome home." They cling to me, refusing to let go.

Seems like they missed me too.

As we approach the car, the boys practically buzz with excitement when they see the Jeep with its doors off. They love riding like this, and it's a perfect day for it. *Not a cloud in sight.*

Cameron bounces on his heels, looking up at me with wide eyes. "Can we go ridin'?"

Ridin'. That's what we call a drive down the expressway—no real destination in mind. Just an opportunity to enjoy the weather and the beauty of one of Argale's most scenic spots—the lakefront.

Lake Emerald features a vibrant, seemingly endless sandy stretch that hugs the shore. A winding path runs for miles along it, drawing joggers, cyclists, and walkers year-round. The views are breathtaking, with the lake's shimmering blue water and the gleaming skyline of Argale in the distance. Its yearly boating event—the Emerald Parade—draws in crowds from all of Alabama.

"You sure you guys aren't too tired from all that traveling?" I tease.

"No!" they shout in unison, racing to claim their spots in the backseat, leaving their luggage behind for me to toss in the trunk. *Typical.*

The ride there is a blast—music blaring from the speakers, wind blowing, the boys laughing. They hold their hands out of the Jeep, letting the wind whip through their fingers as they hoot and howl along with the song. Cameron points at girls in bikini tops, riding electric scooters along the lakefront. *This boy.* CJ shakes his head with me.

These are the moments that I love the most. We park at an ice cream shop to get a treat and chat about their trip. I order my usual—one scoop chocolate chip cookie dough, one scoop strawberry. The boys each double up on their favorites—Superman for CJ and Oreo for Cameron.

"Tell me all about your trip," I say before my first bite. "What'd you guys do? Don't leave anything out."

They recount the week in a blur—a music festival, barbecuing, the beach, fishing with Papa, board games, and breakfast at the country club.

"We swam in the pool *every* day!" Cameron adds enthusiastically.

"And even though it's not Christmas," CJ chimes in, "we still baked and decorated cookies with Grandma."

As expected, Vivian and Wesley planned out a full week for them. I'm glad the boys got to spend some quality time with them. It's unfortunate that it took losing Rachel to bring them closer. They've never asked to have the boys visit like this before. CJ and Cam deserve the bond. God, I hope that Vivian was loving. I hope that she was kind.

"My own mother has never told me that she's proud of me," Rachel once said.

"What did you do while we were gone?" Cam asks, breaking me from my thoughts.

I spent most of it in the arms of a beautiful woman. "Work, mostly. I missed you guys like crazy though. I had no one to boss around, clean up after, or cook for."

We all laugh, and Cameron drops his spoon.

"Oops," he says, frowning.

"It's okay, Cam. Go grab a new one and get us some napkins while you're up there," I call after him as he scampers off toward the counter.

I turn to CJ, wrapping my arm around his shoulder. "I really missed you, CJ."

"I missed you too, Dad."

"How's Grandma and Grandpa?"

"They're alright," he answers, his eyes avoiding mine. Then, he hesitates. "Dad, can I ask you something?"

"Anything."

"Did you cheat on mom?" he asks, and my heart damn near stops in my chest. "Is that why she was mad at you? Is that what you were fighting about?" His questions burst out of him like a rapid stream, each one flowing into the next without a breath.

"CJ, where did you hear that?"

"I heard Grandma Vivian talking to Papa last night," he says, a haunted look in his eye. "She said that it's your fault that mom died."

Goddamn those people. I run a hand over my mouth, closing my eyes and sucking in a deep breath. When I open them, Cameron is on his way back, *oblivious.*

"Let's talk about this later, okay? Just you and me."

CJ nods. Clearly his little brother doesn't know, considering he waited until we were alone to ask. I appreciate his maturity and thoughtfulness. On the ride home, I steal a glance back at him through the rearview mirror. CJ looks sullen, staring out at the lakefront.

Was my lack of an answer too telling?

Later that evening, after tucking Cameron into bed, I make my way to CJ's bedroom. The subject looms over me like a storm cloud. *You knew this day would come, Charlie.*

CJ is at his computer desk playing a video game on his computer. Suddenly, the anger is back again. Why would Vivian be so careless? *Plaguing his little mind.* He was too young to know about this, to understand the complicated lives of adults. But now I have to try to explain it to him in terms he'll understand.

I owe him that much.

"Hey," I say, knocking gently on his open door.

"Hey," he says back, eyes never leaving the monitor.

"Time for bed."

My oldest powers off the computer then gets into bed. I pull his gaming chair up to the bed, taking a seat. I can't seem to swallow the lump in my throat before I begin.

"CJ, I loved your mom," I begin, my mind heavy, voice thick with regret. "She and I had some difficulties, and I'm not proud of some of the choices that I've made. I was wrong, and I take ownership of that. I hurt Mom, and in doing so, I hurt you and your brother, and I hate myself for it." I pause, swallowing hard. *How could I put this on him?* "There's a lot you don't understand about adult relationships, and you don't need to know any of this for a long time. And I know that you may have questions, and I want to be able to answer them for you, but without Mom here, I... I just don't want to paint her in a bad light because she's not here to defend herself." I search his eyes for understanding. "You've lost something that I can never replace, CJ. The bond you shared with her was unique, and I'm so sorry for my part in her leaving us. Someday, I hope you'll find it in your heart to forgive me." My gaze falls to the floor, laden with guilt. "I realize that may take some time"

CJ turns his head slightly, likely wrestling with my plea. It's late, and I've just unloaded a heavy truth on him. He needs time and space to process it. I understand that. I struggle to this day with forgiving my own father for hurting my mother.

Maybe we aren't as well-adjusted as I may have hoped.

I clasp my hands in prayer, hoping that I haven't scarred him permanently. Hopefully, he doesn't grow up resenting me the same way that I resented my father. I beg God that we don't have a lifetime of pain ahead of us.

"Do you have any questions?"

CJ shakes his head.

"Okay." The silence stretches between us, thick and palpable, until I finally break it. "Good night, son."

I don't try to kiss him good night, fearful he might pull away. For what it's worth, I make it back to my bedroom before the tears begin to fall.

Not so well-adjusted after all.

September

Eleven

HOPE

CHARLIE

Doc has a biweekly slot on my calendar. Fortunately, I can see him during my lunch hour, which keeps me from having to make arrangements with Sienna. So far, no new cases have impeded our schedule.

Walking into my therapist's office feels like stepping into a sanctuary—one of the few places I can shed the weight of the outside world and sit with the parts of myself I usually avoid. But the moment I sink into my usual spot on the sofa, that weight tends to shift. Emotions rise to the surface, uninvited, daring me to confront what I came here hoping to avoid.

Suffice it to say, I leave each session adequately drained.

"Welcome back," Doc says, crossing one leg over the other.

"Thanks," I say simply. My mind races with everything I need to unpack, but one topic surges to the forefront of my mind—*CJ*.

"How was your week?" Doc asks.

"Challenging."

"What was challenging about it?"

I run a hand over the back of my neck, preemptively feeling for sweat. "My sons went to visit their grandparents—Rachel's parents—in Tennessee for a week. The night before they came home, my oldest overheard his grandparents discussing my infidelity. And he asked me about it."

Doc's brows rise. "That must have been a shock. How did you address it with your son?"

"I took accountability for my actions, acknowledged the hurt I caused... and I asked for his forgiveness."

"And how did he receive it?"

There's that lump again. "I saw the disappointment in his eyes. He didn't yell, didn't cry. Just looked at me like he couldn't unsee what he'd heard."

Doc lets that settle. "How did that make you feel?"

"Like maybe I'm not much better than my father after all."

"Okay, let's shift gears for a moment. Tell me about your relationship with your father."

"I don't have one."

He nods once, then flips back through his notepad. "You mentioned in our first session that your father walked out on you and your mother. How do you think his absence shaped who you became—as a husband and as a father?"

I take my time, mulling over the question. Doc never rushes me, and I've come to appreciate the space he gives me to find my words. "I think that his absence taught me the significance of being present, both emotionally and physically. I tried to be that for Rachel. For the boys. I wanted my family to feel secure—valued. Like I was someone they could count on."

"Do you think that commitment—to staying, to being 'there'—was what kept you in the marriage?"

"To a certain extent, yes. There was a time that Rachel and I were in love, or at least I'd like to think there was. I'd like to think we weren't doomed from the start." I exhale shakily, resting my forehead against my fist. "Sorry, Doc. This is hard to talk about."

"It is," he agrees. "How do you usually cope with stress?"

Doc's good at reading the room—knowing when to press and when to pivot. I'm grateful for that.

"I work out, and I've come to enjoy reading. My girlfriend's got me reading mystery novels," I laugh.

"That's great! Both are solid stress relievers." He rises and walks over to his bookshelf, scanning the spines until he finds what he's looking for. He hands me a slim hardcover. "Read this at your leisure."

I glance down. *As a Man Thinketh.*

"It's not a mystery," he chuckles, returning to his seat, "but I think you'll find it meaningful. Maybe even journal your thoughts as you go. It's over a century old, but it still holds up."

"Thank you."

I leave the session with more than a new book to read. In the car, I pull out the business card Doc tucked between the pages—*Dr. Bree Perry, Family Therapist.* His assignment: schedule a session with her for me and the boys. He says she's one of the best, but I'm still apprehensive.

Aren't the boys too young for therapy?

But then I remember Gloria. How young she was when her mother died. How her father brought in a grief counselor for her and her sister.

I'm still mulling it over when I return to the department. Graham and I are heading out to follow up on a couple of leads and swing by forensics to check in with Cole. Just as I grab my gear, Sarge's voice stops me.

"Bensley!" he calls, waving me into his office.

"I'll pull the car up," Graham says.

"Be right there." I bump arms with him before stepping into the office.

"Hey, Sarge, what's up?"

He juts his chin toward the open door. "Close it. We gotta talk."

CHARLIE

Sunlight streams in through the bedroom window, floating on the residual hairspray in the air like little motes of light. Gloria stands in the full length mirror in my bedroom, applying a final swipe of maroon lipstick.

I still need to put on my tie, but I've slowed down my own getting ready process to appreciate hers, pretending to adjust my cufflinks for the last five minutes. *She's worth admiring.*

Her wine colored dress hugs every curve, even unzipped. She reaches behind, trying to fasten it herself, feeling for the toggle.

"Can I help?" I offer.

"Sure," she says, smiling at me through the mirror.

I close the distance between us, dropping a kiss to her bare shoulder as I slowly drag the zipper up her back. "Do you think it'll start on time or...?"

She giggles, turning to face me. "You have quite the appetite, sir."

She's referring to the sex we already had today. *She's not wrong.* I bring my lips down to hers with a smiling kiss as I attempt to unzip her dress once again.

"Stop," she chuckles. "We better get going."

I sigh, nodding in resignation as I adjust myself in my pants.

"Let's do this."

The drive to the Urban Garden Center is short, but I find myself wishing for more time alone with Gloria. Today's not just a friend's wedding—it's the first time we'll be seen as a couple. *Publicly.* And I'm more than ready.

When I open the passenger door for her, I catch my reflection in the side view mirror.

"How do I look?" I ask, dubious of this oversized bow tie.

She reads my mind, straightening it for me. My hands slide to her waist, giving her a gentle squeeze.

"There. Perfect," she says with those beautifully painted lips.

"How do you feel?"

Her smile dips a bit, but her eyes stay soft. "Nervous. Ready. But nervous."

"Whatever happens, we're in it together. Okay?"

There's that smile again. "Okay."

We enter the courtyard, hand in hand. It's a beautiful, outdoor ceremony set in a lush garden. The grounds are bathed in the soft glow of late afternoon sunlight. Rows of elegantly arranged garden chairs face a magnificent floral archway, absolutely bursting with pink blooms. The gentle breeze carries the scent of florals, mingling with the soft strains of a string quartet. I smile, recognizing a rendition of a love ballad. The aisle is blanketed with thousands of delicate rose petals in various shades of pink.

Stunning.

"Is that fuchsia?" I whisper in my lover's ear, pointing to one of the shades.

She nods, eyes bright. "Very close."

Once the seats have filled, the bride's procession begins, and guests turn to face the back of the venue, their eyes fixed in anticipation of the bride's entrance. Kenya wears a traditional wedding dress with a wide skirt, looking like she's stepped out of a book of fairytales. In her hands is a bouquet of brightly colored peonies.

Gloria sighs dreamily. "Beautiful."

She squeezes my hand, and I squeeze it back. *So are you.*

As Kenya passes us, I turn to look at Graham. He stands at the altar, eyes brimming with tears, completely overtaken by the beauty of his bride gliding toward him.

What would it be like to watch Gloria walk down the aisle?

I imagine it—me, standing at the altar, waiting for her. Her dress flowing, her smile sure, the soft whispers of the wind and the gentle murmur of our guests would blend into a beautiful prelude to our ceremony. *Our forever.*

It occurs to me now that each passing second of our lives only brings us closer to the moment when I'll see her walking down that aisle, radiant and breathtaking, ready to begin our lives together. Or so I hope. There's a chance we may never see this day for ourselves, but I'm no less excited or grateful for the relationship that we share now. Our love is more valuable to me than one special day or a legal document solidifying our commitment to one another.

I just hope she feels the same.

The music dies down, and the officiant smiles over the crowd. "We are gathered here today to witness the sacred union of Kenya Bell and Eric Graham," he says. "Today we celebrate the love, commitment, and friendship of two people who love each other and wish to spend the rest of their lives together."

The couple stands beneath the arch, exchanging their vows with heartfelt emotion as we all watch on with endeared smiles. When the ceremony concludes, the newlyweds seal their vows with a tender kiss, and we witnesses send them off with hoots, hollers, and hearty applause.

The reception unfolds in the grand ballroom. High lattices wrapped in flowering vines stretch overhead, casting shadows on the ornate rugs lining the stone pathways. The tables are set with pristine white linens and shimmering silverware. An individual candelabra centerpiece sits center of each table, the flickering flames enhancing the already romantic ambiance.

Gloria smiles at me from a distance, beckoning me to catch up to her.

Would she want a reception like this? Something as glamorous as she is?

During cocktail hour, guests mingle over hors d'oeuvres and wine. Soon, we're ushered to our table, and I take Gloria's hand in mine. *It's time.*

Our table is filled with fellow city personnel—Anderson and her husband, Sarge and his wife. I can feel Gloria hesitate as Ms. Judy sidles up to her seat, but rather than back down, she just squeezes my hand a little tighter.

"My, my, my," Ms. Judy beams. "Don't you two clean up well!"

We smile with matching blushes. Then—she notices our hands. Entwined.

Here we go.

I clear my throat, ready to offer some clarification. "Ms. Gatlin here is my plus one tonight. Well, not just tonight..." I gaze at Gloria adoringly. She smiles sweetly before looking to Ms. Judy, anxious—hopeful.

The sweet older woman holds her heart, sighing happily. "I am thrilled for the two of you. Absolutely thrilled."

Gloria's tension softens. "Thank you, Ms. Judy," she says.

Abandoning her spot, Ms. Judy scurries around the table to tear Gloria from my side and wrap her in a supportive embrace. Over their shoulders, Jonas approaches, looking dapper as ever in his signature three-piece suit.

"Bensley," he says, grasping my hand. "Hell of a wedding, right?"

"Spectacular."

Jonas turns to Gloria, now free from Ms. Judy's gentle hold. "It's great to see you outside the office, Gatlin."

"It's good to be out of the office," Gloria laughs.

Ever the gentleman, Jonas pulls out Ms. Judy's chair before taking his seat. Together, we all sit, engaging in lively conversation about the ceremony. I catch Gloria's eye, taking her hand in mine under the table. *That wasn't so bad, now was it?*

Where anxiety guarded her expression, she now sparkles with unabashed happiness.

Just then, the wedding emcee comes over the speakers, readying us for the entrance of the couple. We stand, applauding their debut as man and wife. The music begins, and the newlyweds share their first dance under the soft spotlight. Graham looks happier than I've ever seen him, and my heart bursts with pride for my friend.

When the dance floor opens to the rest of the guests, Gloria and I make a quick escape to the terrace. The night air is cool and refreshing, carrying with it a hint of night-blooming flowers. I twirl my tumblr, watching the ice swirl around the amber liquid.

"What are you thinking about?" Gloria asks.

I shake my head, finding the words. "It's hard not to want this with you." I glance out over the terrace, exhaling slowly. "Has there ever been anyone that made you even consider marriage? Someone you may have once thought you could spend the rest of your life with?"

She ponders before answering. "Yes."

"Okay, what happened? I gotta know. I mean, I'm lowkey grateful that it didn't work out. But, I definitely want to make sure that I don't make the same mistakes as he did."

She smiles secretively. I raise my eyebrows, awaiting her response.

"Who said that it ended?" she whispers coyly.

I gasp aloud, pointing to myself.

She throws her head back with laughter. "Cool your jets. This is all beautiful—the ceremony, the reception, you in that tux. *It's everything.* And I'd be lying if I said that I wasn't moved by this too." She reaches for my bow tie again, straightening it, her smile bittersweet. "But like I said, it's risky. And I love you so much..." She closes her eyes for just a moment, losing herself in the words. "I'm just not willing to take that risk with you. To risk losing you—us—what we have. It's hard enough..." Her voice catches in her throat, eyes watering.

"Babe, I understand. I don't like it," I admit, scrunching up my face like a pouty child. She giggles, wiping a stray tear away. "But I understand. The important thing is always going to be that we're together." Setting my drink on the balcony's edge, I take both of her hands in mine, holding them like a prayer. I kiss her knuckles. "Have I told you how beautiful you look tonight?"

She smiles sweetly. "Thank you, Charlie."

"Sarge!"

The voice comes from behind, belonging to none other than the man of the hour.

"Well, hey," I say, reaching out to hug him.

Graham bypasses me altogether, taking Gloria's hand. "Ms. Gatlin, right?"

"Right," she chuckles, taking his energy in stride. "Please, call me Gloria."

"He used to being called 'Sarge' yet, Gloria?"

"Not yet."

It's true. I'm not used to being a sergeant. It's still so fresh. The pinning ceremony was only last week. Gloria surprised me by attending, standing quietly in the back. I didn't even see her until I posed for a photo with the chief after receiving the new badge.

I still remember the little wave she gave me, the pride in her smile, the way I ached to pull her close. I suppose it's a good thing she slipped out before I could. Her coming out to support me—well, I can't begin to put into words how much it meant to me.

The world.

Maybe someday, she'll be front and center, pinning a new badge on my uniform—as wives traditionally do.

"Hey, cut that out," I laugh, pulling Graham back by the shoulder. We clasp hands, and I pull him into an embrace.

"Thank you so much for coming. Both of you," he says. "You too look great together, by the way. I see you, trying to upstage me and my wife with this debut of yours."

We all laugh. It's such a pleasure to hear him refer to Kenya as his wife.

"Congratulations, by the way," Gloria says, placing a hand on Graham's forearm.

"Yeah, my guy, congrats. I'm so happy for you."

Graham beams at us, looking ten years younger. "Thanks, guys. I'm so lucky."

"Well, I'm going to head back in," Gloria says. "I'll leave you two to chat."

I give her a quick kiss before watching her float back into the ballroom. Over Graham's shoulder, Jonas approaches, raising his glass to Gloria before he joins us on the terrace.

"Gentlemen," he greets, shaking our hands. He holds Graham's hand a little longer, squeezing his arm with his free hand. "Congratulations on the nuptials."

"Thanks, man."

He turns to me, brows furrowed, looking perplexed as if trying to piece together a puzzle with missing pieces. "Are you and Gatlin...?" His thumb points conspicuously over his shoulder where she chats with Ms. Judy.

"Yup!" Graham declares for me.

I swallow my snicker, nodding in confirmation. "Yeah."

Jonas' eyes widen ever so slightly, and I feel every bit as anxious as Gloria did earlier. I brace myself for the judgment that so naturally comes with speculation.

"Ok," Jonas finally says with a nodding grin. "I like it. You two make a great match."

Graham nudges my arm with his elbow. "I know, right?"

"Thanks," I say, lifting my glass to them both. I'm relieved by how well we've been received. I appreciate the vote of confidence. "Being with her—it just feels right."

Through the open French doors, I see Gloria chatting with Ms. Judy. We lock eyes for a moment, and I shoot her a wink. She blushes, focusing back on her conversation. Meanwhile, my conversation has veered back to work-related material.

"Well done on the Minter case," Jonas says. After almost a year of investigating, we finally apprehended the suspect we'd been searching for. He panicked, making our lives a lot easier with a full confession. Even so, a confession does not ensure a slam dunk for the prosecution.

"Jake, I hope we set up a win for you," Graham says.

The victim being a state senator's daughter made the case extremely high-profile, creating a lot of pressure on the department, so closing this case was a huge deal. It felt like we were restoring the community's faith in our unit. Graham did a damn good job as lead on this case. One of my first priorities as sergeant is to see my boy get bumped up to corporal.

"It looks good to me," Jonas says, confident as ever.

"If you win the election, this could very well be your last case, right?"

Jonas nods. "If all goes well."

"It will," I conclude, slapping him on the back.

"Ugh," Graham groans softly. "My mother-in-law saw me."

I turn to see an older woman with a stern expression, beckoning Graham back inside.

"That's the 'get your ass in here' look. You better get moving," I tease, downing the rest of my whiskey on the rocks.

The three of us mosey back into the ballroom just as the lights shift, music bumping.

"Alright y'all!" the DJ projects. "Let's get a Soul Train line going!"

"I feel like falling in love..."

Beyoncé pulses through the ballroom, inspiring dancers to flood the dance floor. Gloria joins me, tugging my hands around her waist to hold her from behind as we watch the processional.

"Judy!" I bellow over the music, cheering her on as she sashays down the line.

It doesn't take long for Gloria and I to join the celebration, busting out old-school moves.

"Come and cuff it, cuff it, cuff it, cuff it, baby. While I buss it, buss it, buss it for you baby..."

We sing to each other, cutting up the dance floor, smiles for days.

The rest of our days, I pray.

GLORIA

Luci and Peter live in a charming cape cod on a tree-lined street in North Argale. It's a safe, cozy block—the perfect place to lay down roots, raise your kids in. With Charlie's hand in mine, we walk up the drive together—flowers tucked under his arm, a wine bag swinging from the crook of my fingers.

I pause on the porch to smooth my skirt and brush a bit of lint from his shoulder. I'm nervous. I cannot believe that I'm this nervous. Luci can be—a lot. I just hope that she's on her best behavior. *Oh God, this was a mistake.*

"Breathe, babe" Charlie reminds me, gently.

I nod and ring the bell before I can change my mind.

The shapes of Luci and Peter approach through the beveled glass. The door swings open to reveal their smiling faces—wider than I've ever seen on either of them before. I'm immediately suspicious. It's like I've brought a celebrity over for dinner.

Please don't make this weird.

"Heyyy!" the two sing-song in unison.

They're going to be weird.

"Come on in!" Pete says cheerfully. I step in first, kissing my brother-in-law on the cheek before hugging my sister. Charlie stands at the threshold, waiting patiently to be introduced.

"Charlie, this is my sister, Luci."

He steps inside, offering her the flowers. She gushes over them like it's her birthday. Charlie shoots me a triumphant look—it was his idea to bring them. *Credit where it's due.*

"And this is Pete, my brother—"

"—in love," Pete interjects, holding out his hand. "Welcome, Charlie. It's fantastic to finally meet you."

Charlie is completely at ease, smiling between them like he's known them for years. "Thank you for having me. You have a beautiful home."

Luci and Pete exchange a pleased glance. *They like him.* My heart does a little pirouette, but I stifle the impulse to dance along with it.

"You're just in time," Luci says. "You two can put the wine in the cooler while GG and I get dinner on the table. I made chicken parmigiana. Hope that's okay?"

"Sounds amazing," Charlie replies.

As he and Pete venture off, I hear Pete say, "So, I hear you're an Eta man..."

Good. They're bonding. I breathe a sigh of relief while I follow Luci into the kitchen. As I set the table, Luci trims the flowers, preparing them for a vase she's filling in the sink.

"Where are the kids?" I ask.

"Down the street at the neighbor's," she says, sprucing the arrangement. "Figured it'd be more fun if we could talk freely, you know?"

Oh boy.

At dinner, the inevitable question comes fast.

"So, how'd you two meet?" Pete asks, pushing his black framed glasses up his nose.

"I told you they work together," Luci says.

"I know, but let them tell the story, honey." He refills her wine glass with a smile.

"Technically, we don't *work* together," I clarify carefully.

"Right," Charlie chimes in. "The night we met, we were both out—socially."

"I didn't even know that he was in law enforcement."

"And I didn't know that she was a prosecutor. I saw her, and time stood still. He grins sheepishly. "Cliché, but true." He looks at me lovingly, setting my cheeks aflame. Snapping out of his trance, he continues to say, "We had a brief encounter. I stepped away for a moment, and when I returned, she was gone."

All eyes shift to me. I shrug, feigning innocence.

"But as luck would have it," Charlie concludes, "we would run into each other a few more times."

We certainly did. My office. The Greek Picnic. I chuckle to myself, remembering how I felt an instant connection at Swank, so certain that it didn't mean anything. *A blip.* It's surreal to hear him tell the story, *our* story—not like a torrid affair to be judged, but a love story to remember.

"So, it was fate?" Luci asks.

"Told ya," Charlie says with pride.

"Happenstance," I rebut.

Pete barks a laugh. "Says the skeptical lawyer type over here."

We all laugh—me included.

"And as you know," Charlie adds, "she helped me out with a case. The rest is history."

After that, the rest of the meal is a breeze. Luci and Pete pepper Charlie with questions about the world of homicide investigations like the true crime enthusiasts that they are. We even touch on travel plans—*Paris.* Maybe someday.

Later, with our bellies full of chicken and wine, Luci and I retreat to the kitchen to pack up the leftovers while the guys talk sports in the other room.

"So..." Luci begins, sealing a Ziploc bag. "You really like him, huh?

I shrug, turning my back to hide my blush. "A little."

"Like Big Love like him?"

I nod. "Yeah."

Her voice booms. "He's a triathlete!?"

"Luci!" I gawk, remembering the inside joke.

She stands with hands on her hips, brows raised. "Well?"

"Yep," I concede. "He swam the moat and scaled that wall."

"Yeah, it looks like he did," she says with a smirk, looking me up and down.

"Oh my *God.*"

"I'm just saying. Love looks good on you, sis."

"Thanks," I murmur, placing a dish in the sink. "It feels good too."

She hugs me from behind. "I wish that Mom were here. She'd love him for you."

"Yeah?"

"Yeah."

On the drive home, I ponder that alternate reality. What would Mom have thought of Charlie? Would she be able to see past what we've done to see what we have?

Would she have condemned me for being just like Evelyn?

Charlie's hand finds mine on the center console, and I'm instantly soothed.

At times, I still don't believe that this is real. In some ways, I'm still preparing my heart for the gavel to fall, certain that I'll wake up one day to a man that thought he was in love with me but realizes it was all an illusion—infatuation at best. Above all, *a mistake.*

But he hasn't. And my foolish heart keeps whispering to my weary mind that he never will. Instead, he continues to build a case against me to prove without reasonable doubt that I'm the one for him.

The woman of his dreams. The love of his life. His soulmate.

I close my eyes, trying to believe it, trying to commit the feeling to memory. I wasn't just a conquest. This isn't just a fling. What we have is by design.

Destiny.

CHARLIE

"I think that went well," I say, squeezing Gloria's hand. She blinks over at me from where she was just staring so pensively out the passenger side window.

"They adore you. I knew they would."

"I'm glad I finally got to meet them. To see that part of your life."

I slowly pull into the circle drive of her building, reluctant to part. She leans across the console, slipping a hand behind my neck and drawing my lips to hers in an unhurried kiss.

"Thank you," she whispers. "Tonight was perfect."

I catch that faint, lingering smile she's been wearing all night.

"So... a triathlete, huh?" I murmur against her lips, letting the words drag just a little.

"Ugh. You *heard* that?"

I laugh softly, smiling against her mouth. "Mmhmm."

"Shit," she whispers, biting her lip. She half-laughs to herself, clearly embarrassed.

"It's cool," I say with a soft smile, brushing my nose along hers. "Should I be flattered..."

She kisses me again—deeper, more deliberate— then rests her forehead against mine.

"Flattered? Without a doubt," she breathes. *"You bring home the gold...every time."*

I kiss her slow and certain—sealing the win. "Wish I could come up."

"I know." She kisses me again, and we sigh into the moment.

I wait until she's safely inside before pulling away, the car suddenly too quiet. As I turn the car toward Jack's house, my heart aches a bit at the rift between us still. All I want is to integrate her into my family, to make her feel like she belongs with us. *It's too soon.*

Jack greets me at the door when I'm walking up the steps.

"Hey," he says. "Let's rap outside."

I follow his lead, sitting next to him on his reclining porch chairs.

"So how'd it go?" he asks.

"It was cool. They're good people. I actually met her sister a while back—at the Greek Picnic. And her brother-in-law is in the frat, so we had that in common."

"Ah, so she got gangbangers in her family too, huh?"

I chuckle. "Yeah, something like that."

"This didn't turn into a Greek playdate for you, did it?"

"Nah."

Jack laughs quietly, then releases a heavy sigh. "So check this out. CJ and I had a long talk this morning."

Dread coils in my gut. "Okay... about what?"

"He asked if he could come and live here with us. Told me what happened with Rachel's parents."

"Man, I..." I drag my hand down the length of my face, fingers raking through my beard. "I've been worried about him. Worried that he'll never..." I just close my eyes and try to breathe through it.

"He loves you, Charlie. He's just upset and confused. And I know you get it. We both know how he feels."

He's talking about our father. It stings, but he's right. That feeling of betrayal when our dad left us. That hollow space he carved out when he walked away—I remember it well.

"The difference is—my son can trust me," I insist. "I'm going to do whatever I have to do to restore us. This... this is what I tried to avoid. I stayed in my marriage for years to avoid this, Jack. Long before Gloria. I stayed with Rachel because I was trying to be better than him. A better father. A better man."

My voice cracks. "Was I wrong to keep trying? To keep hoping things would get better between us? For wanting to stay—for *them*?"

Jack plants a hand on my shoulder. "Bro, I know how desperately you wanted to keep your family together, and you know I know why. Dad really fucked us up. And what's crazy is that we both have sons. I'll tell you this—you are *not* our father."

That damn lump lodges itself back in my throat. "I know that," I choke out, "but lately it's his reflection that I see looking back at me in the mirror."

"Honestly, bro, the way I see it—no matter how or when—it didn't end well. It wasn't ever going to end well between you two."

Silence hangs heavily between us for a moment before Jack cuts into it again.

"Look," he says, releasing my shoulder. "He's a kid. He'll be alright. It's a shitty situation. You let your son down—*so fix it.*"

CHARLIE

Contrary to Dr. Solomon's office, Dr. Bree Perry's office is bright and cheerful. Splashes of color decorate the space in the form of paintings, art sculptures, and even little kids' toys. Somehow, CJ feels simultaneously too old for this space and too young for the things that brought us here. Even so, this is what the doctor ordered, and I'm desperate.

I've read that grief impacts everyone differently. Although CJ is the more mature and stronger of my two, his response to the loss of his mom and my indiscretion is... troubling. He has to be overwhelmed. Despite the charade that he puts on of being okay, I know that he's not.

In fact, it's an eerie reminder of Rachel—that quiet repression of pain.

I don't want CJ harboring resentment, trying to process all this information on his own. The pressure on his young mind is enough to cause a dam to break. As hard as it was to hear, I was relieved to know that he was able to talk to Jack.

I haven't pushed him to talk to me. I know he doesn't want to. It's a miracle he didn't fight me harder on this session. I'm confident that both of my children could benefit from grief counseling, but as it stands, Cameron seems to be coping better. Maybe he'll have his turn when he's older. I'm grateful that CJ hasn't shared the ugly truth with him. Thanks to him, I am able to seek therapy individually—for now. The impact is the heaviest on CJ at this juncture, and I am desperate to help him carry it.

Dr. Perry sits down across from us. Dark brown curls tumble from her sleek updo, framing her face with a soft, natural grace and a touch of playful sophistication. Her golden-brown complexion harmonizes with the warm, inviting hue of her eyes, reminiscent of rich, salted caramel. Her clothes are as vibrant as her surroundings, adding a lively splash of color to the scene.

"Charlie and CJ," she says with a smile, "it's really nice to meet you both. Tell me, what brings you in today?"

I clear my throat, taking the lead. "Earlier this year, CJ lost his mom—tragically. His mother and I were having some marital issues. Recently, he learned of my infidelity, and he has a lot of big feelings about it. He's been *distant*. Which I can understand." I chose not to mention CJ's talk with Jack, not wanting CJ to feel betrayed by his uncle. This needs to be a safe space for him to express himself. "We just need a little guidance on how to move forward—together."

"Okay, well, let me start by saying, CJ, I'm so sorry for your loss."

"Thanks."

"Losing a parent is incredibly tough. And then, on top of that, realizing that our heroes are flawed can be a lot. This may sound like a really silly question, but when you learned about the struggles between your parents, how did that make you feel?"

CJ looks at me for permission to speak freely. I nod, encouraging his voice.

"Angry," he finally says. "Like I wanted to hit something."

I try to hide my shock. Neither of my boys have ever been exposed to real violence, let alone exhibit it themselves. Then, it occurs to me that they saw their grandmother slap their father earlier this year. So maybe violence birthed from anger doesn't feel so foreign after all.

"I get that," Dr. Perry relates. "Do you have siblings, CJ?"

"Yeah, a little brother."

"Oh, I know first hand what it's like having younger siblings. I'm the oldest of four girls. And they used to drive me up the wall. Still do." CJ cracks a small smile.

I like this doctor already.

"Sometimes, our family members do things that frustrate us, " she continues, "but it's important to figure out how to navigate that frustration in a way that keeps our relationships strong. In general, we don't like anger, right?"

"Right," CJ responds.

"It's the way that it makes you feel. Like you've lost control." She pantomimes a small explosion between her hands. "It just feels bad. But when you understand anger, what it's masking within you, it can become a healing and empowering force."

CJ looks a little confused, but Dr. Perry doesn't seem concerned by it. She meets my eyes, looking for my support.

"I have an assignment for the two of you," she says. "I want you two to work together to find healthy ways to express anger." We both nod. "Maybe there's an activity the two of you can do—something active, something creative. I'll let you decide what. But I want you to think it over and bring your ideas next time. Sound good, CJ?" He nods. "Dad?" I nod.

After the session, I pull Dr. Perry aside while CJ flips through a comic book in the waiting area.

"Should I be worried—about the *anger*, I mean? He's never been an angry kid."

Dr. Perry nods sympathetically. "Traumatic experiences like the sudden loss of a loved one can trigger new feelings in anyone—especially a child. Anger is a natural emotion. It isn't the enemy. What matters is how we help him express it."

I nod slowly, digesting her words. "I'm sorry if this is a dumb question but... how do you express anger in a healthy way?

"Don't apologize," she says kindly. "Most of us didn't get taught this as kids. But there *are* ways to vent those feelings without causing harm. And believe it or not—working through anger together can actually bring you closer."

Bring us closer.

On the drive home, CJ and I ride in silence, processing the information we've been gifted in our own way. That's what it feels like—a gift. As shapeless and uncertain as her advice seemed, I'm determined to make something concrete of it.

Fix it, Jack said.

"Thanks for coming with me today, CJ," I say. "You did great in there."

"Thanks, Dad," he says quietly.

It's the sweetest thing he's said to me all week. I grip the steering wheel, holding steady. Not every baby step is worth celebrating, but this one? This one gives me something I've been running low on.

Hope.

October

Twelve

SAFE PASSAGE

GLORIA

The notebook stares up at me from my office desk. I open it carefully, pen dancing idly between my fingers. Inside, I've tucked the page Charlie gave me—the prompts he thoughtfully shared after completing them himself.

Pondering where to begin, I scan the list, then read one aloud. "What is something from your parents that you are still harboring?"

Hmm, I tap the pen against my lips, thinking about it for a moment. *Marriage?* And my disenchantment with it. That's what comes to mind.

"I want to be your husband," he'd said that night in his backyard. The night that he made his intentions clear about this being a *forever* thing. Everything I've learned about him over the past year still amazes me. His

resilience. His strength. His capacity to feel and heal—it runs deeper than I ever expected.

I only have to think of his smile for a quiet pride to settle in my heart.

Charlie has taught me so much—about love, about courage, about what it means to truly support someone. And in return, I want to be everything he deserves. To show up for him. To grow with him.

I'm so proud of him. Proud to call him mine.

My gaze drifts back to the random notebook I picked up while shopping with Luci. It caught my eye as we browsed, its floral cover too pretty to leave behind. Finally, I put pen to paper. *Marriage. I'm afraid—*

Before I can dive any deeper, my phone buzzes. Unknown number.

"Hi, this is Gloria."

"Hi Gloria, this is Jasmine Renee. I'm the owner of Studio Hue. I received your inquiry about hosting an event at our venue."

"Yes! Thank you for following up."

As Jasmine and I speak, the pipe dream I shared with Charlie starts taking shape. I explain my vision: to bring together Argale's art community, showcase emerging talent, and create a space where collectors and supporters can connect. Suffice it to say, Jasmine is on board.

"Are you free to come by today?" she asks.

"Yes," I say, surprising myself.

After a final exchange with Jasmine, I pull up Charlie's contact and shoot him a text.

Sergeant Bensley.

His reply is immediate—*ASA Gatlin.*

My smile deepens. *How are you, lover? Got an hour to spare?*

Not an hour later, I'm downtown, walking toward Studio Hue. The photos online were promising, but Jasmine's friendliness over the phone sealed the deal, making a quick lunchtime visit a no-brainer.

"Gloria?" Jasmine greets me at the door with a bright smile. Her cocoa-brown skin is flawless, and her dark curls fall sleekly past her shoulders, bangs framing her face just right. She's gorgeous and graceful with red-painted nails that catch the light as we shake hands. "Thanks for coming out!"

"Thanks for having me. How long have you had this space?"

She beckons me inside with the wave of her hand. "Oh, just a little over a year now. I moved here from Northwest Indiana to be closer to my father. Visiting him was always a nice little getaway for me, but next thing I knew, I was packing up my life and business and making the big move. My dad can be pretty persuasive."

"Sounds like my father," I laugh.

"Is your dad a salesman too?"

"Worse—a lawyer," I say with a playful grimace, which she mirrors. "Was it a difficult adjustment, moving here?"

"Initially, yes. Business was booming being so close to Chicago, but Argale has its own charms. I've been fortunate. My competitors don't offer the range of services that I do, and when this spot became available, it felt perfect for expansion. We mostly host beauty expos, makeup classes, spa parties—you name it."

Luci would love that. Already thinking of signing us up for one of Jasmine's events.

"About six months ago, I started booking private events, and it's been going well ever since."

"That's amazing," I say, feeling more confident about my decision to inquire.

Just as I'm about to ask more, the door swings open. Charlie steps inside, and my heart flutters at the mere sight of him. Tall. Collected. *Mine*. He greets me with a kiss before turning to Jasmine.

"Jasmine," I say, "this is Charlie. Charlie, meet Jasmine. She's the owner."

"Nice to meet you," he says, ever the gentleman.

"Likewise!" Jasmine beams. "You two look around. I'll be right over there in my office if you need me. Take your time."

Hand in hand, Charlie and I walk the hardwood floors that stretch across the space. The walls are minimal, the lighting warm and gallery-perfect. Everything about it feels right.

"So," Charlie says, "how does this work?"

"Well, I've already started connecting with local artists. At the event, they'll showcase their work, and this venue is a perfect space for an exhibit. It's so versatile. From here, it's just the matter of curating the pieces to be displayed and promoting the event. Luci's already on board to help spread the word."

He nods. "As am I."

"Thank you," I say sincerely.

We wander around for a few more minutes, dreaming about what could be. While checking on availability with Jasmine, I pull out my calendar to see what dates might work. A reminder pops up—*Dad and Evelyn's Anniversary Party*. It completely slipped my mind.

"How about early December?" I suggest.

"It's open," she confirms. "I'll email you the details."

As we wrap things up, Charlie walks me to my car, our hands entwined.

I hesitate for only a moment before saying, "Hey, so—it's last minute, and I know you've got the boys and work..."

"Mmhmm..."

"My dad and Evelyn are hosting a party for their anniversary next month. Be my date?"

"In D.C.?"

"Yes," I say, sheepishly biting my lip.

His smile answers before his words do. "I'd love to."

"Really?"

"Yes," he says, pulling me closer.

It's a date then.

CHARLIE

... 48... 49... 50!

I grunt out the last rep, arms burning as I push myself off the floor. I needed this today. The workday was long, but I decided to hit up the gym anyway. I texted Sienna earlier to see if she could stay a little later with the boys. Thankfully, she agreed. *I owe her one.*

Sitting up to catch my breath, my attention drifts to a guy on the heavy bag, fists flying.

I wanted to hit something, CJ had said. It's been stuck in my head ever since. Dr. Perry gave us an assignment: find healthy ways to express anger. *Maybe...*

While I'm in the neighborhood, I swing by a sporting goods store and pick up something new—just to try. When I get home, Sienna is sitting at the kitchen counter, reading a textbook.

"Hey Sienna," I say, dropping my keys on the counter. "Thanks for staying late."

She glances up with an easy smile. "Hey, Mr. B. No problem. Homework's done." She scribbles a note in her notebook before packing up her book bag. "See you tomorrow."

"See you then," I say, walking her to the door, "and thanks again." Once Sienna is safely in her car, I head to the stairs and yell up, "I'm home!"

"Okay!" one of them sings.

"What's for dinner?" the other chimes in—like clockwork. I shake my head, grinning to myself.

After throwing together a quick meal, we sit down and debrief the day. Nothing too unusual—school, friends, video games. After dinner, the boys help clean up in the kitchen, then scatter upstairs.

In the garage, I open the trunk of my car and pull out the punching bag I purchased for CJ. It's a solid, freestanding one—about six feet tall, black and white, and sturdy but forgiving. I set it up in the corner of the garage, contemplating Dr. Perry's suggestion about finding an activity. *An outlet.*

Upstairs, CJ is lounging in his gaming rocker, eyes glued to the screen, fingers flying across the controller. I take a seat on the corner of his desk.

"Hey."

"Hey, Dad," he mutters, barely glancing at me.

"I've been thinking about Dr. Perry's assignment. Have you?"

He shakes his head. "Not really."

"Okay. Throw on your sweats and meet me in the garage."

"But Dad, I'm—"

"Five minutes," I cut him off as I stand and leave his room.

Right on schedule, CJ sulks into the garage, eyeing the new setup with a suspicious frown. "What's this?" he asks.

"It's a punching bag," I keep it simple. "Boxing can be a constructive way to deal with anger. Like an outlet when you're frustrated. Hitting the bag helps to release tension in the body. Helps you let it go. I think it could help." I toss him a pair of gloves. He catches them, hesitant. "Okay. Hit it."

"Dad..."

"You said you were angry, CJ. And you have every right to be. You said you wanted to hit something. So hit it."

He looks at me for a second, then at the bag. Slowly, he slips on the gloves and squares up. His first punch is cautious, like he's unsure if he should even be doing this.

"Again," I say, my voice steady but firm.

He throws another punch, harder this time. Then another. With each hit, the tension in his face starts to crack. His punches come faster, his fists connecting with more force, more purpose. His breathing grows heavier, and before long, tears form—then fall—streaming down his cheeks, spilling with every blow.

My throat tightens as I watch my son unload all of his pent-up pain. The sight of him hitting the bag—struggling with the weight of what he's feeling—wrecks me.

CJ stops, the gloves dropping to his sides, his chest heaving. I close the distance between us, pulling him into my arms as he starts to sob. Dropping a kiss to the top of his head, I hold him tight, like it's the only thing keeping either of us upright.

"It's okay," I murmur. "We'll get through this. *Together.*"

CHARLIE

The evening is drenched in the rich colors of fall. The sky's reddish-orange glow blends into the fiery canopy of leaves above Peter and Luci's backyard. Standing on their deck, I sip my beer and take in the sunset as it paints the horizon in hues that seem otherworldly.

Meanwhile, Peter is manning the grill like a pro, flipping steaks and chicken with the confidence of someone who's done this a million times.

"You like steak, Charlie?" he asks.

"Almost as much as I love me some Gloria," I shoot back, smirking.

"Good answer," he chuckles, nodding his head. "How do you like it?"

"Medium well."

He cuts into one of the steaks, checking the color. "Almost there."

Glancing out in the yard, I catch Gloria watching me. I swear, her smile makes everything else fade away. With her long lashes lowered, she turns her attention back to the portfolio in her hands. She and Luci are seated on lawn chairs, making plans for Gloria's upcoming art show. As they chat, they keep an eye on the kids, who are tossing a frisbee back and forth, their laughter coloring the air.

Peter's voice pulls me back. "Got any kids, Charlie?"

"Yeah, two sons," I say, a small smile tugging at my lips.

"Nice," he nods. "Ever been married?"

"Yeah."

There's a pause before he asks, quieter now, "Divorced?"

I hesitate now too, the word catching in my throat for just a second. "Widowed."

It still feels strange to say it.

Peter's face softens. "Man, I'm sorry. I... I couldn't imagine losing Luci." His gaze shifts to her, huddled close with Gloria, deep in conversation. "I'm glad you and Gloria found each other. I mean, isn't that something? A second chance at love."

A soft chuckle dislodges from the tension in my lungs. "Yeah, it's... I can't even put into words how grateful I am for her. She means a lot to me."

Peter grins. "Oh, I can tell."

Gloria looks over her shoulder at me once again, catching my eye. My heart swells at Peter's endorsement. I think about how far we've come—the good and the hard, the secrets we kept, and how the truth brought it all crashing down—everything collapsing around us. *But she stayed*. Somehow, despite all the chaos, she stayed. These past months have been a rollercoaster, but she stuck with me when anyone else would've run for the hills. Not only that, she's brought so much joy into my life—more than I ever thought I'd have again.

Peter raises his beer. "Looks like you've got yourself a Gatlin girl."

I lift my bottle to meet his. "Cheers to that."

Later, as we all gather around the table on the deck, Gloria leans in with a curious smile.

"So," she asks quietly, "how's boxing going?"

"CJ likes it. He's been hitting the bag every day. When I saw him watching YouTube videos to learn new techniques, I got him a coach."

"That's great!" She beams at me, clearly proud. "You better watch out. He's gonna get good and be able to take you on one of these days."

"Not a chance," I chuckle. "He starts training at the boxing gym on Fifth Avenue next week."

There's a knowing sparkle in her eyes. "Bensley men—forces of nature."

"Damn right."

Just then, Penelope—Luci and Peter's oldest—leans forward, her tiny voice cutting through the conversation. "Charlie, do you have a girlfriend?" she asks, blushing, a shy smile spreading across her face.

I can't help but smile in return. "I do."

Peter leans back in his chair, clearly enjoying the moment. "Auntie GG is his girlfriend, Nelly."

"Auntie GG has a boyfriend?" Preston shrieks. "Does that make you our uncle?"

"Preston!" Luci gasps, but everyone's already laughing.

I lean forward, meeting Preston's wide eyes. "I'm working on it, Pres," I say, holding out my fist for a bump. He grins and bumps it back.

"Alright, alright, let's say grace," Peter rallies. He clears his throat, clasps his hands, and bows his head. "Lord, we thank you for this food, for family, for friends old and new. We ask that you bless this meal and the hands that prepared it. Watch over us, guide us, and keep us close. Amen."

"Amen," we all echo.

As the plates make their rounds and the conversation flows, I steal another glance at Gloria. She's so comfortable with her family, glowing with the reassurance of being surrounded by the people she loves. A deep well of pride overflows within me—*I'm one of the people she loves.* What more could a man want?

Peter calls it a second chance at love. I call it a second chance at life.

November

Thirteen

From Here I Saw What Happened and I Cried

CHARLIE

The airplane cabin is alive with the bustle of passengers settling into their seats. I tuck our bags in the overhead bin, taking my own seat as a flight attendant moves down the aisle, checking that everything is secure.

"Good morning, ladies and gentlemen," another attendant announces through the intercom, her voice calm and practiced. "We are about to take off for Washington, D.C. We expect smooth skies for the majority of the flight. Please ensure your seat belts are fastened and your seat backs are in the upright position..."

As the staff demonstrates the safety protocols, I glance at Gloria next to me. Her demeanor contrasts with the jittery excitement I'm feeling.

"Excited?"

"Mmhmm." Her eyes sparkle with enthusiasm, but her posture is the picture of calm.

"Me too," I say, trying to match her tranquility. This is my first time flying to D.C., and the anticipation of exploring the nation's capital, especially with Gloria, feels exhilarating. The purpose of this trip adds another layer of significance—her dad and Evelyn's 25th anniversary party, a milestone celebration that feels both momentous and intimate.

Across the aisle, Luci and Peter are engaged in animated conversation, laughter punctuating their chatter. Though their friendliness has always made me feel more at ease, I still can't help feeling a bit like an outsider in this close-knit family's excursion. Gloria's hand resting gently on my knee is an anchor of reassurance.

The plane begins to rumble as it taxis down the runway. We pick up speed, the engines roaring to life. Soon, we're lifting off into blue skies, and the cityscape of Argale fades beneath us—a patchwork of buildings and streets shrinking into the distance.

Gloria winds her hand in mine, and I squeeze it gently in return.

"They know I'm coming, right?"

Gloria giggles, leaning closer. "Yes, they know. Are you nervous?"

"Nah, I'm good."

Her brow lifts in a mix of skepticism and amusement.

"Okay, maybe a little," I admit with a sheepish grin.

She gives me a steadying smile. "Don't worry. If the gatekeeper over there likes you..." She nods toward Luci, who is gazing out the window as the plane climbs higher. "...you'll be fine. I'm pretty sure they'll love you. You make it really hard not to."

The tension in my chest eases a bit. "Thanks." I run my thumb over the silky stretch of her wrist, eager to shift focus away from myself.

"What's the name of that spot you love, the one you told me about, with the cherry blossoms?"

Gloria's eyes light up with the spark of reminiscence. "The Tidal Basin. It's beautiful. The cherry blossoms bloom in springtime, but it's still stunning this time of year. The trees might not be in full bloom, but the reflections in the water and the crisp air make it magical."

I nod, trying to imagine the scene. "Cool. Can't wait to see it."

As the plane levels out, I watch the world pass by outside the window. The clouds below us swirl like cotton candy, and the sunlight glints off their soft surfaces. The view is mesmerizing, and I find myself caught up in the beauty of the journey as much as the destination.

When the seatbelt light turns off, the flight attendants begin their routine of distributing refreshments. Gloria and I share a small bag of pretzels, our fingers brushing each time we reach for the same treat.

When I met Gloria that night at Swank, I never would have guessed that I'd be flying states away to meet her father. This journey is not just about exploring a new city, nor is it solely about taking our first trip together. No, above all, this weekend is about turning the page into a new chapter of our lives together.

After settling into our cozy weekend rental, Gloria and I decide to make the most of the daylight before we're expected at her dad's place for dinner. The crisp November air nips at our cheeks as we meander along the famous Tidal Basin. I clutch a cup of hot cider, its warmth seeping through the cardboard and offering a comforting contrast to the chill. Gloria, meanwhile, has nearly finished her cinnamon-sugar pretzel with a few crumbs scattered along the path behind us.

Her eyes catch the soft, golden glow of the afternoon sun, and I marvel at how seamlessly she blends into this picturesque scene. It feels as if this place was crafted from her childhood dreams—*and now she's sharing them with me.* Ever since the night she told me about the cherry blossoms, I've wanted to see the Tidal Basin transform into a sea of pink and white, just as she described. While the autumn palette is stunning in its own right, I can't help but imagine the springtime beauty she spoke of.

We'll just have to come back.

Taking a sip of cider, I look over at the impressive monuments lining the water's edge.

"Now, I know that one," I say, pointing towards a tall, slender obelisk rising in the distance. "That's the Washington Monument." I beam with the pride of an amateur tour guide, hoping to impress her.

Gloria's gaze follows mine across the water. "Yep," she confirms. "Did you know it's the tallest stone structure in the world? On a clear day, you can see it from miles away."

"Uh, yeah." I joke. "Babe, everybody knows that."

She gives me a playful nudge, clearly enjoying our lighthearted exchange. We continue along the path, my arm draped comfortably around her neck as she leans into me, her arm wrapped around my waist. Autumn leaves drift down in lazy patterns, adding their own touch to the landscape. The crunch beneath our feet provides a gentle rhythm to our stroll.

As we approach the north end of the Tidal Basin, Gloria gestures towards a striking statue. "That's the Martin Luther King Jr. Memorial," she says, her voice filled with reverence. "It's relatively new compared to the others, but it's powerful. The Stone of Hope is a tribute to Dr. King and his vision for equality and justice."

I take a moment to absorb the grandeur of the memorial. "That is powerful," I agree. "You can really feel the impact of his legacy just by looking at it."

We find a bench overlooking the water and settle down, the scenic tranquility wrapping around us like a warm blanket. My arms stretch across the back of the bench with Gloria nestled sweetly against my side.

"This is amazing," I sigh, my gaze lingering on her wind-tousled hair. "I can see why you love it here so much."

Her eyes crinkle at the corners with her nostalgic smile. "I'm glad you think so. This place holds so many memories for me. I could sit here all day."

I glance at my watch and feel a twinge of regret. "Me too, but we should probably head back soon. We're supposed to reconnect with your family soon, right?"

Gloria nods, reluctantly getting up from the bench. "You're right. Let's go."

As we walk back, our hands find the other's once again. With each unison step, I find myself reluctant to leave this moment, committing it to memory. "Thank you for sharing this with me," I say softly, feeling the weight of my words.

Gloria's eyes sparkle with promise. "Anytime," she replies. "There's so much more to see. We'll have to come back in the spring."

My thoughts exactly. "I'm going to hold you to that."

After we meet up with Luci and Peter, the four of us head to the Gatlin condo. The corridor of the complex stretches far ahead, its walls adorned with elegant, textured wallpaper in muted tones. The polished hardwood floor gleams underfoot, embellished with a patterned runner. The space exudes a blend of modern elegance and understated sophistication.

Gloria strides ahead, her outfit commanding attention—a classy long-sleeve crop top paired with high-waist pants. A sliver of skin peeks out enticingly between the two pieces, adding a subtle allure to her already stunning appearance. Her look perfectly complements my slim-fit sweater, plaid pants, and brown leather shoes. We coordinate effortlessly, our neutral tones merging into a harmonious blend of shared style.

"Here we are," Gloria sings, ringing the doorbell with a giddy bounce in her heels.

The door swings open to reveal a classic man sporting a massive grin. He's dressed in a well-tailored blazer, the top buttons of his dress shirt casually undone, giving him a relaxed yet polished look. His graying hair is neatly combed, and the deep lines around his warm, inviting smile mark a lifetime of charm.

"There are my girls!" he cries, arms spreading wide.

Pete and I stand side by side, abandoned by our partners who eagerly cleave to their father's embrace. I see only a sliver of a woman over his shoulder, standing just out of sight. *That must be Evelyn.* We all wait patiently while the three reconnect with a hug that seems to recharge the collective Gatlin battery. Pete is content to bide his time, but anticipation tugs at my patience as I wait for an introduction.

Why am I so anxious?

Just then, Gloria steps out of her father's embrace and slips her hand into mine. "Charlie, this is my father Bennett and his girlfriend Evelyn."

Bennett offers a warm smile and extends a firm handshake, his presence commanding yet approachable. "Good to meet you, Charlie."

"Welcome," Evelyn adds, stepping forward to offer her own hand. The introduction feels like the start of a promising connection, their friendliness instantly easing any lingering nerves I might have had.

Bennett and Evelyn wave us deeper inside the home they share, offering refreshments. The layout of their high-rise home exudes sophistication with its panoramic city views. The walls are adorned with artwork, and soft, ambient lighting accentuates the smooth, polished surfaces throughout. City lights pour into the open-concept living area through the floor-to-ceiling windows.

Just like one of my favorite places on Earth, I muse. *Like father, like daughter.*

The kitchen features marble countertops, top-of-the-line appliances, and a stylish island. A balcony completes the space, offering a private retreat amid the bustling, urban landscape. The whole place feels expansive yet inviting, with carefully chosen decor that hints at luxury without veering into the realm of ostentation.

As we gather around the dinner table, the conversation comes easily, as do the laughs.

Bennett turns to Gloria with a mischievous glint in his eye. "So, what's new, Counselor? Besides the obvious." He nods his head in my direction, and the table bursts into giggles.

"Daddy," Gloria scolds, but an amused smile plays at the corner of her mouth.

"What? I've put two and two together, GG. Back in April, you were seriously considering moving back to D.C., and—"

"What!" Luci exclaims, eyes wide.

"—I thought you were coming back, rejoining the practice, taking over as partner, retiring me..." Bennett continues, his eyes twinkling. "But then, a sudden change of heart?"

Gloria addresses the whole table. "Yes, there was a lot going on at the time. But Argale is my home, Daddy." She glances at me with a look that speaks volumes. "It's where I belong."

I smile back at her, feeling a profound sense of connection.

"Especially now," Bennett sighs dejectedly. "No offense, Charlie."

I raise my hands in surrender. "None taken."

"Yes, especially now," Gloria confirms.

She's all in—ten toes down. Gloria's commitment and her willingness to sacrifice for our relationship hits me hard. It's overwhelming, but in the best way possible—a true testament to the strength of what we share. *We're unbreakable.*

"Ben, leave her alone," Evelyn says gently.

"Alright." Bennett yields with a good-natured shrug. He then stands to make a toast, his voice filled with warmth and sincerity. "Everyone, thank you for being here to celebrate with us. To Evelyn, my love, and our 25 years of love. Cheers!"

"Cheers!" everyone echoes.

As we all enjoy those first sips of wine, I recall Gloria telling me that they count only the years since Bennett's divorce. Bennett kisses Evelyn's hand, and I reach for Gloria's under the table. Our fingers intertwine, and I give her a reassuring squeeze. She responds by running her thumb tenderly over my fingers.

After dinner, the atmosphere is relaxed. Music underscores our mingling as we engage in lively discussion, all the while enjoying an assortment of desserts. Evelyn bought macarons from The Sweet Lobby bakery—apparently Luci and Gloria's favorite. It's a thoughtful touch that adds a sweet note of sentimentality to the evening.

I can't help but wonder how Gloria might be with *my* sons—would she be loving, nurturing, supportive, patient? *Undoubtedly.* The thought of her integrating into their lives fills me with hope, envisioning a future where she complements the family dynamic with the same thoughtfulness Evelyn has shown today. Could this be a glimpse into what might be a harmonious addition to my family?

Only time will tell.

As the evening quiets, Gloria and I stand by the fireplace, watching the flames.

"Your dad seemed disappointed that you won't be returning to D.C.," I say, hoping to unpack both his comment and her reaction.

"He'll live," Gloria chuckles, glancing over her shoulder at Bennett. "I started my law career at my dad's firm. Branching out on my own, emancipating myself—I needed it. I needed to blaze my own trail. I've always been confident in my abilities. I'm a solid attorney, hardworking, but I could never shake the air of nepotism that hung over me like a shadow."

I nod, understanding.

"He knows that I'm not coming back," she smirks.

"But you'd considered it. Leaving Argale, back in April?"

She nods solemnly. "It was... a really difficult time. I'll admit that the idea of a fresh start was tempting. Removing myself from the equation felt like the right thing to do." Her pain is palpable, like I could reach out and hold it in my hands. "But that wasn't what I really wanted—or needed." She meets my eyes with words unspoken—*"What I needed was you."*

My heart aches with the memory of that dark time. I forget how much it impacted her. Feeling responsible for so much pain, the uncertainty. I would have considered running away too. I lift her hand to my lips and kiss it gently. "I'm glad you stayed."

The glow of the fire reflects in her eyes as she smiles. "Me too."

GLORIA

Soft, morning light filters through the sheer curtains. Next to me, Charlie's breathing is steady and soothing. I prop my head onto my hand to watch him sleep. His back rises and falls with each breath, the contours of his muscles gently flexing beneath the rumpled sheets. The pillow cradles his face, and I trace the line of his jaw with my gaze, marveling at the subtle, contented smile shaping his lips. *What are you dreaming about?* I can't help but wonder.

I must be dreaming too. My life has begun to look and feel like a fairytale, and I don't believe in fairytales. It's as though I'm floating in a perpetual afterglow, like a spell that Charlie casts with his every kiss. I can hardly believe how my world has transformed. My heart stays full. My cheeks stay sore from smiling.

Being in love, truly embracing that it's here to stay, I... I keep telling myself not to get used to this, that I don't deserve it.

Quietly, I slip out of bed, moving to the window alcove. It's a cozy nook that frames a perfect view of the morning sky. I curl my knees up against my chest, leaning into the cool touch of the window against my skin. Last night was everything I'd hoped it would be. Charlie with my family was effortless, like a missing puzzle piece finally clicking into place.

"I'm so happy for you, Gloria," Evelyn had said after dinner. Each word sincere, lingering like the scent of her perfume—a blend of fresh flowers and something uniquely her. For a moment, the world seemed to shrink down to just the two of us, her embrace dissolving years of resentment in a single breath.

How could the woman who played such an integral part in the uprooting of my family be so genuine? How could the individual who was capable of something as devastating as homewrecking, be so caring?

I struggle to reconcile the two starkly different versions of the woman twisting in my memories, old and new. The contradiction of Evelyn challenges my perceptions and forces me to confront the possibility that people can be far more intricate and multifaceted than their most painful actions might suggest.

Or am I just looking for absolution?

I wonder if she ever felt this tortured. The woman I resented for so long, the one I thought was so different from me—*did she feel the same way about my father as I feel about Charlie?*

The subject of my thoughts stirs in bed, reaching for me. Charlie's voice is a gentle murmur in the early dawn, his eyes still half-closed. "Hey."

"Hey."

"You okay?"

"Mmhmm."

"Come back to bed."

"I'll be right there," I assure him. He drifts back to sleep, and I'm left alone with my thoughts once again. Everyone loved him last night, as I expected. I'm grateful for their support, but a pang of longing still tugs at my heart. *I wish my mom were here to weigh in.* What would she say? Would she agree that Charlie was the perfect man for me?

Would she approve?

I'd give anything to feel close to her right now, to be wrapped in her arms, to hear her voice offering reassurance—

"Get back in this bed, woman," Charlie grumbles, his tone playful yet insistent.

I smile and return to his side, slipping under the covers. Settling into his arms, I let out an uncertain sigh. "I was thinking about going to see my mom today."

"Do you want me to go with you?"

"I don't know," I admit honestly.

He presses a kiss to the top of my head. "Whatever you decide, baby, just know that I'm here for you."

I smile, feeling the way his love wraps around me. Curiosity nudges, "Do you believe in destiny?"

"Not before you."

"Same. Before I came to Argale, life was going exactly as I'd planned. But I always felt... unfulfilled."

"Yeah, I remember you saying that."

I fondly caress his cheekbone with my thumb. *Charlie, the ever-attentive listener.*

"I think that it was you. That 'something missing.'"

Charlie gives me that smile I'll never get enough of. *I'm so glad I never gave my heart away.*

"It's like my heart was always meant to be yours," I confess. "Only yours."

"I know exactly what you mean," he says. "I mean, like the opposite," he stumbles over his words, trying to clarify. "You know what I'm saying."

I giggle, forever endeared by his awkwardness. "I love you, Charlie Bensley."

He smiles, his eyes twinkling. "How much?"

He doesn't wait for my answer; instead, his lips claim mine as he pulls the sheet over our heads. And just like that, my anxieties, self-doubt, and contrition magically fade away. *This enchanter.* In this moment, nothing else exists but us. Our quiet time always takes me there—our sacred place, wrapped in each other's arms, living out the fairytale that I never believed in until...

Now.

CHARLIE

With Luci and Gloria away visiting their mother's gravesite, I accept Ben's invitation to spend some one-on-one time together. It's an opportunity I hadn't anticipated, but one I welcome with a mix of curiosity and apprehension. Getting to know Gloria's father better—especially under these more personal circumstances—is a chance I can't pass up.

The den has a quiet sort of lived-in charm. Dark wooden shelves line the walls, holding an array of leather-bound books, awards and honors, and framed photographs—a visual biography of a life well-lived.

Ben moves with practiced ease to a console where a crystal decanter sits waiting. "Bourbon alright?"

"Bourbon's perfect," I reply, eyes catching on a photo of a young girl holding a tennis racket. I'd recognize her bright, proud smile anywhere, but I still ask, "Is this Gloria?"

Ben glances over his shoulder with a fond smile. "Sure is, she used to be quite the tennis player." He returns to pouring two generous servings as I steal one more look at the photo—any glimpse into Gloria's childhood feels like a priceless artifact—pieces of the woman I love that I wasn't yet around for.

Handing me a glass, Ben directs us toward the seating area. We settle into the leather armchairs by the fireplace, which burns low and steady.

"You must be really special, Charlie," he says.

Sharing a drink with this man is feeling more and more like a rite of passage. "What makes you say that, Mr. Gatlin?"

"GG's never brought anyone home before. She's a pretty tough cookie—guarded. Not too keen on letting many into her inner circle, let alone her heart."

I take a sip, feeling a swell of pride and a pinch of pressure. "Really?"

Ben nods, leaning back slightly. "Nope. She's not one to show her cards easily. But here you are. Sounds like you broke through her defenses."

A wave of vulnerability washes over me. "Well, sir, she's special to me. It's been a privilege to know her—and a greater one to love her."

Ben studies me as he sips. "So how long have you been seeing each other? Since April, I presume?"

I chuckle, recognizing the angle—playful, but pointed. Curiosity? Nah. He's more than hinting at the suspicion that I might be the reason Gloria chose to stay in Argale. I shift in my seat, struggling with the urge to be entirely truthful. Thankfully, Ben cuts in before I have to find the words.

"You know," Ben continues, "it's not that I have an issue with her living in Argale. I just want better for her. I tease about her returning here to pass the torch, but honestly, I'd be thrilled to see her start her own practice there. She's overqualified, and I'm sure the State's Attorney knew that when they brought her on. I just hate to see her set the bar so low. But I'm only her father, what do I know?"

I nod, my respect for Ben deepening. "I understand. She's an outstanding attorney who seems to love what she does. And she's an incredible human being. Smart, caring, ambitious..."

"Well, I'm glad you recognize that," Ben says, his tone softening.

The room grows still. The silence, heavy and growing unbearable. Finally, Ben breaks it. "Gloria tells me you're a widower."

"Yes, sir." That familiar sting of loss reemerges, sharp behind my heart. It's always hiding there—*grief*—waiting for the next reminder.

"I'm sorry. That must've been hard."

My eyes drop to the patterned rug. "Yeah, especially for my sons."

"You have sons?"

"Yes, sir. I have two."

"How old are they?"

"CJ is twelve, and Cameron just turned ten," I say, as a small, thoughtful smile forms.

Ben nods, internalizing. "Must've been a tough call—getting back out there. How long had it been when you started seeing Gloria?"

I hesitate, feeling the truth gnawing at my conscience. "Actually, I... I met Gloria before my wife passed away."

I finally look up, bracing for the fallout. His eyebrows lift in surprise. "Oh."

"When I began seeing Gloria, my marriage was..." I catch myself, realizing that no explanation I could offer would truly pardon my actions. "There's no excuse. I was wrong, and I'm not proud of it. But I don't regret it either. I never intended to hurt anyone, but I fell in love with her. Your daughter means the world to me, sir, and I hope someday I can convince her to marry me." I pause, making my intentions clear. "And I hope to convince you that I'm worthy of your blessing."

My confession hangs in the air, silence stretching between us, damn near suffocating with all the words unsaid. Ben's contemplative gaze softens, a flicker of empathy in his eyes.

"Well, I'm sure that GG has told you about Evelyn and me," he says a little gruffly, "about how our relationship began. Ev and I aren't proud of our actions either. Sometimes life leads us down paths we never anticipated. I know what it's like to be in a situation where feelings don't align with what's right or expected. My affair with Evelyn wasn't planned or intentional; it was a consequence of a complicated and unhappy time in my life. And while I regret the hurt it caused, I also understand how love can emerge from unexpected places." The faraway look in Ben's eyes brightens as he clears his throat. "That said, I respect your honesty and appreciate you sharing your intentions with me."

We sit in the quiet, two men with pasts neither of us would rewrite.

He tips his glass toward mine in a gesture of acceptance. "Here's to moving forward, then. To making the best of what we have now."

I raise mine, grateful. "To moving forward."

As conversation veers into more comfortable territory—music, travel, fatherhood—a quiet sense of kinship eases my self-reproach. With Ben's empathy, I feel less like the irredeemable villain in my own complicated narrative. *The antagonist.* And for the first time, I begin to see myself not as someone who has merely wronged others, but as a man who has navigated a challenging path and found meaning in the journey.

Cheers to that.

GLORIA

The football game is well underway by the time Luci and I return from the cemetery. I sidle up next to Charlie, who's perched on the arm of the oversized sectional, fully engrossed in the game with the guys.

"Hey, you," he says, wrapping his arms around my waist. "How'd it go with your mom?"

"I'm glad I went." It takes some effort to keep my voice steady around the lump in my throat. "And how about you? Looks like the three of you have something in common."

"Yeah, your dad's a Warriors fan, but I won't hold that against him," Charlie chuckles. Gently tugging me by the wrist, he pulls me into the kitchen where the game is only a hum in the background. There, he leans back against the counter. "I thought I should tell you..."

"What's up?" I murmur, curiosity piqued.

"The subject of April came up again."

I roll my eyes. *Thanks, Dad.* "Sorry. He can be very persistent."

"Like father, like daughter," Charlie teases, and I can't help but smile. He takes both of my hands, his thumbs gently tracing my knuckles. "Listen. He knows that I was still with Rachel when we first met. I know I should've discussed it with you first, but I didn't want to lie to him, babe."

I nod understandingly, sighing as I glance in my father's direction, watching him cheer for his team with Peter. I'm debating ways to pull him away for a private conversation when Evelyn reminds us of our dinner reservation.

Later.

Dinner, for all intents and purposes, is lovely—good food, even better company. It's pleasant enough that I allow myself to set my anxiety aside. After all, I'm surrounded by my favorite people. *There's a time and a place for such conversations.*

I watch as my father throws his head back in laughter at something Charlie's said, the two clearly enjoying a newfound camaraderie. Truth be told, it's surreal having Charlie here. I'm so used to being the fifth wheel, always content with that role, always the standalone in family photos. Now, I'm here with my partner—the man I've grown so close to, the one I can no longer imagine my life without. Charlie is a permanent fixture. *Unbelievable.*

Back at the condo, I find my father in his office, seated behind his desk and reviewing what appears to be a deposition transcript. *No wonder where I get my work ethic.* I wander around the room quietly, just like I used to as a girl when I needed his advice. Smiling to myself, I pull down a framed photo from the shelf—a remnant of my brief tennis career.

"Charlie gravitated to that one, too. He was surprised that you played."

"Was he?" I smile as I return the frame. Now that I have his attention, I turn to face him, arms crossed.

"What's on your mind, Counselor?"

Deep breath. "Are you disappointed?"

He considers the question, then smiles. "No," he answers, his voice a reassuring baritone. "Shit happens, sweetheart."

Relief washes over me. I exhale, my arms falling to my sides as I lean against the console, his stash of bourbon tinkling softly.

"I like Charlie," he continues, lacing his fingers and leaning back in his leather chair. "He was honest, and I respect that. And I trust you. I never doubt your ability to make the right call. Even if you make a mistake, I have faith in your ability to learn from it. From what I can see, you two have found something special in one another. That's what matters." He rises with a soft grunt and joins me, leaning against the console next to me. There's a mischievous glint in his eye as he asks, "He didn't kill her, did he?"

"Daddy! No!"

"I had to ask," he chuckles before a soberness falls over his face. "I know someone who's been in your shoes, GG. It's not an easy road to take. Are you sure this is what you want?"

None of this could have been easy for Evelyn. I try to imagine her explaining her relationship with my father to her family and friends. It must have been difficult to face Luci and me, anxiously seeking our approval, wanting only a small chance at a meaningful relationship with us. *And I didn't take it easy on her by any means.*

I nod, still so certain despite the storm of emotions inside. "Yeah, it is."

"Then I'm happy for you, baby." He wraps one arm around me and pulls my forehead to his lips for a tender kiss. Then he asks, "Does your sister know?"

"Know what?"

My sister's voice sends a jolt through me. I spin to see her standing in the doorway, having clearly overheard the tail end of our conversation.

Luci narrows her eyes. "What are you two talking about in here? What don't I know?"

My heart hammers in my chest with the dread of my confession. *Is this the right time and place for this conversation?* I knew we'd eventually have to discuss it, but part of me hoped for a little more time to prepare. Luci is that one juror that isn't easy to win over—convincing her will be an uphill battle. I knew she'd have to be sold on Charlie first, which is why I wanted her to see him for who he is before learning what he'd done. *What we'd done.*

Dad squeezes me on the shoulder reassuringly.

Another deep breath. "Lu, Dad and I were just talking about my relationship. Charlie and I have been seeing each other for more than a year—secretly." Luci's face twists in confusion, and I brace for impact, going on to say, "Our relationship began as an affair and—"

"Wait, what?" Luci gasps. "Wh-Why would you do that?"

My mouth opens then closes as I search for a plausible explanation, but I don't have one. Luci blinks at me like I'm a stranger before turning to our father with a fiery glare.

"This is your fault," she snaps. "You and Evelyn—you *mock* marriage, acting like your life is perfect because you chose to forgo it. Like it was the secret formula to a lasting relationship. Look at what you did." She points an angry finger at me, her gaze following to bore holes of disdain in my watering eyes. "And *you*! How could you be so selfish?"

Each word stings, but not so much as the look in her eyes. Behind their glare, all I can see is our mother's disapproval.

Gloria, just explain it to her, my mind pleads. *Tell her that Charlie is everything she wants for you—wonderful, loving, kind. He's not what he appears to be, but he is everything that he seems.*

But my voice is trapped behind that persistent lump in my throat. I'm not prepared for this. I needed more time, and now her disappointment feels like acid on my skin. I hear Peter's voice echo in my mind—*"But only because she loves you, GG."*

I am selfish, I acknowledge—recognizing how my choices have rippled, affecting yet another innocent person.

"Luci," I choke out, "you wouldn't understand. I—"

"And I don't want to," she bites back. With that, Luci turns on her heels and storms out of the room, leaving me standing there, stunned and disheartened.

"Gloria, just give her a minute..." my father is saying behind me, but desperation has taken hold of me. I follow my feet like I'm a child again, chasing after my sister.

"Luci, wait..."

I turn the corner to see her shooting a venomous glance at Charlie before she retreats to the balcony. Confused and concerned, Peter follows. Through the glass, I can't hear their words—only the muffled emotion of them as Luci recoils from her husband's gentle touch. There is deep-seated disdain etched on her face when our eyes meet one last time before she turns away.

She's disgusted. I disgust her.

"Everything okay?" Charlie asks, arms already open.

I can only shake my head, tears brimming in my eyes. Wordlessly, he pulls me in and my head lands softly against his chest, protected by the shelter of his arms.

Refuge.

"It'll be okay," he whispers.

Facing the fallout of our choices was inevitable, and this is only the beginning. If we want to share a life together, we will have to face the judgment of our loved ones, no matter how harsh it may be.

But knowing the battle is coming doesn't make the wounds any less painful. But knowing the storm is coming doesn't make it any easier to endure.

"We'll get through this," Charlie murmurs in my ear, and I cling to him. "We will."

We have to.

Fourteen

BETWEEN THE MARGINS

CHARLIE

The ride back to our rental is painfully quiet, the kind of quiet that makes every bump in the road feel like an electric shock. What should be a mundane, even pleasant transition from one place to another feels like a test of endurance, each minute stretching longer than the last. One could choke on air so thick with unspoken tension.

Gloria keeps her face turned toward the window, her expression resigned. I can't blame her—today didn't unfold exactly as planned. Luci's reaction to my marital betrayal is like a punch to the gut. I get it, she's protective of Gloria, and her anger is rooted in concern. I just hadn't anticipated how deeply it would cut.

Back at the rental, I find Luci in the kitchen, her back turned as she rummages through the pantry. Her calm exterior, contrasting with the frustration I know she's feeling, makes me uneasy. I take a deep breath and approach her.

"Luci," I say, my voice tentative. "Can we talk?"

She straightens up, turning slowly to face me. Her eyes meet mine, and I see a familiar coldness there—a look that tells me she's not ready for any excuses or explanations.

But I have to try.

"I realize today's revelation was upsetting," I start, trying to choose my words carefully. "That I've made it difficult for you to trust me. But Luci, I—I would never hurt Gloria." My voice is earnest. "I can assure you—"

Luci cuts me off, her expression hardening. "And how is that exactly?"

"I was wrong for being unfaithful in my marriage," I continue, struggling to maintain my composure, "but my relationship with Gloria is different. I'm in love with her. Our relationship means everything to me. I'd never do anything to jeopardize it."

Luci's gaze doesn't soften. Instead, she crosses her arms and takes a step back. "Your words mean nothing. As far as I'm concerned, you're a liar and a cheater. And I don't trust you—and neither should she. In fact, I'm shocked that she does." Luci shakes her head, her frustration clear. "And I'm not worried about you hurting my sister because I won't let you."

Her words sting, and I can see the genuine hurt in her eyes. How can I convince her that my past mistakes don't define me—the man that I truly am? But the more I speak, the deeper I dig myself into this hole. Before I can form a response, Luci storms past me, done with the conversation.

She doesn't even take any food with her, appetite lost or sacrificed to be further from me and my meaningless words.

I've lost the battle before it even began.

Peter steps into the kitchen just as Luci storms out. I brace myself for another round of tough conversation.

"She's a fierce protector," he says simply. "It's an important part of who she is, protective and passionate, especially when it comes to her sister."

I nod, feeling somewhat defeated. "Yeah, I can see that."

Peter leans against the counter, eyes kind. "Luci's reaction isn't just about you. I think she's stunned by the whole situation, given their family history."

"I get it," I reply, but my voice sounds pinched. *I'm barely keeping it together.*

Peter gives me a sympathetic smile. "It's going to take some time. Luci just needs to see that your intentions are genuine. She'll come around. I know for a fact that Luci really likes you for GG. This whole thing is just a shock to her, and she needs some space to process it." He adds with a reassuring smile, "She's a processor."

All I can do is respond with a tight nod.

"For what it's worth, I believe you're a good guy, Charlie, and I think you two make a great couple. I'll talk to her. Just give her some time—she won't be upset forever."

His words are a comfort in this storm I'm navigating. "Thanks, Pete."

Grabbing a bag of chips from the pantry, he pats me on the back as he heads out after his wife. "Hang in there."

With Peter's vote of confidence, I feel the tension in my chest ease a bit. His support doesn't fix everything, but it helps. There's still a long road ahead, and earning Luci's trust will be challenging. But knowing that Peter is willing to advocate for me is huge. He sees my commitment to Gloria, and that helps lift some of the weight off my shoulders.

He's a good guy.

I take a deep breath and pour a glass of water from the fridge's filter. The knife-twist of failure still carves away at my soul, but I haven't completely bled out. There's still a steady pulse of determination that refuses to cease.

Proving my commitment to Gloria will take more than just promises.

For now, all I can do is remain consistent and hope that, in time, Luci will see the sincerity in my efforts. Maybe someday she'll give me the chance to prove myself—to show her that I am dedicated to building a future with her sister.

When I return to the bedroom, Gloria is lounging on the chaise, reading a book. I place the glass of water on the end table beside her before settling at the foot of the chaise. Reaching for her feet, I gently ease them into my lap, hoping a massage might offer some comfort.

"You starting a new book without me?" I ask, glancing at the unfamiliar cover.

"I hadn't planned to," she says with a half-smile. "Your copy's in my bag. I just needed a distraction, I suppose."

"Is it working?"

"Nope," she chuckles emptily to herself, the sound betraying her sadness.

"I don't trust you—and neither should she. In fact, I'm shocked that she does." Luci's words still echo in my mind, harsh and exacting.

"Do you trust me, Gloria?"

She pauses, blinking with surprise. Then, her eyes meeting mine with a sincerity that makes my heart ache. "Yes."

"Your delay is a little disheartening," I admit, frustration seeping through.

"I'm sorry."

"Don't be. I'm the one who cheated. I planted this seed of doubt. I've given you every reason to question—"

"Actually, you haven't," she interrupts. "Yes, I'd be naive to ignore what happened, but Charlie, baby, it's never crossed my mind. Not even once. I think you asking me made me stop to consider whether I've been naive for not giving it any thought at all." She inches closer to place a hand on my cheek, gently guiding my gaze to hers. "But I haven't, and I don't plan to. I trust you—with all my heart."

Her resolute words are like a balm to my wounded pride, and I can only nod, emotion getting the better of me. She leans in, pressing a sweet, tender kiss to my lips.

"I could never hurt you, Gloria," I whisper against her mouth.

"I know," she smiles. "I could still use a distraction..."

And a distraction I am happy to provide. We're tangled in bed in no time, spooning between the sheets, skin to skin, our limbs drawn tight, bodies aligned like we were tailored to fit—*perfectly*. I drag lazy kisses from the sensitive spot behind her ear, down the curve of her neck, and over her shoulder—slow, lingering—letting her feel every ounce of love I carry for her in the softness of my lips.

She lets out a moan that curls in my chest, breathy and broken, already undone by anticipation. Her hips shift back into me, guiding my arousal to the space where her body calls to mine. The invitation is silent, but clear. Needy. *Familiar.*

"Charlie..." she whimpers, her voice breaking somewhere between want and weariness.

Following the tug of her hand, I trace down past her navel to find her—already warm, already wet for me. I take my time, drawing slow circles until her hips begin to grind against my touch, her breath hitching as she starts to unravel beneath my fingers, coaxing her higher. Her hand finds mine and holds it there, anchoring us together.

When I enter her, it's not a thrust but a slow, deep slide—the fit so perfect. This moment, too fragile to be rushed. She parts her legs wider for me, urging me closer, deeper, giving me everything. Welcoming all of me. Her body curves into mine, her back arching just enough to press us closer, making room for the depth I know she needs.

Our legs knot beneath the covers. I move inside her with aching precision, my hips tilting to match the rhythm of her breath. Her moans start soft—hushed, then rise, growing desperate, spilling from her in pulses.

"Stay with me," she gasps, and I do—*always will.*

She cranes her neck to kiss me as she gives in to the power of her climax. Her moan disappears into my mouth as I kiss her through the height of it, shattering in my arms. I follow her over the edge, releasing the day's built-up tension.

Sex may not be the solution to the issue at hand, but I'm always grateful for our physical connection. So far, no matter what, making love only deepens our bond.

It seems—no seed of doubt could outgrow our love.

GLORIA

The spa chairs are an island of calm in a sea of tension. Evelyn knew exactly what we needed, directing us to her favorite spot to unwind and reset. Luci and I are nestled into plush, blush-pink chairs, each one fitted with a curved back and a bubbling foot bath. The flower wall behind us is a vibrant tapestry of multicolored blooms, brightening the muted serenity of the salon. The water jets hum a soothing song as we settle in for our pedicures.

Beside me, Luci sighs deeply. It took a bit of convincing to get her here, but I'd hoped the spa's softness might help smooth things over and give us space to talk. She's uncharacteristically quiet. Her face is relaxed, but her eyes are distant. Lost in thought, her fingers absentmindedly trace the edge of her chair. I know she's still processing everything from the day before. Learning about the affair was a shock, and it was clear from her reaction how deeply it hurt her.

"So," I begin, trying for levity, "what do you think of this place?"

Luci glances around, her expression still guarded. "It's... pretty."

It's better to just come out and say it. "Lu, I'm sorry."

"For what?" She's not being sarcastic or passive-aggressive, just genuinely seeking clarity. "You don't owe me an explanation."

"For not being straight with you. In the beginning, I didn't mention Charlie for obvious reasons. But I should've been upfront about our situation before I brought him into your life. I know you're disappointed. And I'm... deeply ashamed of what I've done. I completely understand your frustration. If Peter had ever betrayed you like this, I'd hate him for it. It would be unforgivable."

Luci's gaze sharpens with genuine curiosity. "Then why? Why a married man, GG? You could have any man you want."

There it is. The question that's been haunting me—that I've spent so long trying to answer. *Why Charlie?* It's not easy to articulate exactly how I feel. Every time I try, the words slip away like trying to catch sunlight in my hands. It's not the kind of love you can neatly define, box up, or label. There's no category for it, no checklist that makes it easier to understand. It's not about grand gestures or fleeting moments of passion. It's deeper than that—*wider*.

But how do you define something that feels like it's woven into your soul? Maybe that's the point. Maybe our love is the kind you just experience quietly, without needing to explain it. A love that can't be defined—not because it's confusing, but because it's too infinite to fit into something as small as words.

"You could have any man you want..."

"You may be right," I admit. "And I don't have a convincing explanation, not one I can articulate perfectly."

Luci looks at me, her expression a mix of skepticism and concern. "I just don't see how you can trust him."

I take a steadying breath, fully understanding her worry. "I recognize how Charlie must seem now, and how your impression of him has probably shifted after learning about the affair. It's hard not to let something like that color your view of someone. But what happened doesn't define who he is. I'm not making excuses for him, and I'm sure he wouldn't either. He's owned up to it and taken full responsibility for the hurt he caused. That part of his life isn't a secret he's trying to bury—it's a mistake he's learned from, one that's made him more intentional, more careful with his heart and with others."

"Charlie isn't pretending to be someone he's not. You have every right to be cautious, but please don't let what you now know erase everything you've seen in him before. And please... try not to judge him too harshly. He's not perfect, but he's real. And with you, he's been nothing but sincere. And I love him."

I love him.

Luci's gaze shifts away as she processes my words. She doesn't say anything, just sighs with weary resignation. And I suppose—*I can live with that.*

Trying to lighten the air, I pivot. "So, what are you wearing tonight?"

Luci cracks a wry smile. "I brought a few options..."

As the pedicurists finish up, Luci and I fall back into safer conversation. The distance between us begins to shrink, but it's clear that healing will be a process.

There's still so much left unsaid.

How do I even begin to explain the situation with Rachel? If the affair was such a shock for Luci, what on Earth will she think when she finds out about the tragedy that followed? I can't drop another bombshell on her—not now, not when she's still reeling from our indiscretion...

Should I wait until the dust settles? Give her a chance to absorb everything before I bring it up? I need a plan—*no, I need more time.* The last thing I want is for Luci to feel like I'm hiding more from her, but if I tell her now, I'll be adding fuel to the fire that I'm trying so desperately to put out.

What do I do?

CHARLIE

The evening is in full swing. Ben and Evelyn's luxury condo is packed with guests celebrating their anniversary. It's as dazzling and polished as you'd expect from such a great couple. They have impeccable taste, refined and upscale but far from pretentious, and despite their success, they're down-to-earth and welcoming. Ben's attire matches the champagne silk of Evelyn's evening gown, which sparkles under the overhead lights. That same golden lighting blankets a lavish spread of food and drinks that speaks to their shared talent of hosting. The hum of cheerful conversation inspires the atmosphere, decorated with the clinking of glasses and the gentle strains of piano underscoring.

"So, is this how you see us in 25 years? Like Oprah and Stedman?" I tease, gesturing toward her dad and Evelyn, referring to their unmarried yet opulent lifestyle. We stand apart from the various groups, taking in the charming atmosphere.

She laughs from somewhere deep and genuine, eyes sparkling with amusement. "Depends on what you mean. Incredibly wealthy?"

I raise a brow. "You know what I mean."

"Oh," she says, tying her arms around my neck. "You mean celebrating a milestone."

I fall into her beautiful eyes, tempted to kiss her. "Yep."

She grins—*so cheeky.* "Then yes. This is how I see us—together."

Just then, Ben steps to the center of the room, tapping his glass to get everyone's attention. The room falls into an anticipatory hush as he clears his throat.

"Ladies and gentlemen," he begins, surveying the crowd with a proud smile, "Ev and I would like to take a moment to express our deepest gratitude to all of you for being here today to celebrate this special occasion with us. What a love story we have, Ev." His gaze settles on her, who beams back at him. "A rather unconventional one, I'd say, but timeless nonetheless. We didn't take the traditional path, but that's what makes our story unique, not perfect—love never is—but real, enduring, and undeniably ours.

"Through every plot twist and turn, we've written our own story—one filled with laughter, adventure, and an unshakeable bond. To new love," he says, tipping his glass toward Gloria and me. Our hands tangle at our sides. "To a solid love," he adds, nodding toward his eldest daughter and her husband. Luci smiles tenderly as Peter wraps his arms around her from behind. "And to a forever love," he finishes, raising his glass to Evelyn. "You've been my partner, my confidante, and my greatest love. Here's to 25 years of living our own version of happily ever after, and to the many chapters still waiting to be written. Cheers, my love."

The guests erupt into applause. Gloria and I raise our glasses high, our eyes locked in a shared moment of reflection and appreciation.

As the crowd begins to disperse, I see Luci approaching.

"Charlie, got a minute?" she asks, her tone gentle yet unmistakably firm.

I exchange a quick glance with Gloria before nodding. Luci and I step out onto the balcony, away from the lively chatter of the party. The cool night air greets us, and I take a deep breath of it, watching puffs of air vanish into the night sky.

Luci turns to face me, and for the first time, her expression is... not soft, exactly, but less guarded. "I wanted to apologize for the way I acted last night. You'll have to forgive me. I'm still trying to wrap my head around what happened between you and my sister."

I shake my head, brows furrowing. "No apology needed, Luci."

She pauses, her gaze searching mine as if weighing her next words carefully. "Look, I really do like you for my sister, Charlie. She's happy with you, and that means the world to me. But..." She exhales slowly, her stare sharpening. "I still have my reservations. I'm choosing to believe you, to trust what you said—that you'll *never* hurt her. Don't make me regret it."

"I won't." I pin the weight of that promise securely on my heart like a badge of honor.

Luci sighs, a hint of exasperation in her expression. A trace of reluctance lingers in her eyes, as if she's not quite ready to let her guard down completely.

I can understand that.

I want to reassure her—to make her believe me—but instead we stand in silence, listening to the muffled sounds of the party. Finally, Luci breaks the quiet, offering a small, tentative smile. "I'm gonna head back inside."

"I'll be right behind you."

As Luci disappears into the warmth of the penthouse, I linger on the balcony, the November breeze cooling my skin.

"I'm choosing to believe you, to trust what you said—that you'll never hurt her."

Winning Gloria's trust and the trust of her family isn't a task I take lightly. I've broken a promise like this once before. But not this time. Not with Gloria.

Never again.

Through the glass doors, Gloria dances with her dad. They're deep in conversation, their faces glowing. After a moment, Evelyn places a graceful hand on Ben's shoulder. He kisses Gloria's forehead just before she steps in to take her place.

That's my cue.

I step back inside, joining Gloria on the dance floor. She smiles tentatively, lifting a curious brow as I approach, hand extended. She places hers in mine and I twirl her, then pull her in close.

"I can't stand to see you alone on the dance floor." I say, sliding my arms around her waist. We sway to the music, content to lose ourselves in each other for a stolen moment. Still, with my cheek pressed to her temple, I can practically hear the questions gnawing at her mind.

"All good?" she asks.

I pull her deeper into my arms. "All good."

It's the truth. For now, we are good. As we dance, relief makes way for a sense of contentment. In spite of the challenges and uncertainties, what truly matters is this woman in my arms—her love, her trust, her heart.

All good.

GLORIA

This isn't just any evening. Tonight, I stand in front of my full length mirror, adjusting the final touches on my dress—a strapless number with a floral appliqué that hugs me in all the right places. I run my hands over the delicate, raised petals, smoothing the fabric like I might smooth my nerves.

Just days ago, we returned home from D.C. where Charlie met my entire family. Tonight, it's my turn—I get to meet his. It's Jack's birthday party. His brother. My first real introduction to the rest of Charlie's world. My heart beats a little faster at the thought of it.

Earlier today, Luci stopped by. I'd invited her over to talk—it was at the top of my checklist after returning home from D.C. I told her everything—about my relationship with Charlie. A situationship that evolved into something neither of us planned but couldn't seem to stop.

Then, I walked her through the heartbreaking details of that tragic night between Charlie and Rachel, and how I was ready to run back to D.C. to escape the pain of it all.

"It was horrifying," I admitted, voice hoarse with emotion, *"to know that my actions—our actions—sent her to such a dark place. And Charlie has to wear those scars for the rest of his life. All because I—I—"*

I didn't finish. Luci pulled me into her arms before I could. Her embrace stunning me to silence. I'd braced myself for her verdict, for her to condemn me—but she didn't. I didn't expect her eyes to well up too, for her to bear the weight of my shame with me. For that moment in my sister's arms, that burden lifted—if only temporarily.

"I'm so sorry, Gloria," she murmured in my ear. *"That's awful. I can't imagine how you must have felt—or even what you're still carrying. And Charlie... Thank God he survived."* She loosened her grip on my shoulders, her gaze catching mine like she needed me to know she meant it. *"GG, I wish you'd told me sooner. I could have been there for you. But... I understand why you didn't."* She paused, her face twisting with reluctant admiration. *"I hate how great he is."*

I laughed, still weepy. *"Yeah, me too."*

"And his ass better stay that way," she said matter-of-factly, pointing at me with narrowed eyes. *"Because if he tries that shit with you..."* Her voice dipped, sharp with sisterly threat. *"I'll bury him in a place where no one will ever find him. He won't survive this time, GG."*

I smiled lightly, sighing in acceptance. *Duly noted. "And I'll bring the shovels."*

Seeing past what Charlie and I did couldn't have been easy for her. We didn't just cross a line. We trespassed. We betrayed. And yet, there she was, standing by me anyway. *I love you, Luci.*

"No more secrets, okay?"

"No more secrets."

There was a soul-deep relief in knowing I'd no longer have anything else to hide from her—my sister, my *ride or die*, my closest friend. She stuck around a little while longer, helping me decide what to wear tonight. I needed the distraction just as much as I needed a second opinion. After a few duds, I modeled the floral dress, spinning around, showing off how it kissed my curves.

"That's the one," Luci crowed, her tone playful. *"Charlie better know how lucky he is."*

I only smiled in response, thinking, *I'm the lucky one.*

Luci's tone shifted after that. More cautious. *"Do they know that you were... his mistress?"* The awkward word hung between us like smoke. Ugly and accurate. Still, I appreciated her attempt to tread carefully on such delicate matters. On her care in how she said it.

"His mom and his brother know," I replied, the knot in my stomach returning with a vengeance. *"I'm not sure about anyone else."*

With the dress decided, Luci offered a final dose of wisdom before she left.

"Take tonight as it comes—don't overthink it."

Now, standing alone before this mirror with my hair and makeup done, I'm already struggling to heed her advice. My nerves are alive and whispering. Family dynamics are tricky, and rumors can spread like wildfire. The side eyes, the whispers, and the judgment that comes with being *her—the other woman*. I've told myself I can handle it, but it doesn't stop the knot in my stomach from tightening by the second.

A buzz from my phone breaks the spiral. A text message.

Charlie.

Be there in 5—followed by a heart emoji.

I take one last look at myself in the mirror, feeling the anxiety of the night ahead coil in my chest. With a deep breath, I slip into my heels, grab my bag, and head for the door. My chest still tight, but my spine straight. The nerves are still there, but I know I can't turn back now. Tonight, it's my turn to meet his family, and I can only hope for the best.

The venue is a swanky supper club with plush velvet seating that oozes decadence. The air feels alive with the smooth rhythm of soulful beats, rich and mellow. Each note vibrates with a steady groove, filling the space with a laid-back yet magnetic energy that competes with the laughter of its stylishly well-dressed guests. Waiters glide through the crowd, trays of hors d'oeuvres balanced effortlessly, while colorful lights dance across the walls like reflections of the mood.

As we step deeper into the room, I sneak a glance at Charlie, and a smile tugs at my lips. He looks incredible tonight—his navy blue suit, sharp and impeccably tailored, the black turtleneck beneath adding a sleek, modern touch, while the fuchsia paisley pocket square, tucked neatly into his jacket, coordinates perfectly with the flowers of my dress. It's as if we planned to complement each other.

In most ways, we do.

"Ready?" he asks.

I nod, even as my heart flutters in my chest. I can already feel eyes on us, hear the whispers tucked beneath the bassline. But Charlie takes my hand, and somehow, everything feels a little more manageable. I admire how he carries himself—quiet, but commanding. Like presence alone is a language, and his speaks volumes.

"There they are," he says, leading me through the crowd toward his brother Jack and the beautiful woman beside him. When we reach them, Charlie wraps his arms around Jack in a tight, brotherly embrace, clapping him on the back. "Happy birthday, bro!"

"Thanks, Charlie." Jack's smile is contagious, his energy as kind and easy-going as his younger brother's. The woman at his side is elegance incarnate in a sleek, black dress.

Charlie slips an arm around me as he introduces us. "Jack, Aries, this is Gloria."

"Finally!" Jack exclaims, pulling me into a warm hug. "Great to meet you, Gloria."

Aries follows suit, her eyes soft as she embraces me. "Your dress is stunning," she adds sincerely, and I feel a little of the tension in my shoulders release.

"Thank you," I say with a gracious smile. Despite their warm welcome, nerves still hum beneath the surface. After a few minutes of light conversation, we make our way over to the bar. The bartender greets us with a polished smile, offering a list of signature drinks. Charlie orders for us—two sparkling cocktails that seem to glow under the hypnotic lighting. I take a sip, letting the bubbles calm me, just as Charlie's arm grazes mine. Before I can sink into the moment, his gaze shifts over my shoulder.

"I'll be right back," he says, flashing me a quick smile before disappearing into the crowd.

Curious, I turn and spot him returning moments later with a beautiful older woman on his arm. She's poised and regal, her jet black pixie cut neatly styled, presence commanding. *Just like Charlie.* I don't need an introduction to know. This is his mother.

Breathe, Gloria.

"Mom," Charlie beams, his smile wide and proud. "This is Gloria."

I extend my hand, keeping my composure. "Ms. Bensley, it's a pleasure to meet you."

Rather than accept my hand, her response is a tight-lipped smile, perhaps an attempt to distract from the contempt in her eyes. "You're quite beautiful," she says after a heavy beat. "I can see why Charles is so mesmerized by you."

I blink, unsure of how to respond. The words sound like a compliment, but land like a slap. I know a jab when I hear one. My stomach tightens as I force a polite smile. "Thank you?"

Her gaze lingers, dissecting me, and the meaning is clear. She thinks this is all physical for him, that I'm just some fleeting attraction. Her disapproval is palpable, and I'm left wondering if she'll ever see me as anything more than her son's—mistress.

"Mom?" Charlie says, picking up on the underhanded comment.

She looks at him, her expression unreadable. "You two enjoy your evening."

As she turns and walks away, Charlie's brow furrows, a mix of disappointment and defeat across his features. He turns to me, voice low. "I'm sorry."

"Don't be," I say, placing a reassuring hand on his arm. "It's fine."

He shakes his head, exhaling slowly. His frustration is evident as he brings his glass to his lips and gulps down its contents. We find an unoccupied highboy table in a quiet corner where we can watch the party unfold.

"Sit tight," he says. "I'll grab us some hors d'oeuvres."

"Great idea," I say with a smile, my stomach rumbling at the thought of food. Today's anticipation left me without an appetite, and now that I'm here, I'm absolutely starving.

Just as Charlie steps away, Aries sidles up to the table, her warm smile instantly disarming me. "Hey, I just wanted to check in on you," she says, leaning casually against the highboy table. "I saw that little exchange with Mona. Meeting the family can be... challenging."

"Thank you," I say, grateful for her kindness. "Yeah... just a little."

Aries nods knowingly. "I get it. When Jack first brought me home to meet their mom, she wasn't exactly thrilled then either." Her eyes twinkle with humor. "Granted, I was three months pregnant at the time. Can you imagine the look on her face?"

My jaw drops, genuinely surprised. "How did she react?"

"Oh, she was furious," Aries says with a laugh, shaking her head at the memory. "I thought she was going to have a heart attack right there at the dinner table. Let's just say it made for a very memorable Thanksgiving."

I laugh along, imagining the chaos unfolding over the cranberry sauce. "Sounds intense."

"It was," she agrees. "But she came around—eventually. Once she realized I wasn't going anywhere, and that I loved Jack. It got better. Just takes time."

Her words offer a comforting perspective. "Thanks, Aries. That really helps."

She gives my hand a reassuring squeeze. "Anytime. You're doing great."

Just then, Charlie returns with sustenance, a plate of mini crab cakes and bruschetta. He flashes a grin at us. "What'd I miss?"

"Just girl talk," Aries replies with a wink as she departs.

With Aries' encouragement, the night continues on a more joyful note. I meet more of Charlie's relatives, each one welcoming me with smiles and conversation. We dance the night away, the DJ spinning hit after hit, only pausing briefly to lead the room in singing "Happy

Birthday" to Jack. Laughter and cheers fill the air, and when the music picks back up, everyone rushes back to the dance floor.

As the DJ slows it down, Charlie pulls me close, his arms wrapping around me securely. He leans in and starts to sing the lyrics:

"I... I'm so in love with you.

Whatever you want to do,

Is alright with me..."

I feel light as a feather, floating on the melody.

"You make me feel so brand new.

And I... want to spend my life with you."

We dance until my feet ache. After all the tension of tonight, I'm still reminded of the feeling of being in the best place in the world—his arms. He gazes down at me, his eyes shining with sincerity. "I'm really happy you came tonight."

"Me too. I just hope your mom can one day see me as more than... you know."

"She will," he assures me, gently tilting my chin up for a kiss that sends butterflies aflutter. "Let's go home."

I swing by the ladies room before we depart. Standing at the mirror, I thumb open a text from Luci—*How's it going? Which shoe did you decide to go with?*

I smile to myself, grateful for her support. Before I can type up a response, a toilet flushes, and the stall door creaks open.

Mona.

She strides to the sink, her stark presence consumes the space. Her reflection meets mine briefly before she speaks.

"It's clear you've forgotten your place," she says, lathering her hands under the running water. "It's certainly not on my son's arm, out in public." Heat crawls up my neck, but I refuse to let it show.

Relentless, she continues, her voice dripping with disdain. "The audacity of you—standing by his side like you're... significant." She shakes water from her hands into the sink, splattering droplets onto the polished countertop before reaching for a napkin. "See, it's women like you that make it easy for men like my son—good men—to lose their way. You swoop in like a fantasy with your promises of escape, of excitement. Dangling temptation in front of them, and they fall for it because it's easy."

Easy? The word echoes bitterly in my mind.

But Mona isn't through with me yet. "Do you have any idea what it's like to build a life with someone? To invest years into a marriage, into a family, only to have some... *woman* waltz in and think that she can fill your shoes?" Her words slice through me, each one a cruel distortion of the reality I'm entangled in. "You don't belong here," she states, her tone as sharp as the edge of a knife. "You're his mistress. You don't get a promotion just because his wife died. Rachel's gone, but as far as I'm concerned, that's all you'll ever be." There's something truly mournful in her voice when she says, "And my son is a fool to believe that he can replace what he's lost with someone like you."

Someone like me.

With that, she tosses her used napkin in the trash bin, as if discarding something unworthy. The door swings shut behind her, and I'm left staring at my flushed reflection, grappling with the weight of her words. It's easy to stand here and allow myself to feel defeated. Her words sting like acid on an open wound. Her point is clear, and her pain—undeniable. Both are valid.

But that doesn't mean what Charlie and I have isn't real.

I close my eyes, trying to block out the crushing weight of guilt and doubt, desperately seeking any semblance of comfort. And then, in the thick fog of my mind, I see Charlie's eyes—steady and warm. Then, his smile, that gentle curve that always seems to center me even in my darkest moments.

Before we left D.C., Evelyn pulled me aside.

"Make peace with your mistakes," she advised, holding my hand in both of hers. *"Some will be determined to never let you forget them. You have to hold fast to your love."*

Get it together, Gloria, I tell myself, standing a little straighter. *The man you love—the man who loves you—is waiting.*

Exiting the restroom, I immediately spot Charlie, waiting for me. His brow is furrowed, frustration etched across his face. His jaw ticks as he asks, "Did she say something to you?"

He must have seen Mona walk out. I shake my head, trying to force a smile, to assure him everything's fine. But the effort feels heavy—*hollow.*

"Babe?" he insists, his hand cupping my cheek. The compassion in his touch instantly melts away the worthlessness I'd felt so deep in my bones just moments ago. Still, a stormy conflict remains, roiling beneath my unspoken words.

Instead, I slip my hand in his and quiet the tempest inside. "You ready?"

He's not convinced, but that's alright. I'm content to let that dreadful conversation stay behind that door forever. What good would it do, telling Charlie that his mother had verbally torn me to shreds?

No good at all.

December

Fifteen

INTERLUDE

CHARLIE

The lock on Gloria's front door disengages, dislodging the memory from not so long ago. There was a time when I could only imagine what it would feel like—reaching into my pocket, pulling out my very own key, and unlocking this door. It seemed so impossible then, like a dream just out of reach. And now... here I am. *Destiny fulfilled.*

I drop the key in the bowl by the door right next to hers, calling out, "Babe?"

"Hey, I'll be out in a minute!" she sings from the bedroom.

"Need some help?" I ask, knowing full well she doesn't.

"Tempting!" she chimes, a playful lilt in her voice. "But no, Charlie, your kind of help will most certainly make us late."

I chuckle to myself. *She's right.*

Standing in front of Gloria's Christmas tree, hands in my pockets, I can't help but admire the beautifully painted spectacle. It's a true work of art, from the intricately designed ornaments to the twinkling lights to the perfect balance of colors. I can't stop myself from reminiscing about last year, the night we trimmed the tree together. We laughed, sang, danced—it was the kind of night you want to freeze in time. A night I'll cherish forever. That night, I realized my life would never be the same, that this—*she*—was what I'd been missing.

My eyes land on the novelty ornament I gave her last year. The gold interlocking C & G shines like a beacon, hung high and center—a place of honor. *Damn.* I hate that I missed decorating with her this year. Work's been relentless, and I've been called to scenes day and night, working cases around the clock. It feels like I've been in a constant blur, but standing here, I feel grounded again.

"How do I look?"

Her pillowy soft voice pulls me from my thoughts. I turn on my heel—and stop breathing.

She's radiant. Her beauty stealing the air from my lungs. The silk of her dress clings to her like a second skin, deep green that catches the light with every step. The neckline dips just enough to tease, while the fabric falls in soft waves over her curves like brushstrokes brought to life. She's a masterpiece standing in front of me, bold and effortless all at once.

But it's not just the dress. It's the way she looks at me—that familiar spark in her eyes... that reminds me all over again why I fell for her. She's more than beautiful—*she's everything.*

It turns out that I will be speechless more than once tonight. Less than an hour later, I find myself standing in awe before a portrait of Gloria—the one I painted all those months ago. But here, under the intentional lights of the gallery, it feels like I'm seeing it for the first time. I had no idea that she planned to use it in the show. Her coy words play at the back of my mind...

"Only if you'll be my featured artist."

A breathless laugh escapes me. *She wasn't kidding.*

The portrait looks different now—better, more vibrant. She's added color to the background, transforming it into a stained-glass window that frames her visage. The painting feels more alive now that it's a collaboration.

Jack walks up from behind, nodding in appreciation. "That's dope," he says, leaning in to squint at the placard. "Anonymous."

I smile, my eyes drawn to the faint, interlocking initials *C* and *G* that she's tucked into the bottom right corner. It's subtle, but certainly there—only for me to recognize, I presume.

"She's an attorney, right?" Jack asks, pulling me back to the present.

"Yep. But as you can see, she's got a profound love for art."

We both turn to survey the gallery, the energy of the event buzzing all around us. The space is alive with activity—people mingling and admiring the carefully curated artwork, their thoughtful conversations blending with the soft underscoring by local musicians.

Jack nods, taking a sip from his drink. "She's really pulling this off. It's a great event."

"Yeah, she is. She's been working on this for months."

Gloria moves gracefully through the room, effortlessly shifting from guest to guest, her face glowing with excitement. Her radiance is electric here, illuminating the room like a source of light herself and captivating me entirely. She's always been impressive but seeing her like this, completely in her element, hosting and showcasing the artists' work with such elegance… I didn't think my already fathomless admiration of her could go any deeper.

Gloria catches my eye from across the room and smiles—a bright, genuine smile that lights up my heart with pride. I return the gesture with a wink, watching as she expertly guides another guest toward a painting.

Some of our closest friends and family came out to show support. Ms. Judy busies herself at the refreshments table, talking animatedly with another guest as they load their plates with tapas. Across the room, Jonas settles into a seat next to a charming stranger, striking up a conversation. Standing before a series of sculptures, Luci, Peter, and Aries appear to be getting along very well, laughing and chatting amiably. It's nice to see them bonding, especially after being introduced less than an hour ago. It feels good, bringing our families together like this.

It feels right.

"Hey, how are things going with her sister?" Jack asks, following my gaze. "Good people, by the way."

"Yeah, they are," I reply. "We're in a good place." I'd already briefed Jack on the misadventures of D.C., so he's well aware of my drive to prove myself. "But just when I feel like I'm climbing out of one hole, it's like I'm digging myself into another."

Jack's brows furrow. "What do you mean?"

I sigh. "Mom." The one word acts as an all-encompassing explanation. I can imagine how hard it must be for my mother to see past what Gloria was to me before—my paramour—but she's so much more than that. *Always has been.* My most recent phone call with her had been especially difficult. "She thinks I should break it off with Gloria and… date someone else. Her exact words: '*Anyone* else.'"

Jack sighs deeply, taking it in. "Fuck that."

We both laugh, but it's a knowing, exhausted kind of laugh—a laugh we've earned from years of navigating our mother's resentments.

"Mom means well and all," he says, "but this is your life, and that's your woman. She just has to respect that."

I nod, grateful for his support.

"Hell, you took two bullets for her," he adds with a grin. "This shit better work out!"

I bark out a laugh. "I know, right?"

"She's been good for you, bro. Anyone can see that. And Aries and I—we're rooting for you two." He raises his beer in a toast. We clink our drinks together before making our way over to the collective's camaraderie.

When Gloria joins, I seize the opportunity to steal her away, even if only for a moment.

"How do you feel?" I ask, my pride unmistakable.

She beams at me, eyes wide with glee. "It feels like a dream. Is this really happening?"

"It's really happening, babe," I say, tugging her closer. "I'm so proud of you. We all are." I brush aside a few loose curls from her cheeks, cupping her face as I drop a soft kiss on her head. "And—I bet your mom is peacock-proud right now too."

"You think so?" she asks, her voice full of hope.

"Oh, yeah."

She looks around the room, drinking in the night. A grateful sigh passes between her perfect lips. "I never would have done this without your encouragement. Thank you, Charlie."

Just before I can lean in to kiss her, my gaze snags on two familiar faces over Gloria's shoulder. Graham and Kenya weave through the crowd toward us with wide, impressed smiles. As they approach, I can't help but feel incredibly grateful for this night—for the chance to stand beside Gloria and witness her success—for the way the art community has rallied around her. And most of all, I'm grateful for the support of our friends and family.

Our friends. Our family.

CHARLIE

Far from the elegance of the art show, life at the Bensley house has been a back-to-back takeout meal kind of affair. Tonight, the kitchen smells like pizza, and the boys are already perched on their stools at the island, chatting away like they always do. I catch snippets of their conversation as I move around the counter, setting plates down in front of them.

"I heard it's Marvel-themed this year," CJ says, leaning toward a wide-eyed Cameron.

"For Real!?" Cameron practically bounces up and down in his seat. "You think Spider-Man's gonna dress up as Santa? And maybe the Avengers will be elves?"

CJ snorts, and soon they're both cracking up, their excitement bubbling over. I smile with them, walking over with the pizza box in hand. I set it down on the island and let them dive in.

"What are you two talking about?"

"The holiday windows!" CJ chirps, grabbing a slice. "We're going this year, right?"

The holiday windows. Every year, downtown Argale transforms with all sorts of festive displays in shop windows—some traditional, some wild and creative, and some with themes from books and movies. The boys look forward to it every year; it's become our own little holiday tradition.

"Of course we're going."

Cam looks worried for a second. "But what if you get called into work?"

"Well," I say, pretending to think it over, "let's just hope the criminals take a day off. Otherwise, I can always ask Sienna to take you guys. You wouldn't mind that, right, CJ?"

CJ freezes mid-bite, and I catch the faintest blush creeping up his cheeks. Cam notices too, a toothy grin spreading across his face.

"I think CJ looooves Sienna," Cam sing-songs.

CJ bursts into laughter, pizza flying out of his mouth, and before long, we're all laughing.

But then, as kids do, Cam shifts gears on me with a question I wasn't entirely prepared for. "Dad, do you still love Mom?"

The laughter dies down, and for a second, the only sound is our chewing.

"First of all, Cam, don't talk with food in your mouth."

"Sorry," he mumbles.

"And, yeah. I'll always love your mom."

He nods thoughtfully before firing off another. "Are you gonna get a new wife?"

I pause, glancing over at CJ, who's watching me carefully, like he's reading my face for the answer before I even say it. "Well... that depends," I say, stalling for a second. *What can I say in this situation?*

"On what?" CJ asks, his tone a little more skeptical.

"On if wives go on sale at Macy's," I say with a cheeky grin.

Cam giggles, wiping his hands on his napkin. "Dad!"

"What?" I chuckle. "Wives are expensive, son. I never told you two that?"

"You can't get a wife at a store!"

I raise an eyebrow. "Oh? Where do you find one, then?"

He shrugs, clueless, but CJ's still watching me, his curiosity piqued. My eldest asks, "Where'd you meet Mom?"

"In college," I say, smiling at the memory. "We met in college."

Cam, always the thinker, jumps in again. "Dad, I think you have to ask someone out on a date first. You know, before you get married."

I laugh, shaking my head. "And how do you know all of this, Cameron?"

He shrugs again, pretending to be innocent.

"So, I need to ask someone out on a date first, huh?" I ask, playing along.

"Yep," he says confidently, nodding like he's some kind of expert. "Sean's dad has a girlfriend, right, CJ? Maybe you can ask him where to find one."

CJ's best friend Sean has been a constant in his life, supporting him through the tough times after Rachel passed away. Recently, Sean's dad, who has been divorced for a while, introduced his new girlfriend to Sean. I've been wondering how that went.

CJ huffs a lighthearted sigh, shaking his head at his brother. "Cam, that's not how it works."

I snicker. "No worries, Cam. I'm sure that I can figure it out. And maybe you guys can come with me—help me out."

Both boys stare at me like I've just said the weirdest thing in the world.

"What?" I ask, keeping a straight face. "You know, to let me know what you think. You can be my wingmen."

CJ looks confused. "What are *wingmen*?"

"Someone that looks out for you. Someone who's got your back."

"Like The Avengers?" Cam gasps.

"Exactly."

CJ narrows his eyes at me, still processing. "You want us to go on a date with you?"

"Sure, why not?" I lean back against the counter, acting casual. "We're a package deal, right?"

Cam nods eagerly. "Right!"

CJ doesn't say anything at first, but I can see the wheels turning in his head. He's still not sure how to feel about all this, but at least he's not shutting it down completely. *Progress.*

"Alright, you two clean up," I say, stretching my arms over my head, ready to head upstairs. "I've got some work to finish."

Halfway up, I overhear Cam whisper to CJ, "Do you think Dad might like Miss Ledwell, my math teacher? She's pretty, and I might get a better grade in math if he did."

"Cam!" CJ groans, exasperated by his little brother's innocent antics.

I chuckle under my breath as I climb the rest of the way, shaking my head at their conversation. As many times as I've imagined introducing them to Gloria, I never thought they'd be so open to the idea of me dating again. It makes me pause for a second, wondering if it's too soon, if they're ready... *if I'm ready.*

Maybe it's time to find out.

GLORIA

Christmastime. My favorite time of year.

The air is crisp with that early December chill, and the downtown streets of Argale are alive with the bustle of families bundled up in their winter-wear, strolling hand-in-hand as they take in the festive window displays. It's almost magical, but my stomach twists with nerves. It's half-excitement and half-anxiety, wholly making a mess of me.

Is it too soon? Am I ready?

Ready or not, I spot Charlie and the boys up ahead before they see me. CJ and Cameron are standing side by side, captivated by a window display. Charlie hovers protectively behind them, hands in his pockets, looking after them in that familiar, steady way of his.

I catch a glimpse of myself in a nearby window, wondering if I look as flustered as I feel. My heart races, unsure how to make sense of all my emotions—excited to finally meet the boys, anxious for their approval, overwhelmed by the pressure of it all. Meeting Charlie's boys for the first time feels monumental, a step that once seemed impossible when I'd resigned myself to being nothing more than his secret.

Last year, I walked down this very street, watching families stroll by, but one family stood out—a man with his sons. I remember daydreaming about the bond Charlie might have with his own boys, imagining what it must feel like to be a part of that closeness.

And, here I am—about to meet the two most important people in Charlie's life, about to step into that once-imagined scene. But now, it's real.

Oh, God. It's real.

I still can't fully grasp everything that's happened—that Mr. Old-Fashioned and I are something more. And that more keeps evolving into something that excites, grounds, and inspires but also terrifies me.

Breathe, Gloria.

What if they don't like me? What if they take one look at me and decide that this is a waste of time because no one could ever compare to their mother? It wouldn't be surprising, and honestly, I wouldn't blame them. I'd understand. I'd never be so bold as to try to take their mother's place. The force of my panic threatens to blow me away entirely, and for a second, I contemplate escape. I thought I was anchored the other night at Jack's party, but Mona's brutal blows knocked the wind out of me.

How will I handle a rejection from the boys?

But then Charlie glances over his shoulder. The moment his eyes find mine, everything softens. His expression is warm and reassuring, chasing away my mounting anxieties. I offer a tentative smile and wave, taking a deep breath as I close the distance between us.

"Hey," Charlie says as I approach, reaching out awkwardly to pull me into a hug. It's the kind of embrace that feels performative, like we're both hyper-aware of the significance of this moment. We hold each other, but there's an air of formality—like this is the first time we're meeting again in a different context, trying to navigate what this all means.

"Hi," I practically whisper.

"Ay," Charlie calls out to the boys, drawing their attention away from the window display. "This is... Gloria." He hesitates for just a second, glancing at me before continuing. "Gloria, these are my sons, CJ and Cameron."

Cameron, the younger one, beams up at me with adorably curious eyes. He's got that unfiltered enthusiasm that only kids have. "Hi, Gloria!" he says, bouncing on his toes a little before raising his fist for a bump.

I grin, meeting his fist with mine. "Hi, Cameron! It's nice to meet you."

CJ, on the other hand, is more reserved. He steps forward and offers his gloved hand for a polite handshake, his expression thoughtful but guarded. There's a maturity in his eyes that makes me instantly aware of just how significant this is for him. I meet his gaze, feeling a flicker of understanding between us.

"Hi, CJ," I say, shaking his hand. "It's really nice to meet you too."

He gives a small nod, studying me for a beat longer before stepping back. His behavior isn't cold like his grandmother's was. It's more like he's watching, observing, taking it all in. His demeanor reminds me a bit of how Luci and I felt when we met Evelyn for the first time—curious, but cautious.

Charlie's smile says it all—*It's going well.*

Looking at his boys, I can't help but reflect on how much has changed. For a long time I thought moments like this were out of reach, but now here we are, standing together under the holiday lights of Argale. Meeting them feels like a bridge between two parts of my life—the secret and the open. This is the future I never imagined I could have. These days, it's exactly what I've begun to long for, even if it's complicated.

"It's really nice to meet you both," I say again, meaning every word.

We stroll down Main Street together, the boys darting ahead to examine each new display. They are completely absorbed by the scenes unfolding behind the glass, every window more elaborate than the last—skating penguins, nutcracker ballet scenes, snow-covered castles. I try to relax, to take it all in—the lights, the festive cheer, and the way the boys are buzzing with excitement—but I can't shake the awareness of what this moment means. *A new level.*

Charlie and I keep our conversation light, chatting about the decorations, the music, and how the businesses seem to outdo themselves every year.

"You look nervous," he finally says, breaking the ice.

"I am nervous," I admit, smiling faintly. "Kids are so... intuitive. They can detect evil."

Charlie laughs under his breath. "But you're not evil. A little naughty at times," he adds with a playful grin, "but definitely not evil."

I laugh, a bit of the discomfort shaking loose. We follow the boys, stealing quiet moments to talk, but mostly just enjoying being in each other's presence. It feels surreal, being out in the open with Charlie and his boys, even if we're pretending this is the beginning of something new.

In a way, it is.

Suddenly, Cam beckons us over. We approach a storefront window featuring elves on skateboards, weaving around a snowy landscape. His sweet face lights up. "Dad, do you think elves really know how to skateboard?"

I glance at Charlie, just as curious about his answer as Cam is.

"I'm sure they do," Charlie insists. "But I'd think they'd be even better at snowboarding, with all the snow at the North Pole." He looks at me, drawing me into the conversation.

"Oh, definitely," I chime in with as confident a smile as I can muster.

Soon we arrive at a quaint little café trimmed in bistro lights and a nearly life-sized gingerbread house in the window. A sign out front advertises hot chocolate.

Charlie turns to me with a boyish smile. "Want to grab some?"

"Absolutely."

"Ay!" He calls out to the boys again, who are a few windows down. Once they scamper back to us, Charlie shepherds us all inside the warm and cozy café. The rich scent of cocoa and peppermint permeates the air, creating a perfect retreat from the bustling world outside. The boys rush to the counter to place their orders, their energy contagious. Charlie and I hang back, watching them with quiet admiration.

"This is nice," I say softly, leaning closer to him. "They're amazing, Charlie."

He glances at me with a gentle grin. "Thank you."

I nudge him. "That Cam's quite charming, kinda like someone I know..."

Charlie blushes, a faint holiday glow reflecting in his eyes as he nudges me right back. Once we're suitably stocked with steaming cocoa and more flavored marshmallows than sense, we settle into a cozy corner by the window. A fireplace crackles nearby, and the lights outside flicker in perfect rhythm. It's as if we've stepped out of real life and into a holiday postcard.

As we sip our hot chocolate, Cam excitedly launches into a conversation about superheroes. His words tumble out with enthusiasm as he describes a whimsical holiday window display where the Avengers band together to save Christmas from an evil villain.

"That sounds amazing," I say, leaning in with a smile. "And did the Avengers save Christmas?"

"Of course!" he exclaims, his grin wide beneath a cocoa mustache.

Meanwhile, CJ takes a quiet sip of his drink. The more reserved of the two, he listens to Cam's speech before adding his own thoughts. "I liked the Christmas Village with the train. It looked exactly like Argale. I could even see our school."

"Really? I bet it was beautiful. Christmas villages are such a holiday classic. I really like them too."

Our conversation flows easily enough, but I can sense that CJ is still holding back, unsure about me. His guardedness isn't hostile, but I know I have to earn his trust. Even so, he's engaging—and for that, I'm grateful.

"So," I ask, shifting the topic, "have you guys seen the big Christmas tree yet?"

"Not yet," Charlie replies.

Cam's eyes immediately light up with excitement. "Can we?"

Charlie turns to CJ. "What do you think, CJ? Wanna go see the tree?"

CJ shrugs. "Sure."

Charlie stands and helps me into my coat, his touch warm as he holds the garment open for me. I slip my arms into the sleeves and smile up at him in thanks. As CJ pulls on his own coat, I notice his expression soften just a little.

"Gloria," CJ says unexpectedly, "did you know this year's tree is a tech tree? It's lit by fiber optics. It can change colors—like, every day if they want."

"How creative," I muse, intrigued by the blend of tradition and technology. "I love to see artists exploring that intersection where art and tech collide to create something truly magical."

CJ's eyes flicker with interest at my response, and for the first time, I see a small spark of connection between us. The moment feels significant, as if this simple conversation about a Christmas tree is a small step toward something bigger.

Outside, the tree towers in the distance. *Unlit.* According to a passerby, it won't illuminate until the festival. Still, we stand beneath its magnificent height, admiring the sight. It's like gazing at a blank canvas and the colors that sit waiting, knowing that you have the makings of something truly special—something beautiful.

Patience, I whisper to its grandeur and to my heart as I glance between the unlit Christmas tree and the three Bensley boys beside me. No, it's not hard to imagine how beautiful it will be—*this will be.*

In its time.

CHARLIE

I never could have imagined how well CJ and Cam would take to Gloria. It's only been a few weeks, but I feel like they've made a solid connection with her, each in their own way. I feared that it was still too soon, that introducing someone new into their lives after everything we've been through might unsettle our delicate balance.

But instead, they've enjoyed her. Seeing how naturally Gloria fits into the equation makes me think that maybe—*just maybe*—this could work.

After our initial outing to view the holiday windows, the four of us met up a few more times. We built gingerbread houses at the children's museum, ice skated around the newly lit tech tree at the roundabout, and even checked out the illumination trail at the Argale Botanical Garden. Stepping into the massive glass conservatory felt like stepping onto the set of a holiday movie. Glowing evergreens lined the winding path of the garden, their rich greens contrasting with the deep reds of the poinsettias while ice sculptures sparkled under twinkling lights. *Festive.* And the unabashed amazement on the boys' faces—priceless.

Gloria was beautiful, even more than usual with festive cheer coloring her cheeks. Strolling beside her through a tunnel of lights with carolers harmonizing in the background was overwhelmingly romantic. Not to mention the pesky mistletoe hanging in every single doorway—taunting me. It took everything in me not to scoop her into my arms, kiss her, and tell her how much I love her, how much all of this means to me. At one point, I even had to resist dropping down on one knee and convincing her to marry me right then and there. Needless to say, both the enchanting scene and "Carol of the Bells" were stuck in my head for days afterward.

We've kept things pretty platonic-looking for the boys' sake, careful not to rush into anything that might make them uncomfortable. We're mindful of how we act around them—no hand-holding, no lingering looks—just keeping it light and casual. But there are moments when all I want to do is reach for her hand, pull her closer, and let them see what she really means to me. Show them—*this is what love looks like.* Still, I know we have to take it slow, give the boys time to adjust and make sure they feel secure in this new dynamic before we take that step.

Today's adventure brings us to the trampoline park. It's hard to focus on the festive decor when all I see is chaos—kids bouncing in every which direction.

"Ready?" Gloria asks from the sideline of the dodgeball court, her eyes sparkling with that playfully competitive edge I love as she pulls her hair into a quick ponytail.

I smirk. "You don't want none of this, babe."

"Yeah, we'll see, Coach B," she teases, giving me a playful shove before stepping onto the trampolines. I watch as she bounces over to the boys, sexy as hell in her twist-knot t-shirt and yoga pants that cling to her round, supple ass almost as closely as—*Charlie, focus.* I shake my head, trying to snap out of it. There has got to be some kind of penalty for this. *Unsportsmanlike conduct for being so damn distracting.* I chuckle at the thought. She's effortlessly stealing my attention, and honestly, I don't even mind.

It's a losing battle, and I know it.

The trampolines are sprinkled with fake snowflakes that spring up with each bounce, adding to the wintery atmosphere. The dodgeballs are large and white, designed to look like oversized snowballs—perfect for launching across the court in playful battles.

Still a big kid at heart, I playfully dart out to join my crew. Other jumpers break into teams, and Cam is already calling dibs.

"Dad, come on, you're with me!" he shouts.

CJ and Gloria take the opposite side, game faces on as we prepare to face off. Cam is amped, ready to throw dodgeballs at anything that moves. CJ, on the other hand, is more calculated—his eyes sharp, scanning for weak spots in our defense, strategizing.

Gloria and I lock eyes. She cracks a smile, and I shoot her a wink just as the buzzer sounds—*game on.*

Before I can react, CJ fires the first shot—a fastball aimed directly at me. I dodge it, barely, the ball ricocheting off the net behind me.

I flash him an impressed grin, adrenaline kicking in. "Nice try!"

Cam flings a ball at Gloria, but it flies wide, missing her by a mile. He's unfazed. His grin could power the court.

"I'm coming for you, G," I say, grabbing a loose ball, hopping up and down to find my rhythm. I take aim and throw it at Gloria, but she twists away, laughing as she narrowly avoids getting hit. The ball whizzes past her just as CJ lobs another one at me.

A combo? *Impressive.* I have to admit, babe's got skills—I underestimated her. Never again. Gloria waves her index finger like Dikembe Mutombo, grinning.

"That's a cute little team y'all got over there!" I shout playfully. "Come on, Cam, we've got to step it up!" My youngest slaps my waiting palm, ready to take them down. He laughs as he ducks under a shot, his energy contagious, and we throw ourselves into the game, dodging, bouncing, and launching dodgeballs. The whole court is alive with the thrill of it.

Gloria fires a ball that barely grazes Cam's side. He throws his hands up dramatically, falling to his dodgeball "death."

"You got me!" he groans, dropping flat onto the trampoline in exaggerated defeat. I can't help but laugh at his theatrics. "Look, Dad, I'm making a snow angel," he says, flapping his arms and legs in the fake snow before he scurries to the side, sitting just out of bounds to watch what's left of the game.

This boy.

Without Cam, it's a showdown between me, Gloria, and CJ—the last three standing. I can see the determination in CJ's eyes. I make a move, trying to bounce closer, and that's when CJ sees his opportunity. With a quick, calculated throw, his dodgeball hurtles toward me. I leap, trying to dodge it, but he's too fast—I'm hit.

"Whyyy!" I howl in mock agony, channeling my inner Cam, dropping to my knees before collapsing dramatically onto the mat. The soft layer of fake snow puffs up around me, and I just lie there for a second, laughing at myself. *Game over.*

When I look up, CJ's face is bright with a victorious grin. He's taken down his old man and clearly feels pretty damn good about it.

Gloria laughs at my dramatics and raises her hand for a high-five. "Nice one, CJ."

He returns the gesture with a quick slap of her palm.

Gloria's already heading my way, a grin lighting up her face as she leans down, offering me a hand. "Officer down?" she teases, her voice full of playful concern.

I reach up, grabbing her hand with a smirk. Before she can react, I tug her down, and she lands softly on top of me, her laughter mixing with mine. The snowball dodgeballs roll around us as we bounce slightly from the force of our fall, but all I can focus on is her—her eyes sparkling with amusement, her breath labored from the game, and the way she's so close, our bodies tangled together in this spontaneous moment.

Our laughter fades, and for a second, we just lie there, looking at each other. The playful energy between us shifts, softens, and before I know it, we're inching closer, my hand still wrapped around hers. My other hand finds the small of her back, pulling her close as my eyes drift to her lips. The world around us fades, and it feels like it's just the two of us, suspended in this winter wonderland...

But then, out of the corner of my eye, I catch a glimpse of CJ. He's standing a few feet away, watching us with a stiff expression, his shoulders tense, eyes betraying the discomfort he's trying to hide. My joy dims, and I realize this moment—*our* moment—has a much larger impact than I realized.

Gloria must sense it too. She glances up, following my gaze, and the playful smile on her face fades the second she sees him. She shifts quickly, untangling herself as she presses off my chest and rises to her feet. The air becomes heavier. The moment—dissolved. And CJ's discomfort is unmistakable.

We've got to tread carefully.

I sit up, brushing the fake snow off my shirt, trying to shake off the awkwardness settling in. Gloria gives me a quick look—understanding, apologetic—and then turns her attention back to the boys. I push myself to my feet, forcing a smile.

"All right," I say, clapping my hands, doing my best to bring the levity back. "I want a rematch. You two are going down."

January

Sixteen

THE ECLIPSE

GLORIA

I could get used to this.

It's downright domestic, sitting in Charlie's kitchen, watching him stir the pot on the stove. Garlic and other savory spices seem to season the very air around us.

"Smells good," I say. "Can I help?"

Charlie glances over his shoulder, a playful smirk tugging at his lips. "No, you cannot. You're a guest."

I tilt my head, raising an eyebrow. "Am I?" I tease, knowing full well that I've spent more nights here than I can count. I've become quite familiar with every inch of this house—the cracks in the tile, the various creaks in the wooden floors, the way the sunlight hits the windows just right in the morning. The last thing I feel like is a guest. At least, not in the usual sense.

Charlie catches my meaning and shakes his head, grinning. "At least for tonight," he concedes. Then, almost as an afterthought, he adds, "Actually, there is something you can do. C'mere."

I round the counter, crossing to where he stands at the stove. He's stirring a pot of white chicken chili—always keeping my dietary choices in mind. He grabs a clean spoon, scoops up some chili, and blows gently on it before holding it out to me.

"Taste this," he prompts softly. "Let me know what you think."

I lean in, tasting the spoonful. The flavors explode on my tongue, warm and creamy and seasoned to perfection. "Mmm," I hum in approval. "Sensational."

He leans in, lips brushing mine—but I pull back just enough to glance around, scanning for the boys. *The coast is clear.* I steal a kiss, quick and sweet, before slipping back to the other side of the counter.

I don't want to push CJ any further, not after the other day at the trampoline park. The dodgeball game was fun, but I can't forget the way CJ looked when Charlie and I nearly kissed—uncomfortable, confused, maybe even a little disapproving. The array of unpleasant emotions that crossed his young face was a sobering reminder that we still need to be careful, to take it slow.

For their sakes.

When Charlie invited me over for dinner, I took it as a good sign, like we were still on the right track. As it stands, CJ doesn't seem to be distant or apprehensive, at least not any more than usual. I've enjoyed earning his admiration. I want to keep moving forward.

"Babe," Charlie says, pulling me from my thoughts. "The food's almost done. Can you grab the boys? They're playing video games."

"Sure."

Upstairs, I knock lightly on the doorframe of CJ's room. "Hey, guys. Dinner's ready."

Cameron jumps to his feet, easily abandoning the game. "I'm starving!" He rushes past me, the smell of good food drawing him downstairs.

CJ, on the other hand, takes his time, wordlessly powering off the game console. When I turn to follow his younger brother downstairs, his voice calls me back.

"Gloria?"

I turn. "Yeah?"

His eyes meet mine, uncertain, searching for something. "Did you know my dad when he was married to my mom?"

Panic flares up in my chest, constricting my throat. "Yes," I manage to say. "I did."

Where will this line of questioning lead?

His voice is timid. "Were you dating him then too?"

My heart pounds in my ears against the suffocating silence in the room. I don't know where to search, where to find the words to make this okay. I look around, as if the answer might be hiding somewhere in this room. "CJ, I don't think that—"

"Never mind," he cuts in. His voice is razor sharp, slicing deep, but beneath it is something more fragile. *He's hurting.* "Just so you know, my dad really loved my mom, and he'll never love anyone like he loved her again."

I feel—small. My heart fractures as my chest tightens. His words land like a hammer on our tenuous connection. I want to shrink into myself, to disappear from this conversation, but there's nowhere to go. His pain is so real, so raw, and I can feel the sharp edge of his resentment. It's well directed, after all... *I'm responsible.*

"No one can ever replace her," CJ continues, matter-of-fact. "Especially not you."

With that, he pushes past me and storms out, leaving me hollow and shaken.

Somehow, I find my legs and make my way downstairs, wearing my best attempt at normal. Dinner feels... strained. Nonetheless, Cameron chatters away, oblivious to it all. Charlie seems to notice CJ's withdrawn mood—quiet, barely touching his food—picking up on the awkwardness, despite my best efforts to hide it. Across the table, his eyes are full of quiet questions. He doesn't say anything, just asks with a concerned look: *Everything okay?*

I answer with a solemn smile, but it's a poor disguise for the turmoil I feel inside.

"Do you want to come?" Cam asks.

Lost in my thoughts, I'm not sure what I've even been invited to. "I'd love to, Cameron. Thank you," I say, catching CJ's slight eye roll. "But I have plans that day. Raincheck?"

Truth is, I don't have plans—I just can't bear to add to CJ's discomfort. I refuse to hurt him any more than I already have.

CHARLIE

Beep beep.

My watch chimes, reminding me of today's session with Dr. Solomon. I close my office door, take a steadying breath, and open my laptop, logging into the virtual meeting. I'm eager to discuss what happened the other night. After dinner, Gloria confided in me about her conversation with CJ—how he asked if she knew me while I was still married to Rachel. He confronted her, basically put her on the stand. She brushed off the impact it had on her, but I could see the hurt beneath her brave face, even if she wouldn't let herself admit it.

"Maybe I put too much on them too soon," I tell Dr. Solomon, my voice quieter than I'd intended. *How do I handle this?*

"Maybe," he says evenly.

I lean back in my chair, rubbing my temples. "I don't know. I thought we were doing okay. I thought the boys were adjusting. But now... I just don't know."

Doc nods. "It's a time of uncertainty for everyone. You're exploring a new relationship with Gloria while repairing a fractured one with your son. There's no easy way through that."

I sigh. "I just... I don't want them to feel like I'm trying to replace their mother. CJ—he made it pretty clear to Gloria that no one could. And I get that. I just don't know how to assure him that this—what I have with Gloria—isn't that."

"Instead of focusing on reassuring CJ that you're not trying to replace his mother, maybe it's more about reinforcing that his mother is irreplaceable. You can acknowledge how important she'll always be and explain that Gloria isn't here to take that role but rather to bring something new and supportive into their lives. Sometimes, when children feel their memories are safe, it's easier for them to accept change."

Makes sense.

But still, even as our session comes to a close, the questions linger, heavier than before. How do I help CJ? How do I guide all of us through this without causing more damage? Closing my laptop, I sink back into my chair, peering out the window at the cityscape, tracing the skyline as if the answers might be hidden there.

One step at a time, as Doc would say.

Step one: get back to work. The only upside to a full caseload is that it keeps my mind off my personal troubles. It lets me disconnect—if only for a little while.

I'm halfway down the hall carrying a load of laundry when I hear Cameron's voice drift through the cracked door of CJ's room.

"Do you think Dad's going to marry Gloria?" he asks.

I freeze, the basket in my arms suddenly feeling impossibly heavy. I hold my breath, waiting for CJ's response.

"No," CJ says flatly. *No hesitation.*

I swallow hard. I knew he had his doubts about her, but hearing it like this hits different.

"Why not?" Cam presses. "He likes her, I can tell. And I kinda like her too."

"You like everybody, Cameron," CJ mutters, his voice edged with frustration. "Dad still loves Mom."

My heart sinks. The laundry in my arms feels irrelevant now, like a burden I should've put down long ago. I lean against the wall, fighting the urge to walk in and interrupt.

"Then why does he act like that with Gloria?" Cam presses, undeterred.

"Like what?" CJ snaps, clearly defensive, like he knows where this is going but doesn't want to admit it.

"Like he *likes* her," Cam says. "Mom and Dad weren't like them."

A lump sits like lead in my throat. It's the kind of observation only a kid can make—blunt, honest, intuitive. He's seen the difference, the way things are between me and Gloria, how it doesn't mirror the life I had with Rachel. *The love I had with Rachel.*

"Look, I'm tired. I'm going to bed," CJ says finally, cutting the conversation short.

"But it's not even late," Cam protests, clearly confused by his brother's mood shift.

"Cam, will you go to your room, please?" His wavering voice breaks my heart.

"Okay, okay, geez..."

I hear footsteps, and for a second, I think the conversation is over. I'm about to move, maybe pretend I didn't hear any of it, but then CJ speaks again. "I'm sorry," his voice low and contrite. "I just miss Mom."

"I miss her too," Cam says, every word smaller than the last.

Their grief is heavy and fragile at the same time, filling the silence in a way that words never could. I stay rooted in place, holding still, bearing witness. I should have known better than to force my happiness onto them—to bypass their grieving process for the convenience of my relationship. They weren't ready.

Maybe none of us were.

CHARLIE

For the first time in weeks, a Saturday morning actually feels like a Saturday morning. There are no meetings, no calls, and no housekeeping errands to run that can't wait another day. With the boys still sleeping, the house is uncharacteristically quiet. I get up to refill my coffee, glancing at the calendar on the fridge. The weekend is wide open for them too. No soccer games, no birthday parties, no school projects—just an empty square staring back at me.

The sound of footsteps shuffling down the stairs stirs an idea free from the cobwebs of my mind. When Cameron and CJ stumble into the kitchen in their pajamas, still half-asleep, I'm already devising a plan.

"Morning, guys," I say as Cameron pulls the milk from the fridge and CJ grabs a box of cereal. They slump into chairs at the table.

"Mornin'," Cameron mumbles, rubbing his eyes.

CJ grunts, barely awake.

I take a sip of coffee. "I was thinking..." I start slowly, gauging their reactions. "How about we finally check out that waterpark you've been asking about?"

I recall seeing the commercial for the waterpark during my hospital stay. It's one of those massive, indoor centers with towering slides that snake through the air like rollercoasters. The advertisement featured a lobby lush with artificial palm trees and wave pools crashing against fake beaches. A place made for kids to run wild, and it's long overdue. Cameron and CJ begged us to go that last summer with Rachel. But we never made it.

I've been given a second chance at life. I cringe to think of how I put off another opportunity to take them. Another opportunity, taken for granted.

I won't let it slip by again.

The words barely leave my mouth before they're both wide awake.

"For real?" Cam's eyes glow, as CJ's head snaps up, his tiredness forgotten.

"Yep," I say with a grin. "Let's make it happen."

"Yes!" they shout, practically jumping out of their seats.

Cam bounces over, nearly tripping over the belt of his robe as he asks, "Is Gloria coming?"

The question catches me off guard. I glance at CJ, and I catch the flicker of uneasiness on his face the second Cameron says her name. It's subtle, but it's there.

"Nah, bud. Not this time."

"Aww, I like when she comes," Cam whines, oblivious to his brother's reaction.

"Well, this weekend is for men only," I say with a grin, hoping to smooth things over. "That alright with you, CJ?"

CJ nods, a small smile surfacing out of his discomfort.

"Alright. Go get washed up and pack your bags—it's about an hour drive, and we can grab breakfast on the way. The Bensley Express leaves in t-minus sixty minutes!"

They don't need to be told twice. Cam bolts upstairs, and CJ follows close behind, abandoning the milk and cereal on the table as they strategize which slides to hit first. After their footsteps thunder up the stairs, I lean back against the counter and exhale slowly. *God, I need this.* Time—carved out for just the three of us. A chance to remind them—and myself—just how important they are to me.

This weekend, it's just us. *The Bensley men.*

GLORIA

How did we get here?

The warm water from my bathroom sink soothes the cold skin of my hands. I reach for the towel hanging nearby, my eyes drifting to the little stand where Charlie's toothbrush sits next to mine on full display. A soft chuckle escapes my lips at the sight.

We clearly go together.

Soft music hums from the living room speaker, inspiring me to light a few candles and lean into the mood. I pull a chilled pitcher of sangria from the fridge, slices of fresh fruit swirling inside. Charlie should be here soon, so I pour the wine into two glasses to wait on standby for his arrival.

The jingle of keys announces his arrival. At the sight of me, he smiles, loosening his tie. He's still in his work clothes, his dress shirt slightly wrinkled from the day and his service weapon still holstered at his hip, a silent reminder of his world outside these walls. Wordlessly, he hangs up his overcoat, drops his backpack, and closes the distance between us with a kiss.

"Mmm, dinner smells delicious," he murmurs against my lips. "What are we having?"

I peck his lips again before saying, "Seafood paella."

"Sounds good, babe," he sighs with that warm, easy grin of his.

He's off to the shower a few minutes later. The faint hum of his electric toothbrush has me smiling like a fool. *That toothbrush.* It's such a simple thing, but it means so much. *We've come so far.* He's in the bathroom now—my bathroom—shedding the weight of the day. Part of me wants to slip in and join him, to melt under the water with him, but I'd better keep an eye on the food.

Once the paella has simmered to perfection and Charlie is refreshed, we sit at the breakfast bar, steaming plates before us.

"How are the boys?" I ask between bites.

"They're good," he says, twirling his fork. "Our mini weekend vacay was much needed."

"The 'three wild and crazy guys' trip?" I fondly recall the text he sent to let me know that he'd be busy.

He laughs. "Yeah, something like that."

My next question catches in my throat before it leaves my lips. "CJ doing alright?"

Charlie hesitates for just a moment. "Yeah."

"I know exactly how he feels," I admit. "For a long time, I resented Evelyn. She was like... the Wicked Witch of the East, and I was determined to drop a house on her." I take a swig of sangria as Charlie chuckles darkly. "I mean, just the fact that she was in my dad's life, that she was special to him... It was enough to fuel my fury. I couldn't stand the thought of someone else stepping into my mom's place. And even when Evelyn tried to be kind or patient, I'd just shut her down. Every time she reached out, I'd wall up. I didn't realize how hard it was on her—just being there, trying to belong in someone else's story." I shake my head, my newfound understanding bringing a whole lot of regret to the surface. "CJ probably sees me as just... intruding." *Just like I did.*

Charlie's face softens. "He just misses his mom."

I only nod in response. *I did too.*

"He reminds me so much of her," he sighs. "Strong-willed." He smiles at that, his eyes warm but distant, like he's looking through a window into his past.

It occurs to me that I don't know very much about Rachel. "Tell me about her." I say, propping my elbow up on the counter, resting my chin on my fist, listening intently.

Charlie blinks at me in surprise. "What do you want to know?"

"How'd you meet?" I ask, genuinely curious. I want to know more about the woman who once had his heart. *Their love story.*

"We met at a Greek service event," he says, smiling at the memory. "I saw her and spit my best game at her."

I roll my eyes, teasing. "And?"

"And... she was like, 'Boy, if you don't get the hell outta my face...'" We both burst into laughter at his poor impression of a woman's voice. "Eventually we started hanging out, then dating, and then we were a thing. Before I knew it, we were graduating, and I just knew I loved her. We were so young when we got married."

"Do you think that was the reason... that it didn't work?" I ask, my words tentative. "Timing?"

Charlie shakes his head with a certainty that makes my throat tighten and my heart loosen all at once. With a gentle smile, he says, "No. Let's just say, it took a while for me to realize that our colors didn't suit each other. Not like fuchsia and navy do."

I desperately try to hide my blush behind another sip of sangria. Despite his reassurances, there's a part of me that wonders if, given more time, they could have found their way back to where they started. *In love.*

As the evening progresses, Charlie doesn't let my insecurities stay for much longer. His kisses chase them away, and his caresses remind me that he's here to stay. We make love with my legs straddling his lap, our arms locked tightly around one another. While his fingers trace my spine, mine draw languid circles on the back of his neck, nails catching on his cropped hair.

Being this close to the man I love feels like surrender and sanctuary all at once, an intentional excavation of all the walls I've built up, crumbling under the warmth of his touch. There's nothing left of my fortress but rubble at his feet. In his embrace, every pent-up part of me finally exhales, safe and understood in ways I've come to associate with only him.

Our heartbeats sing in time, his soothing mine like the cadence of a love song, steady and intimate—the perfect rhythm to make love to. Each beat pulses against me, syncing with my own, drawing me deeper into him. Our bodies dance to this shared rhythm, like we're writing a ballad that only we know.

It's almost too much to fathom. As I give myself over to the quiet intensity between us, his eyes shine up at me. You see, Charlie's smile is a sight to behold, but it's his eyes that I could truly get lost in. Absolutely carried away like sitting before a blank canvas, brush in hand—inspired by the flecks of gold that circle his irises. An entire world waits for me in them. Eager to see what colors will emerge, what story will unfold, and how each stroke might reveal something new and unexpected.

A jazz classic from the living room breezes into our lovemaking—a familiar, soft melody.

"I love this song," I whisper, craning my head back as Charlie devours my neck. Lowering my eyes to his, I start to lip-sync the words, my voice barely above a whisper.

"When I fall in love, it will be forever..."

His hands trace familiar paths along my back.

"... Or I'll never fall in love."

Charlie presses our foreheads together, swaying side to side ever so gently to the croon of Carmen McRae's serenade.

"And the moment I can feel that
You feel that way too

Is when I fall in love with you..."

As the song fades, I murmur against his mouth, "I love you, Charlie Bensley. Like navy loves fuchsia."

He smiles, enraptured, as his masterpiece eyes lock onto mine.

"I know."

February

Seventeen

THE ART OF CONVERSATION

CHARLIE

The bell above the door chimes as it closes behind me, welcoming me into the lovely little shop on Main Street. My mind feels foggy and distant, so I try to let the scent of fresh flowers and damp earth to ground me as I approach the counter. The florist, a kindly older woman with a weathered smile, looks up from her work.

"What can I do for you today?" she asks, hands busy arranging a bouquet of roses.

"White tulips," I reply. My voice sounds steady, even though my mind is far from here.

Her smile lines deepen. "Anniversary? Birthday?"

"No," I say simply, offering only a polite smile as clarification.

She tilts her head with a knowing shimmer in her eyes. "Oh, so you're a 'just because' kind of man."

The truth is more complicated, but this is neither the time nor the place to get into such matters. I smile again, reaching into my coat pocket to retrieve my wallet. "How much for a bouquet?"

"Thirty-five for a dozen." She nods approvingly as she starts selecting the stems. "You know, that's my favorite kind of man," she continues. "My husband's a 'just because' man too—well, at least he's learned to be."

I let out a short laugh, releasing some tension. "Smart man."

She chuckles along as she wraps the tulips in brown paper with careful hands. There's a gentleness in her movements, a quiet reverence that draws me in. For a moment, I get lost in the simple beauty of it.

"Here you go," she says, handing them to me once the transaction is complete.

"Thank you." The scent of the tulips is faint but familiar. I give her one last nod before stepping outside into the bitter cold of a February morning.

For what feels like forever, I can only stare at the letters of her name.

Rachel Simone Bensley.

The gravestone is cold, permanent, and etched eternally. *A reminder of all I can't undo.*

I clutch the base of the bouquet tighter, the paper wrapping crinkling loudly in this quiet place. I crouch low, placing the flowers gingerly against the stone. The stillness in the air almost feels like permission to speak, if I can find it in me to break the silence.

"I brought your favorite," I say softly. "Tulips. Just like the ones you carried, floating down the aisle on our wedding day. Do you remember that, Rach?"

It's not that I don't realize where I am or the solitude of my being here, but somehow, her silence feels achingly familiar.

"Rachel, do you love me?"

I remember asking her once, when our future together felt like a mystery—when I'd questioned if she was still in it with me. *When I'd felt alone in our marriage.*

That same silence haunts me now, washing over me like it always did in those last few years. It's the kind of silence that isn't just about words unspoken but rather about feelings left unshared. It's the kind that makes you feel more alone in someone's presence than when you're actually by yourself.

"That's a stupid question," she'd finally said in response—but it wasn't a real answer.

I sigh, watching my breath cloud in front of me in the cold air. Standing, I brush the dried, shriveled leaves off the top of her headstone, like somehow that gesture might make this moment feel any less suffocating.

"I'm angry, Rachel." The words come out sharper than I intend. "You may not think that I have the right to be—but I am. Angry at you. At myself. And I'm trying to let it go, but..." I glance up at the sky, at the way the clouds drift slowly by, unbothered by the hurts that humans cause to one another.

I don't want to be angry anymore.

"Therapy's been helping," I admit. I know now that the anger only keeps me stuck, trapped in the worst night of my life.

I close my eyes. There were good times, weren't there? When we laughed more than we fought, when we shared dreams instead of that dreaded silence?

"It's brought me a long way," I continue, quieter now. "I've found ways to work through my emotions and right my wrongs." I pause, looking down at the patch of frost-covered grass around her headstone. "That said... I'm sorry, Rach." *Forgive me.*

The breeze picks up for a moment, rustling the leaves around me. I don't know if it's a sign or just nature doing its thing, but it feels like... *she's listening.*

"I hurt you," I croak, composure faltering, "and I struggle with that, I struggle with not recognizing the pain you were in too." I take another breath, this time a little steadier, thinking about our boys. "And CJ—our son—God, he's just like you, Rach. He suppresses. But he's gonna be alright. Cam's already doing so much better too. They're both gonna be alright—I promise." I smile a little, thinking about the small ways she saturates their lives. "CJ misses your chili dogs, by the way. Apparently, I can never get the recipe right." My bittersweet laughter fades, and I'm left with this ache in my chest. "The boys miss you. And I..." I swallow the lump in my throat, my voice barely a whisper. "I miss my friend. I miss—the good times."

For a long time, I just stand there, watching the wind gently rustling the tulip petals. It feels like she's still with me somehow. Maybe not in the way I used to hope for, but she's here. And I know what I need to say before I go.

"Love you, Rach. Always will."

Later that night, I sit cross-legged on the floor, eyes closed, focusing on my breath.

In through the nose, out through the mouth...

Eventually, I hear the door creak open. A soft shuffle of footsteps follows. I know it's CJ before he even says a word.

"Hey," I say without opening my eyes.

"Hey, Dad. What are you doing?"

"Meditating." I crack one eye open to glance at him. He's standing by the door, curious but a little hesitant.

"Why?"

I take another deep breath, exhale slowly, and open both eyes. "It helps quiet my mind. It's something I picked up in therapy. In fact, I've learned a few ways to keep myself centered—like this and journaling."

CJ looks at me, a little unsure, but I can tell he's listening.

"Wanna try it?"

He shakes his head, a frown forming. "Not really."

"Come on," I urge, tapping the space next to me. "Just for a minute."

CJ sighs, like I've just asked him to clean the entire garage, but after a moment, he slumps down next to me, exasperated, but here. Present. *It's a start.*

"Alright, let's start simple," I instruct. "Close your eyes. Focus on your breath. In through the nose, out through the mouth." I peek to see if he's doing it. His face is tight, like he's trying not to laugh, but he's giving it a shot. "Just relax, CJ. One minute. That's all we're doing."

We sit in near silence, only the sound of our unison breathing to underscore our thoughts. After the minute passes, I open my eyes and say, "Good job."

CJ cracks one eye open—just like I did before. "That's it?"

I nod. "That's it."

He lets out a little breath of relief.

I grin, hoping to keep the momentum going. "You know, all the greats meditate. LeBron. Steph Curry. Kobe did too." I pause, giving him time to digest that. "It helps them stay sharp."

CJ doesn't say anything, but I can tell the mention of his favorite athletes has piqued his interest, even if just a little.

"Speaking of great," I add, nudging him lightly. "You were incredible in the ring today. Those combos? Dude, you were killing it out there. I was so proud of you."

CJ's face lights up, a gleam of pride flashing across his features. "Thanks, Dad."

I feel the shift in the air before I even say it. "Mom would be proud too."

His expression falls, that glimmer of pride fading into something more solemn. I shake loose the tension in my chest with a deep breath, deciding to go deeper. There's something I've needed to say to my son for a long time.

"You know, when Mom and I found out we were having a boy, I was over the moon. I used to lie awake at night, thinking about what you'd look like, what kind of person you'd grow up to be, what interests you might have. But more than anything, I knew that I loved you. Before I ever held you—I loved you. And that I'd always be here for you."

CJ's eyes stay glued to the floor. He doesn't say anything, but he's still—*present.*

"CJ, when I was your age, I didn't have my dad. I wanted so badly to look up and see him in the stands at my football games, cheering me on, telling me he was proud. There was so much I didn't understand back then about adult relationships. With your mom, I was afraid of what would happen to you two if we ever split. I guess... I wanted you and your brother to have the kind of life I didn't. I didn't want to deprive you of a parent—make you choose between us just because we weren't a good match for each other anymore." I turn to face him now, my voice softer. "I'm sorry, CJ. For hurting you. I would give anything to bring your mother back to you."

CJ doesn't move, his face unreadable. Still, I press on.

"You and your brother are my highest priority. After Mom died, I should've put all my focus into making sure you were okay. I took for granted how strong you are. How much you were handling. I lost sight of meeting all your needs. And that's on me. And for that—I'm so sorry, son."

The room feels heavy with the silence that follows.

I search for the words that matter the most. "I love you, CJ—more than anything. That'll never change"

A beat passes, and then I feel it—a small shift as CJ leans into me.

"Love you too, Dad," he whispers.

I wrap my arm around my son, pulling him in to kiss the top of his head. He stays close for a moment, resting against me. But then I hear his voice, small and unsure.

"Dad?"

I loosen my hold and look down at him, raising an eyebrow. "Hmm?"

He sighs, and I can tell he's working up the courage to ask whatever's on his mind. "Do you... Do you love Gloria?"

It's a quiet question, but it feels loaded. He's bracing himself for the answer. I'm bracing myself to provide it. *Honestly.*

"Yes. I do."

CJ fidgets with his fingers, still not looking at me. "Are you going to marry her?"

I want to. Gloria's stance on marriage has left her uncertain of that next step. I realize this is too complicated for CJ to understand right now, so

I keep it simple. "I don't know, CJ," I answer. "And, honestly, son... I don't want to make any big decisions without your support."

CJ looks up at me for the first time, his eyes clear.

"So..." I continue, "for now, let's just say... we'll see what happens. Cool?"

CJ nods, the tension easing from his brow. For the first time in a long while, I feel like we're starting to understand each other again—finding our way back.

He's letting me lighten his load.

GLORIA

I came to the bookstore to browse, but ended up lost in the cover of a romance novel that's been on my TBR for weeks. The cover art features a fierce woman with a lusty disposition that's starting to feel a little too familiar. I shift my weight, balancing a few other titles in my arm, most of them just as steamy as this one. I'd only come for two books, but the stack is growing. It's fair to say that lately, my reading preferences have taken a turn for the...spicier.

The hum of the bookstore fades as I read the blurb, the fantasy of a dark romance pulling me in—until a young, familiar voice slices through my reverie.

"Gloria?"

I blink, startled, and look up. Standing at the end of the aisle is CJ Bensley, hands shoved in his hoodie pockets. He looks so young, and yet... something about the way he carries himself reminds me of his father.

"CJ! Hey," I say, trying to steady the surprise in my voice. "How are you?"

"I'm okay," he shrugs, calm but hard to read—*as always.*

"That's good." I glance behind him, half-expecting Charlie or Cameron. But he's alone. I certainly miss spending time with all of them.

CJ's sudden appearance catches me completely off guard. Still reeling from our last encounter—his words, fierce and sharp, cut deeper than he probably knows. A nervous flutter rises in my chest, my pulse ticking upward. I fumble for something, anything, to say.

"So, are you a bookworm?"

"Do graphic novels count?" A hint of a smile tugs at the corner of his mouth.

"Absolutely. In my opinion, they definitely count."

CJ's eyes flicker to the stack of books I'm holding. Suddenly self-conscious, I instinctively tuck the covers closer to my chest. No need for him to see that I'm swapping out my usual thrillers for these steamy romance novels. *I can practically feel the woman on the cover giving me away.*

"Is that what you're here for? Graphic novels?" I ask, hoping to divert his attention.

"Nah," he says, looking over his shoulder. "My best friend Sean and I are looking for gaming books."

"Oh, okay." I nod, the space between us filling with silence again. The weight of our last conversation presses between us like an invisible wall. It's hard to forget—his bold, painfully honest confrontation about my relationship with his dad, paired with his fierce loyalty to his mom's memory. He's only twelve, but that night, his words held an intensity well beyond his years.

I should address the confrontation, acknowledge his feelings. *But how?* How do I express how much I regret being part of the disruption that reshaped his world? *What can I say?*

"CJ, about the last time we talked..." I pause, choosing my words carefully. "I'm so sorry. I never intended to..."

"CJ, check this one out!" another young man around CJ's age walks up—Sean presumably. He's flipping through the pages of a magazine. "It's got codes and everything."

"Sean," CJ says, "this is Gloria."

Sean looks up, eyes bouncing between me and CJ, his curiosity piqued.

"My dad's... girlfriend," CJ adds, almost like he's still getting used to the idea himself. Even as my own pulse leaps, I can see how he's internalizing it, letting the words sink in, just like I am. *His dad's girlfriend.*

I extend my hand. "Nice to meet you, Sean."

Sean shakes my hand and smiles. "You too." He then pulls out his phone, glancing at the screen. "My dad just texted—he's outside waiting in the car. We've gotta go."

CJ nods, looking back at me. "See ya."

I smile, waving as they turn and head out of the aisle, watching until they disappear. I stand frozen for a moment, mentally replaying the gentle ways he's let me in—cracking a hesitant smile at one of my jokes, his guard slipping for just a second. Sharing his gumdrops to help me decorate my gingerbread condo that day at the children's museum. Small gestures. Tiny offerings. *Puzzle pieces.*

Each moment could be deemed insignificant, but I see them contributing to something bigger—a picture I hope we're still building together.

"My dad's girlfriend."

His words ring in my ears. There was no hint of disdain or even an errant eye roll—just... a simple statement that, admittedly, set my heart racing the moment he uttered it. He didn't have to do that—to say those words. But he did. *What do they mean to him?*

I may very well be sensationalizing a well-mannered young man's attempt at being polite. CJ's the type to be courteous even if he's uncomfortable. *Like his father.*

I can't believe how perplexed I am by the actions of a twelve-year-old. Even so, it felt good to be acknowledged in that way, especially by him. I allow hope and every other comforting feeling to ease away, grasping at reality, physically shaking my head as if I can shuffle my thoughts before I head toward the checkout.

"Gloria."

CJ.

I freeze, heart skipping a beat. Same tone he used the night he confronted me. My whole body goes still.

He's come back—alone. Undoubtedly with something to say. We were interrupted earlier, after all.

"Yes?" I brace myself, swallowing hard as I prepare my heart for the worst. The aisle seems to narrow around us as he steps closer, something unreadable flickering in his eyes.

Here we go.

Eighteen

PAST TIMES

CHARLIE

A chill sharpens in the nighttime air, but no brisk weather could stop us from moving forward with our fresh take on movie night. The boys have been excited all week, talking non-stop about our outdoor theater setup. The fire pit comes to life under my command, with the help of a healthy dousing of fire starter. Meanwhile, CJ carries out blankets through the patio door, and Cameron sets up our concessions—marshmallows, chocolate, graham crackers, and popcorn, of course—or at least he was until he got distracted, pausing to stare in awe as the projector screen inflates.

Ding dong.

My brow furrows at the sound of the doorbell. *Who could be here this late?* I head for the door, curiosity piqued as I glance at the security monitor on the way. The image comes into focus, and stops me cold.

Gloria?

Her familiar figure stands illuminated, framed by the glow of the porch light, hands tucked into her coat pockets, a soft smile playing on her lips as she shifts from foot to foot. I feel a wave of surprise, followed by something warmer—a thrill, really, at seeing her here. I open the door, my grin already carved in place as I take her in. She's radiant with her hair tucked behind her ears, styled with a middle part that highlights the perfect symmetry of her features.

"Hi," I say, grinning. I don't even try to hide my delight.

"Hey," she replies warmly.

"What are you doing here?" I ask, with absolutely zero disappointment.

"I was invited," she says, eyes drifting over my shoulder.

I follow her gaze to see CJ walking from the living room back out to the backyard, an extra blanket tucked under his arm. "Hey, Gloria," he says casually on his way out, as if this is the most normal thing in the world.

I glance back at Gloria, still puzzled. *CJ invited her?* I step aside, holding the door open wider. "Well, come on in."

Gloria gives me a secretive smile as she strides by, like she's in on a secret I haven't caught up to yet. Outside, the fire crackles, the snacks are prepped, and the air is just cool enough to draw us close. When the movie starts, I cozy up next to Gloria on the outdoor sofa, our bodies naturally gravitating toward each other. Well, not *too* cozy, but close enough to share each other's warmth. I drape a blanket over our laps, the cool night air giving me a perfect excuse to pull her close. Cam and CJ sit near the fire, faces glowing, marshmallows turning golden as they rotate them on sticks.

This scene—*the four of us*—feels better than I ever imagined.

I drape my arm around Gloria's shoulders. "You warm?" I ask, tugging her a little closer.

She smiles. "Yeah."

"So, how'd this come together? The invitation?"

She chuckles to herself. "I actually ran into CJ at the bookstore. Total coincidence. He asked me not to say anything—wanted it to be a surprise."

I look at my son, who is entirely engrossed in the film, seeming all at once like the little boy he is under the pressures of becoming a young man. It's a reminder that, despite his age, he is capable of processing difficult emotions. I'm overwhelmed by his thoughtfulness, blinking back tears that most certainly have nothing to do with the movie.

Man, I love him.

As the credits roll, the boys say their goodnights and head inside for bed. With the backyard all to ourselves, Gloria and I settle in, sharing a drink and small talk. I bring up random, meaningless things, just to keep her here. In this house. In this moment. *With me.* Her being here feels big, like we've turned a page. When I can't hold back anymore, I lean in and kiss her—soft at first, sweet and slow.

Gloria pulls back and instinctively glances around, checking for young eyes. She's still a bit cautious—*makes sense, I probably should be too*—but it's been over a week since I last saw her, and, well, I've missed her more than I can express with words.

With the coast clear, I capture her lips again—hungrier this time. We're making up for lost time with each push and pull of our tongues, punishing each other for the distance with the gentlest of nips. My lips trail down her neck, maneuvering past the cowl of her sweater, my free hand weaving into her hair.

"Charlie," she whispers, breathless.

"Stay the night with me," I murmur.

"Absolutely not," she chuckles, firm and a little hesitant, but I can tell she wants to. She leans into my touch even as she tries to stand her ground.

"Why not?" I whine, unzipping her coat slightly to gain more access to the stretch of her throat that might make her reconsider.

She pulls back, giving me a pointed look. "Babe, I just got out of the doghouse with CJ, and you're trying to get me in trouble. I need to tread lightly."

I can't help but smile, loving how much it means to her to earn the respect of the boys. I stroke her cheek with my thumb, and she turns into the touch, kissing it gently.

"But..." I persist, not above begging.

Gloria groans, throwing her head back in mock exasperation, making me laugh.

Her eyes return to mine. "Are you waiting for me to let you off the hook?" I ask, teasing her.

"Yes, actually, I am. You're supposed to say, 'Gloria, I understand.'"

"Gloria," I say with mock-seriousness. "I understand."

She glares at me, but there's no denying the relenting quirk of her lips. Her resolve wavers with every kiss, her body leaning in even as her words hold back. "Okay. But I'm leaving first thing in the morning, before they wake up."

As much as I want to protest. I agree. "I'll check in on the boys."

Hand in hand, we sneak inside, feeling like two teenagers tip-toeing around in the dark. Upstairs, Gloria shoots me a wink before retreating into the master bedroom. I peek in only to find the boys are already knocked out in their beds, limbs hanging every which way.

With my heart thrumming all the way down to my fingertips, I make my way to the bedroom. The door to the en suite is slightly ajar, and candlelight flickers from within. I press my hand to the wood, pushing the door open, and there she is—dipped luxuriously beneath a blanket of bubbles in the bathtub. Her dewy face and shoulders rest just above the surface, and her knee, like an iceberg, peeks out of the foam. She looks like she belongs here.

Probably because she does. This is her second home.

The seduction in her eyes contrasts the sweetness in her smile. She's so damn beautiful I forget how to breathe. Just the sight of her overwhelms me.

"Take your clothes off," she whispers.

Request granted.

I lock the door behind me and strip down. Her hungry eyes sample my body as she bites her lip, blushing at the sight of my arousal. She lifts a hand to beckon me with her finger, suds rolling down her hand. I slip into the water behind her, pulling her back against my chest, and she lets out a soft sigh, melting into the moment with me. I know exactly how she feels. Finally, another piece of our puzzle is locked in, looking more full. Almost complete.

With featherlight fingers, I trace her slippery skin, up and down—from her collarbone to her navel. Gloria leans her head back against my shoulder, her breasts peeking out of the water, nipples tight and eager. Slowly, I slide a finger inside of her. With a shaky breath, she reaches back, hooking her hand behind my neck and throwing her leg over the rim of the tub—asking for more.

Not yet.

I withdraw, lips at her ear, "Come with me."

After toweling off, I lead her to the bed, watching as she stretches across it, knees pressed together, gaze coy but smoldering. The sight is enticing, and I'm ready to sink between them and kiss away every last inhibition. Suddenly, I'm reminded of a little secret she'd let me in on that night at the loft...

Blindfolded or handcuffed?

"Both," she'd said.

"Don't move," I whisper.

Gloria is my obedient girl, waiting patiently. I return with a tie from my closet and my cuffs dangling from the crooks of my fingers, a question in my gaze.

Her lips part with a gasp, but she nods ever so slightly, closing her eyes. I wrap the tie snuggly over her dark lashes as she drapes her hands above her head. Carefully, I fasten the cuffs around her wrists, securing her to the iron frame of my slate-gray canopy bed. She squirms with curiosity, not knowing what to expect but trusting me completely.

Her drink sits, nearly empty on the nightstand, so I throw back the contents. The sound of the ice against the glass pulls her attention in its direction. I let a cube from the tumbler rest on my tongue.

Gloria jolts when I press the cold ice just below her belly button with my tongue, dragging it up past the well of her navel, between the peaks of her breasts. It leaves a watery trail in its wake. Her body arches up off the bed, shivering with the cool sensation.

Her luscious lips open against mine, our kiss slow and deliberate. I inch my way back down her wonderland, pausing to tease each nipple. They perk up under the melting ice just before I wrap my lips around them, suckling until she winces with pleasure. Her bottom lip caught beneath her teeth makes my manhood twitch. The look of lust on her somehow making her even more appealing to me. *Irresistible.*

Her body is ready, as is mine but I'm not done. I want to watch her lose herself at my command, I want to feel her body writhe beneath my touch, I want to hear pleasure travel from her sweetest spot up past her lips. *I want to make her come.*

Continuing my exploration, I trail kisses past her navel. She spreads her legs for me, hands gripping the iron headboard. The ice has melted, heat radiating from her center. I run my tongue along her slit, parting her folds until I find her most sensitive spot—the spot that I could find with my eyes closed. Gloria's sweet, warm, and so very wet. Her mouth falls open into a silent scream as I languidly lick at her rosebud with deliberate circles. Gloria's heels arch up off the bed, toes press into the mattress as she bites down, trying desperately to muffle her moans. She's probably concerned about the boys hearing her, but I'm not; they're not light sleepers.

She can cry out all she likes.

Wrapping my lips around her clit, I suck in time with her body's rhythm. I won't release her until she peaks. Gloria gasps breathlessly, her close-lipped moans fill the air like a hummed love ballad, just for me. The cuffs around her wrists clatter against the frame with every jolt of pleasure. *Sweet percussion.*

Hands flat on the mattress, I hover over her, easing down for a kiss. Her lips follow me even as I pull away. I reach between us, positioning myself to dive deep into her passion. Her legs wrap tight around my waist, ankles locked behind me, anxiously pulling me towards her. But I'm in no rush. This'll be a slow burn. I've got her until first light, and no matter how eager she may be right now, I'm going to take my time. I'm sure she'll thank me later. Teasing, I only feed the crown of my arousal to her greedy center, slipping in and out.

"Charlie," she whimpers.

"Yes, baby."

"Don't play with me." Her voice trembles, more command than plea.

I can't help but chuckle at her threat as I claim her eager lips, easing in inch by inch until she's served, full, and satisfied. I swallow down her moans like aged bourbon—they're utterly intoxicating. I pull myself upright, my hands gripping her waist as I move within her. Making love to Gloria is like stepping into a quiet storm—intense, consuming, but with a calm at its center that pulls me in. The blindfold heightens her senses, stripping away distraction until all that's left is sensation—raw, electric, and deeply primal. I work into her until I feel her inch closer and closer to her limit. A limit I intend to test. I pick up the pace feeling myself drift into an ecstasy beyond my own comprehension. *Euphoria.*

Gloria is everything. Everything I need, want, desire. Everything I love.

Tonight, we explore sensation. The tickle of my breath on her skin, the caress of my tongue, the bite of the ice, the heat of my release...

Our bodies are like two lit matches, catching fire. *Flame and friction.* Before I lose myself completely, I pull out, stroking my length until the warmth of my fire erupts, spilling onto her skin like hot wax, branding her with my release. *Mine.*

She gasps, lips parted, chest rising and falling as she gulps in air, trying to catch her breath. I collapse onto her, pressing a passionate kiss to her lips, eager to meet her gaze. Carefully, I ease the blindfold off, and her eyes meet mine—dazed and glistening.

"You alright?" I ask softly.

"I'm... *glad I stayed.*"

GLORIA

Another perfect day with him.

Today is the kind of day that stirs up reckless thoughts, like—*this is it.* This is the man I want to spend my life with. I just want to shout it to the world, tell everyone that we've found "the one" in one another. I can't even hide it anymore—I'm in love.

Charlie, I'd go anywhere you'd go. Where to, my love?

We walk side by side in easy silence, the late afternoon sun filtering through the trees, casting dappled light onto the sidewalk. I love this neighborhood. It feels familiar, welcoming, like it could be ours one day—*the four of us.* The possibility makes me pause, taking in the houses nestled close together, each one with its own quiet charm. Welcoming front porches, perfectly trimmed lawns, wreaths hanging on doors... I've never pictured myself here, on this kind of street, in this kind of life—but now? I can see it all so clearly.

It wasn't long ago that I thought I had it all, cherishing the solitude of my single life, a life that felt luxurious in its simplicity. I basked in quiet nights in my cozy condo, a glass of wine in hand, soft jazz playing in the background as the skyline glimmered beyond my windows. It was *Sex & the City* perfect, each night an ode to independence—the kind of life Carrie Bradshaw herself would admire: independent, stylish, and all mine. I'd crafted that life carefully so each detail and ritual stood as a testament to my freedom. My version of happiness, and mine alone. For the longest time, I was certain it was everything I wanted.

But here I am now, enchanted by the thought of trading my view of the bustling city for the stillness of the suburbs—the brilliant reds and golds of autumn leaves drifting down from a towering maple, the sound of kids' laughter echoing from the cul-de-sac. Somehow, it doesn't feel like a compromise. In fact, it feels almost... better. *How could that be?*

Just as I'm wrapped in that comforting thought, we come across an open house viewing. As prospective buyers wander up and down the front steps, Charlie and I simply stand on the curb, admiring the house before us. It's a grand, two-story brick building with a style that is modern in form but classic in the details. Its elegant, stone-framed entrance and tall windows promise spacious rooms inside, like something straight out of a magazine.

"What is this? A Georgian?" I ask, taking in its stately charm.

"Let's find out," Charlie says with a smile, tugging at my hand like a kid on an adventure.

Inside, the realtor greets us warmly. "Please have a look around," she says before moving to welcome another group entering behind us.

Charlie grabs a property listing sheet from the entry table as we step further in. "Four bedrooms," he says, raising his eyebrows playfully. "One for you and me, one for each of the boys. And maybe an art room?"

I laugh. *How good does that sound?* "Don't try to butter me up with an art room."

"Okay," he grins, "then how about... a nursery?"

The word hits me softly, but with impact, like a pebble tossed into still water. *A nursery.* I've never seriously considered being a mother before. The idea always felt distant, like it belonged in someone else's story, not mine. But now... *could I? Should I?* I mean, if I ever had a child, it'd be with Charlie.

I find myself drifting through the room, picturing it—not as it is now, but as it could be. The white walls soften into a pale pastel. There's a crib in one corner, a changing table with soft linens in another, and a teddy bear perched on a shelf. I see myself in a glider by the window, gently rocking an infant drifting off to sleep. My heart clenches with a strange, new warmth.

Could I really be a mother?

I move closer to the window, leaning against the sill, and for a moment, it isn't a nursery I see anymore. It's my own memory, a younger me, staring out of the window, watching my father leave on that fateful day that he moved out for good. His figure grew smaller and smaller as he walked away, the weight of that goodbye still unsettled somewhere deep within me.

"Hey."

Charlie's voice pulls me back to the present. I turn to see him leaning against the wall, arms folded, watching me with those thoughtful eyes that somehow make me feel safe and vulnerable all at once.

"Hello, you two," the realtor says, peeking around the doorframe with a cheery disposition. "So, what do we think?"

"It's amazing," Charlie replies smoothly. "We're gonna take some time to think about it."

Outside, we continue our walk, but the easy rhythm between us has shifted. There's a slight awkwardness now, a silence that's thick with unsaid words. Hand in hand, we stroll quietly, the sound of our footsteps louder than before. I stop, turning into him, needing to know, needing to clear the fog.

"Is that a dealbreaker?" I blurt out. "Not having a baby—" I struggle to bring my eyes to his, scanning the peaceful beauty of the neighborhood, desperate for a soft place to land, afraid of the truth—of what this could really mean to him. *For us.*

"G," he calls softly but still with that unmistakable note that commands my attention. I look up, finally meeting his gaze, bracing myself. His eyes search mine, intent and unwavering. "No," he says firmly, a steady answer that stills the air around us. But then, his expression softens, and I watch as something shifts—a quiet acceptance, like he's wrapping his mind around a reality he may have once dreamed of but is realizing he might have to live without. "Are kids off the table too?" Now, it's his turn to brace, waiting for a truth that's only fair to ask.

I shrug, feeling conflicted. "I don't know. It's just... kids get hurt when relationships end." The words hang in the air, and I feel the old ache resurface, the memory of how much it hurt to watch my parents fall apart.

Charlie's gaze stays unwavering. "Are you going somewhere? Because I'm not."

I blink, my heart twisting at the simplicity of his words. "But... I'm sure you've felt this way once before."

Her name doesn't need to be spoken. She lingers in the air between us now, a quiet reminder of the life he had before me, of promises he once made to someone else. Charlie's jaw tightens, his gaze slipping past me, into the space where memory lives.

"All I'm saying," I add softly, "is that so many relationships fail."

"This one won't," he combats, a quiet strength in his voice. When he locks eyes with me, it's with a conviction I envy. "And I know you know that."

I do, I want to say. *I really do.* No matter how much he shows me that there's no other place he'd rather be, no other woman he'd rather love, my heart still shields itself from the inevitable—*loss*. We keep climbing higher and higher, only making me more fearful of the fall.

"Yes, relationships fail," he continues. "You and I both know that all too well. But this—" He gestures between us. "—you and me? We're solid, babe. We're one in a million. Like Oprah and Stedman. Ben and Ev." His eyes crinkle with his smile, inspiring one of my own. His assurance is enough to make me believe, even for a moment, that we might be different. Charlie points to a nearby tree. "Should we just go ahead and carve our names right now? 'Chloria.'"

I just laugh, shaking my head at him merging our names like we're a celebrity couple.

"'Relationships fail,'—ha!" he chuckles to himself. "You're stuck with me, woman." His smile fades a bit as he sobers. "Babe, I won't lie, the idea of us making our own little masterpiece together is..." The fantasy floats around in his eyes, only for him to tuck it away for safekeeping. He pulls me close, dropping a sweet kiss on my lips. "I love you, Gloria Gatlin."

I slide an arm around his waist as he drapes his over my shoulders, sinking into the warmth of his embrace as we continue our walk. This man is my safe place to land—my home.

Charlie presses a kiss to my temple as he declares, "An art room it is."

GLORIA

The abstract painting hanging on the wall of this waiting room is a swirl of blue and yellow lines weaving into a complex, blended knot of verdant greens. It's funny how abstract art never really makes sense but is oddly calming.

"Ms. Gatlin?"

The nurse in her signature pink scrubs calls from the doorway, motioning me back. I follow her down the hallway to the exam room where I change into a gown and perch on the padded table, flipping through a magazine without actually reading it.

A soft knock precedes a familiar, melodic voice.

"Hey, Gloria!"

Dr. Green steps in, smiling with the easy warmth that always puts me at ease.

"Hey, Dr. Green."

"How's everything going?" she asks, pulling up my chart on her tablet.

"Really well, thanks," I say, and it's true. Everything has been good—better than good, really. *Wonderful.*

"Good! So, what brings you in today?" Dr. Green murmurs, half to herself as her eyes skim the screen behind her modern black frames. A second later, she answers her own question. "Ah, your annual."

"Yep."

Time passes in the usual way—running down the standard checklist of questions: diet, exercise, sleep, stress levels. It's familiar, almost comforting in its routine.

After a few taps on her screen, her brows lift slightly. "And it looks like we're at the five-year mark with your IUD."

"Oh, okay?"

"Technically, yours can last up to twelve years, but I always like to check in around this point." She glances up. "Any adverse reactions?"

I shake my head. "No, none."

"Great." Her smile is gentle, that same calm I've come to know and trust. "Given any thought to family planning?"

The room stills—just for a breath. I should've expected the question—it's one she's asked routinely for years. Reasonable. Standard. And I've always had an answer. But this time, it lands differently. And for the first time—I don't.

Family planning.

The words settle in the space between us, gentle but echoing. My mind drifts back to the conversation with Charlie, prompted by the idea of a nursery. The truth is, *I have.* The thought sneaks in when my mind is quiet—inopportune, uninvited, but not unwelcome. Charlie let it be. But my mind hasn't.

Dr. Green tilts her head, her slow smile soft but knowing—as if she can sense that something has shifted. It's been years since I started this journey with her, back when I was so sure. *No kids.* That decision felt firm, clear. But now...

Do I want to have a baby?

The fantasy is there, fragile and flickering behind my defenses—more real than I ever expected it to be. *"Our own little masterpiece,"* he'd called it.

Masterpiece.

Anticipation flutters in my chest, a quiet joy edged in fear.

Of course I do.

Why tempt fate, though? She's been so kind to me already—more than I deserve. I'm happy. Dangerously happy. Wanting more, a child, seems selfish. My life is so full already. I have more than I could have ever hoped for—Charlie and the boys. *Purpose.* I'm complete.

"A question for another day," Dr. Green concludes kindly, pulling me back from my spiral. I nod, exhaling a breath I didn't realize I was holding as I ease back, settling onto the crinkling paper. She hums a light tune as she begins gathering materials for the exam. The soft snap of latex gloves follows.

"Alright now, Ms. Gloria," she says playfully, rolling her stool closer. "I think we have some catching up to do. I'm guessing that glow has a name—and maybe dimples?"

I blush, the warmth rising to my cheeks before it spreads into a full smile. *I plead the fifth.* Which, ironically, feels like it speaks louder than any confession. Dr. Green is undeterred and undistracted. And with perfect timing—and not an ounce of mercy—she sing-songs, "Details..."

My gaze lingers on the fluorescent light overhead. The details—are messy and marvelous and...

Where do I even begin?

...May

Nineteen

SWEET ON YOU IN BLUE

GLORIA

The familiar scent of paint mingles with the fresh air wafting through my open windows. I gaze at the skyline of my forever home. The view of the city stretches out like a postcard. It's stunning, truly—a beautiful canvas of vibrant colors and sharp edges against the backdrop of a bright, blue sky, my muse for the landscape portrait I'm creating. Each stroke of my brush strives to capture the essence of the place where I fell in love, where I found a part of myself I never knew was missing.

Argale cradles my heart.

My canvas is positioned perfectly to catch the light, the view just a glance away. Within that same glance is a framed article on the wall—a clipping from the Argale Post. The headline boldly proclaims,

"Local Art Enthusiast Wows with Stunning Debut: Art Show Draws Rave Reviews and Packed House." Beneath it, a photo of me beaming alongside J.N. Nettles, a young, celebrated local artist and the epitome of *Black Girl Magic*. Charlie had it framed for me, a symbol of his unwavering support.

What an incredible night, I think, reflecting on the evening as one I'll never forget.

The days are growing longer, and a flock of geese—much like the flying "V" I've captured in this portrait—soar just above the city's towers, returning home. *Home.* Just the other day, I spotted a pink magnolia tree bursting into bloom, its petals reminiscent of cherry blossoms. All signs of springtime, the time of year that melts away the remnants of winter and makes way for new growth. A beautiful metaphor for my life.

The boys and I have grown closer over the past few months, and I've worked so hard to earn their trust. These days, it feels like I spend more time at Charlie's than in my own sanctuary. It's surprising, really. My condo has always been my retreat, yet I don't mind trading that solitude for time with them. I value the moments we share, the laughter echoing through the kitchen as we create messy homemade pizzas, the evenings spent around the table playing board games, and the thrill of cheering for CJ at his boxing matches. I become a little emotional glancing at a picture on my phone, a snapshot of the four of us just before Cameron's school dance. *The Spring Fling.*

I've been so warmly welcomed into this family, not only by the boys. Just the other day, I was thrilled to receive an invitation from Aries for tea and *tea*. I can't help but smile, remembering the advice she'd offered about my relationship with Charlie's mom. Mona isn't very supportive of Charlie and me, but I'm hopeful that one day she will be, especially for Charlie's sake. I know how important she is to him. Maybe someday, she'll give me a small chance to show her that I'm more than the portrait she's painted of me—that I love her son more than there are stars in the sky. *A girl can dream, right?*

For now, I'm happy to heed Aries' advice: *patience.*

We've even had a double date night with her and Jack. They remind me of Luci and Peter—so connected. So inspirational. Being surrounded by such healthy relationships has truly changed my outlook on what real love looks like. *Big Love.* Naturally, Luci still has her reservations about Charlie. *Understandably.* Even so, she's making an effort, going as far as inviting Charlie and the boys to Sunday dinner. As soon as Luci met Cam and CJ and witnessed the bond they share with their father, I could see the ice begin to thaw. *Progress.* Her laughter that night felt lighter, less guarded. She even teased Charlie about his love for hammock naps. It's not full acceptance—*not yet*—but I'm grateful for the small steps forward. It's surreal—almost perfect, just like the breathtaking view outside my window.

With Charlie's birthday approaching, I was wise to remember the cabin he mentioned that day in the hammock. Jack and Aries shared the details, and before I knew it, Charlie and I had locked in a getaway, just the two of us. I can hardly wait.

I rest my brush on the edge of the easel, resigning myself to stop for the day. Stretching my arms above my head, I feel how my body aches, craving sustenance. I glance at my watch—about half past six. I always seem to lose track of time in this room, hours passing. When was the last time I'd eaten?

I'm starving.

GLORIA

The house is still quiet this early in the morning. It's cozy like the sunrise framed perfectly outside the Bensleys' kitchen window or the fragrant aroma of herbal tea brewing. Cozy, like being wrapped in my plush robe, the belt cinched snugly around my waist, or Charlie's soft fleece house shoes. I wiggle my toes inside them, loving the texture while I try to adjust to the extra space. The Keurig chimes, and I clumsily shuffle over to grab my mug of tea. His shoes are way too big on my feet—I nearly tumbled down the stairs this morning trying to keep them on.

Note to self. Leave a pair of slippers at Charlie's.

My fingers work at untwisting the tie on the bread bag, the faint scent of my hot tea rising in the cool morning air. Then I hear it—soft footsteps on the stairs. I glance up just in time to see CJ coming down.

"Good morning," I say, my voice gentle so as not to disturb the calm.

"Morning," he yawns.

"You're up early."

He shuffles over to the counter and climbs onto a stool, sitting across from me. "Sean and I have been working on programming our own video game for weeks," he says, a spark of excitement lighting his voice. "I wanted to get some more work done."

"Wow, CJ," I say, genuinely impressed. "You're programming your own video game?"

The corner of his mouth lifts into a shy smile. "Yeah."

"Want some toast?" I offer, my hand already reaching for the bread.

"Yes, please," he says, always so polite.

I pop two slices of wheat bread into the toaster. "What phase of programming are you in?" I ask, turning back to him.

He shifts a little in his seat, clearly eager to talk about it. "I've been up for a while creating animations for characters and working on level design. I'm in the beginning stages, creating keyframes and filling in the in-between frames."

"That went completely over my head, CJ," I admit with a laugh.

CJ's eyes widen slightly. "Oh, sorry. I mean, I'm creating the characters' movements. Like, if the character is jumping, the keyframes would be the start of the jump, the peak of the jump, and the landing." As he explains, he uses his hands to demonstrate.

"That's really cool. Is that what you want to do when you grow up? Be a programmer?"

He grins, nodding his head. "Yeah."

"Do you know any programmers?"

"No."

"CJ, my brother-in-law, Peter, works for a major software company. We should talk to him. There might be an opportunity for shadowing or maybe even a summer internship you could do."

His eyes light up. "Really?"

"Yeah," I say, glancing at the clock. "Let's FaceTime him later this morning. It's still pretty early. I don't think anyone else in the world is up right now besides you and me." We giggle at the thought of it, the two early birds waiting for their morning toast.

Soon, I'm spreading cinnamon sugar over two slices, carefully removing the crust like I know he prefers. I pour him a glass of orange juice and slide it across the counter to him.

"Do you think Sean can come too?" he asks, hope flickering in his eyes.

"I don't see why not," I say with a smile, watching his smile widen even more as he takes a bite of his toast.

This quiet moment together means a lot to me, more important than I expected. The connection that I feel with him is unexplainable, slowly growing into something I never thought possible. I'm grateful for it—*for him.*

"She's not trying to be your mother," my dad would say about Evelyn when Luci and I made things hard for her. *"She just wants to be in your life."*

Now, standing here with CJ, I finally understand.

"CJ," I say softly, feeling a lump forming in my throat.

He looks up at me, eyebrows raised over the rim of his glass as he swallows a gulp of juice. *Adorable.*

"I know it probably doesn't mean a whole lot coming from me, but for whatever it's worth—I'm proud of you."

His eyes soften, and he gives me a small, almost imperceptible smile before taking another bite of his toast.

That's all I need.

GLORIA

"What's something that you can't live without?"

It was a question Charlie once asked me that I couldn't seem to find a solid answer to. Now, on this scenic drive to the cabin with warm springtime air rushing through the open top of his Jeep, I want him to ask it again. I glance over at Charlie behind the wheel, his profile aglow with the late afternoon sun. He looks my way, and my smile reflects in the mirrored lenses of his sunglasses.

This man holds the key to my heart. He unlocks something inside me, something that was waiting, holding its breath all this time...

Ask me again, Charlie. It's you.

My unlikely friend, my lover, my man. Somehow, Charlie makes the world around me feel smaller, more focused, more right. It's not the same unexplainable spark that I felt the night we met; no, it's deeper now, more like a powerful current running through us as we hold hands, his thumb tracing soft circles on my skin. We collided like we were always meant to, and it feels like I've waited lifetimes for this. I never believed in fate before I met Charlie, I suppose I've finally jumped on his bandwagon; perhaps...we were meant to be all along.

I bite my bottom lip to anchor myself, the tiny sting reminding me—

Yep, it's real.

We pull up to the cabin—a chic retreat with just enough rustic charm to feel like we've left the world behind. Inside, a Latin man steps out from around the corner, a sleek black chef's jacket fitted to his frame.

"Charlie? Gloria?" he asks, hand outstretched.

Charlie is caught off guard but accepts the handshake. "Hello. You are...?"

"I'm Omar, your personal chef for the evening."

Charlie shoots me a look. I tuck my smile away, feigning bashfulness, as if I'm not responsible for pulling out all the stops to make this weekend unforgettable.

"Dinner will be ready in about an hour, and I believe you're all set for massages upstairs," Omar says.

Charlie's brows lift in surprise. "Massages?"

"You're not the only one who can be romantic," I murmur.

Upstairs, we're side by side on plush massage tables in a dimly lit room, the air scented faintly of eucalyptus. Soulful slow jams underscore the masseuse's hands as she works out the tension in my shoulders, coaxing each stubborn knot into surrender. The room melts away as my lashes lower, sinking into the moment, the world narrowing around the soft, soothing sound of Charlie's contented sigh. When I open them again, he's smiling at me—that timeless sight, tenderness softening his gaze. He lowers his hand between the tables, a quiet invitation. Our fingers brush, then tangle. He squeezes twice, and I squeeze back with the same sentiment folded into my touch.

Love you, he mouths.

Love you, I reply.

Later, I stand alone in front of the bathroom mirror in a soft white spa robe, letting it hang open. From my luggage, I draw out a piece of delicate lingerie, my fingers tracing along the fine lace. I hold it against my body, studying my reflection, imagining the silk against my skin, how his gaze might linger a little longer. I tilt my head, a quiet thrill building as I picture the look in his eyes.

Suddenly, the man of my fantasies is behind me, leaning casually against the doorway, in his own matching robe, his bedroom eyes locked on mine in the reflection.

"I like it," he says. His hand finds the curve of my neck, thumb brushing upward as he tilts my head. His breath warms the stretch of my throat. "Put it on," he murmurs against my skin.

My breath hitches, almost helplessly. "Charlie..." I gasp, fighting to stay composed but tempted to use the five minutes we have before dinner... *wisely.*

"Yes, baby?" His voice, that silky baritone, sends a shiver down my spine.

"Dinner's ready... and we aren't even dressed," I protest softly, clinging to the last thread of restraint.

He lets out a quiet groan, pressing his lips to the side of my neck, ignoring my gentle protests as his hands slide around my waist, pulling me closer. His mouth tracing a slow, deliberate path to my jaw, as if savoring every stolen second before we have to rejoin the evening.

"Dinner can wait," he murmurs, his voice a deep, tempting whisper, making it nearly impossible to desire anything else. With the promise of what's to come, I managed to convince him that this ensemble—along with a few other surprises I packed—would be worth the wait.

We forgo our dinner attire, deciding instead to stay comfortably wrapped in our matching robes. Downstairs, a rather romantic setup waits for us, the dining room glows—candlelight flickering, rose petals scattered, soft music drifting in the air. The table is beautifully arranged, two silver cloches keeping our food warm.

Over the next hour, Chef Omar and his team present each course—succulent ribeye, scallops, roasted potatoes, black rice, asparagus, and brussels sprouts. Every bite is rich, carefully prepared, and utterly delicious. After dessert is served, Omar and his staff discreetly pack up, leaving us alone to savor the best course of the evening—each other.

"So, what do you want for your birthday?" I ask, savoring a bite of cheesecake.

He leans back in his chair, nodding toward the outdoor shower just visible through the window. "To check out that outdoor shower."

I smile, intrigued—and, well, undeniably horny—*ready for whatever he's imagining*.

I slip away to the restroom, gathering my hair into a loose updo with a clip. When I return, Charlie is already outside, head bowed beneath the stream of the outdoor shower. Water cascades over the carved lines of his muscles, giving each ridge and hollow a glistening sheen. My robe falls to the ground, softer than a whisper, as I join him under the spray. He hums low in approval when I slide my arms beneath his, embracing him from behind. I press my cheek to the warm plane of his back, and together we sigh—two currents meeting in the same river.

My fingers graze the faint traces of his scars—now healed. *Thank God.* Charlie places his hands over mine, following my lead as I roam across his chest, down over the grooves of his abs. I explore him slowly until I reach the heat of his shaft. He's already growing hard for me, when I take him in my hand and let him guide my strokes. With each passing second, he grows harder, heavier, heat radiating from him in waves.

Before I can finish him, he turns, eyes dark. His fingers slip into my hair, loosening the clip and tossing it to the ground. I couldn't care less. His mouth claims mine, urgent, starving, as if the rich dinner we shared left us hungrier still. *The way we consume each other.*

Soon, my hair is dripping wet, fisted in his hand. He tilts my head back, his tongue tracing the vulnerable length of my throat, as his other hand urges the small of my back forward, pressing us intimately together. All I can do is wrap my arms around his neck and hold on, caressing the back of his head and dragging my fingernails through his cropped hair.

"Mmm," I moan as a cool breeze cuts through the night air. Steam curls from our smoldering bodies, clashing with the evening's chill. "Charlie..."

"Yes?" he murmurs, nipping at my collarbone.

"Let me taste you."

Charlie's grip loosens. He watches, unblinking, as I sink to my knees, never once breaking eye contact. I drag my tongue along his length, testing the size of him against the open hinge of my jaw before sucking him down, inch by glorious inch. Charlie groans, fingers tangling in my wet hair. He can't keep his eyes off me as I work.

"Shit...Ah, babe." The guttural sound coils heat low in my belly.

Water slicks over his shoulders and down his torso, adding a decadent glide to my movements. I don't know what turns me on more, his sensual sounds, the silky sensation of his bulging veins against my tongue, or the sheer rush of owning his pleasure. His hips twitch, but he lets me set the rhythm. *Control*, a gift he's giving me—and one I wield with deliberate precision.

His brows draw tight, chest heaving, eyes fixed on me with an intoxicating mix of awe and desperation.

"Gloria," he grits out, voice frayed.

His hand cradles the back of my neck, gently guiding me the way he likes. And I let him—his submissive conquest. Pressure builds in my own core as I ache to feel him deep inside me, but I can taste how close he is. I'd be content to finish him right here, my mouth coaxing every drop of release.

But Charlie has other plans. With one hand at my throat and the other under my arm, he urges me to my feet. Our lips collide so desperately, dizzying and deep, until I have to cling to him for balance.

I twist the shower handle off, water trailing down our skin in cooling rivulets, our smiles mingling between kisses. Taking his hand, I lead him to a nearby double lounger.

"Sit," I command, and he obeys, looking up at me like something to be worshiped.

There's no one around to hear my strangled moan as I sink down, claiming every inch of him. Inverted, I ride him in reverse, my hips meeting his steady, but hungry tempo. We find a rhythm—slow at first, deliberate, my body rocking back into his every thrust. The stretch of him, the deep exploration, makes my toes curl against the lounger. His hands grip my waist, guiding the tempo, hitting every deep, devastating angle. The night air brushes over my damp skin, goosebumps rising, but his heat keeps me anchored as my satisfaction, slick and warm, coats his pleasure, even as we shiver in the cold.

I glance over my shoulder to catch his eyes—half-lidded, jaw tight, his teeth sinking into his lower lip—a look of pure ecstasy. The sight alone makes me clench around him, and his groan vibrates up my spine. And then, his eyes drift open as if he's been awakened from a dream, only to realize he wasn't dreaming at all.

I too find myself caught up in the rapturous intensity of it all. Love drunk, my hazy gaze settles on the lake's surface. It's so still, it almost looks unreal, a perfect mirror to the sky—black silk dusted with glittering stars. One star burns brighter than the rest, a tiny beacon among countless lights. My eyes drift upward to the beautiful, navy blue expanse, where constellations scatter like love stories waiting to be told, stretching endlessly.

"Do you know what a red nova is?" Charlie's voice echoes in my memory, low and reverent. I can still picture his steady gaze, lips slightly parted as if the words carried more weight than he could bear to hold back. *"It's a stellar explosion."*

A rare occurrence.

Back then, I was captivated by the poetry of his cosmic metaphor. Tonight, it's a prophecy fulfilled. His words resonate with a depth that stretches far beyond anything I could have ever imagined—those many nights ago.

"A red nova. Stars destined to collide—a grand design."

Destined, like stars hurtling through the cosmos, bound to meet in this destructive but breathtakingly beautiful way.

Charlie sits upright, cupping my breasts and holding onto me for dear life as my head falls back onto his shoulder.

The stars twinkle above us, bearing witness—*blessing this union.* It's so beautiful that my eyes blur with tears as I come, unseen by my lover but blissful all the same.

A grand design.

GLORIA

The cabin's kitchen glows warm in the morning, honeyed light streaming through the windows and draping everything in softness. I stand at the island in a satin cami set, slicing vegetables for omelets, while Charlie, shirtless in his pajama pants, whisks eggs across from me. His gaze finds me, and I sense it before he speaks.

"What are you thinking about over there?" His voice is teasing, but fond. "You look so lost in thought I'm scared you're gonna slice a finger off."

I snicker, pausing mid-chop.

"So?"

"So, what?"

"What's on your mind, babe?"

The unthinkable. My eyes drift back down to the cutting board. "My life, I suppose. I was thinking about my life."

He's quiet, still whisking, but watching me intently. "What about it?"

I glance up at him, my heart swelling with emotion. "I was thinking about meeting you. Falling in love with you."

He smiles—a genuine, quiet smile. *Go on,* it seems to say.

"Meeting your family. You meeting mine. And the boys... they're wonderful, babe." My voice wavers. "I don't deserve it, but my life is so full with you. And I'm so grateful. I love you, Charlie. I love every moment that we share. Just the other day I thought about the night we met—your smile—and how I've been helpless ever since." I admit, concealed behind a playful eye roll. "How you make me feel—*safe*."

Something in Charlie's eyes shines brighter. "I'm glad to hear you feel that way. I'll always love you, Gloria Gatlin."

His words, I hear them differently than I ever have before. They sound like—*confirmation*. Like I can finally put to rest my incessant need to give up before we try, to brace for the fall, to clip our wings before we fly away.

My heart races, my insides bursting with realization, as if his declaration was the final piece to our puzzle, the remedy to my madness, the confidence that I need to put my everything in his hands without fear of losing it all one day.

The freedom to love him like he loves me—fearlessly.

"Charlie?" I finally say, setting aside the vegetables. "I have something to ask you."

His head tilts, curious. "Okay, shoot."

For a moment, I find myself trying to translate my heart's deepest whisper—to shape it into something breathable, something my lips can carry, though it feels too sacred for speech.

A question—that doesn't feel like a question at all...

"Actually it's not a question though," the reality I murmur, more to myself than to him.

He chuckles. "A statement, then?"

"No..." my voice trails.

Concern flickers in his brow. He sets the whisk down, walks around the island, and folds his arms around my waist. "Okay. If it's not a question or a statement, what is it? We're running out of options here, babe."

"I know," I huff with an exasperated laugh. "It feels more like... a plea."

His expression softens. "A plea? Baby, is everything okay?"

I exhale, my heart racing, butterflies rioting. Disoriented by a clarity that knocks the wind from my chest. I shake my head. "No—and yes. Clearly, I'm all over the place."

"Talk to me. Whatever it is, we can figure it—"

"—Marry me."

The words come out just above a whisper, and my body goes still, feeling the profound weight of what I've just said.

Charlie's eyes widen, stunned. "Excuse me? What did you say?"

"Nothing."

"Bullshit."

I sigh—a strangled sound. "I know this is coming out of nowhere. I told you that I didn't want marriage, didn't want to risk it. And I *still don't*, because I love you—and the boys—and losing you all would be..." My breath catches. "...unbearable."

His silence guts me.

"I'm rambling," I murmur. "Just... disregard. I sound like a crazy woman."

"Oh, hell no," he draws out, lifting my chin with the crook of his finger, forcing me to meet his eyes.

"No, seriously, I—"

"Did you just try to rescind a proposal?"

I blush, biting my lip. I can't bring myself to answer.

"Now, try that again," he says tenderly. "What did you say?"

Be brave, Gloria. "I said... I want this. Forever. I want you. Forever."

His smile grows, but I can tell he's waiting for those words. *Those special words.*

"Marry me—please."

"I accept your plea," Charlie declares, and before I can even process it, he's kissing me with that forever kind of love. *Offer accepted.*

"Yeah?" I ask when we part, still breathless from the kiss.

"Yes," he answers with another kiss. He pulls back, grinning. "Yes!" he says again for good measure. "Now, do I need to remind you that this is a life sentence?"

I snicker at his word choice. "No."

"Good." His hands find my face again, pulling my lips to his, sealing the promise again and again. Then he pulls back, a wild look in his eyes. "Let's do something crazy."

"Like what?"

"Let's have a baby. A daughter."

"Charlie..."

"Baby, I know you're scared, but you don't have to be. And I'm not saying I wasn't already sold on the idea of us just being Oprah and Stedman, but I can't help but imagine—our baby girl, with your beautiful eyes. A little piece of us to raise together."

My heart feels like it might burst. *Oh, Charlie...*

"I want this with you," he says fiercely. "Gloria, I love you more than the air that I breathe. Always will."

And with my whole heart, I believe him.

His eyes suddenly widen with realization. "Damn, babe, I'm sorry. We just got engaged, and here I am already trying to get you pregnant."

"*Got* me pregnant," I correct softly.

The world pauses. A moment passing where neither of us dares to breathe.

His eyes snap to mine. "Wait, what?"

"You said, 'Let's have a baby.' And I was going to say... 'Okay.' Because—we're already having a baby."

He stares, stunned. "We're... having a baby?"

I nod, a tentative smile trembling.

Tears shine in his eyes as the biggest grin spreads across his beautiful face. "G, baby—we're getting married *and* having a baby?"

"Yes," I laugh softly. "I mean—if you still want to."

He scoops me into his arms. We share a laughing kiss as he slowly lowers me back down to the ground. Forehead pressed to mine, voice rough with joy, he whispers, "Thank you—for loving me."

"You make it really hard not to." I smile, my heart overflowing. "Happy Birthday, Charlie."

"Thank you, baby." His kiss is slow. Reverent. Timeless.

"Best birthday ever."

The Journey Continues...

The Masterpiece

Book Three ~ The Series Finale

Coming In 2026

Acknowledgements

Thank you for letting me be myself... *again*.

I heard this song while writing these acknowledgments and thought—how fitting.

So—*thank you*.

Lord, the giver of every good gift, thank You for trusting me with this one.

Mom, we did it...again! Thank you for always believing in me. No matter what, I know you'll always be there. I pray that you're proud. I love you. We are your legacy: *the writer, the musician, the artist.*

RACHEL BORGO! My editor and friend. If being grammatically incorrect is wrong, then I don't wanna write, right! I love you. You're invaluable. Thank you! Still reaching for the top, RB. You coming with me?

To thee good Rev. Dr. Christopher E. Dodd, my pastor and friend—thank you for blazing the trail, sharing your resources, and most of all, for praying for me and filling my growth gaps. How can I ever say thank you enough? By telling the world how great my PASTOR is...

Taja Ferguson—thank you for another amazing cover design. The road to Charlie was winding, but you went along for the ride with me. And in the end, you nailed it. Thank you!

Aubrya and Nicole, what can I say? You two balance me out. Thank you both for your friendship and for how you've contributed to this enduring literary love affair. I'll love you both forever, my friends—the shrink and the detective.

A very special thank you to my incredible beta readers and contributors: Aubrya, Chris, Nicole, Sherry, Tomika, and the Bougie Black Girls Book Club—Celeste, Felicia, Maggie, Monique, Rhonda, Suzanne, Valencia, and Veleda. Thank you for your honest feedback and encouragement. Your insights made this story sharper, stronger, and better. I'm grateful beyond words for you.

To my writing circle, readers, family, friends, and everyone who has joined me on this journey—thank you for coming back after *The Paramour* and for letting me take you deeper into Charlie and Gloria's story. You have my gratitude for every prayer, every word of encouragement, and every nudge forward.

With love, I thank my husband, Jerald, and my daughters, Maleah and Janelle.

Maleah, my inspiration, my cheerleader—I miss you. Without you, my rose-colored world is a hue dimmer. You are my most wonderful thing. Thank you for the endless support. Your light and your love inspire me even in your absence. Every word is written in memory of you, and every page is proof of how deeply you continue to shape my life.

No worries, sweet girl, I'll tell your story for the rest of my life. *Rest well, Leah B.* ♡

About the Author

V. Kay Martin is a devoted daydreamer and storyteller, continuing her journey in the world of romance with her second novel, *The Muse*, following her riveting debut, *The Paramour.*

V. believes immensely in the "secret place" that resides only in the imagination of dreamers—a place that comforts, stimulates, heals, and liberates true romantics. To her, there is nothing better than seeing the world through rose-colored lenses.

When the Chicago native isn't creating characters, building worlds, twisting plots, and shaping storylines, she's indulging in a good swoon by way of a dreamy and *hopefully* steamy romance novel or movie.

She aspires to continue coloring the world with charming love stories that imbue adventurous readers with a healthy dose of sentiment and spice in equal measure.